VICTORIA
GOTTI

The Senator's Daughter

A TOM DOHERTY ASSOCIATES BOOK
NEW YORK

This is a work of fiction. All the characters and events portrayed in this book are either products of the author's imagination or are used fictitiously.

THE SENATOR'S DAUGHTER

Copyright © 1997 by Victoria Gotti

A Forge Book
Published by Tom Doherty Associates, Inc.
175 Fifth Avenue
New York, NY 10010

Forge® is a registered trademark of Tom Doherty Associates, Inc.

ISBN: 0-812-57176-2

First edition: February 1997
First mass market edition: May 1998

Printed in the United States of America

0 9 8 7 6 5 4 3 2 1

This book is dedicated with love to my parents John and Victoria, who together have always given me the courage, hope, and strength to continue on.

To my children, the gifts in my life, Carmine, John, and Frank; for the unconditional love, joy, and happiness they have brought me, convincing me there is no greater love than that of a parent for a child.

Carmine, for your support, love, and dedication: I will always be there for you. To my siblings, John, Peter, and Angel—I love you all—and my brother Frank and my daughter Justine, the angels who've passed through my life and live forever in my heart.

Acknowledgments

The characters and events in this novel are fictional. The background, however, is real, and I am grateful to those who unselfishly gave of their time.

My deep gratitude goes to Linda Sheffield, Richard Rhebok, and Anthony Cardinale, for sharing their courtroom experiences and knowledge.

Frank Weimann, my agent, for his patience and many hours of working with me. Your dedication is so appreciated.

Andrew Zack, my editor, for keeping me focused and guiding me in the right direction.

Tom Doherty, president and publisher, Linda Quinton, Jennifer Marcus, Steve de las Heras, and all the staff at Tor/Forge Books.

My friend Trish, for all her help, advice, and a great listening ear.

To Sue Pollock, my dear friend, for convincing me it was all possible.

My appreciation to Angela Carillo, who patiently transcribed and typed the manuscript over and over.

And finally to my friend Fr. Thomas Arnao, for all his assistance in researching the Catholic Charities.

Victoria Gotti

SHE WALKS IN BEAUTY

She walks in beauty, like the night
 Of cloudless climes and starry skies;
And all that's best of dark and bright
 Meet in her aspect and her eyes:
Thus mellow'd to that tender light
 Which heaven to gaudy day denies.

One shade the more, one ray the less,
 Had half impaired the nameless grace
Which waves in every raven tress,
 Or softly lightens o'er her face;
Where thoughts serenely sweet express
 How pure, how dear their dwelling-place.

And on that cheek, and o'er that brow,
 So soft, so calm, yet eloquent,
The smiles that win, the tints that glow,
 But tell of days in goodness spent,
A mind at peace with all below,
 A heart whose love is innocent!

—*Lord Byron*

PART ONE

The Hit

LATE MAY – EARLY JUNE

1

The bloodthirsty, the perverse, and the merely curious: all crowded the entrance of DeCiccio's Restaurant for a view of the corpse. As far as Debra Gova knew, the corpse still lay inside, where it had fallen.

She threaded her way through the crowd, just another eager bystander until she ducked under the yellow ribbon that blocked entry to the popular restaurant. Then people noticed her—a plain woman with short brown hair, wire-frame glasses, and a slender body not endowed with curves.

Gova nodded to a cop in uniform, who opened the door for her. She stepped quickly inside, into the middle of a murder investigation, the last place she wanted to be on the Thursday before Memorial Day weekend.

The restaurant seemed almost as familiar to her as her own kitchen. In recent years, the place had become a lawyer hangout, a favorite haunt of the courthouse crowd. Just two days ago, Gova had enjoyed the arugula special, a cappuccino, and *biscotti*. Most of the *biscotti* still sat in her refrigerator. You never had to worry about the anisette-flavored biscuits getting stale and hard. They started out that way.

Crime scenes, on the other hand, grew stale pretty fast. People trampled the evidence or outright destroyed it while attempting to help the victims. Worse, the overly ripe victims tended to be stuffed under a bed or in a car trunk for a couple of weeks. Thank God for small favors; Joe Sessio had been dead less than an hour.

When word of the murder had reached her office, Gova had hesitated only a moment before she tagged the case a Priority One, the equivalent of an assassination of a political figure. All available resources would be used in gathering evidence and hunting for suspects.

Ironically, her office had been trying to put Sessio away for the past several years. As the leader of the largest dock union in Boston, Sessio had long walked the thin line between organizer and racketeer. Gova's office felt he'd crossed that line a few too many times and went after him. Unfortunately, he already had been acquitted in one case, but another trial was pending. At least, it had been pending until an hour ago. Now, irony upon irony, her office would be expending every effort to capture and prosecute the individual who had put him away permanently.

Forensic technicians hustled around, busily dusting for prints at a table near the front of the restaurant. But most of the activity took place at the rear of the room, where a pair of legs protruded from under a table. She headed in that direction, but stopped when she saw a man with a short neck and a wide girth, his back to her. She recognized him before he spoke; it would be difficult to mistake Charlie Schultz, the chief detective at the 13th Precinct, for anyone else.

Schultz faced three young men wearing standard busboy attire, white uniforms with long, white aprons. The men had their backs against a wall near the swinging door leading into the kitchen.

"What is this, Chicago? What is this, 1919? Guy takes a couple slugs to his mug at point blank range, in a restaurant in broad daylight, middle of town, and no one saw a thing? C'mon."

Gova started to call out a greeting when Schultz suddenly stabbed a finger at one of the men, a guy with a ponytail and a stud in his ear. "My name's Schultz. So what's your name, punk?"

"Schultz." The kid grinned at the detective.

In a flash, Schultz's open hand slammed the side of the kid's head. He yelped and grabbed his ear.

Great, Gova thought, battering a witness at the crime scene. The city could be sued for several hundred grand for this kind of macho, tough-guy crap.

"But his name *is* Schultz. Billy Schultz," one of the other busboys said.

Schultz ignored the kid and turned to see who had witnessed his assault. His face, with that square jaw and pale skin now flushed with excitement, reminded Gova of some character actor down on his luck. Schultz had to be pushing sixty, she thought, but looked as if he could still defend himself in a street fight. His gaze stopped on Gova, but he didn't look too concerned. His mouth swung into a mocking smile as he walked over to her.

"Well, hello there, Ms. Attorney General." His smirk widened. "I mean, Ms. Gova."

"That's getting old, Detective."

A couple of months ago, *The Boston Globe* had profiled Gova after her office had succeeded in prosecuting several police officers who had provided protection for a fencing operation. The case had proven her power to overcome the notorious "blue line," the unwritten code of honor that kept officers from testifying against other officers and made it extremely difficult to prosecute corruption in the department.

The article had compared her to the President's Attorney General, putting her on the fast track toward a higher office. She knew that Schultz meant his remark as a compliment, but suspected it also acknowledged the indisputable comparison between her looks and the "plain Jane" Cabinet member.

Although the Attorney General had twenty years on Gova, they shared more than similar appearances. Gova also loved her work, her life centered around it. She had almost no social life.

"So what's going on here?" she asked. "Why'd you hit that kid?"

Schultz clearly didn't find Gova's presence intimidating, which annoyed her. "Hey, I'm just doing what his mother shoulda done. These clowns don't want to be witnesses. They're afraid."

"Maybe they didn't see anything."

"Listen, the chef told me there's another busboy, a black kid, who just happened to disappear about the same time as the murder. No one saw him leave. No one saw nothing."

He gestured to a couple of uniforms, and they moved in on Ponytail, who still clutched his left ear with both hands and moaned about a busted eardrum. Schultz had him hauled out of the restaurant.

"The kid'll get a free ride to the hospital," he said quietly to Gova. "He'll get a few dollars, maybe a couple of tickets to the Celtics will end up in his pocket. Everybody goes home happy. More or less."

"Not me," she replied.

In spite of the well-publicized effort to root out corruption in the police department, Schultz conducted himself as usual. She considered him one of the last of a breed she would be happy to see go extinct. She often wondered if he had any respect for her at all.

"What? You don't approve of the old-school style? The fact is, Ms. Gova, sometimes you gotta nudge these punks to get anything outta 'em. That's the way it is, that's the way it's always been."

"Spare me the history lesson, Detective."

Schultz touched her shoulder lightly, and when he spoke again, she heard self-pity in his voice. "I gotta tell you. When we was all guys, it was easier. But now we got you women cops, women detectives, women lawyers. Even women DAs like yourself. It's not as easy as it used to be."

Gova stiffened, glanced at his hand; his arm dropped to his side and he smirked again. "So it makes it hard, you know what I mean?"

"Not really. Why don't you spell it out for me?"

He waved his hand impatiently. "Aw, hell. You lawyers are all alike. Never mind."

Schultz turned back to the other two men and addressed the one who had spoken to him.

Jerk, she thought. But Schultz had clout and she couldn't very well order him off the case, not without paying for it. If she went after him, made an example of him, it would backfire. Any further efforts to prosecute police officers or even file a complaint would look like overkill. It would work against her. She had to deal with the situation as it existed.

In the long run, it seemed better for all concerned to have Schultz as the lead detective than to have some young, aggressive investigator who might poke around in the wrong places. And in this case, danger zones proliferated. Her future, in fact, hinged on its resolution.

Gova went over to where Sessio's body lay. His chair had toppled backward from the blast of the gun. The body lay sprawled near the wall. A pool of blood had drained onto the blue tile floor and rivulets ran along the grouted depressions between the tiles.

A bloody napkin covered Sessio's face. But even with his face covered, she recognized Sessio by his trademark Harris tweed suit coat and gold cuff links. "Only a favored few were ever seated at that table," Schultz remarked, coming up behind her. "And Joe Sessio was probably at the top of Alfonse DeCiccio's list."

Like most of Boston, Gova knew the client pecking order and that civil servants were at the bottom. "Odd that he didn't wear Italian suits." She said it more to herself than to Schultz, but he exploded with laughter.

She'd meant it as an observation, but it didn't surprise her that Schultz had taken it as a joke. Crime scenes affected investigators strangely. Some cracked jokes, others went about their business, doing what they had to do so they could leave. Everyone, she thought, had a way of dealing with the immediacy of murder or violent death and the sight of a victim.

Even in cases like this one, in which investigators didn't hold the victim in high regard, you still felt the weight of your own mortality. Hell, she felt it and guessed that even an old hand like Schultz did, too.

Gova hesitantly lifted a corner of the napkin covering Sessio's face. She'd seen plenty of murder victims during her stint in the DA's office, but the effect of a close-range blast from a large caliber weapon hit her in the pit of her stomach. She glanced at the gaping hole, bits of brain, and shattered bone, then looked away, dropping the cloth back into place.

"Some mess, huh?" Schultz seemed pleased by her reaction to the wound. It apparently confirmed his belief about women and police work.

Gova ignored the comment. "Was DeCiccio here when it happened?"

"He was in the kitchen. He's been zero help. When I got here, he was sitting back in the wine cellar, blubbering about hoodlums and the passing of the old order. He's still back there with the cook, who's feeding him brandy and trying to calm him down or knock him out. You can talk to him, but you won't learn anything that I didn't hear from him back twenty years."

Weeks, Gova thought. Or months. Yeah, it would probably take them months to collar the perp, if they ever did. The field of potential suspects spanned the spectrum of the city's underworld. In Sessio's business, jealousies and infighting abounded. She credited him for remaining on top as long as he had.

Schultz grunted as he squatted next to the body. His knees creaked loudly enough for Gova to hear. He used a handkerchief to pull Sessio's wallet out of his back pocket. He opened it and flipped through the money, flashing hundred dollar bills. "Looks like robbery wasn't no motive. I'd say there's about two grand in here." He passed her the wallet. "You count it and we'll go by your count."

She thought he might be suggesting they divide the money and resented the implication. "Don't worry. It'll go into evidence with a complete listing of the contents," she told him.

A uniform shouted to Schultz from the other side of the room. "Call for you."

"Excuse me," he said, and hurried away.

Gova glanced through the wallet and paused on a photo of Sessio's three children, taken as youngsters. Cute kids, she thought, ordinary kids. But how ordinary could they be living under the same roof as old Joe Sessio?

Schultz returned awhile later, his face lit up like the fourth of July. "You'll love this. We've got the perp. Ponytail came through. He spotted the kid down by the wharf. He's already cuffed and in the squad car. We're taking him in."

"Taking him in for questioning?"

"Taking him in to charge him."

"On what evidence? Where's your witness? What's the motive?"

"Listen, we've got plenty of probable causes with that kid's behavior. As for motive, someone hired him. What else? He shot him, got scared that someone saw him do it, and ran. He'll confess when we get him downtown."

For a moment, she imagined Schultz beating a confession out of the suspect with no attorney present, a confession that would be thrown out of court. "What's the kid's name?"

"Tommy Washington."

"Have your men found a murder weapon?"

"We're looking for it."

The phone rang again, someone called Schultz's name, and he lumbered across the room once more. Gova glanced again at Sessio's body, then turned away, grateful for her empty stomach.

She wandered into the kitchen, where Alfonse DeCiccio slouched in a chair against the wall, a handkerchief pressed to his face, his chef fussing over him like a Jewish mother. "Please, take another sip, Alfonse."

The chef held out a snifter of brandy, but DeCiccio pushed it away and rattled off something in Italian. Then he saw Gova in the doorway and raised his arm, pointing at her. In a thick, Italian accent, he snapped, "You, get out of my kitchen!"

"Excuse me, sir," she said, coming over. "I'm Debra Gova, the district attorney."

He sniffed and wiped the back of his hand across his nose. "I have nothing to say. I was . . . was back here when it happened."

"Did you hear anything?"

DeCiccio shook his head. "I was in the freezer." He pointed across the kitchen at the large walk-in freezer. "The door was shut."

Gova looked at the chef. "What about you? Did you see or hear anything?"

He straightened his lopsided white chef's hat. "Big boom. I run over to the freezer, open the door, and tell Alphonse to . . . to come quickly. We went into the restaurant and there he . . . he was, Mr. Sessio. . . ."

"I covered his face with a napkin," DeCiccio said, and his eyes teared up.

"How long has Tommy Washington worked for you, Mr. DeCiccio?"

"Who?"

"He's one of your busboys."

DeCiccio waved his hand impatiently. "I have many busboys, how am I supposed to keep them all straight?" He rubbed his plump, dimpled fingers over his face and shook his head. "Bad business, very bad. I tell Joe he must be careful, I always tell him that. But he doesn't listen. He thinks he is . . ." He hesitated, seeking the right word, then spat out something in Italian.

"Invulnerable," the chef translated.

"Yes, invulnerable," DeCiccio agreed. "Joe he walks around the neighborhood like anyone else. And now . . . now . . ." His face squashed up and he broke down again, sobbing into his hands.

Gova thanked the chef and hurried out of the kitchen. She nearly walked right into Schultz. "Ms. Gova. You'll love this."

Ha, she thought. "What is it?"

"We found the ski mask he was wearing and the gun, a .38. The turkey tossed both into a trash can between here and the wharf. We're running the prints on the gun now, but you can bet your ass his prints are on it. We got our man."

2

<hr>

For Taylor Brooke, the news on WBZ radio summed it up.

"If you're coming into downtown this morning, you can expect long delays on most routes. Just forget about being on time. The reason: dueling funeral processions.

"One funeral is for Joseph Sessio, the notorious boss of the docks, a man whose influence was widespread. The other is for Monroe Morgan, who is, of course, the father of Senator Franklin Morgan. Services for Morgan will be held this morning at Trinity Church, with the cortege moving from the west on Beacon Street to Harvard Bridge, across the Charles and out Memorial Drive to Mount Auburn Cemetery.

"Sessio's procession will be . . ."

"Damn," she whispered. "Damn them both." She hit the heel of her hand against the steering wheel of her seven-year-old Saab.

Since she'd gotten over the bridge, she hadn't moved more than a few yards in five minutes. She'd never seen incoming traffic this congested on a weekday. At this rate, she wouldn't arrive at the office until well after ten.

Senator Franklin Morgan's voice filled the car. She angrily stabbed at the buttons on the radio until she found music. A melodious sax. Resigned to the wait, she chided herself for not paying more attention to the news over the weekend.

Her thoughts drifted back to the younger Morgan. Whenever she heard his name, a coldness crept through her. The senator had come up in conversations at the office several times during her two years at the firm and she usually either excused herself or directed the conversation elsewhere. If she heard his name on the news, she found another station.

Denial and evasion, she thought.

But since the elder Morgan's death, her long-standing hatred toward everything connected to Morgan had been mixed with a new curiosity. The combination disturbed her deeply and recently had spilled over into her work. More than once in the past couple of days, she'd caught herself snapping at one of the paralegals for some insignificant reason. She reminded herself to apologize to Eileen, her assistant.

She turned back to the first station and listened to a female broadcaster extolling the virtues and accomplishments of the Morgan family. "*Monroe Morgan was the patriarch of a business and political dynasty that has often been compared to the Kennedys. However, the Morgans are Episcopalians, with Puritan ancestors in their family tree.*"

"And skeletons in their closets," Taylor murmured.

She started to change the station again, but the car in front of her shot ahead fifty feet. She grabbed the steering wheel and brought her foot down hard on the accelerator before another car could cut in front of her.

"*A widower for the past twenty years, Morgan had managed the family fortune shrewdly,*" the broadcaster continued. "*After the death of his eldest son, James, Morgan turned his attention to his son, Frank, and was considered the behind-the-scenes manager of his political campaigns. He suffered a minor stroke in 1990 and, after that, conducted his affairs from a private suite of offices in his home. In recent years, his public appearances have been rare and brief.*"

Taylor turned the radio off. She'd heard and read enough. She knew the Morgans had begun building their family fortune before the Revolution with a successful blacksmith shop in Boston. Ezekial Morgan gradually had added stables and a small tavern and later had started a stagecoach service between Boston and Worcester.

According to family lore, Morgan had used the stagecoach line to pass messages among patriots during the revolution. But more than one historian had said that Ezekial Morgan had been in cahoots with the British.

Taylor believed the historians. From her own experience, the Morgans smelled like traitors.

Monroe Morgan's father, among the fourth generation of Morgans residing in the U.S., invested in mills and factories in New Bedford, Fall River, and other surrounding towns during the late nineteenth century. But by the beginning of World War I, most of the Morgan wealth had been shifted from those smoky, soot-stained manufacturing towns to banks and financial institutions that managed to weather the closings of the 1930s.

A few of the Morgans still operated small businesses around New England and Monroe Morgan had inherited pieces of some of these enterprises. Dovecote, a manufacturer of fine china sold worldwide, seemed to interest him the most. The company had proven to be particularly successful and today Frank Morgan remained connected with the company, quietly overseeing its operation from a distance.

The Morgans also prospered in real estate. Monroe had been despised by East Boston residents for joining forces with the head of the Massachusetts Port Authority, which ran Logan Airport, during the sixties and seventies.

In that era, air traffic out of Logan had made Boston and other areas practically unbearable and new highway construction had razed whole chunks of established neighborhoods. But Monroe Morgan hadn't given a damn.

Morgan's death had followed Sessio's by two days, and the passing of the two legends seemed to mark the end of a political era. Since Sessio had been murdered, his burial had been delayed until the coroner's office released the body. As a result, the two funerals had been scheduled on the same day.

One of those little chuckles the universe sometimes enjoyed, Taylor thought.

In each case, authorities expected between twelve hundred to three thousand people, with the Sessio funeral ending in a memorial at the docks later this afternoon. City traffic authorities, alarmed at the prospect of a massive, day-long gridlock, had negotiated with both families on the routes the processionals would take.

Taylor switched lanes and moved ahead a quarter of a mile. She glanced at the clock on the dash, then punched out a number on her car phone. On the second ring, her paralegal assistant answered.

"Good morning, Taylor Brooke's office."

"Hi, Eileen. I'm stuck out here in traffic. I should be there in about twenty minutes. Any calls for me?"

"Mr. Simpson wants to talk to you as soon as you get here." She lowered her voice. "He seems very anxious to see you."

"Great," Taylor moaned. Just what she didn't need. "Pass on the message that I'll be there as soon as I can. By the way, I want to apologize for snapping at you yesterday. I really do appreciate your work."

"No problem."

"See you soon."

She couldn't tell from Eileen's voice whether her apology had been accepted or not. But frankly, she worried more about Ogden Simpson wanting to see her.

Simpson had headed the firm for years and remained a virtual symbol of its long-standing traditions. When the firm had recruited her straight out of law school, Simpson had taken a special interest in her, which had puzzled her. But in recent months, she'd had very few dealings with him. So now she tried to figure out what he might want, what she might have done wrong.

At least half of her time during the past six months had involved Bureau of Prisons advocacy work, pro bono cases. Simpson initially had encouraged her to take the cases. But one afternoon a month ago, he'd suggested she tie up her pending cases so she could begin working more with the firm's private clients.

Maybe now he simply wanted to check on her progress. Or maybe his concern centered on her commitment to advocacy work. She knew attorneys who worked as BOP advocates, helping prisoners with legal matters, risked becoming radicalized by the very nature of the work.

She'd met a couple of other lawyers, both women, who were so committed to working with prisoners that they took other cases only to pay their expenses. But Simpson & Willis hardly led the way in prison reform and that sort of commitment wasn't likely to go over well with the firm.

Five minutes after arriving at the office, Taylor abandoned her small cubicle and slipped into the restroom. She pulled her thick blond hair over one shoulder and brushed it vigorously, a mindless, nervous brushing, then let it drop against her shoulders.

She knew she was an attractive woman, tall and slender, with a certain guarded look that deepened the bluish green of her eyes. She dressed well and had an intuitive feel for the kinds of clothes that enhanced her appearance. But she didn't see herself as the knockout that other people seemed to perceive. Even now, at twenty-eight, when she studied herself in the mirror, she saw herself through the critical lens of her childhood. To her, the eyes seemed too large and intense for her face, the nose seemed too narrow, the mouth too generous. The woman in the mirror still harbored the little girl, the unwanted waif, the outsider, who'd been told by others she would never amount to anything.

Other people, though, seemed to think her looks would be better suited to a life on the modeling runway rather than in the courtroom. More than once, she had caught the eyes of jurors—even judges—wandering over her figure, their attention clearly focused on something other than the case.

She stepped back into the hallway and readied herself for a possible confrontation. Maybe one of the judges had sent word to Simpson that she had violated the parameters of advocacy in challenges to the court. She'd taken strong positions in two particular cases that she could think of. But the case that had inadvertently thrust her into the public eye involved a female inmate who recently had been released into a halfway program.

A guard from the prison where the woman had been incarcerated, a man she'd been having sex with, had gotten in touch with her shortly after she'd entered the halfway program. They'd resumed relations, then she'd vanished from the halfway house for nearly a month. When the police had found her, she claimed the guard had held her prisoner, that their so-called relationship in prison had been consensual rape because she'd been trading sex for privileges.

The police had found numerous locks and security devices in the guard's home that indicated he *had* been keeping her captive. But the woman, after being charged with escape from the halfway house, had landed back in prison for another two years. The guard had lost his job, but claimed his firing was racially motivated.

Right from the start, the case had felt all wrong to Taylor. The woman had only three months left on her sentence in the halfway house. Why would she jeopardize that to hole up with the guard?

She'd won a retrial, which had made headlines, and in the media blitz that had followed, her relationship with Simpson had changed. He didn't just pay special attention to her; she had his ear whenever she wanted.

So what the hell had she done?

Maybe he'd heard that in the other case, she'd been threatened with contempt. But other than that, what had she done that might reflect badly on the firm? Taylor flipped through a mental file of the cases she'd handled. She couldn't come up with a damn thing she'd done that any other attorney in her position wouldn't have done.

She headed down a gloomy passageway lined with ancient walnut bookcases. Along one side ran endless rows of leatherbound copies of Massachusetts statutes dating back to the seventeenth century. Jammed on the other side were paperbound volumes of more recent vintage. There were also copies of *U.S. Law Week,* the *Harvard Law Review,* and other materials that Simpson referred to as "ephemera."

He recently had suggested that the ephemera be moved down the hall and placed in what the junior staff called "the pit," a small, dirty room with a linoleum floor and glaring fluorescent lighting. Clutter dominated the room—Styrofoam cups and packets of Sweet 'n Low left on the battered library tables, magazines tossed here and there, soft drink cans spilling from the trash bin.

Taylor doubted that Simpson had looked into the room lately. The metal shelves lining the walls already overflowed with cardboard boxes of files and briefs. But Simpson would get his way. After all, he had run the firm for decades and his presence suffused every aspect of its operation.

She greeted Clara, Simpson's secretary, who had been with the firm nearly as long as Simpson himself. She smiled and retreated into her boss's office. Taylor started to sit on the couch, when Clara told her to go inside. Simpson met her at the door and ushered her into his office, his paternal manner easing her nervousness.

Despite the pleasant seventy degree day outside, the temperature in Simpson's office barely reached sixty. The staff joked that Simpson had ice in his veins. Old Man Winter, they called him. Spring and summer seemed to turn him sour, but his disposition improved during the interminable Boston winters.

"Make yourself comfortable, Taylor."

From the cherry wood desk and matching chairs to the antiques in the sitting area to the art on the walls, everything in the room had been designed for comfort. Taylor claimed one of the chairs in front of his desk, her body sinking into the soft, cream-colored cushion. The Persian rug under her feet invited her to kick off her shoes and stay awhile.

"I completely forgot about the funerals this morning," she said quickly, just in case he was going to mention her tardiness. "If I'd known there was going to be such a traffic problem, I would've left hours earlier."

Simpson's soft, rolling chuckle echoed briefly in the air. "You're much too quick to blame yourself for things, Taylor. I know you're here until ten or eleven almost every night.

Your work has been nothing less than superior. I'm extremely proud of you.''

Her relief, she knew, didn't escape Simpson's notice. She fulfilled the expectation of all junior attorneys, putting in twelve- and fourteen-hour days, six days a week. Given a larger office, she probably would install a comfortable couch and sleep on it to save on commuting time.

''Thanks, Ogden.''

He opened a file on his desk. ''I've got to leave in a few minutes for the Morgan funeral. Fortunately, I can walk over to Trinity in five minutes.''

''I didn't realize you knew him.''

''Roe and I went back a good many years.''

News to her, she thought. But considering the circles in which Simpson moved, it didn't surprise her that he'd known Monroe Morgan.

''This afternoon there's going to be a big memorial service down on the docks for Joseph Sessio. I'd like you to be there, Taylor.''

Now *that* surprised her. ''You would? I mean, sure, if that's what you'd like. Will I, uh, be representing the firm?''

''In a sense, but that's not the point. I'd like you to get a firsthand look at Sessio's constituents and hear what his friends have to say about him. You're going to be hearing a lot about Joe Sessio in the coming weeks and months.''

''Why's that?''

''Because this firm is going to be defending Tommy Washington, the man who's accused of killing him.''

''I thought you didn't want any more pro bono cases.''

''This case is special. It was also assigned to us by Judge Cornwell.''

''How'd that happen?''

''Kyle Nelson was in court waiting for a preliminary hearing on another case when the public defender's office informed Cornwell that they have a conflict of interest with Washington. One of the prosecution's witnesses is being defended by the public defender in another pending case.''

"So Judge Cornwell appointed Kyle to take the case?"

"He appointed the firm to take it. I'd like you to talk to the defendant tomorrow."

"Sure. Of course." She sat straight in her chair and wondered what, exactly, her role would be.

"This isn't an ordinary pro bono case, Taylor. It will attract a lot of attention and publicity for the firm. And for you."

"I don't understand."

"I want you to lead the defense." His smile seemed to cut his aging, yet handsome face neatly in two. "I think you're ready for a homicide case."

She didn't agree with him, but she appreciated his confidence. "Thank you, Ogden. I'll do my best."

"There's never been a question about that."

He handed her the file on Tommy Washington, then stood up. "I've got to get going. Kyle has already been informed that he'll assist you in the defense." He extended his hand. "Good luck, Taylor."

Taylor's walk to the harbor took her through a neighborhood with a playground where, years ago, she and the other kids at St. Mary's had played. She stopped and gazed through the wire mesh fence, her ears ringing with the phantom shouts and laughter of those children.

In the bright June light, she could almost see herself out there, a nine-year-old girl alone, shunned, unwelcomed by the others, and embarrassed at their questions. Bastard child, homeless waif, burden of the church: she still felt the sting of the cruel names they'd called her. Even though Sister Catherine and Father Carl James had tried to console her, Taylor had known she would never fit in with the others.

After all, the other girls had a place they called home. They had mothers, fathers, brothers, and sisters. They returned to their families on weekends and holidays, while Taylor remained behind. She saw that young girl sitting on the merry-go-round, alone and crying as one of the other girls taunted her. *"Bastard girl is crying. Got nowhere to go for Christmas? No mommy and daddy? No one wants the shame . . . no one . . . no one. . . ."*

Taylor turned away quickly from the playground, their taunts echoing through the years, touching all the painful scars she kept hidden from the world.

She expected several hundred people to show up for Sessio's memorial service. Instead, an undulating wave of humanity spilled across the docks of Boston Harbor. It looked as if half the city had turned out.

She'd known that Sessio had been loved and respected on the docks. As one of the biggest shippers in the business and a friend to the unions, he'd paid scale without protest and had sometimes paid more than scale. Joe Sessio might be called the working man's hero. But c'mon, she thought, didn't it matter to any of these people that the wages were subsidized by illegal activities?

After leaving Simpson's office, she'd gone through the slim file that contained the original police reports. This included the investigation of Sessio's death, the arrest of Tommy Washington, and a report from a public defender who had talked with the accused. She also found a statement from Sal Ravigno, the prosecution's key witness, that said Washington had been bragging about how he was going to waste "the big shot on the docks."

This conversation apparently had taken place when Ravigno had bought crack from Washington on a street corner in Roxbury, a place Taylor and her Saab would never be seen, even in broad daylight, without a police escort. Ravigno claimed Washington was high at the time and "shootin' off his mouth 'bout all kinds of shit. . . ." Ravigno said he asked Washington why he'd want to off a big shot like Sessio, and Washington had replied: "Ain't my idea, dude. You wouldn't believe who I'm doin' it for. . . ."

Taylor made her way along the edge of the dock, past the throngs of casually dressed people. She'd figured her dark suit would be ideal for a funeral; instead, she stuck out, and she didn't particularly like it.

She finally found an opening in the crowd and threaded her way through it, murmuring, "Excuse me, excuse me." She headed toward the front, where the podium stood.

The case, at least as it stood now, favored the prosecution. It appeared that Washington had put on a ski mask (but apparently had forgotten gloves, since his prints had been lifted off the gun), shot Sessio at point blank range, then fled the restaurant. He'd shoved the gun and ski mask into a trash can near where he'd been arrested. Another busboy had said Washington had been acting strangely just before the shooting. That brought her back to Ravigno's statement.

Ravigno, crackhead and crook, she thought.

The public defender who had initially talked to Washington said that the kid insisted he hadn't shot Sessio, that he'd left the restaurant because of a call he'd received about his sister being in trouble. Part of Kyle's job entailed getting a copy of the phone records for DeCiccio's on the day of the shooting.

Taylor stopped as she reached the front of the crowd. Here, jeans gave way to jackets and ties and a few dresses. Michael Sessio stood at the podium, adulating his father, his voice booming through speakers that had been set up. In the younger Sessio's version of reality, he painted his father as a demigod who had vanished from the planet, a hero in the classical sense, right up there with Apollo and Luke Skywalker.

As she watched him, it became apparent that even if he never reached the level of his father's fame, Michael Sessio commanded attention. It went beyond his good looks and his intensity, but it took her several moments to pinpoint. The younger Sessio believed what he was saying. And any time a man believed something with this sort of passion, it convinced others. Televangelists knew it. Political candidates knew it.

"My father knew every face on the docks, even the guys who'd been out here only a week. He could attract an audience with the tip of his hat, his toothy smile, and his affectionate handshake. He possessed a kind of magic and was respected everywhere he went."

She doubted that Sessio's son would mention that last year,

his father had been charged in a case designed to ferret out criminal influence among the unions operating in and around the port. It had been a flimsy case. And the government's attempt to portray him as the ghost of Jimmy Hoffa had backfired big time. Sessio had been acquitted.

In the aftermath, Sessio and his entourage had paraded through the streets. As word of his appearance had spread, the crowd of spectators had grown and the media coverage had intensified. Sessio seized advantage of the situation by setting up shop at a table outside a cafe.

There, like some Gypsy fortune-teller, he'd held court with the "commoners." Housewifes in aprons, men in business suits, and young guys who all wanted to talk to "Mr. Sessio."

Taylor hadn't just watched the circus on television; she'd been glued to her set, just like the night O. J. Simpson had fled in his white Bronco. TV had made the bizarre instantly accessible. The people who'd gotten an audience with Sessio included a young woman who'd been abandoned by her husband of four years, leaving her with two small children to support; an aging man whose daughter's infidelity had split up a family of six; and an elderly widow with no money.

Sessio had nodded his big, bald head, had dispensed a hug here and there, then whispered to one of his men, presumably instructing him how the problem would be handled.

As a result of the government's pursuit of Joseph Sessio, respect for him among the "commoners" had grown tremendously. For Joe Sessio, it had been business as usual; he simply went about doing what he'd always done, ministering to the underclass.

"Well, hey, look who's here," said a soft, male voice behind her.

Everything inside of her went tight. But she somehow managed to turn, to smile, to speak. "Hi, John. You slumming or what?"

"I was just about to ask you the same thing." He smiled, his pale eyes crinkling at the corners.

At one time in her life, she'd wanted to drown in those eyes. John Stark, now pushing forty, remained a ruggedly handsome man possessed of an indisputable charisma. His blond hair had begun to fade to white at the temples. His blue eyes held just the right blend of triumph and tragedy, and when he smiled, a piece of her heart broke off and floated away.

"I'm here on business," she said.

"Business." He looked amused. "And what kind of business would that be, Taylor?"

"I'm defending Tommy Washington."

His eyes widened. He might have suspected, she thought, but hadn't known for sure until she'd said it. Now he stepped back, his brows shot up. "Really? Then we'll be seeing a lot of each other."

The blood drained from her face. Stark, the deputy district attorney, would be prosecuting the man she would be defending. Full circle, she thought. She and Stark had come full circle.

"How interesting," she murmured, then started to turn, to move away from him, but he touched her arm, freezing her in place. She looked at him; he removed his hand. But she felt the phantom burn of his fingers on her skin.

"I think the son ordered the hit on his old man, Taylor, and your client carried it out."

Anger poured through her. His arrogance breathed in the way he'd touched her arm, in his self-confidence, in his blatant attempt to intimidate her by referring, however obliquely, to their past. "A crackhead is hardly a credible witness, John."

He laughed, the bastard actually laughed. "Witnesses don't have to be credible. Once Debra and I nail Washington, we go after the son. Everyone knows he had his old man wasted. It was some sort of power play. Sessio senior and Sessio junior never saw eye to eye on any issue. Besides, there was a lot of revenue at stake. Sessio is going down, Taylor. That's really what it's about, payback where payback is due."

She started to say something, but a thunderous applause ripped across the docks. On the podium, Sessio's fist pounded the air above his head, a gesture of unity, not a salute of defiance. Then he slipped down from the platform.

"Make me gag," Stark murmured, and his hand touched her back, touched the space between her shoulder blades.

"Good luck, Taylor. You're going to need it."

Then, just that fast, he disappeared into the crowd.

Taylor just stood there, blinking hard against the bright June light, her ears ringing with the applause, with Stark's parting words. She thought of what Ravigno claimed Washington had said: *"You wouldn't believe who I'm doing it for."* If Stark could link Washington with Sessio, then the kid was screwed. She would just be going through the motions.

Which would be exactly what Stark wanted.

*M*ichael Sessio made a beeline through the crowd and slipped into his waiting limousine. Nikko, his trusted friend, waited inside.

"It's a goddamn circus, Mike," Nikko remarked, his eyes glued on the crowd outside the limo. "The old man would get a kick out of this."

Sessio nodded, but his thoughts were elsewhere.

"You okay?" Nikko asked.

"Yeah, I'm fine." A lie, he thought. He knew very well that the ramifications of his father's murder would wreak havoc throughout Boston, his company, and, most of all, through his inner circle.

"You can't lie worth a damn," Nikko said.

Sessio glanced at the other man. Nikko's salt and pepper hair looked just as thick now as it had been when he was twenty. His soft brown eyes barely wrinkled at the corners, his body had remained trim and muscular from regular workouts. The passage of time didn't seem to have touched him.

Years ago, Nikko had defended Sessio against a neighborhood bully and had lost most of his teeth, part of an index finger, and much of the flesh on the right side of his jaw. Sessio's father had paid his hospital and dental bills, then hired him to do exactly what he now did for Sessio: cull information. But for years, Nikko had been far more than an employee; he was Sessio's closest friend.

"So let's go through it again," Nikko said. "How're you doing?"

"Bad," Sessio replied.

Nikko patted him on the shoulder. "That means things will improve from here on out."

Sessio doubted it and knew that Nikko did, too. "Now who's lying?"

Nikko grinned. "Guilty," he murmured, and they both fell silent as the limo sped away from the docks.

3

The elevator at the county jail moved slowly upward, groaning like an animal in pain. Taylor Brooke found it a thoroughly depressing ride. Every time she came here, she had to remind herself that, as a visitor, she could leave any time.

When the elevator doors opened, a wave of oppression crashed over her. The pall of gloom that emanated from this place felt like an invisible wall she had to move against.

The sensation bore disturbing similarities to the emotional prison she inhabited in her childhood. The inmate who mopped floors just down the hall could be Taylor, scrubbing the floor at St. Mary's. The guard who stood nearby, watching the inmate like a hawk, could be Sister Irene, her dark, mean eyes scrutinizing everything Taylor had done. She wondered if the inmate feared the guard to the depth she'd feared the nun.

She walked over to a counter where she registered with a sullen guard, who obviously hated his job and wanted everyone to know it. Another guard escorted her through clanking steel doors and down a hallway that literally screamed for fresh paint. Despite repeated visits to jails and prisons, the darkness of confinement, of wasted lives, never entirely left her.

Talk to him and get it over with, she thought.

A guard took her to a small room with a table, two chairs, a barred window. She sat down so that she faced the door and opened her leather briefcase. She removed a file folder, a notebook, and a mini cassette recorder. The folder now included Washington's adult criminal record. Even though he had a juvenile record as well, she hadn't seen it yet.

He'd been arrested three times and convicted twice—for crack possession, and a B&E. The other arrest related to the murder of a teenaged kid, which disturbed her. The charge had been dropped, but it implied that Washington spelled bad news.

The entire case spelled bad news, though, and Taylor wondered for the umpteenth time why Ogden Simpson had assigned the case to her instead of to a more experienced attorney. She figured Simpson had pegged the case as a sure loss. Given the media attention that would surround the trial, the firm would get exposure either way, she would get her feet wet, Washington would be found guilty and go to jail. End of story.

The door clattered and Tommy Washington shuffled into the room, his feet shackled, his hands cuffed to a belly chain. He stood at least six feet two, weighed about two hundred pounds. His shaved head looked slightly darker than the scar that ran several inches along his jaw. "I'll be right outside the door," the guard said.

"Thanks." Then, to Washington: "Have a seat, Mr. Washington." He sat, the guard left, and she added: "I'm Taylor Brooke, your new attorney. Do you mind if I tape our conversation? It will help me in your defense."

He eyed the recorder with suspicion. "Who else hears the tape?"

"Just my assistant."

"I guess it's okay. What happened to my other lawyer?"

She turned on the recorder. "There was a conflict of interest. The judge assigned your case to me."

Washington frowned. His huge, dark eyes seemed genuinely perplexed. "I don't understand."

"The public defender is defending a man named Sal Ravigno in another case and Mr. Ravigno is now a witness for the prosecution in this case. That's considered a conflict of interest."

"Ravigno. He Italian?"

Taylor smiled. "That's a good guess."

"Never heard of no Ravigno."

In the notebook, she jotted: *Find out where Ravigno buys his crack.*

"Listen, lady, I didn't kill nobody." He sat forward, his long fingers laced together on the tabletop. His nails were chewed to the quick. "Mr. Sessio he always left a tip for me when I bussed his table. He didn't have to do that, but every time I bussed for him, there it was, five or ten bucks. I didn't shoot him, didn't shoot nobody. Maybe this Ravigno dude killed him, huh?"

"Tell me what happened last Thursday, Mr. Washington."

He stared at his hands as he started talking. Occasionally, he pulled his fingers apart and gnawed at his thumbnail. "I got a call in the kitchen. Some dude tells me he has my sister and he's gonna cut her real bad. He says, 'You know what this is about, man. If you don't want your little sister hurt, you better git your ass down here fast.'

"I told him I couldn't hear what he was saying, because of the dishwasher. I was stallin' for time, tryin' to figure out what to do. So he says it again. He tells me where I better meet him. I don't know what it's about, he won't tell me, he just keeps sayin' I know what it is."

"So you left."

His shaved head bobbed up and down; he raised his eyes now. "Had to. Kitara, she's only thirteen, just a kid. So, yeah, I tore outta there."

"How were you dressed when you left, Mr. Washington?"

"Dressed?"

"Don't the busboys wear whites?"

"Yeah, sure. But I ripped off my whites before I tore outta there. I was in jeans, a shirt, my sneakers, the clothes I wore to work. I tear ass down to where I was s'posed to meet this dude, but no one's there. I thought maybe I was s'posed to wait for somebody to pick me up, so that's what I did.''

"Did you think the call was gang-related?"

"I figured some crew was messin' with me for something from before. They never leave me alone.''

"Where were you supposed to meet him?"

"On the wharf. Down there by the stand for the airport water ferry."

She nodded; Washington had been arrested at the wharf. "Do you know what time you left the restaurant?"

"Yes, ma'am. At one-forty-nine. I looked at the clock. I wanted to be able to tell Mr. DeCiccio how much time to dock me."

Taylor jotted the time in her notebook and next to it wrote: *Police records indicate J. Sessio shot between 1:55 & 2:00 p.m. & that T. Washington was arrested at 2:22 p.m.*

"How long did you wait? Do you remember?"

"Twenty or thirty minutes, something like that. Then a cop car pulls up. They got Billy Boy—that's Billy Schultz, another busboy—and he starts pointin' at me, identifyin' me to the cops. Then the cops they're stickin' guns in my face and shouting at me to lie down on the sidewalk and shit. I couldn't believe it. I said for what? Skippin' outta work? Next thing I know, I'm in here and they're tellin' me this crap 'bout how I shot Mr. Sessio."

"Have you heard anything about your sister?"

"Sure thing. My mama says Kitara's fine. Nothin' happened to her."

"What can you tell me about the caller's voice? Did it sound familiar?"

He shook his head. "Guy was talkin' real soft."

"Do you think it was a black man?"

"I dunno. He was talkin' shit like a lotta the guys I know, but I can't say for sure he was a black dude."

"Has anyone at the restaurant ever said anything about Mr. Sessio?"

"People talk 'bout him all the time, 'cause he gave such good tips. Mr. D. he gave Mr. Sessio a lotta respect. He was always tellin' us to do whatever Mr. Sessio wants. Fill his water glass, get him more bread, whatever. But I don't remember anyone badmouthin' him, uh-uh, no way. Y'know what I think? I think this is some sort of game, like in a movie I saw where this guy goes to jail for twenty years for somethin' he didn't even do." He sounded angry now. "That's what it is, right? Yeah, I know that's it. I'll go tell the judge and jury, too."

"That's part of what I'm trying to find out, Tommy. May I call you Tommy?"

"Uh, yeah, sure."

"Do you own a gun?"

"A gun?" Like he'd never heard the word before.

"Yes."

"No, ma'am. I don't own no gun."

"The police found a gun with your prints on it, Tommy." She made a point of not mentioning the type of gun or where it had been found.

"I, uh . . ."

"Look, Tommy. I've got to know the whole truth to be able to defend you. Because, quite frankly, right now it doesn't look very good."

He kept lacing and unlacing his fingers, but didn't say anything.

"Do you understand what I'm saying, Tommy?"

"Yes, ma'am."

"So tell me about the gun."

"I bought it from a dude on the streets. I bought it 'cause the crew they was givin' me shit back then and I thought . . . I thought I needed somethin' to keep Mama and Kitara safe. Couple weeks ago, I looked in the drawer where I kept it and it was gone."

"Gone?"

"Uh-huh."

"Had your apartment been broken into?"

"The window looked like it'd been jimmied. But nothin' else was gone, so I didn't tell Mama."

"What kind of gun was it?"

"A thirty-eight. Had me a box of bullets, but it was gone, too."

And a .38 had been found with his prints on it. "Do you know what the date was?"

"Sure. May thirteenth Mama and me we took Kitara out for her birthday. Next day, the gun wasn't where I put it."

Taylor brought a pocket calendar from her briefcase and handed it to Washington. "You're sure about the date?"

He glanced at the calendar, nodded. "Yes, ma'am."

"Why were you looking for it?"

"I figured I'd better hide it somewhere that Kitara wouldn't find it."

"What time did you get home?"

He thought a moment. "On Mondays, I work from eleven to seven. We went out as soon as I got off and got home around ten."

Even though the recorder still whirred, she jotted it in her notebook. "Can't you tell the judge I was set up?" Washington asked.

"I've got to prove that you were. And to do that, Tommy, I need you to be thinking about anything you've heard at the restaurant concerning Mr. Sessio."

"But I already tol' you I've never heard nothin' bad about him."

"I want you to think back over the last few weeks. I want you to think about who you might have told about your sister's birthday, that you were going out that night. I want you to think about it so hard, Tommy, that your head aches."

The gravity of her voice must have made an impression, because he nodded solemnly. "One other thing," she said. "Ravigno claims you sold him crack."

"Look, I got in trouble with that stuff. I even did a couple of break-ins, 'cause I needed cash to get high. And I got caught. But all that's behind me. I've been clean for almost a year. I didn't sell no crack, not to this Ravigno or anyone."

"Okay. Did you tell anyone that the gun was stolen?"

He thought a moment. "Don't think so, ma'am. How long do I have to stay locked up here?"

"You've been charged with first-degree murder, Tommy.

You can't be bailed out. So you're going to be in here until the trial. Within six weeks, a grand jury will consider the prosecution's indictment. At that time, if they think the evidence presented is enough to warrant a trial, they'll endorse the indictment and you'll be arraigned. At that time, we'll enter a not guilty plea and Judge Cornwell will then set a date for the trial. Once it starts, you'll be in court every day and be brought back here at night.''

''This lawyer named Stark talked to me yesterday. He said if I just tell him 'bout Michael Sessio, everything will go a lot better for me. He asked if I knew Sessio hit his old man. I told him no. He said it was just a matter of time before they pinned him. Asked if I wanted to plea.''

Stark and his slick tricks, she thought. ''Did Mr. Stark ask if you wanted your attorney present?''

The kid shrugged. ''I guess so, but I didn't know who my lawyer was. They brought in that red-haired guy for a couple of minutes the other day. But I didn't see him no more.''

''That was Kyle Nelson. He'll be assisting me with your defense. If the police or prosecutors ever want to talk to you again, tell them you want me present. If I'm not available, ask for Mr. Nelson. It's your right.''

He nodded.

''What did you tell Mr. Stark?''

''The truth. I don't know any Michael Sessio. Never heard of him, neither.''

''He's Joe Sessio's son. The prosecution thinks he hired you to kill his father.''

Fire leaped into Washington's eyes and he brought his fist down hard against the table. ''I didn't kill Mr. Sessio,'' he hissed. ''I didn't kill nobody. I done some bad things in my life, but I never killed nobody—not for drugs, not for money, not for shit. That's the God's honest truth.''

Then the fire seemed to die in him and he began to cry, his fists pressed against his eyes. He reminded her of a small child suddenly confronted with something huge and terrible. Taylor leaned forward and touched Washington's arm.

''I'll do my best for you, Tommy. You have my word.''

His hands dropped away from his face, he ran the back of

his hand across his nose and sniffled. "They got me in isolation."

"I can ask the judge to transfer you into the general population, but I think you've been separated for your own safety."

"Yeah. Forget it." He sniffled again. "This guard he tol' me if I was with the other guys, I wouldn't have to worry about being found guilty. I'd be dead before the trial. He said I popped the wrong guy. But I didn't pop nobody."

Kyle Nelson paced back and forth across his office, the telephone cord stretched out behind him like a leash, the receiver pressed hard to his ear. "Hi, Burt. Thanks for getting back to me so quickly. What did you find out?"

"Well," boomed Burt Hallas, "according to my source at the phone company, no calls came into that number at DeCiccio's, during the time frame you stipulated."

Kyle shut his eyes, elated that it had worked. "You're positive, Burt?"

He knew, of course, that Hallas wouldn't have called otherwise. His reputation as a private eye had been established long before Kyle had come to work for Simpson & Willis. The man prided himself on his thoroughness and discretion; he remained the only gumshoe Simpson ever used.

"Absolutely certain, Kyle. It's a public phone that DeCiccio keeps in the kitchen for his employees to use. Lots of calls go out, very few come in."

In the background, Kyle heard another phone ringing. "I'll let you go, Burt. Let me know when you've got something on this Ravigno character."

"Will do, Kyle. Talk to you later."

Kyle hung up and continued to pace, his head racing. He caught a glimpse of himself in the window and it shocked him. He looked strung out. His unruly red hair needed to be cut, his clothes screamed for a hot iron, and the dark circles under his eyes attested to a lack of sleep. The comparison people often made between him and Tom Sawyer hardly fit today, he thought. And shit, innocence hadn't been a part of his nature since the age of thirteen.

So forget it, asshole, he thought, and picked up the phone. He punched out a number. A woman answered with a wary, "Hello."

"It's Watson. I just wanted to let you know your contact at the phone company deleted the call that came in."

Silence at the other end, then a harsh laugh that grated on him. "You doubted it?"

"Let's just say I wanted to be sure."

"So now you're sure. Good. Anything else?"

"No."

The line went dead. Kyle slammed down the receiver.

Taylor walked along the wharf, enjoying the sea air and the crowds of people. Every spring and summer, tourists flocked to Boston and they loved the wharf, this stretch of waterfront on Atlantic Avenue.

When Taylor had returned to Boston after years away, she'd spent a lot of her free time here on the wharf, sampling the restaurants, poking into the shops, enjoying the history of the place. But then, history characterized Boston and traditions formed a bridge between the Massachusetts Bay Colony of 1630 and today.

At one time, warehouses and docks along Atlantic Avenue had catered to the prosperous China trade. Now, condos and offices, shops and restaurants, all crowded the waterfront. Back then, the harbor provided a gateway to other, unimagined worlds; now landfills had left it landlocked.

And yet, Taylor could still gaze across the six and a half miles of harbor and imagine what it must have been like back then.

As a child, Boston had loomed like some sort of fantasy city, impossibly huge but infinitely mysterious, steeped in a history that had seemed too remote from her concerns to be relevant. But when she'd returned here as an adult several years ago, Boston's history had become a living, breathing entity. It had fascinated her. She'd devoured books on the topic, had spent her weekends playing tourist, visiting museums. Once she and Stark had begun seeing each other, he'd acted like a tour guide, showing her the city from a personal, intimate perspective.

They had toured Paul Revere's house, gone to the Boston Pops, visited Bunker Hill, taken the ferry to and from Logan Airport. And she'd loved every minute of it. For the first time in her life, she'd felt connected to this city.

That feeling had only intensified in the years since her arrival.

She passed Rowes Wharf and the sign for the Airport Water Shuttle, where Tommy Washington had been arrested. She wondered where he'd eaten the night of his sister's birthday. Probably not at one of the expensive places, unless Washington or his mother or both had saved up money for the occasion. A fast food place seemed more likely.

She passed the New England Aquarium. During the winter, tourists lined up for the whale-watching cruises; today there were no lines. She ducked into the Cornucopia on the Wharf and claimed a table for two at one of the windows, where she had a clear view of the neighboring wharfs and the harbor.

She was supposed to meet her neighbor, Cathy Spelling, for lunch and since Taylor had arrived first, she perused today's *Globe*. She saw two large color photos, one of Joseph Sessio's casket being carried by pallbearers, the other an aerial shot of Monroe Morgan's funeral procession.

Contingents of Boston's finest, in dress blues, had marched in both processions, she read. Precincts serving Beacon Hill and the Back Bay escorted Morgan's cortege; those from the North End and South Boston accompanied Sessio's procession.

Taylor turned to an inside page, a spread of photos on the two funerals. Because of the memorial service on the docks, far more people had honored Sessio, but Morgan had attracted a number of out-of-state dignitaries and famous faces. The photo display, Taylor decided, looked more like scenes from a political convention.

She turned the page again and read a farewell column on

the editorial page that described how the two men, despite their differences, had grown to depend on each other. One man came from wealth and privilege, the other had risen from poverty. But when Monroe Morgan had directed the senatorial campaign of his son, Franklin, he had called upon Joseph Sessio for assistance.

The younger Morgan had been popular in the affluent suburbs, but lacked a strong base in the city. The black communities, the Irish and Italian wards, had been skeptical, if not hostile toward the candidate. But Joseph Sessio's support for the senator had swayed enough votes, in particular the union vote, to win the city for Morgan and usher him into Congress for a second term. In return, the senator had dispensed a few federal jobs to his city supporters and promised to support legislation that would have a favorable economic impact on the inner city.

"Sorry I'm late."

Taylor glanced up as Cathy Spelling, her neighbor and closest friend, joined her at the table. "Well, I was early, so we're even." Taylor folded the newspaper and set it aside.

"Some coverage for those funerals, huh," Cathy remarked.

"Incredible, actually. So how's the interior decorating business these days?"

"Not as interesting as your world. Lunch is on me, by the way. Maybe we should order a bottle of wine to celebrate your good news."

Taylor shook her head. "Thanks, but let's save the wine for another day. I've got a million things to do this afternoon."

"You nervous about defending Washington?"

Taylor nodded. She'd told Cathy about it last night when she'd gotten home, the two of them exchanging confidences in Cathy's kitchen. "Yeah, I'm nervous."

"You're going to do great, Taylor, I just know it."

"I wish I had your optimism."

"So what's the scoop on Sessio's son? My God, he's gorgeous, charming, and oh so mysterious."

Taylor shrugged. "I don't know what he's about. I don't want to know."

"Well, anyway, you'll do fine."

Cathy looked like the prototypical all-American girl, a cheerleader type. She had a dynamite figure, large hazel eyes that dominated her pretty face, an expressive mouth that swung quickly into a smile, and short, dark hair that sprang from her head in tight, shiny curls.

As they chatted, catching up on news, Taylor spotted Debra Gova, the district attorney, heading toward their table. Not now, she thought at Gova. Go away. But Gova strolled right over and stopped, smiling amicably.

"Excuse me for barging in like this, but aren't you Taylor Brooke?"

"Yes, I am."

Gova introduced herself to both women and Taylor introduced Cathy. "I just want to wish you the best in the Washington case, Ms. Brooke. I understand you're the lead defense attorney."

"That's right."

Gova twisted one of the gold earrings she wore, a clover with a bright green emerald in the center of it. "It'll be great exposure for you, but don't get your hopes up on this one. As I think you know, it doesn't look very good for the defendant."

This woman, Taylor knew, loved psyching out the opposition and refused to let it get to her. She smiled politely, revealing nothing. "We'll see what develops."

Gova's dark, intense eyes scrutinized Taylor without apology and for a moment or two, she felt as if the DA were peering down inside of her. It made her distinctly uncomfortable.

"Well, nice meeting both of you." She started to leave, then turned back to Taylor. "By the way, my assistant, John Stark, will be the acting prosecutor in the case." A quick, mocking smile, then, "You know John, don't you?"

"We've met."

Gova flashed a deprecating smile and appeared ready to offer a retort, then apparently changed her mind and walked off.

"What a bitch," Cathy murmured.

"She's tough."

"She knows about you and John, too."

"So what. The relationship has been over too long to make a difference in this case."

Cathy didn't look convinced. "You'd better be sure of that before you go into court, Taylor."

Taylor's thoughts turned, briefly, to Stark. He remained a fresh, bright wound in her life, a detail that Gova surely would try to use to her advantage.

"Where's that waitress, anyway?" Cathy glanced around.

"I think I've lost my appetite."

"Oh, c'mon, don't let that cow get to you." She studied the menu. "I think I'll have my usual, the grilled salmon squares with lobster vinaigrette, a side order of baby artichokes and a cup of chowder. I'm famished."

Taylor tried to put the incident with Gova out of her mind and concentrated on the menu. Codfish cakes with baked beans and Boston brown bread sounded good. They ordered when the waitress came over, then Taylor asked Cathy about her latest romance, a question that never failed to provoke an interesting conversation.

Although Cathy's interior decoration business flourished, her personal life begged for an overhaul. Her judgment about men had been consistently flawed and as a result, she bounced from one bad relationship to another, ever hopeful that Mr. Right might turn her corner, but always missing the mark.

It appeared that Cathy's new relationship followed faithfully in the usual pattern: an attractive, financially stable, and older man with whom she didn't have much in common. And yet, she remained hopeful.

"I've worked with this guy for a year and a half without realizing he was interested in me," she said. "Sometimes you overlook the good stuff that's right under your nose. He's kind, a gentleman. He always goes out of his way to help me."

"Is he an interior decorator?"

"No, a corporate guy. VP. He's in charge of my accounts. He's forty-five, fit, no bulging belly, a full head of hair, and deep gray eyes."

Taylor heard the unvoiced *but*, the caveat of Cathy's life. She wondered why it was so easy to spot flawed patterns in other people's lives and so difficult to see her own. "But what?"

Cathy shrugged. "I'm mad at him right now. He's married and he didn't tell me until the day before yesterday, after our second date."

"Have you stopped seeing him?"

"Sort of. But I suppose there're some advantages to the situation. I don't have to worry about commitment. He's already committed."

"Be careful, Cathy."

Her eyes met Taylor's. "Oh, that's right. John Stark was married."

"*Is* married."

"What happened between you two, anyway?"

Ironically, the conversation had turned back to the subject she'd been trying to avoid. "Let's talk about it when we get together over a bottle of wine."

To Taylor's relief, Cathy didn't push it. She just nodded and veered the conversation toward other, simpler things. But Taylor felt a lingering unease about Stark, Gova, the whole stinking case.

4

Taylor lived in a townhouse near Cambridge, twenty minutes from her office on a good traffic day, twice that on a bad. The cobblestone streets, lined by old-fashioned lampposts and beautiful oaks and maples, echoed earlier, simpler times.

Even though she could easily afford a larger apartment now, she felt attached to this one bedroom townhouse, perhaps because she'd lived here since her return to Boston. But this morning she wished she lived closer to her office. She'd overslept and decided to drive into town.

By the time she got into Boston, all the convenient parking spaces had been taken. She had to drive around looking for a place to park in the midst of three and a half centuries of Boston's famous architecture.

She passed the glass-walled John Hancock Tower, Bulfinch's golden-domed State House, the Union Oyster House. Each place had a particular memory attached to it, a Stark memory that was part of his tourist guide routine in the early days of their relationship. She'd wondered then, as she did now, what he'd told his wife on those occasions.

"Going out with the guys, hon. Be back at midnight, hon."
Ridiculous. She'd been two years younger then and much
more naive.

She finally circled back and resorted to the underground
parking garage. She detested it. Gloomy and dimly lit, it always made her feel like a little kid again, spooked by shadows
that pooled in corners.

She parked, locked her Saab as she got out, and hurried
toward the elevators. Her heels clicked against the concrete,
the noise filling the garage. The pooled shadows seemed to
deepen and expand with every step she took. She kept glancing around nervously, almost expecting something to lunge at
her from the shadows.

Bogeymen, she thought.

Now she heard a second pair of footsteps, one beat after her
own. Someone trailed behind her. Every muscle in her body
tensed, adrenaline poured through her, she nearly broke into a
run.

Relax, it's just another person headed to the elevators, she
thought.

And suppose it wasn't? Thoughts of her estranged husband
filled her imagination; the footsteps grew louder, closer, and
quickened as she picked up her pace. She focused on the green
elevator door. Kept her eyes glued to it.

Hurry. . . .

She heard a dry cough; her husband always had coughed
when he was nervous. The gap between them narrowed.

Not him, please don't let it be him, please. . . .

She shouldn't have parked in here. How stupid, how incredibly stupid. She broke into a run, arms pumping at her
sides, her briefcase banging against her hip, her heart hammering.

"Taylor!"

She stopped cold and looked back. Kyle Nelson loped toward her, a tall, thin man with red hair and freckles. "My
God, Kyle, you scared me. What're you doing here?"

"Christ, I'm sorry. I couldn't tell for certain that it was

you." He touched her elbow and they continued toward the elevators. "You were really spooked."

Spooked, for sure. "Who'd you think I was?" she asked.

"I couldn't tell. The walk looked like you, but it's so dark down here I just wasn't sure."

Kyle, already known for his ingratiating ways, had been with the firm less than a year. His youth and his Tom Sawyer face often misled people into believing he lacked the qualities of a savvy attorney. Kyle used this trait to his advantage when it behooved him. Taylor considered him an asset and felt grateful to have him on her team.

As they waited for the elevator, she told him about her encounter with Debra Gova, but didn't mention Gova's snide remark about her and Stark. "I don't know where she gets off thinking this is such an open and shut case. Their major witness is a crook."

"That's Gova for you. By the way, I've got the scoop on Ravigno."

"That was fast."

Kyle grinned. "That's what women always tell me."

She laughed and suddenly wondered what kind of women Kyle dated. Sweet young things barely of age? Older women? Model types? No telling, she thought.

"Ravigno's waiting to go to trial for loan-sharking, extortion, and burglary. He served six years of a fifteen-year sentence for second-degree murder for killing his cousin back in 1975. Your basic sleaze."

"My guess is that he's feeding the prosecution information in exchange for getting a couple of charges dropped." Taylor stepped into the elevator, Kyle right behind her. "And who's to say he didn't just make up the story about Washington? That's what it boils down to."

Kyle nodded. "Yeah, it *is* kind of odd that a nineteen-year-old black kid would spill his plans to kill Joe Sessio to a fifty-six-year-old Italian guy. Unless they were in it together."

"I don't know, but Debra Gova sounds like she's got something else we don't know about yet." She recalled what Stark had hinted at during the memorial service. "It might have something to do with Sessio's son, Michael."

"Sessio orders his old man killed. Ravigno pulls the trigger and blames Washington, who's been set up."

"Maybe," Taylor said cautiously. "Seems to me, though, that Ravigno would be staying as far from the case as possible if he were the shooter."

"Maybe he's stupid."

She thought about the gun with Washington's prints on it. "There're a couple things I'd like you to check out, Kyle."

He removed a notepad and pen from his shirt pocket. "Go ahead."

"I want the phone records for every call that came into DeCiccio's last Thursday."

"I already checked. There's no record of a call coming into the public phone in the restaurant kitchen."

"You're right on top of things."

Kyle beamed with pleasure. "What else?"

"Ask Burt Hallas to dig more deeply into Ravigno's life."

"Right-o."

The elevator doors opened and they walked out into the sunlight. She felt more at ease out here. The tension drained from her neck and shoulders and she took a deep breath of the warm June air. They followed the sidewalk to the corner and crossed the street to the old courthouse.

With its majestic columns and portico, the building seemed ghostly, surreal, a throwback to another time. The "new courthouse," built in the 1920s, remained the building used today, but Taylor often cut through the historical old building en route to her office, just for the mood it conjured.

As she climbed the steps that rose toward the building's massive columns, she felt a jolt of pleasure and pride that she belonged here, that she played a small role in the history of the place. The towering bronze doors at the top of the steps swung open as she and Kyle entered the building.

The distinct smell of the place washed over her, an odor that reminded her of museums, of age and permanence. They passed through the huge foyer, went down a hall, and out another door. After crossing the street, she and Kyle were on "Lawyers' Row," and entered the building where the law offices were housed.

The young security guard nodded as they approached his desk.

Taylor smiled. "Hey, Bobby Tee. How's it going?"

"Not bad, Miss Brooke. How about for you?"

"Pretty good."

"Nice shoes."

"Thanks."

"He didn't say anything about my shoes," Kyle remarked as they walked on.

She laughed.

In a sea of gray, black, and pinstripe suits, the security guard took note of the colorful and feminine touches in Taylor's apparel and never failed to comment when he spotted something new. Some days, he simply flashed her a wordless thumbs up. Other days he singled out a particular article of clothing or an accessory.

The shoes he'd noticed were Gucci black lizard pumps, ridiculously expensive. But she'd been working hard lately and felt she deserved the perk. Her appearance inside the courtroom was important. Nicknamed the Looks, Taylor was often sent out to "play" a jury, particularly when a guilty verdict was expected.

They got into the elevator with half a dozen other people. As the door whispered shut, Taylor caught a vaguely familiar scent. It took her a moment to identify it but when she did, goosebumps erupted on her arms. English Leather aftershave. Her husband used to douse himself with the stuff when they'd gone out on Saturday nights in Fall River.

That made it twice within the last hour that she'd thought of her ex-husband, an abusive S.O.B. named Eric Serle. Coincidence? Or a nudge from the universe telling her to snap to it and pay attention?

Eric Serle.

Just the thought of his name filled her with dread and forced her to acknowledge that they weren't legally divorced. Eric, Fall River, her flight from that past nearly five years ago. Now, with the scent of English Leather swirling in her nostrils, those Saturday nights in Fall River rushed back at her.

When Eric had been in a good mood, their nights out had

consisted of a pizza, a movie, maybe a beer afterward at one of the local pubs. Except that for Eric it had never been just one beer. He couldn't stop at one beer. And the more beers he'd put away, the more suspicious and verbally abusive he'd become.

"Just because you're taking courses over at the college you think you're some kinda Einstein. Well. I got news for you, babe. You're not so smart. You're not very smart at all. Don't think you're going anywhere, either. We're staying here. This is where we live. I'll never let you go. Never."

The elevator stopped at the seventh floor. As she turned sideways to let a woman squeeze past her, she quickly glanced around at the other people, reassuring herself that Eric wasn't among them. Of course not, he couldn't be. He had no idea where she was, no way of finding her. She had a different name now, a different look. The hour or so that separated Fall River and Boston loomed as large as a continent. He would never find her. Besides, after all this time, he couldn't possibly be looking for her.

He couldn't, but in her heart she knew otherwise. She believed her flight had enraged him and that rage had festered inside of him all these years, smothering whatever impulses he might have had toward creating a new life for himself. Eric wouldn't know how to pick up the pieces and move on.

When her prison advocacy work had hurled her, however briefly, into the public eye, her first thought had been that Eric would see her on TV. That he would recognize her. Come after her. For days after the initial media blitz on the female inmate case, her terror had lived and breathed inside of her like an unborn child. She'd slept poorly, barricaded herself into her apartment at night, refused to answer the phone until the machine had picked up. She'd slept with a baseball bat next to the bed.

But the months passed and he didn't resurface in her life and her terror coiled up into a tight ball and hid inside of her. It became a shadow that pursued her in her dreams at night, the invisible wolf that crouched in the darkened corners of the underground garage. It waited, like a succubus, in the wings of her life, waited for the right moment to seize her, cripple her.

Only Cathy knew about Eric and that part of her life. Stark might have suspected some dark secret, but she'd never confided in him. Good thing, too, since she would have to face him in court. She suspected that Stark figured their past affair would make her vulnerable. He saw her as the weakest point in Washington's defense, the pretty but naive lady lawyer whose bed he'd shared, the white knight to his powerful black queen. He knew that if he could screw her up on a personal level in court, then he could blow holes in her defense and send Washington away for the rest of his life.

Taylor and Kyle parted company as they got off the elevator. He headed off to his nook and she made a beeline toward hers, mentally running through her checklist of things to do this afternoon.

She stopped at Eileen's desk, just outside her office, to pick up her messages and mail. "Not much in the mail," Eileen said, handing her a packet of what looked to be mostly junk. "Mr. Simpson wants to see you around four."

"For what?"

Eileen peered at her over the rims of her round, wire-framed glasses. "He didn't say. I didn't ask."

Even though Eileen was about Taylor's age, she made a concerted effort to look much older. Her glasses had gone out of style in the sixties and hid the dark, liquid softness of her compassionate eyes. Her flawless complexion, the kind you saw in women's magazines, needed a dash of blush, if only to bring out her prominent cheekbones.

But Eileen didn't bother with blush. She didn't bother with any makeup except mascara. She didn't bother trying to minimize her chubbiness with the right clothes or colors. In short, Taylor mused, Eileen reminded her of a piece of raw stone, waiting for a miracle like Michelangelo to release her true beauty.

"What?" Eileen asked, cocking her head, smiling a little.

Taylor realized she'd been staring at her. "No other messages?"

"Well, there was one other call. He didn't want to leave his name, so I forwarded him to your voice mail." Her smile widened. "He sounded cute."

Taylor laughed. "What does cute sound like?"

Eileen shrugged. "Oh, you know, six feet tall, great eyes, nice bod. . . ."

"Keanu Reeves?"

"Older. De Niro."

"Damn. I'll be sure to check my voice mail."

They both laughed and Taylor went into her office and shut the door. She tossed her mail on her desk and called Cathy at work. "Sorry to bother you, Cath. I just wanted to check to see if you were still going to be able to walk my pup this evening."

The woman who regularly walked and fed Taylor's black lab had left for the summer and Cathy had agreed to fill in for her. But Taylor wanted to remind her.

"Of course. I haven't forgotten. Lady and I are going to have a good walk together."

"I hate leaving her home by herself so much." Lady had become the child Taylor had never had, the family she'd longed for. In a sense, her pet, her trusted companion, had become her only form of personal attachment, the perfect expression of unconditional love.

"Don't worry about it," Cathy said. "She's in good hands."

"Okay. You know where the key is."

With dog business taken care of, she picked up her voice mail. It didn't amount to much: one call, no message, just a click, then a dial tone. So much for Robert De Niro, she thought, and sat down at her desk and went to work.

Shortly before four, Eileen knocked at her door and said that Mr. Simpson was outside. Taylor shot to her feet. "Good thing you reminded me. I forgot all about my appointment with him."

"Relax. He's just got someone out here he wants you to meet."

Taylor brushed self-consciously at her skirt and came out from behind her desk. She followed Eileen out of her office and stopped cold. Blood rushed into her face. She didn't see Simpson, she saw a crowd.

"Surprise!"

Everyone from the firm stood there—attorneys, paralegals, secretaries, interns. Someone popped open a champagne bottle. The crowd parted, revealing a long table draped with a pink cloth and covered with plates of hors d'oeuvres. Tradition, she thought. She'd forgotten all about the traditional celebration when an attorney assumed first chair in his or her inaugural murder trial.

Simpson moved toward her, grinning like a proud grandfather. He slipped an arm around her shoulders and walked her forward. Then he addressed the crowd. "I don't think there's a question in any of our minds that Taylor is going to do a great job and that she is going to perpetuate this firm's reputation for excellence."

Applause, cheers. Then all eyes fixed on her. She found her voice. "Thank you. I'll certainly do my best. This is a real surprise."

Someone started filling the champagne glasses, people filed through the food line. "Congratulations," said Clara, the boss's secretary. "I just know you're going to be the firm's new star."

Simpson appeared moments later and shepherded her away from the food. "Eileen tricked me, Ogden. She said there was someone you wanted me to meet."

"There is," he replied, just as Clara escorted a man from Simpson's office into the common area.

Everything around her paled, then screeched to a halt. Her champagne glass slipped from her hand and shattered on the floor. In the brief flurry of subsequent activity, as several people rushed over to clean up the glass, her body seemed suspended, as if trapped in Jell-O.

The man in front of her looked more distinguished in person

than he ever had on television; his square jaw, cleft chin, and piercing eyes echoed the color of her own. "Good luck in all your endeavors, Ms. Brooke," said Senator Frank Morgan, and raised his glass of champagne. "All my best to you."

She somehow managed to smile, to murmur her thanks, then excused herself and hurried into the hallway, her head in an uproar. As soon as she reached the hall, she broke into a run and charged into the restroom.

She hadn't realized that Simpson knew Morgan, but it didn't surprise her. Simpson had known Monroe Morgan, had gone to his funeral, so naturally he would know the son. But what the hell was he doing here?

She rushed over to a sink and turned on a faucet. The water ran cold and she splashed it on her face, then grabbed towels from the dispenser and held them to her face.

In her mind's eye, she saw Morgan's face, saw him raising his glass of champagne to her, toasting her. Bile rose in her throat.

She splashed more cold water on her face, grabbed towels from the dispenser, patted her face dry and looked at herself in the mirror. Her own face faded and in its place she saw Talia, the young girl she had been, her face pressed to a tall, smoky pane of glass in an ornate wood door, the door of Frank Morgan's home on Commonwealth Avenue.

The longer she stared, the clearer the image became: the thirteen-year-old girl with her small hands up against the window as she tried to peer inside the mansion where her father lived. The vivid emotions of that horrible day rushed back to her, her excitement, her anxiety, the hollow pit in the center of her stomach.

She had broken into the administration office at the children's home where she'd been put when her mother had died. She'd found her records, with Frank Morgan listed as her father. A note inside said to notify him only in the event of Talia's death.

Several days later, on her thirteenth birthday, she'd taken a bus uptown to Commonwealth Avenue. The Cinderella in her wanted to believe he would put his arms around her, embrace her, whisper how sorry he was that he'd let her remain in the home for four years. She'd wanted a happy ending.

After pressing her face to that smoky glass, she'd rung the bell of the enormous brownstone and stepped back, waiting for someone to answer the door. She'd tried to smooth the creases in her worn jumper. She'd kept glancing into that smoky glass, studying her reflection: the brown hair was unkempt, the pale oval face, the pathetic waif that she was. She'd wondered which parts of her face had come from him. Her chin? Her ears? The shape of her mouth?

And then a woman in a white uniform had opened the door. She'd stammered that she was here to see her father, Frank Morgan, and the woman had smiled as though she were a cute, but not very bright puppy.

"Mr. Morgan has only one daughter, young lady, and she's at boarding school in Switzerland."

The housekeeper started to close the door and Taylor had lost it. She'd jammed her foot in the door and shrieked, *"I'm his bastard daughter and it's my birthday!"*

The housekeeper had drawn back in surprise and kept saying, *"Ssshhhh, sshhhh, don't make me call the police."* Suddenly, Frank Morgan had appeared in the doorway, staring at her, looking down at her, eyeing her as if she were an annoying bug that had crawled out of the woodwork.

She clearly remembered the cold darkness of his eyes, like the dark side of the moon. *"I don't know who you think I am, but if you don't stop making such a racket, I'll be forced to call the police."* Then he'd stepped out of sight, receding like a wave, and the housekeeper was standing there again, thrusting a fifty dollar bill at her.

"On your way, young lady."

"But you're my dad," she'd whispered as the door slammed shut.

"Taylor? You okay?"

The images in the mirror vanished; in their place she saw Eileen, standing in the doorway, frowning. "I'll be okay. I guess it was something I ate."

"Maybe you should take the rest of the afternoon off." She

stabbed a thumb over her shoulder. "Don't worry about people out there."

"Would you mind getting my briefcase and purse for me? If Ogden asks, just tell him I didn't feel well."

"Sure, no problem."

"I'll be at home if there're any emergency calls."

"Don't worry about it."

A few minutes later, Taylor slipped out of the office, grateful that she didn't have to see the senator again.

5

Dusk crept like a thief into Fall River, Massachusetts. It darkened the waterfront and stole across the south end, swallowing the shops along Water Street. It filtered over the bars on Sicklin and the decayed factories that still covered acres of city land. In the evening twilight, the peeling paint and rotting wood faded as darkness fell; the shabby neighborhood almost regained the beauty of its bustling youth.

A vintage Dodge Charger, a muscle machine from the early seventies, roared down Water Street and screeched to a stop in front of an apartment building, one of the bleak three-deckers that housed the town's lower middle class. The spotless Charger had a completely restored paint job that mirrored the precise shade of its original orange finish.

Eric Serle switched off the engine, a massive 421-cubic-inch V-8. He leaned over and locked the passenger door and rolled up his window. You could never be too careful in this neighborhood, Eric thought. Thieves ran rampant.

He passed his hand over the dash and admired the interior, also in mint condition. The only personal touches were the sheepskin that covered the driver's seat and the rabbit's foot that dangled from a piece of rawhide that hung from the rearview mirror. He rubbed the rabbit's foot between his thumb and index finger, then got out.

Eric loped along the sidewalk, a warm breeze licking at his face. A yellow wrapper from a fast-food burger pinwheeled down the street. Eric paused briefly outside the door and glanced up and down the block. He didn't know what he expected to see, but for days now he'd sensed a change in the wind, something headed toward him. He didn't know if that something was good or bad. The way his luck had been running lately, though, he figured it was bad.

He ducked into the building and bounded up the stairs, taking the steps two at a time. The nosy old biddy on the second floor, the unofficial super of the building, opened her door a crack, the chain still in place. "Oh, Mr. Clapton," she murmured, and quickly shut the door.

He'd told her his name was Eric Clapton, thinking she would laugh. But she'd believed him. She hadn't found the name unusual. She apparently had never heard of *the* Eric Clapton, which Eric found inconceivable. You'd have to be living on another planet never to have heard of Clapton.

At the top of the stairs, he stopped in front of his door and crouched down, checking to make sure the matchbook cover was still there. It was. This didn't mean, of course, that no one had entered the apartment; the intruder, after all, might have noticed the matchbook cover and simply put it back into place when he'd left. So he entered the apartment quietly, slipped off his shoes, and moved silently through the darkness, his senses jammed into a kind of hyperalertness.

His eyes swept through the living room, but he didn't sense anything unusual here. He paused in the kitchen doorway, listening. The old fridge chattered and clanked, nothing more. He moved on to the next two rooms, opening closets, peering under the beds. Nothing. Certain now that his private spaces hadn't been violated, he returned to the living room and turned on the lights.

Chaos and clutter reigned. Beer cans, gun magazines, *TV Guides,* and old newspapers littered the floor, the couch, the coffee table. A twenty-seven-inch television filled one corner of the room. A folding snack table in front of the faded sofa held the remains of last night's frozen dinner. Flies buzzed around it.

Eric picked up the tray, carried it into the kitchen, and swept the food into the garbage can. He folded the soiled tray and set it against the wall. In the old days, cleaning had been his wife's responsibility. Now he had no wife and since he hated cleaning, he didn't bother with it unless the trash overflowed or the clutter blocked his way.

Eric tossed his keys on the kitchen table and emptied the pockets of his jeans. He unsnapped a leather scabbard, which held an Eddie Bauer hunting knife with an elk horn handle, from the back of his belt. On one side, the blade was jagged, filled with tiny, pointed teeth for scaling fish. A beauty.

He opened the fridge and helped himself to a beer from the case on the bottom shelf. The other shelves looked pathetic, nearly bare—a quart of milk that had probably gone bad, half a loaf of bread, an egg carton, and a jar of mayonnaise. He slammed the door shut and popped the top on the Coors.

Eric shrugged off his windbreaker and tossed it over the back of one of the cheap kitchen chairs. Under his white T-shirt, the muscles in his shoulders and chest were tight and well defined. He bent his left arm and flexed the muscles, pleased at how hard they were, wanting to show them off.

He'd stopped at Harbor Terrace on his way home, one of the older housing projects in town, looking for action. He'd waited at the curb for awhile, watching the balconies. A pale-faced girl in a checkered shirt had appeared briefly on one of the balconies, stared at him, then turned and slammed the door. It pissed him off. Her attitude needed some correcting, he thought.

Apparently the word had spread on Water Street that he had beaten up a few of the girls. He'd been warned to stay away by several local guys—pimps who looked after the girls.

Back a couple of months ago, the toughest of these pimps, a husky French Canadian named DuPré, had cornered him in one of the grimy bars at the wrong end of Water Street, and threatened him. "*Next time you slap anyone around, next time*

*you put a knife to a girl's throat, it won't be the cops you'll
be dealing with. Got that, man?''*

''*Sure thing, DuPrick,*'' he'd replied.

Then the bastard had grabbed Eric's hand and bent two of
his fingers back so hard he'd ended up in the ER later that
night. He'd worn a metal splint for more than week, which
had made him clumsy with his tools.

He'd told the guys at the garage that he'd hurt his hand
putting up shelves in his apartment. His boss hadn't believed
him, though. He didn't like Eric much and had threatened to
can him if he messed up one more time. Eric felt like telling
him to shove the job, that he didn't need it. But he couldn't
afford to lose the goddamn job.

He tried to think about something else, to push away any
thoughts about his boss, the sluts, DuPré, the whole stinking
lot of them. He shuffled into the living room, flopped back on
the couch, and turned on the tube. He cruised through the
stations, found a cop show and watched it for a few minutes.
An undercover cop tracked a drug dealer and put his own life
in jeopardy. Eric cheered for the dealer.

He polished off the beer and during the commercial break,
got up for another. Maybe later tonight he would cruise the
bars outside North Dartmouth or Fitchburg to see what kind
of women he could find outside the city limits. He made that
trip regularly now just to avoid DuPré the Prick and his buddies on Water Street. Besides, he'd already played with most
of the merchandise available locally.

He wandered back into the living room. His gaze strayed to
the battered photos on top of the TV, pictures of him and his
wife . . . when they were getting along. When she hadn't decided that she was better than him. The bitch had run out on
him more than four years ago.

Eric picked up an old belt draped over the back of the sofa.
The leather was worn, stretched, limber. He wrapped it around
his fists and stretched it until he felt the tendons in his forearms
tighten. The buckle bit into his palm. He sat forward on the
couch, watching as the undercover cop slammed the drug
dealer to the floor, and snapped the belt a couple of times.

He slipped lower on the sofa; the cushion cupped his head

like a pair of large hands. Between swigs of beer, he wrapped the leather around his left hand, let it unwind, then wrapped it around his right. Then he held it up to his face. He imagined that the faint scent of leather was actually his wife's perfume. The bitch had been wearing perfume the night she'd left him.

He shut his eyes and let the imagined scent drift through him. He was almost able to feel the leather wrapped around her throat, could feel her squirming against the pressure, and immediately he became aroused.

The thought of her squirming below him, begging him to stop as he hit her harder and harder, thrilled him. He imagined her crying, helpless, whimpering. That was when he would shove it into her, just like in the old days.

Afterward, she would lay there, sobbing silently. Yeah, he thought, smiling. The good ole days.

Four years, six months, and three days ago, those good times had ended and his life had never been the same since. When he found her again—and he would, he'd never doubted that for a second—she would pay big time. No bitch ever walked out on Eric Serle, especially not Talia.

Sometimes, at odd moments during the day, Michael Sessio glanced appreciatively around his opulent office and marveled at his own accomplishments. Surrounded by the accoutrements of his success, he might easily have forgotten all that had brought him to this particular point in time. But he'd never forgotten.

He pushed away from his desk and walked over to the picture window that faced Boston Harbor. He gazed across the miles of blue broken up by the docks and ships. My world, he thought.

And this world allowed him to buy the best of everything— the Armani suits, the fast cars, the yachts, the good life. And yet, at the center of himself, he sensed a loneliness that had burgeoned in the days since his father's death.

More than two decades ago, at the age of twenty-two, he'd started Sessio Shipping on a hope and a prayer. It had floundered in the beginning, but he'd kept at it, working fourteen-hour days, and then, twelve years ago, the huge profits had begun to roll in.

And now, he thought, the company shone among the competition, larger and more powerful than he'd ever imagined. His father, however, had always believed it would happen and at the very least, Sessio owed his father—and himself—answers to the questions that haunted him.

He turned, strolled over to the phone, punched out Nikko's number. As it rang, he went back to the window, drawn by the ineffable tug of water and sky and summer light. "Nikko here."

"Hey, it's Mike."

"What's up?"

"You have time to hunt down some information for me, Nikko?"

"You bet. Shoot."

"I want everything you can find about a young woman named Taylor Brooke. She works for Simpson and Willis. I want to know what restaurants she frequents, who she eats lunch with, what she does during her leisure time, who her friends are. I want to know what kind of food she likes, what books she reads, what movies she sees, what men she dates, what animals she likes, her favorite flowers. Everything."

"It'll take a few days. I'll call you when I've got something, Mike."

"Thanks. Talk to you soon."

Sessio hung up, stood for a moment with his hands jammed in the pockets of his slacks, then opened his top desk drawer and removed a newspaper photo of Taylor Brooke. He passed his thumb lightly over her face and sought the right adjective to describe her. Beautiful? Magnificent? Striking? Yes, he thought. Striking.

Sessio had spent so many years married to his work, it had been years since he'd felt more than brief moments of passion for any woman. But this Taylor Brooke, he thought, fascinated him.

He slipped the article back into his drawer, grabbed his Armani jacket from the back of his chair, and buzzed his secretary. "Please have my car brought around to the front, Janet."

"Right away, Mr. Sessio."

Speak and they jump, he thought wearily. His father had relished such power, but lately he'd found himself bored by it. Power as an entity unto itself no longer satisfied him. He needed a new challenge and suspected that Taylor Brooke might well be it.

That face.

Those eyes.

That mouth that promised paradise.

6

As soon as Taylor reached her neighborhood, the day behind her fell away. During the years she'd been here, this area had become her refuge, her sanctuary. Several blocks away, the Charles River ran through the summer greenery, a wide blue ribbon with its own history. The place suited her.

She nosed her Saab into a shady resident permit-required parking spot at the curb and got out, locking the doors behind her. Between the students and the employees and the tourists, parking in Cambridge was at a record premium.

The evening loomed ahead of her, a desert of time to fill. She would run with her dog, review her notes on the Washington case, maybe just kick up her feet and read. The stack of books on the floor next to her bed grew by at least one every time she browsed through the Coop in Harvard Square.

Taylor let herself into the apartment, a corner one-bedroom on the ground floor. She whistled for Lady, who bounded up the hall, seventy pounds of puppy exuberance. The lab leaped and her front paws landed on Taylor's chest, nearly bowling her over.

"I know, I know," she laughed. "It gets lonely here by yourself."

Lady slathered her face with wet kisses, then leaped down and trotted into the kitchen, Taylor following her. The black lab went over to her empty bowl, nudged it with her muzzle, and barked. "I'll fill your bowl up right away." Lady barked again and sat back, panting and eyeing Taylor as she picked up the bowl and scooped out dry food from the bag in the cabinet.

The phone rang, she let the machine get it. She didn't feel like talking to anyone right now. Her taped message ran its course, the machine beeped. No one spoke. But she heard breathing on the other end. She hurried over to the machine and turned up the volume, listening for background noises.

A ringing phone, that was all. Then there was a click and the line went dead. She quickly hit the SAVE button on the machine and played back the tape. Eric, she thought.

Couldn't be. Eric didn't know her as Taylor Brooke and even if he did, her number was unlisted.

"Let me get out of these clothes, Lady, and we'll go for a walk." Lady barked and trotted over to her leash, which hung on the back of the utility room door. "Yeah, yeah, just hold on."

Taylor went into her bedroom and stripped off her clothes, leaving them wherever they fell, a luxury of living alone. Eric, she remembered, had complained bitterly every time she'd done it and yet had never cleaned up after himself.

Don't think about him, about all that, she told herself.

The four-poster mahogany bed that dominated the room was the first piece of furniture she'd bought for herself when she'd moved in. She'd picked it up at a flea market and months later had found a mahogany dresser and a large wicker chair with pastel cushions. Most of the rest of the furniture in the apartment was eclectic, odd pieces she'd picked up here and there.

Yes, she could afford to toss out all the old stuff and buy new everything. But she'd become attached to some of the older pieces simply because they connected her to her early days in Boston. The brass floor lamp, for instance, had cost her five bucks at a garage sale she'd run across in the Berkshires one Saturday. The wooden chest at the foot of her bed was a nicked wreck when she bought it from an antique shop. She and Stark had stripped it one Saturday afternoon, then refurbished it.

The pealing of the phone interrupted her reverie. Certain it was the breather again, she hurried back into the living room and stood over the machine, waiting for the caller to speak.

"Taylor, it's me. Cathy. I saw your car—"

"Hi," Taylor said, picking up. "I got a breather call, so I wasn't going to pick up until I heard a voice."

"Oh, I used to get them all the time when my number was listed."

My number isn't listed, she thought. "Thanks again for walking Lady today."

"We had fun. Listen, I'm making some fettuccine and I've got a bottle of wine. You want to come over here for a bite to eat?"

"Bring the stuff over here and we'll mess up my kitchen. Let me just walk Lady first."

"Great. See you in a while."

Cathy arrived thirty minutes later, bustling into the apartment with a tray of food and a bottle of Chilean wine tucked under her arm. If only for this evening, Taylor wouldn't have to think about Morgan, about Washington, about any of it.

"You're my guinea pig, Taylor. If you like the fettuccine, I'll make it for Roger."

"Who's Roger?"

"That guy I was telling you about when we had lunch."

"Oh, right. The one you're mad at."

"Well, I'm not that mad now. He called me this afternoon. He wants to get together over the weekend."

"Where's his wife going to be?"

"Out of town."

She moved with utter ease around Taylor's kitchen, popping slices of French bread into the toaster oven, dishing up the fettuccine. She even added several spoonfuls to Lady's dish.

Awhile later, they opened the bottle of wine and Cathy filled the glasses. "Toast," she said. "To the soon-to-be-famous lawyer."

"You won't believe what happened to me today," Taylor said, and told Cathy about the surprise party and Franklin Morgan's appearance.

Cathy didn't say anything, didn't interrupt. She just listened as Taylor described her shock at seeing the man who had been tucked away in the back of her mind, like a dirty, shameful secret, for most of her life.

"What I don't understand is why my so-called father is showing up now in my life, Cathy. I mean, what the hell does he think he's doing?"

"Maybe he's just curious," Cathy offered.

"Curious." She spat the word. "Give me a break. What'd he think, that I was going to turn out to be a bag lady or a hooker or something? Or maybe he figured I'd try to get money from him. Or that I'd announce my existence to his prissy wife. *'Hi, Mrs. Morgan. I'm Frank's long-lost illegitimate kid.'* "

Lady whined at the tone of Taylor's voice and she glanced down at the dog, sprawled next to her chair on the floor. "It's okay, girl," she said gently. "I'm not talking about you."

"Maybe he wants to set the record straight."

"Twenty-eight years after the fact?" She knocked back the rest of her wine. "He's a little late. Before I left the room, my impression was that he'd waited all these years to see if I was, I don't know, infected or something. Now he realizes I'm not some hopeless working-class slob."

"Doesn't he have another daughter?"

"Yeah, it said in the paper that she's dying of leukemia. Now I guess I'm supposed to take her place."

"I think you're being too hard on him, kiddo. Maybe he's just curious."

"What I think he's most curious about is whether I'm going to tell someone his dirty little secret. Now that I've got some credibility, it wouldn't be as easy for people to dismiss my story." She nodded to herself. "Yeah, I think that's what it's about. I think he figures he'll beat me to the punch, tell my boss, maybe, or his D.C. buddies. What's his prissy wife going to say to that?''

''It sounds like a midlife crisis to me,'' Cathy remarked.

''Men like him don't have midlife crises. He's got everything he wants. If he plays his cards right, he'll probably run for the White House someday. And he'll probably make it.''

''Not if the press brings up his past.''

''C'mon. None of that stuff makes any difference these days. Who cares if his old man paid off coeds from Vassar?''

''I thought it was Mount Holyoke.''

''One of those seven sisters.'' Taylor waved her hand impatiently. ''The point is that when I left Eric, I shouldn't have come to Boston. I should've run off to Montana or Hong Kong.''

''You didn't have enough money to get to Hong Kong.''

''You know what I mean.''

''Yeah, I do know.'' Cathy reached across the table and patted Taylor's hand. ''And frankly, I think you've done the right thing ever since you left Eric. You put yourself through two and a half years of law school on scholarships, loans, and sheer will power. You're with one of the best firms in the country. You're about to take on a big case that's going to change your career. . . .'' She shook her head. ''I mean, if that isn't about right choices, what is?''

Her words struck Taylor where they always did, right in the heart. It had been that way since they'd met, complete honesty and total support for each other. They each knew what to say to the other and when to say it.

After that, she felt better, more in control of the situation and of herself. But as they talked, she began to see analogies between Morgan's relationship with her mother and her marriage to Eric. In both instances, the women had fallen for an illusion.

Her mother, she knew, had been taken in by Frank Morgan's money, his family name, his gentility, his good looks. Eric had never had money and his family was blue collar, not blue blood. But Taylor had been sucked in by his all American good looks, his charm, his fast-talking smoothness.

They'd met at a friend's wedding, during a time in her life

when she'd felt particularly lonely and hungry for a family of her own. She'd just graduated from college and had gone to work in a lawyer's office, basically doing grunt work that she hated. She'd been vulnerable; it was the only rationalization she could come up with for why she'd married the man.

For the first six months, they'd enjoyed the proverbial honeymoon. The turning point had come when she'd registered for law courses. Eric already felt threatened because of their education differences; she had a BA, he had an associate degree. Now, suddenly, she wanted to work toward a law degree, which would put her in another league entirely, not just educationally, but financially. His insecurities had burgeoned and he'd taken it out on her.

He had become violent, cruel, abusive. Often, without apparent provocation, particularly when he'd been drinking, he would turn on her, attacking her verbally. Everything she did upset him. If she left early for work in the morning or came home late, he accused her of screwing someone else. Twice he followed her to campus. Once, he made a scene at the law office and she nearly lost her job.

The first time he beat her up, he'd come home six sheets to the wind, enraged because he'd been fired from his job, fired, his boss said, for missing work one day too many. She ended up in the emergency room, too ashamed and humiliated to tell anyone what had really happened to her.

The next morning, Eric cried and begged her not to leave him. He swore he would never touch her again. And for months, he didn't. He went to AA, he found another job, their lives went on, things seemed to improve.

Then, fifteen months into the marriage, she discovered she was pregnant. The news appalled Eric, but filled her with an elation she'd never known before. Despite his abusive behavior in the past, she'd convinced herself a child would make the difference.

She couldn't have been more wrong. The day she'd registered for more law courses, Eric had been fired from another job and she'd ended up in the emergency room with three fractured ribs, a dislocated shoulder, and she'd lost her baby—and her dream that the marriage would work.

A young nurse had whispered to her, "You can leave him. We can help you. All you have to do is say yes."

And she'd said yes.

For the next three months, she'd planned her escape, saved for it, and drew comfort and courage from a battered wives' group that she attended once a week, on the nights Eric went to AA meetings. That, too, was somehow fitting. In a sense, they suffered from the same disease; it had merely manifested differently in each of them.

The day after she'd fled and taken a train to Boston, she'd called one of the women in her group, who had wired her a thousand dollars. It was enough for her to rent an efficiency apartment. She'd legally changed her name from Talia Serle to Taylor Brooke, grew her hair long and dyed it blond. She enrolled in law school at Amherst and found an administrative job on campus to help pay her tuition.

She had never filed for divorce, fearing that Eric would find her.

In a sense, she had lived out the nightmare that would have been her mother's life if she'd married Frank Morgan. The potential for violence, duplicity, and cruelty that had existed in her mother's relationship with Morgan had manifested in her marriage to Eric.

Now, nearly five years later, her past seemed to be crowding in on her, like a battalion of ghosts. She had the deeply uneasy feeling that it would get worse, a lot worse, before it got better.

Easy, Eric thought, take it nice and easy, just the way these hot little numbers liked it. Sip some wine, sweet thing. Try this pill, honey.

The hooker accepted everything he offered. They liked being high, these women. They needed it. They couldn't function without it. He'd brought the wine, rotgut shit that probably would leave her puking in the morning, but the pills belonged to her, little treasures she pulled from here, from there.

The woman, maybe all of nineteen, had hair as dark as Talia's and a body like hers, too, slender with curves in the right places. The kind of body, Eric thought, that a man could lose himself in.

Their motel room, small but not bad, had a tiny fridge in the wall, an incredibly soft bed, and mirrors on the ceiling. They hadn't tried the Jacuzzi in the bathroom yet.

Her name was Ginger, like the spice, and she had a rolling Southern accent that made him think of bayous and banyan trees, of steaming Southern mornings when the air smelled of grits and home fries. She seemed classier than the other hookers he'd known and she cost more, seventy-five an hour and that didn't include the room.

"So what d'you like, hon?" She straddled him, her nimble fingers working at the buttons on his shirt. "I do just about anything."

Eric whipped a scarf out of the back pocket of his jeans. "Let me blindfold you," he said.

She giggled, a small, girlish giggle, eyes wide. "That's okay."

She rolled off him, onto her back, and stretched her long, pale arms over her head, stretching like some lovely, lazy cat. Her silk teddy stretched across her breasts; her panties had tiny red hearts on them.

Eric remembered buying Talia a teddy, bringing it home in a pretty box with a big red ribbon on it. And he remembered the disappointment in her expression when she'd removed it from the box and held it up, a sheer, black teddy.

"You don't like it," he'd said, unable to mask his disappointment.

"It's beautiful, but I never wear these."

He'd snatched it out of her hand, stuffed it back into the box, and stomped out of the room.

Ginger wouldn't do that. Right now, she poured them more wine, her hair falling like a dark veil on either side of her face. She hummed to herself, a soft, disjointed tune.

"One more sip for bliss." She slugged down half her glass, then handed it to him. "Your turn."

He drank it down too fast and the rotgut blew his brain wide open. Suddenly, he found himself in the apartment with Talia, the two of them arguing, shouting. Dressed for her night classes, she looked too perfect—makeup just so, a dab of expensive perfume, clothes too tight. Eric *knew* she was meeting another man, some lawyer that she wanted to screw.

And he swung at her.

His fist sank into her stomach and she gasped, eyes bulging in their sockets, air rushing from her lungs. *"Bitch, you can't do this to me,"* he hissed, and swung again and again and again. She rolled across the bed, trying to escape his fists, but he grabbed her by the hair, jerking her back, and her arms flew up, covering her face, and she sobbed, *"Please, no, don't hurt me, oh please, God. . . ."*

Something snapped in his head, he could hear it, the sound of a dried branch as it broke in two. He wrenched back and stared at the woman on the bed, the brunette who wasn't Talia.

The hooker named Ginger.

Jesus God, what have I done?

Torn teddy, torn panties, blood: he panicked. Eric leaped off the bed, breathing hard, his fists aching and bloody. He looked down at himself, naked from the waist down. He'd been screwing her, screwing her and beating her up.

Get out fast, now, c'mon, c'mon, where're your clothes?

He stumbled back, his heart hammering, the woman's sobs slapping the air. He swept up his clothes and pulled on his jeans, dancing around on one leg. He scooped his wallet and loose change off the dresser, stuffed everything into his pockets, grabbed his windbreaker off the back of a chair.

He reached the door and realized he'd forgotten his shoes.

He spun around, ran over to the bed, dropped to his knees, and looked under it. He grabbed his sneakers, but couldn't reach the socks. He flattened out on his stomach so he could reach farther and just then, the woman leaped onto his back. She pounded him with her fists, pounded and sobbed, "Bastard, you bastard, you ruined my face. . . ."

Eric reared up, throwing her off, then grabbed her by the arms and hurled her onto the bed. Her head struck the wall, she slumped to the mattress, motionless.

"Christ, oh man, Christ. . . ."

Run! shrieked the voice inside of him, and he tore toward the door, his socks forgotten, a sneaker in either hand.

He poked his head outside first, checking the lot. Clear, everything clear. Then he charged toward his car, scrambled behind the wheel, and forced himself to drive slowly out of the lot.

Ginger belonged to DuPré; the bastard would be looking for Eric soon. DuPré and his buddies would stalk him with their fists, their brass knuckles, their knives.

He would toss some things into a suitcase, take what he needed, and lay low for a while. Very low.

As soon as he hit the highway, he opened the Charger up as wide as she would go.

7

────────────

She runs to answer the ringing phone, but it's as if she's on a treadmill, running and going nowhere. The phone keeps pealing, her legs move faster and faster, blurring beneath her. Her breath explodes from her mouth. Then suddenly she shoots forward like a stone released from a slingshot, and flies toward the phone.

"Hello? Hello?"

"Hi, bitch," says Eric.

She slams down the receiver, but it begins to ring again and she races to answer it and charges right out of the dream. . . .

Taylor bolted awake, her face damp with sweat, the phone next to the bed ringing. Eric.

No, impossible.

She snatched up the receiver. "Yes? Hello?"

Breathing, then: "If you want to live to see thirty, back off from the Washington case."

"Who is this?" she demanded.

But the caller had already hung up. She quickly punched

out *69, a feature she'd recently gotten on her phone service. An automated voice said, ''The last number to call you was five-five-five, nine-six-eight-zero. If you wish to call this number, press the pound key.''

She hit the pound key. The number rang twice before someone answered. ''Yeah,'' said a gruff male voice. It didn't sound like the same man who had called her.

''Hi, is Tina in?''

''Ain't no Tina here, lady. This is a phone booth and I'm waitin' for a call.''

''A phone booth where?''

''Downtown,'' the man replied, and hung up.

She glanced at the clock; it was barely eight. Eileen probably hadn't left for work yet. Taylor called her at home.

''Eileen, it's Taylor. I'm sorry to bother you at home.''

''No problem. What's up?''

''I got a disturbing call a few minutes ago. It apparently was made from a phone booth downtown somewhere. Can you check it out for me and get the address?''

''You bet. What's the number?''

Taylor gave it to her. ''I'd appreciate it if you didn't mention this to anyone else.''

''Sure. What'd the person say?''

She told her.

''Maybe you should report it to the cops, Taylor.''

''I'd rather not do anything yet. Just find the address for now.''

''Okay. What time will you be in?''

''Around nine-thirty. And thanks, Eileen.''

She showered, dressed, fed herself and Lady, then took Lady for a walk. The entire time, she kept hearing the man's voice in her head. She fixed it in her mind, the rhythm, the tone, the slick smoothness of the words. If she heard it again, she would recognize it, of that much she was certain.

On the way back from Lady's walk, she remembered that before the Eric dream, she'd been dreaming of her mother again. Her mother as an apparition in a white, flowing gown, her mother with arms outstretched, and herself as a girl, as

Talia, her own arms extended as she sobbed, *"Don't leave me, please don't leave me . . ."*

Eric, her mother, her father, the spiraling episodes of her past: when would any of it cease to haunt her?

On her way into town, her cell phone rang. "Taylor, it's Eileen. I've got an address for that number." She reeled it off. "I figure that puts it down on the wharf somewhere."

Yeah, Taylor thought. Not too far from the Cornucopia, where she and Cathy had lunch. "Thanks a million, Eileen. See you in a few minutes."

She walked into the office at 9:30 on the nose. Eileen handed her some phone messages. "Kyle said to buzz him as soon as you get in. He wants to go over some things. Oh, I almost forgot. When I picked up the mail out front, this was with it." She handed Taylor a padded envelope without stamps or a return address.

"Thanks." She ran her thumb over the bulge in the middle. "Did De Niro call back?"

Eileen laughed. "Nope. I didn't forward any calls to your voice mail."

"Well, if he calls," Taylor said with a smile, "be sure to put him through."

She went into her office, dropped the package and her messages on her desk, started to buzz Kyle, then decided to open the package first. She cut it open with a pair of scissors and tilted the envelope so the contents would slide out.

A cassette tape in a plastic container dropped onto her desk. She popped open the container, removed the tape. No label. She stuck her hand into the envelope, looking for a note, a letter, something, but the envelope was empty. She opened the bottom drawer of her desk and brought out the regular tape recorder she used for dictating correspondence.

Taylor dropped the tape into place, hit the PLAY button. Static. Then she heard snatches of a man's voice, saying something about a Detective Schultz, the detective in charge of the Washington case.

The voice she heard, however, didn't belong to Schultz.

"Yeah, he's certain they got the one that did it. The busboy was s'posed to shoot him, then get rid of the gun and the ski mask. Then he was s'posed to sneak in the back door of the kitchen like he'd never left."

"You really think that's it?" A surly voice; it grated on her.

"That's what they say. I got this right from a cop who works with Schultz. The kid panicked and ran. Or maybe he went around to the back door and it was locked. He runs a few blocks, tosses the shit into a garbage can, then runs down to the wharf."

"That's bullshit."

"Joe Sessio went down because someone ordered it. That's what they're saying. But the kid's not sayin' squat about who hired him."

"Are you going to shoot or not?"

"It's your shot, not mine."

Clicks, a series of them, one right after another. Music played in the background, there were more clicks. Pool, she thought. The two men were playing pool and one of them had recorded the conversation.

"If I were you," the surly voice said, "I wouldn't go around telling that story because it don't fly, man."

"What're you telling me, Ravigno?"

Taylor stopped the tape, backed it up. ". . . telling me, Ravigno."

My God, she thought. The surly voice belonged to the prosecution witness.

"What I'm telling you, man, is that the kid, Washington, didn't shoot nobody. I know for a fact that the whole thing was set up to make it look like he did it."

"Yeah, right."

"You callin' me a liar?"

"Okay, you're not a liar. So what's it about? Tell me that."

"Fuck you, man, I told you too much already. Just forget I said anything. Play pool, for Christ's sakes. You're pissing me off with these questions."

The tape ended. A hissing sound filled the room. Taylor pressed the STOP button, rewound the tape, listened to the whole thing again and timed it. Two minutes and eighteen seconds of tape that would destroy the prosecution's witness and get Tommy Washington acquitted.

She buzzed Kyle. "Get up here fast," she said.

"What happened?"

"Just get up here."

"I'm on my way."

He hurried into her office a few seconds later and tapped his chest with his palm as he made an exaggerated effort to gasp for air. "How's that for speed?"

"Sit down. We've got a miracle," she said, and hit the PLAY button.

Kyle listened with rapt attention, not interrupting, barely moving, until the two minutes and eighteen seconds of tape had finished. Then he rewound it and listened again, a frown burrowing down between his bushy, reddish brows.

"I can't believe this," he exclaimed. "If it's the real thing, Ravigno is out. Hell, they won't even be able to convince the jury, even with the gun as evidence. Not beyond a reasonable doubt. That jury is going to have all kinds of doubts."

Taylor grinned. "You got it."

"What's our next move?"

"I want you to go down to the Thirteenth Precinct and get a copy of the taped interview with Ravigno. They'll probably try to give you the transcript, but insist on a copy of the tape. In the meantime, I'll get in touch with a voice analyst. If we can prove it's Ravigno, we'll ask Judge Cornwell to throw out the case. It won't even go before the grand jury."

"I'll make a copy of the tape and put the original in a safe place," Kyle said.

She knew she could entrust the tape to Kyle, but she didn't intend to risk something going wrong. "I'll make a copy at home tonight. Just get down to the precinct."

Kyle slid off the corner of her desk and saluted. "I'm on my way."

She hadn't felt this elated since the night she'd fled Fall River.

Debra Gova frowned when her secretary's voice came over the intercom. "Ms. Gova, there's a man on the phone who insists on talking to you."

"Ellen, I said no interruptions. Take a message and I'll call him back."

"He, uh, doesn't want to leave a message. He said to tell you it's Mr. Watson. What do you—"

"I'll take the call." Gova dropped her pen, reached for the receiver. "Thanks, Eva."

A click, a hum, then a hoarse whisper. "It's me," said Kyle Nelson. "I—"

"Hello, Mr. Watson. I got the call, Ellen."

Another click: her secretary had disconnected.

"I told you never to call me here," she snapped, her voice quiet but sharp. "Give me your number and I'll call you back on—"

"Fuck the rules," he snapped. "We've got a major problem."

"Are you at a phone booth?"

"Yes." He reeled off the number, they hung up.

Gova opened one of her desk drawers and took out a blue phone, her private line, her safe line. It better be good, she thought. She hadn't gotten where she was by taking unnecessary risks. She punched out the number.

Nelson answered on the first ring. "Okay, here's the—"

"Hold on a minute. We need to be real clear on the ground rules. This could've waited until tonight, when I'll be home."

"No, it can't wait," he replied and proceeded to explain.

Gova felt ill. She shut her eyes and squeezed the bridge of her nose, massaging it as he spoke. Her head spun with options.

"No violence," he said. "You promised me, you know. No one gets hurt."

"You aren't in any position to be giving me orders. But don't worry about it. It'll be clean, squeaky clean."

Gova hung up and immediately made another call. She left

a brief message and the number for her private line. Then she
paced as she waited, paced and mulled over her options. They
were pitifully few.

Six minutes later, the blue phone rang. She said what she
had to say. "Any questions?"

"No. It'll be taken care of."

"It's got to look like a botched B&E."

"Of course."

She hung up and a wave of despair crashed over her. Sweet
Christ, how could it come down to this? Sure, she could be
ruthless in getting things her way, but she didn't like violence.
The whole thing made her sick. But what other choice did she
have? The stakes had shot too high to do otherwise. And the
bottom line, she thought, was that Taylor Brooke didn't have
a clue what she'd stumbled into and so it would remain.

Taylor took a late lunch and walked down to the wharf by
herself. She found the phone booth easily enough, two doors
away from the Cornucopia. She went over to it, picked up the
receiver, listened to the dial tone.

She wished, suddenly, that the simple act of touching the
receiver would yield an impression of the man who had called
her apartment and warned her to back off. But she felt only
the warm plastic of the receiver against her hand and a vague
disgust. She replaced the receiver, brushed her hands together,
and walked on.

At a fast food stall, she bought a bowl of New England
clam chowder and a salad and went over to one of the tables
near the water to eat it. Gulls pinwheeled through the warm,
blue afternoon, their shrieks ringing out across the wharf, as
much a part of this place as the line of sailboats in the distance.

"If you want to live to see thirty. . . ."

She touched the side of her purse and felt the shape of the
tape.

*"What I'm telling you, man, is that the kid, Washington,
didn't shoot nobody. I know for a fact that the whole thing
was set up to make it look like he did it."*

"Let's hope you're right," she said softly to herself.

"The practice of law has been known to cause people to talk to themselves. Mind if I sit down?"

And just that fast, John Stark pulled out the other chair at her table and joined her. "I don't recall saying yes," she said.

"C'mon, Taylor. Knock it off, okay? You've made your point. I'm the schmuck. I made terrible choices right down the line and now I've got to live with those choices."

So do I, she thought, but didn't say it. She refused to let him know how badly scarred he'd left her. "So what'd you do, Stark, follow me from the office?"

"Sure. I follow women every day."

"As a stalker, I suppose."

"You've got me pegged."

He took off his sunglasses and slipped them in the pocket of his striped blue shirt. He wore light gray summer slacks that fit him well; his jacket fitted neatly over the back of his chair. His tie, typical for Stark, looked as if some rambunctious kid had flicked his paintbrush at it. Ties apparently remained Stark's single rebellious statement.

"Your wife pick out that tie?" she asked.

"Actually, my sister gave it to me."

"She needs glasses."

He laughed and looked down at the tie. "I don't know, I sort of like it. So how's the defense holding up?"

"I was just about to ask the prosecution the same thing," she shot back.

Stark polished off half of his fried fish sandwich, then dabbed at his mouth with a paper napkin. "You're going to make a fool of yourself in court, Taylor. But it won't be through any fault of your own."

She felt like telling him what he could do with his unsolicited advice. Instead, she laughed. "Is that supposed to make me feel better?"

"Just a friendly warning."

"You and Gova make quite a team, John. I'm impressed. She figures she'll take first crack at psyching me out, then she'll send you in to finish the job. I mean, please." She rolled her eyes. "What I figure is that you two must be sweating bullets, otherwise you wouldn't be bothering with me."

Stark's eyes fixed on her and for moments, she squirmed inside like an impaled bug. "Is that what you think?" His eyes suddenly seemed wounded, his voice too soft.

"It's what I *know* John. You haven't given me any reason to think otherwise."

"Well, you're wrong. Washington is going to be convicted. The evidence is overwhelming. And I just don't want to see you make an ass out of yourself in court."

"So don't come to court."

"I'm afraid that's not one of the options."

"So did you hire someone to threaten me on the phone?"

"What're you talking about?"

Her patience snapped and she leaned forward, mimicking the caller's voice, that insidious low rasp. " 'If you want to live to see thirty, back off from the Washington case.' Sound familiar, John?"

With that, she pushed back her chair, picked up her empty paper dishes and plastic utensils, and walked away from him. She pushed everything into the trash can and headed back toward her office.

"Taylor, wait up." Stark trotted to her side and fell into step with her. "I honestly don't know what you're talking about."

"Then ask Gova, maybe she knows. Did you give her my home phone number?"

"Please." He touched her arm and a kind of electricity leaped between them, a burning current that shot through her elbow and into the rest of her. The feeling smacked of the past, familiar for all the wrong reasons. She jerked her arm free of his grasp and didn't slow down. Neither did he. "C'mon, talk to me, Taylor. When did you get this call? Did you report it?"

She stopped. Looked at him. "Leave. Me. Alone. I can't make it any clearer than that."

Then she hurried up the street, unable to swallow around the huge, swelling lump in the middle of her throat. Images of their brief affair drifted through her, as lazy as swans.

They had met in the law library one Saturday, she and Stark, both of them researching cases. They'd hit it off, gone out for coffee, and spent three hours talking down by the wharf.

It had lasted only a handful of months, intense passionate months in which she'd lived at the edge of some terrible abyss. She'd waited for his calls, waited for the sight of his face coming down her sidewalk, waited for the warm certainty of his hands, his mouth. She'd waited like Rapunzel in her tower, waited for John Stark, prince, to liberate her.

Yeah, right.

She'd known from the beginning that in terms of Stark's priorities, she fell somewhere behind his wife, career, and political aspirations. She'd known that Stark and his wife had an arrangement, that divorce had never been an option and never would be. But it hadn't mattered to her. She naively had believed that he remained in the marriage because it would cost him a king's ransom to get divorced.

But she eventually realized that for years, his marriage had been the harbor to which he returned after his tumultuous affairs in the real world. His wife suited his political aspirations; she looked right, knew the right people, had the right connections. He didn't want to divorce her. He merely wanted to have the freedom to screw around when it suited him.

And Taylor had suited him.

They had suited each other.

My God, twenty-eight years old, she thought, and her personal history seemed weighted with complexities. Would her own marriage one day be nothing but a convenient arrangement? Would she have younger lovers on the side? Why bother to get married at all?

De Niro called again," Eileen said.

"You're kidding. Did he leave a message?"

"I forwarded him to your voice mail." Eileen nudged her glasses higher on the bridge of her nose and leaned forward, her voice soft, confidential. "I'm dying of curiosity, Taylor. Find out if he's got a single friend."

Taylor laughed and went into her office. She called her voice mail. "This is Michael Sessio, Ms. Taylor. We need to talk. Could you please call me at five-five-five nineteen hundred? Thanks."

She hung up the receiver, thought a moment, then called the number Sessio had left. A young woman with a crisp voice answered. "Sessio Shipping. How may I direct your call?"

"Right to the top," she said. "Mr. Sessio."

"Just a minute, please."

The next female voice sounded like a clone of the first. "Michael Sessio's office."

"Mr. Sessio, please."

"Who may I say is calling?"

"Simpson and Willis, the law firm."

"Just a minute, ma'am."

Click, hum, click and hum, click and hum, over and over and over again. The netherworld of HOLD, she thought. She grew inexplicably nervous. Her hand gripped the receiver, the back of her throat felt dry. She thought of Sessio the day of his father's funeral, standing out there on the docks, handsome and charismatic.

Forget it, she thought.

Then a man's voice boomed over the line: "Ms. Brooke. Thanks for calling back."

"What is it we need to talk about Mr. Sessio?"

"I'd rather not discuss it over the phone. Can I meet you someplace for dinner?"

"No. I'll meet you on the airport ferry at five."

"Make it six."

"Six is fine." She hung up.

Hey," *Eileen* said as she was leaving later that afternoon. "Does De Niro have any friends?"

"It wasn't De Niro."

Eileen looked disappointed. "Then who was he?"

"Armand Assante."

Eileen looked perplexed. "Who's that?"

"*The Mambo Kings, Belizaire the Cajun, Blind Justice, Hoffa, Fever....*"

"Oh, yeah." She snapped her fingers, her eyes widened. "I know who he is. Intense, sexual, incredible eyes ... that the guy?"

"You got it. See you Monday."

As Taylor headed out the door, Eileen called after her: "Hey, Taylor. Don't forget to ask if he's got any single friends."

*M*ike Sessio looked forward to this meeting, anticipated it, actually couldn't wait to sit across from her, talk to her. He admired her decision to meet in a public place; he would do the same in her shoes. He needed her. Taylor was the only one who could give him an insider's view of the case—the information he needed to put all the pieces together.

How much should he tell her? How honest should he be? Play it by ear, he thought, and hurried on toward the wharf, feeling like a young man about to meet his blind date for the evening.

8

The wharf bustled with activity this Friday evening, as locals and tourists converged on restaurants and the outdoor stalls. Rollerbladers had come out in full force, bicyclers whizzed past. At Rowes Wharf, Taylor got into the ticket line for the next water shuttle to Logan.

The trip took only seven minutes, dock to dock, plenty of time for Sessio to say whatever he had to say. She dug eight bucks for the ticket out of her wallet and was one person away from the window when a man behind her said, ''I hope you like cappuccino.''

She glanced back at Michael Sessio, dressed casually in slacks and a cotton shirt, a pair of sunglasses riding on top of his head, holding two Starbucks cups. Up close, he actually did bear a resemblance to Armand Assante, handsome in an unconventional way, muscular without looking like a body-builder. His smile came quick and easy, his manner struck her as scrupulously polite. And yes, those smoldering eyes seized her, eyes that surely had broken a few hearts over the years.

"I love cappuccino," she said, accepting the proffered cup.
"Thanks."

"I'd rather not talk on the shuttle. I don't want to risk being overheard. How about if we walk along the harbor?"

"That's fine."

Sessio touched her elbow, guiding her through the crowd. She noticed that he kept looking around and she finally asked, "You expecting company or something?"

"I'm just making sure we aren't being followed."

"And who would be following us, Mr. Sessio?"

"The possibilities will become clearer as we talk. What did you think of the tape?"

Taylor's eyes widened. "How did . . . *You* sent it?"

He nodded. "The man who was playing pool with Ravigno has worked for my family for years. I hired him the day after Dad's funeral. I can't depend on the police to find the truth."

"If that tape proves to be the real thing, Mr. Sessio, it blows the prosecution's case against the man charged with killing your father."

"Good. Because Tommy Washington didn't kill him. He was set up. I think you know that."

"Set up by whom?"

"I don't know yet."

"But you have a theory."

"Do you know who Richard Adler was?"

She nodded. Adler, a high-powered corporate attorney, had been killed several months before in a car-jacking in the affluent suburbs outside of Boston where he'd lived. As far as she knew, the car jacker had never been found.

"I think Adler's death is connected to my father's murder."

"They knew each other?"

"Quite well. For political and business reasons, though, they kept their friendship very low key. That may be one of the reasons the police haven't drawn any connection between the two deaths."

"How do you know they haven't?"

"Because I discussed the possibility with Detective Schultz. He said he checked it out, there's nothing to it. As far as he's concerned, Washington did it, end of story."

Not exactly, she thought, certain that Sessio knew he hadn't been dismissed as a possible suspect.

They had reached the Marriott Long Wharf and settled on the low wall outside. "Why do you think there's a connection between the two deaths?" she asked.

"I know that Adler was in possession of some important papers of my father's. I don't know what the papers concern, but I remember overhearing him talking to Adler about it a couple of times."

"If they're legal papers, another attorney would have taken over."

"In ordinary circumstances, yes. But I don't think these papers concern anything ordinary. I think they contain information that led to my father's death. Someone doesn't want that information made public."

"Where are the papers?"

"I don't know."

"You're making a lot of assumptions, Mr. Sessio."

"Maybe, maybe not. Mrs. Adler, however, has refused to take my calls since Papa's death."

"Have you tried to see her?"

"Once. Her housekeeper said she wasn't home. But as I was driving away, I saw her peering out of a window."

"She can be subpoenaed."

"I doubt she'd talk. I think she's too scared to talk about whatever it is she knows."

"There's been some speculation that you hired Washington."

This elicited a pointed look from Sessio. "Speculation on whose part?"

"Rumors." She didn't want to bring Stark into the conversation.

"The cops grilled me for a couple of hours. Any idea what my motive is supposed to have been?"

"I haven't heard." Stark hadn't gone that far in his accusation about Sessio. "But if they had any evidence, you'd have seen the inside of a cell by now."

"There's no evidence because I didn't do it. There's no motive, either. Why would I kill my father? I had nothing to gain by it. If anything, my power base has been weakened by his death.''

''Maybe this isn't connected to what you've been saying, but I got a call early this morning warning me to back off from Washington's defense.''

Sessio frowned. ''What'd the person say exactly?''

She told him, then explained that the origin of the call had been traced to a public phone on the wharf. ''I have no intention of dropping the case, but I do plan on getting a caller ID machine.''

''Good idea. By the way, that tape you've got is the original. I know a copy won't stand up as well in court.''

''True enough.'' Copies could be edited, things taken out or put in.

He crumpled his empty paper cup and tossed it into a nearby trash can. ''How about if we stay in touch and talk again when one or both of us has new information?''

''The first thing I need to do, Mr. Sessio, is verify that the voice on that tape belongs to Ravigno. If it's him, then we'll talk again.'' She stood, tossed her cup in the trash, and extended her hand. ''Thanks for your candor.''

His hand lingered against hers a shade too long and his eyes, she thought, scrutinized her with astonishing openness. For a beat or two, she stood frozen, unable to move, her thoughts clouded. The Sessio charisma, she thought, and finally withdrew her hand, smiled, and walked away.

By the time she got home, it was near seven and she was bushed. Lady greeted her at the door, with her leash in her mouth. ''So Cathy hasn't been by to walk you yet? I'll have to talk to her, girl.''

Lady barked and trotted after Taylor as she went into the bedroom to change clothes. She put on jogging shorts, a tank top, and her New Balance running shoes, then snapped on Lady's leash and off they went, into the dusk.

She'd been jogging only a few months, whenever she could squeeze it in, two or three times a week. She usually did two miles, a route that took her along the Charles River.

Lady had a chance to run and the dog's presence, of course, allowed her to run at night. The lab protected her, the reason she'd bought the dog in the first place. She still couldn't shake the bone-deep fear that Eric would find her, break into the apartment, and kill her. Always, that irrational fear lay in the back of her mind, crouched like a waiting mugger, and affected everything she did.

As she left the apartment, she slipped on a pair of headphones. She connected them to a Walkman radio clipped to the waistband of her running shorts and fiddled with the station dial until she found a local jazz station. Lady barked, Taylor unhooked her leash, and the lab trotted alongside her, pausing here and there to sniff, then hurrying to catch up.

Half a mile into her run, the music ended and the local news came on. The Sessio murder and investigation had top billing. *"Eight days ago, Tommy Washington, a nineteen-year-old kid from Roxbury, allegedly shot union leader, Joseph Sessio, while he was dining at DeCiccio's. The murder weapon and a ski mask were found in a trash can near the restaurant shortly before Washington's arrest at the wharf.*

"Washington's prints were found on the murder weapon. He claims, however, that the gun, which was unregistered, was stolen from his home several nights before the shooting of Sessio. Washington claims he bought the gun on the street to protect his mother and sister from the gang that he was once a part of.

"Less than a year ago, Tommy Washington was present when another teenager from his project was set on fire by gang members. The boy died three days later. Although there wasn't enough evidence in that case to prosecute Washington, District Attorney Debra Gova is confident it will be different this time."

Gova turned up next, but Taylor didn't want to listen to her. She turned off the radio, hooked the headphones around her neck, and ran harder. When she reached the bridge that marked her turnaround point, her breath came in short staccatos and she had a stitch in her side that forced her to stop. She sank to her knees in the grass that led down to the river and watched Lady run around.

Washington. Gova. Stark. Sessio. The tape.

The tape. How the hell could she have forgotten about the tape?

She whistled for Lady, who ignored her. Five more minutes, she thought. Let Lady run for another five minutes, then they'd go back to the apartment and she would make a copy of that tape.

He had watched her leave.

He had watched her jog up the sidewalk with the black mutt on a leash. Her ponytail bounced, her beautiful butt didn't. Her long legs ate up the sidewalk with the exuberance of a young colt. Jesus, what a piece of work, he thought.

Two minutes after she'd vanished around the corner, he'd left his car in a parking lot several blocks away and walked back to her building. From a pocket of his windbreaker, he removed a zippered Baggie with several chunks of raw steak inside that had been soaked in a liquid tranquilizer. There was enough in it to bring down a dog twice the lab's size. He tossed a chunk over near a bush, where the lab would see it. He wanted the pooch on its way into dreamland before it got into the house.

He found a spare key to her place under a flower pot on the porch, unlocked the door, wiped off the key, and returned it to its hiding place. He slipped quickly into the apartment, pulled on gloves, and hurried up the hallway. The place was odd, not quite what he expected. She made plenty of dough and yet the furnishings looked like a flea market hodgepodge, as though she hadn't really found her taste.

But here and there, he noted a special piece, something that stood out. The antique rocker, for instance. And a handmade quilt that some blind woman in the hills of West Virginia had probably stitched together square by square.

He'd expected the latest electronic equipment—a sophisticated CD player, a wall screen TV, a PC that operated at the speed of light. But he found none of these things. He did, however, run across an expensive tape player, one that could make copies of other tapes. He found the tape he'd come for in the bottom of her purse, which she'd left on the kitchen table.

He pocketed it, then checked the tape player to make sure she hadn't made a copy yet. He searched the living room and the kitchen, the pantry and the hall closets, the bedroom and adjoining bathroom. Not much of interest. But at least he knew where to hide now.

He put the other chunk of steak into the dog's bowl, burying it under a layer of dry food. Then he went into the utility room, turned off the electrical switches for the kitchen and adjoining dining room. Anything else? He glanced around, then ducked into his hiding place to wait.

Lady loped along ahead of Taylor on the way back to the townhouse. On the last stretch, she vanished around the corner. Taylor followed and saw her pawing through the bushes and gobbling up something.

"No, bad girl, spit that out." Probably a mouse or something. Taylor snapped her leash back on and headed toward the steps. As she unlocked the door, Cathy stepped out of her apartment.

"Hey, I was going to walk her," Cathy said.

"Beat you to it." Lady tore away from her and bounded into the apartment, barking. "You going to be home tonight?"

"Looks that way. Why don't you c'mon over?"

"I've got some stuff to do first, but I'll be over in time for *Millennium.*"

"It's a repeat, but it's one we missed."

"Great. I'll bring the popcorn."

Millennium, a tradition with her and Cathy, highlighted their Friday nights, when neither of them had anything else to do. She followed Lady into the apartment. The dog stopped barking. "Lady?" she called.

No answer. Frowning, Taylor hurried up the hall to the

kitchen. Lady, curled up in a corner of the dark kitchen, whimpered softly when Taylor dropped to her knees beside her.

"I guess that ol' mouse you gobbled down is giving you indigestion, huh, girl?"

Lady licked the back of her hand in response, then growled softly. Odd, that Lady would growl at her, she thought, and worried now that she was in pain.

"Let me get the light on, girl." She stood quickly and hit the switch on the wall. Nothing. Great, just great. An electrical problem. "I'm going to call the vet, Lady. Just hold on."

As she picked up the receiver, she heard something behind her and started to spin around, but not quickly enough. Something slammed into her head, stars exploded inside of her eyes, her knees buckled, and she slumped, unconscious, to the floor.

Debra Gova snapped awake on the first ring and grabbed the receiver before the phone rang again. Without preface, she said: "So tell me what I want to hear."

"It's done."

How strangely comforting his voice was, she thought. "And you have the tape?"

"Got it right here."

"Suppose she made a copy?"

"No copy was found."

"How, uh, is she?"

"I'm told she'll have a helluva a headache, but no permanent damage was done. It'll look like a robbery."

"Okay. I hope you're right on both accounts." She just wanted to get off the phone now, to go to sleep, to get on with her life.

"We should get together soon, Deb. It's been awhile."

"Yes, it has." She knew how long it had been, knew right down to the week, day, hour, and minute. "But you haven't exactly been breaking down my door to get over here."

His laugh was quick and deep. "Maybe I'll have to change my ways."

"Maybe we both will," she replied.

"We'll talk soon."

He hung up; the hollow emptiness of a dead connection echoed across the line.

9

_____

She floats in a cold, gray place that gradually takes on shape and substance. Buildings, a street, traffic. She tilts her head back and peers up into the sagging gray sky, the falling snow. She opens her mouth, catching the snowflakes. They taste sweet and cold.

"Hurry," Mama says, tugging on her hand. "It's starting to snow harder, Talia."

She and her mother hurry through the snowy streets. The sidewalk is already slippery. Her mother warns her to watch her step and grips her hand so hard her fingers begin to ache. But Talia doesn't mind. She welcomes Mama's nearness, her attention. So often, Mama seems angry at her, angry that she has no father, that they have no money, that her clothes are worn.

Mama drinks sometimes at night, when she thinks Talia is sleeping. She drinks and cries and paces around her bedroom like some restless ghost. Only last night, her mother staggered past Talia when she was on her way to the bathroom. Her makeup was smeared, her eyes were bloodshot, she couldn't walk in a straight line. She glanced at Talia and hissed, "... child ... ruin my whole life ..." Then she stumbled over to the couch and passed out.

Eva Carlino suddenly stops, sets her bag of groceries on a sidewalk bench, and fusses with Talia's coat. "Button up, sweetie. I can't have you getting sick. God knows we can't afford the doctor."

She picks up the grocery bag and they hurry forward again. The snow sweeps across the sidewalk now. It slides down the back of her neck, melts, and rolls in cold drops down the middle of her spine.

They finally reach their apartment and Mama quickly unlocks the door. It's cold inside, but not as cold as it is outside. Mama sets the bag of groceries on the table and fumbles in her coat pocket for a cigarette. Eva Carlino smokes and drinks too much. Talia knows it, but also knows that if she thinks about it too much, something bad will happen. So she tries not to think about it at all.

She shrugs off her coat and drops it over the back of the nearest chair. "Talia," her mother snaps. "That isn't where your coat goes."

"Sorry."

She is always sorry. Sorry for being a bastard child, sorry for causing her mama to live in poverty, sorry for just about everything. Even though she's only nine, she knows a lot about her mother's past. She knows her father left shortly after she was born and that her mother's friend, Bob, wants to leave his wife and marry her. But Talia's mother doesn't love him, she loves Frank.

Her mother is a "bad girl," who got pregnant while trying to trap a rich man's son. That is the story Talia has heard from neighbors, from other kids. It must be true if so many people know it. The man, Talia's father, left her mother and denied that he fathered a child.

"We have to go back out, Talia. I forgot something at the store and with this snow coming down like it is ..."

––––––––––

Taylor? C'mon, kiddo, wake up. That's right. How many fingers am I holding up?''

Taylor turned her head, looking at the source of the voice. The face blurred, but the voice belonged to Cathy. ''How many fingers?''

''Fo . . .'' Her tongue felt thick and awkward, disconnected from the rest of her mouth, just lying there inside of it like a chunk of old meat. She squeezed her eyes shut and concentrated hard on forming the word she needed. ''Four.''

''Okay, good. Hey, she got the fingers right. What's that mean?''

''That she can see,'' said another voice.

Kyle. Taylor tried to smile, but didn't have the energy. ''Ky,'' she murmured.

''Yeah, I'm here, Taylor,'' Kyle said, leaning close to her, so close she caught the soapy scent of his skin. ''Listen, you're going to be all right. The docs say you've got a concussion and you had to have some stitches where the bastard hit you.''

''Lady? Is Lady okay?''

''She's fine,'' Cathy said. ''I've got her at my place. Just take it easy and don't move around too much, Taylor.''

Her vision began to clear, but the fierce ache in her head didn't improve. ''You found me?''

''When you didn't show up for *Millennium.*''

''It was him,'' Taylor said. ''I know it was. I'd gotten those hangup calls . . .''

''I already told the police about Eric,'' said Cathy.

''Who's Eric?'' asked Kyle.

''The tape,'' she said. ''It was in my purse.''

''They took your purse,'' Cathy said. ''And some other stuff.''

The tape, gone.

Her head raced. It had to be intentional, but who would benefit the most? Gova? Probably. Stark? Possibly. But would he intentionally hurt her? What about Sessio? she wondered. Perhaps he'd set her up from the beginning and had had the tape stolen to deflect suspicion from himself. He claimed he hadn't made a copy: those words remained clear in her mind.

But why hadn't he made a copy? Michael Sessio, she thought, wasn't a man to be trusted.

"I'd like to sleep," Taylor murmured, and rolled over on her side and shut her eyes.

Her head continued to pound. Those last few minutes in her kitchen unrolled like a movie inside her eyes. Lady. The lights that didn't work. The noise. The blow to her head. She should have paid attention to Lady, the way she'd been acting, the way she'd growled. And the light, of course he would turn off the lights.

How had he found her?

Even if Eric had made the hang-up calls she'd been getting, she knew he hadn't been the one who told her to back off from the Washington case. And Eric wouldn't give a damn about the tape or any of her belongings.

Then who had done it?

She dozed again, woke, and lay there thinking of her mother, of that horrible winter day nineteen years ago. If they'd never gone back out to pick up whatever groceries her mother had forgotten, perhaps she would still be alive.

She remembered waiting at a corner several blocks from their apartment, waiting for the red light to change. She'd stared at the red light and tried not to blink until it changed. This little game she played made her forget that her fingers felt frozen and the wind bit through her coat.

"I think the light's broken," her mother had said, and led her out into the street.

Taylor had been looking at her feet, afraid she would slip, when her mother had suddenly gasped. She glanced up and saw a car rushing toward them. Her mother shoved her out of the way and she had fallen back against the pavement.

She'd heard the impact, the sickening thud of the car hitting her mother. Then her mother's body lay sprawled in the snowy street and the car kept right on going.

A week later, her mother's boyfriend, Bob, accompanied her to St. Mary's Children's Home. He treated her much better than he ever had when her mother had been alive. But she knew she wouldn't be seeing him again after today.

Her room, small and sparsely furnished, depressed her. The

single metal-frame bed boasted a lumpy mattress; a small desk and stool attested to the home's lack of funds. Sister Mary handed her a sheet and a pillowcase and told her to make her bed, unpack her things, then to go downstairs to the dining area. She started to cry and the nun told her bluntly that her mother had died, that this would be her home now. Right then, words from a Byron poem that her mother used to read her had run through her mind:

> *One shade the more, one ray the less,*
> *Had half impaired the nameless grace*

She told Sister Mary that her father's name was Frank and why couldn't they call him? But the nun replied that her father had passed away several years earlier.

Yeah, good ole Frank, she thought. He'd passed away, but had gone on to become a U.S. senator. Some trick.

Kyle slipped quietly into Taylor's room and approached her bed. Her blond hair spilled over the white pillowcase, her eyes were shut, and she appeared to be sleeping comfortably. The evening visiting hours had just begun and he'd come early, hoping to get a chance to talk to her alone.

"Taylor?" he said softly.

Her eyes snapped open. "Kyle." She sat up, ran her fingers through her hair, and reached for the robe at the foot of her bed. She shrugged it on and swung her legs over the side of the bed. "All I do in here is sleep."

"Enjoy it while you can. Once you get out, you'll probably wish you were back in here. How're you feeling?"

"Good enough to leave tonight. But the doctor has to take another look at me tomorrow morning, then I'll be discharged."

The attack on Taylor still upset him. Gova had reassured him there would be no rough stuff. But a concussion definitely qualified as rough stuff.

"How's your head?"

She smiled. "Still in place. How're things at the office?"

"Okay. I'll update you on everything when you get back."

"Has anyone been arrested yet?"

"Not that I've heard."

Kyle knew Taylor had been married, but he hadn't known anything about Eric Serle until Cathy had filled him in. The most fascinating bit of information he'd learned was that Taylor's terror of this guy had prompted her to change her name. The existence of a madman ex-hubby remained the best news he'd heard in days.

"So tell me about this Eric fellow," Kyle said.

Taylor glanced away, embarrassed. "There's not much to tell, except that we aren't divorced. I was too scared to file. I mean, I left him, changed my name, invented a new life, and I knew if I filed for divorce, he'd find me. So I didn't do anything."

"Do you have any idea where he's living now? It would help the cops."

"I told the detective I spoke to yesterday that he's probably still in Fall River. That's where we were living when I split."

"I think you'd better get the locks changed on your apartment."

Change her locks, change her address, change her name, change her identity again. She suddenly wondered if her future from this moment forward would simply be a repeat of her past. No more running, she thought. She couldn't. She'd claimed her life and now she intended to keep it.

"Cathy already took care of the locks. I hope to be in by noon tomorrow, Kyle, so let's meet and go over everything. See where we stand."

"Great." He gave her hand a quick squeeze. "I've got to scoot. See you tomorrow."

Kyle left the hospital and stopped at the first public phone he spotted. He called Gova's home number and hung up as soon as she answered. Forget the phone routine, he thought. He wanted to speak to Gova face to face and screw her objections.

Gova's neighborhood seemed pleasant enough—trees, beds of colorful hydrangeas and marigolds, ivy blanketing the yards. Gova's home didn't stand out in any particular way, which fit Gova herself, he thought.

Kyle parked at the curb and got out. He thought, suddenly, of his father, of his pride in his son, the lawyer, and how disappointed he would be if he knew what Kyle had gotten involved in. But his father didn't know the half of it. Throughout college, Kyle had managed to hide his gambling habit while squandering his modest inheritance. By the time he'd received his law degree, he'd plunged thirty grand into debt. Since then, the sum had doubled.

Gova knew about his gambling habits, had capitalized on them. Fifty grand had made him a traitor.

He rang the doorbell and covered the peephole with his hand. She opened the door a moment later, the chain still on. ''Christ, Kyle,'' she snapped. ''I told you to never . . .''

''Open the goddamn door. We need to talk.''

''Okay, hold on.'' She opened the door and motioned him in. ''You pull shit like this again and our deal's off.''

''You can't win this case without me.''

''Spare me the arrogance. Now what's so important that a phone call wouldn't do the job?''

She leaned against the wall, arms folded across her chest. She hardly looked like a hotshot prosecutor, he thought. She wore cutoff jeans, a baggy T-shirt, and no shoes. She'd pulled up her hair and fastened it with a clip. Ms. Plain Jane.

But to her credit, she listened without interrupting. ''Fall River? She thinks he's still there?''

''Yeah.''

''Go find him. Get him involved. Get to him before the cops do.''

''Go *find* him? I've got a job, you know. I can't just take off and traipse all over Fall River looking for this guy.'' And suppose the cops got wind of it? He would be brought in for questioning, he might crack under pressure, and then it would all spill out. How Gova paid him off, how he gambled, the whole sordid mess. His father would be disgraced, he would lose his job, he would be disbarred. And worse, he might do time.

"I'll see what I can do."

Gova rocked forward on the balls of her feet, her face inches from his. "That's not enough. I need a stronger commitment from you."

"Then it's going to cost you another fifteen grand on what you owe me."

"Fine, no problem. Look, Kyle, I know you don't want to see Taylor hurt. I don't, either. But you've got to make a choice. It's going to be you or her. It comes down to that."

"I know, I know. I'll find Eric Serle and tell him where she is."

"That's better. I'll arrange for your package to be delivered to the pickup point by midnight."

He left shortly afterward, astonished that she could raise cash just like that. Where did she get it, anyway? Prosecutors didn't make six-figure salaries. And Gova didn't have inherited money. So who funded this deception? And, more the point, what were the real stakes here? It smelled larger than just winning a case, he thought. Much larger.

Flowers had arrived from the office, from some of her clients, even from Michael Sessio, which she tried not to think about. And now Cathy sailed in with another bouquet and the latest chapter in her love life.

The married executive had told her he "needed more space." Cathy claimed she felt relieved, but Taylor knew otherwise. She could see the weary resignation in her friend's eyes, the hurt and confusion.

The TV droned in the background and although Taylor hadn't been paying much attention to it, she suddenly heard her name. She reached for the clicker and raised the volume. Her photo flashed on the screen and she winced.

"Oh, great. This I don't need."

"I forgot to tell you," Cathy said. "There was an article in this morning's *Globe* about you."

"Terrific. And now my picture is splashed all over the evening news."

Detective Schultz, who had interviewed Taylor yesterday, appeared on the screen. The reporter asked if he thought the attack on Ms. Brooke might be related to the Joseph Sessio case. The detective's reply had caution stamped all over it. "We're well aware that Ms. Brooke is defending the man accused of killing Mr. Sessio, but at this time we have no reason to believe there's any connection to the assault and break-in. On the contrary, we have information that it might be related to a completely different matter that I'm not at liberty to discuss."

Taylor and Cathy glanced at each other, both of them thinking the same thing: Eric. But her conviction about Eric had begun to waver. Even though she never saw the man's face, he seemed too large to be Eric. The scent didn't fit Eric, either, just a faint odor of soap and sweat. Not Eric's scent at all. Besides, Eric probably would have been wearing English Leather.

She remembered how the scent of the English Leather had mixed with the smell of his skin when he'd flown into a rage. Her attacker hadn't been enraged, only methodical.

Cathy turned off the TV. "It doesn't do any good to listen to that crap. They'll get Eric, Taylor. Don't worry about it."

"Suppose it wasn't Eric?"

"Then they'll get whoever did it."

"Be sure of it," said a man's voice from the doorway.

Taylor and Cathy looked around just as Frank Morgan walked into the room with a vase of roses and baby's breath. "I was in the neighborhood, Taylor. I hope you don't mind my dropping by."

"You're Senator Morgan," Cathy exclaimed, and shot to her feet, a peon greeting royalty.

Morgan flashed his politician's smile. "And you're—"

"Cathy Spelling, a neighbor," Taylor said.

"Where should I set this?" Morgan asked, indicating the vase.

"Here, I'll take it." Cathy set it on the windowsill, with several other bouquets from people at the office.

Taylor wished he would leave. She wished he'd never come. She wanted to dress and get out of here. She sat up, tightened the sash on her robe, ran her fingers self-consciously through her hair. She felt awkward and clumsy and knew that Morgan knew it.

"I'll, uh, be moving along," said Cathy. "I'll be by to pick you up in the morning, Taylor. Just give me a call when you know what time."

"I will. Thanks."

Cathy left and Morgan walked over to the window and re-arranged the flowers he'd brought her. She stared at his back, willing him to leave, but of course he didn't. She got up, went into the bathroom, shut the door. She turned on the water, ran a cloth under it, wrung it out, and pressed it to her face.

Go away, she thought at him. Get out of my life.

Nineteen years ago, she would have given anything to have this man in her life. But not now.

Yet, he'd waltzed in here as though none of that had happened, as though the last nineteen years had never been. Screw him, she thought, and marched back out into her hospital room.

Morgan was seated in the chair near the window, his body leaning forward slightly, his fingers laced together. He looked at her, she looked at him, the silence loomed like a continent between them.

"Look, I really don't have anything to say to you," she blurted.

His head tilted downward, in what she perceived as shame. "I understand. But I have something to say, Taylor. I'm sorry. Sorry for everything."

Sorry? He was *sorry?* "And that's supposed to erase nine-teen years?" She nearly choked on the words and then she laughed, a cold, hard laugh. "You died on my thirteenth birth-day, Frank Morgan."

"What I did that day was wrong, Taylor. But I didn't know what else to do. I . . . I was caught between the proverbial rock and a hard place." He paused for what seemed an eternity.

"Your mother and I were kids. . . . My father never approved of my relationship with your mother and I . . . I didn't know how I would explain you after all those years."

"And now your father's dead and your daughter's dying of some terrible disease and you figure you'll just walk in here and make amends." She shook her head and looked down at her hands, close to tears now. "I don't need you. You're not my father. Just stay out of my life."

A nurse entered the room before Morgan could say anything. "Excuse me, Ms. Brooke. This came for you." She handed Taylor a vase with a long-stemmed rose in it.

"Thanks." Taylor set the vase on the nightstand and opened the card. The only thing written inside was: FOUND YOU.

"Oh my God," she whispered, and crumpled the card and threw it to the floor.

"What is it?" Morgan asked, hurrying over. He scooped the card off the floor, glanced at it. "Who found you? What's going on, Taylor?"

"Nothing." She grabbed the vase and dropped it in the wastebasket. "Nothing's going on. Just leave me alone." Then her voice cracked and she began to cry.

"Let me help you," Morgan said gently, coming up behind her, but not touching her. "Please."

She shook her head, grabbed tissues from the box of Kleenex, and blew her nose. And then, to her utter horror, the story of Eric and her marriage spilled out, the words coming fast and furiously.

"I'll hire security for your townhouse," he said when she'd finished. "I'll make sure this man doesn't bother you again. I'll get the police right on it."

He would do this, he would do that. . . . His words echoed in her head and her rage bubbled up from someplace deep inside of her and leaped away from her. "I don't want your help," she spat. "I don't want you in my life. Just leave me the hell alone." Then she hurried over to the door, opened it. "Leave, just leave."

Morgan nodded and crossed the room. He paused at the door, in front of her. "I'm not going to give up on you, Taylor. I kept you out of my life all these years because of what other people felt was best for me. But not anymore. It might seem too late to you, but not to me, Taylor. I'm prepared to do whatever it takes to win you over.''

She didn't say anything, she merely glared at him.

Morgan walked out into the hall and she slammed the door.

*M*ike Sessio walked quickly along the wharf, arms swinging loosely at his sides. He felt good this evening. The day had gone well and his business dinner had yielded new opportunities and deals. But the best part of the day would happen five minutes from now, an exclamation point at the end of a long and busy week.

He passed the restaurants, the fast food stalls, the usual throngs of locals and tourists out enjoying the evening. On a side street off the wharf, he ducked into a bar frequented by many of the dock workers. The air inside smelled of smoke, music blasted from a jukebox, every stool along the bar was occupied.

Sessio greeted half a dozen people, men who had worked for him for years, bought them a round of drinks, then went into the pool room in the back. The man waited for him in a booth, a glass of beer in front of him, a cigarette burning in a nearby ashtray, his hand resting on a folder.

''You work fast, Nikko,'' said Sessio, sliding into the booth.

''Not like I used to, but hell, I'm older.''

''C'mon, man, you look younger than I do.''

''Some days I feel like I ought to go play Thoreau up at my cabin in the Berkshires and just forget all this shit.''

Then he grinned, just to let Sessio know he wasn't serious. His white teeth lined up in his mouth like a newly painted picket fence. Most of Nikko's teeth had been capped, the result of the street fight decades ago in which he'd saved Sessio's life.

''So what've you got?'' Sessio asked.

''Plenty.'' Nikko opened the folder and removed a dozen color snapshots of Taylor Brooke.

Sessio went through them slowly, relishing each one. Here:

Taylor hurrying across a street downtown. There: Taylor jogging along the Charles with a black dog on a leash. And here: Taylor on her way into the city jail. All of the photos depicted Taylor going about the normal routine of her life and all of them utterly exquisite.

"She has a fondness for Italian food." Nikko slipped on a pair of reading glasses and glanced through a pocket-sized notepad. "She likes fish, doesn't seem to eat much meat. She runs two or three times a week along the Charles. Her black lab is named Lady, a pup less than a year old. She stops at Cardero's Gourmet Shop a couple times a week. It's a couple blocks from her place. She buys a couple of paperbacks whenever she grocery shops, usually popular fiction. She went to law school at Amherst, graduated with honors, made the *Law Review,* and Simpson and Willis recruited her right out of school."

"Family?" Sessio asked.

Nikko peered at him over the rims of his glasses. "That's where it gets tougher. She doesn't appear to be married, doesn't have any kids. I don't have a clue about her parents. According to her bio in the American Bar Association, she did her undergrad work at Boston College. But I couldn't find any record of a Taylor Brooke having graduated from there. In fact, Taylor Brooke doesn't seem to have existed until about five years ago."

Fascinating, Sessio thought. "Nothing on her early childhood?"

"Nope."

"Birth records? Marriage records?"

Nikko held out his hands, palms up, and gave Sessio a look. "C'mon, Mike. If the source exists, I checked it."

Of course, Sessio thought, and regretted asking. "What about current men in her life?"

Nikko flipped through the pages in his notepad. "No one now, at least not that I could find. But according to a secretary in the DA's office, Taylor had a fling with John Stark awhile back."

"The guy who intends to nail Washington for the murder of my father." He shook his head. "Incredible."

"It gets better, Mike. She doesn't seem to have many friends. Her neighbor, Cathy Spelling, seems to be her closest friend. Cathy's an interior decorator, single, sort of messed up about men in general."

"That's written somewhere?" Sessio asked, suddenly curious about how Nikko got his information about the neighbor.

Nikko laughed. "Hardly. Once I knew she was a decorator, I asked her to take a look at my house here in town and give me an estimate for redoing it. You'd be surprised what people will tell you, Mike, when you ask the right questions."

"And they're close, you said."

"Seems so." He removed another photo from the folder and passed it to Sessio. "Not bad looking, either."

Not his type, Sessio thought, studying the picture, but certainly a knockout. "Single and searching," he murmured. "Wouldn't you say that qualifies as a pattern, Nikko?"

Nikko grinned again. "You got it."

"By the way, did you happen to make a copy of the Ravigno tape?"

He shook his head. "You wanted it fast, I didn't get a chance."

Sessio nodded, then pulled out his wallet and handed Nikko a check for five grand. "Keep looking for information on the woman to fill in the gaps. I don't care how long it takes."

Nikko folded the check neatly in half, pushed the folder toward Sessio, then stood and left.

Sessio sat in the booth awhile longer, going through the photos of Taylor, reading Nikko's thorough report, and smiling to himself.

PART TWO

The Investigation

10

────────

Eric crossed the room and stood to the side of the window, peeking out from behind the blinds. Waves of heat rippled above the silent street below. A July scorcher, he thought, and not a moving car in sight. But why should there be? People on this street worked regular nine to five jobs.

And yet, he couldn't shake his certainty that he was being watched.

He'd quit his job and moved into the rooming house the day after he'd beaten up the hooker, moved because he knew the pimps would be looking for him. His room, basic and cheap, had a private bath, a hot plate, and two windows. One faced the street and the other faced the railroad tracks behind the house.

He had so little money left, he did odd jobs around the place for the old woman who owned it. He made a little cash on the side doing the same sort of odd jobs for the old woman's friends, most of them aging widows who lived alone. The old ladies liked him, didn't ask too many questions, but he didn't know how much longer he could stand it.

Some nights he lay awake in this room, listening to the clatters and gasps of the old AC unit in the window and thinking about Talia. He knew that if he stayed here much longer, he would lose his mind.

He went over to the TV and VCR on his dresser, popped in the videotape he'd watched nearly every day for the last five weeks, and hit PLAY. The news broadcast from a local Boston station concerned an assault on the attorney defending the man arrested for the murder of Joseph Sessio. An attorney named Taylor Brooke.

He froze the tape on the photo of Taylor and stepped back from the TV, studying her face. He clenched his fists and the old rage welled inside of him. But he held it back, refused to let it get away from him, and after a moment, it withdrew, hiding where it always hid, in some deeply buried pocket of his soul.

He leaned close to the TV screen and drew his fingers lightly over her face. Her appearance had changed: blond hair now, a fuller face, and a well-kept, wealthy look, utterly confident. But the eyes were Talia's eyes, that bluish green shade of Bahamian waters, and that mouth was definitely Talia's mouth, hesitant to smile too quickly, to reveal too much. He didn't understand how she'd gotten as far as she had in just five years, but it didn't really surprise him. Her ambition and intelligence always had outshone his.

Mrs. Eric Serle, he thought.

He knew her name, that she lived in Boston, that she worked for a hotshot firm called Simpson & Willis. When he felt ready to find her, he would go to the firm and wait outside until she appeared. He would follow her home. He would pay her a little visit. And when he got done with her, she would be sorry she ever left him.

Just the thought of it aroused him.

He reached into the pocket of his shorts and pulled out a slip of crumpled paper. The number for Simpson & Willis. He'd called once, but had been told she was in a meeting. The secretary had forwarded his call to her voice mail and the sound of her voice had sent him into a rage. He'd hung up before he'd said anything.

Eric put on his boots, stepped outside his room, locked the

door and went downstairs. An eerie quiet pervaded the rooming house. People were out and about, living their lives.

Gotta get a life, Eric thought.

Or, better yet, move into Taylor's life.

Outside, the morning air smelled of deep summer. He walked along the railroad tracks, behind the row of houses that were identical to the one where he was living. It was a shabby section of town, a forgotten pocket of Fall River, a place where people lived in quiet desperation. Lawns were overrun with weeds, junker cars occupied driveways, fat women in curlers chatted over fences as they hung their laundry on clotheslines.

He reached the end of the block and stepped out onto the sidewalk. His eyes swept through the street, checking things out. No one around.

So why couldn't he shake the feeling that he was being watched?

He set his change on the counter, punched out the number for Simpson & Willis, then fed the quarters into the phone. He kept glancing around as the number rang.

"Simpson and Willis," said a cheery female voice. "How may I direct your call?"

"Taylor Brooke, please."

"One minute."

Then, another cheery female voice: "Taylor Brooke's office."

"Ms. Brooke, please."

"Who may I say is calling, sir?"

"Jim Fenton."

"Just a minute, Mr. Fenton."

He counted silently to himself, marking off the seconds. At seventy-five, she picked up. "This is Taylor Brooke."

The sound of her voice filled him with a bittersweet nostalgia. But behind it smoldered rage, bubbling like a pool of lava in the pit of his gut. He clenched his teeth to keep from saying her name.

"Hello. This is Taylor Brooke."

He slammed his fingers over the disconnect bar, dropped the receiver into the cradle. Then he stood there with his hand on the receiver, his eyes squeezed shut, and struggled against the tidal wave of anger that crashed over him.

The bitch had left him.

He would find her.

She'd lied to him.

He would make her pay.

She was still his wife.

He would kill her.

Eric's eyes snapped open, he jerked his hand away from the receiver, and wrenched back from the pay phone. He jammed his hands into his pockets and hastened back the way he'd come. His thoughts absorbed him so deeply he failed to notice the dark sedan driving slowly past, a camera to the driver's eye.

A cough. Shoes scraping against the floor. Papers rustling. Every noise punctuated the silence in the courtroom. Taylor, Kyle, and Tommy Washington waited in the back of the courtroom, where they'd been for nearly an hour.

The air felt warm and sticky and Taylor fanned herself with a legal pad. Next to her, Tommy Washington squirmed inside his white dress shirt and tie. Beads of perspiration dotted his forehead, sweat marks darkened his shirt.

Two days ago, the grand jury had indicted Washington; today he would be arraigned. A long wait, she thought, for a short hearing in which Washington would enter a not guilty plea.

The fact that Michael Sessio hadn't been indicted reconfirmed Taylor's belief that Ravigno had been telling the truth on the tape. But if she'd made a copy of that tape as soon as she'd gotten it, Washington probably wouldn't be here today.

On the other hand, Washington's story hadn't held up well. The phone records for incoming calls to DeCiccio's on May 30 showed that only two calls had been made to the public phone in the kitchen around the time Tommy claimed he'd gotten the call about his sister. They concerned personal matters for two of the employees. If, indeed, there had been a call, then someone had tampered with Ma Bell records.

A hacker probably could do it. And so could an employee with access to computer records. The DELETE button on a computer would wipe out the call, especially if enough money crossed a palm somewhere along the way. Her head ached with the possibilities, but it always came back to the same central question. Who had benefited most from Sessio's murder? His son? His enemies? Which enemies?

Judge Karen Cornwell moved on through the docket of arraignments and preliminary hearings. She looked, Taylor thought, more like the stereotypical librarian than a judge—middle-aged, plump, with her salt and pepper hair twisted up into a bun at the back of her head.

She studied the screen on her notebook computer for the next case, called out another name. Each time, she turned from her computer and peered over her half-moon glasses at the attorney and defendant. Even though Washington's arraignment clearly outweighed every other case on the judge's docket, she hadn't separated it from the others.

Two more cases were dispatched before the court clerk called out, "The People versus Tommy Washington."

Taylor motioned for Washington to stand. He looked clumsy and awkward as he got up, an Ichabod Crane with stooped shoulders and clothes that hung on his tall, narrow frame. They approached the bench, with Stark just a few paces behind them.

She glanced surreptitiously at Stark as they stopped in front of the bench. He looked perfectly at ease. Even though he wore a jacket, he seemed impervious to the warm stickiness of the air.

"Mr. Washington, the grand jury has carefully considered the evidence presented by the prosecution," said Judge Cornwell. "They've decided to charge you with first-degree murder. You're here today to be arraigned on that charge." She pinned him with her eyes. "Do you understand the charge against you?"

"Yes, ma'am."

"And how do you plead, Mr. Washington?"

"Not guilty, Your Honor," Washington murmured, then added, "I didn't do it."

Behind them in the courtroom, someone began to weep softly. She didn't have to glance back to identify the weeping woman as Tommy Washington's mother.

"As with all first-degree murder charges, bail is denied. I'm setting a trial date of September tenth. Will that date allow you sufficient time to prepare a defense for your client, counselor?"

"Yes, Your Honor."

Cornwell looked at Stark. "Does the prosecution have anything to say, Mr. Stark?"

"Not at this time, Your Honor."

"That'll be all."

As they turned to leave, Tommy Washington's mother suddenly stumbled forward, sobbing, "My boy didn't kill no one, he ain't no killer, my boy . . ." And Bertha Washington, who stood about five feet tall and probably weighed two hundred pounds, threw her arms around her son's waist and buried her face against his shirt.

The judge slammed her gavel, a murmur rippled through the courtroom, and several deputies hurried over to take Tommy away. In the seconds before Bertha let go of her son, Tommy rested his chin against the top of her head and hugged her tightly, whispering, "Don't cry now, Mama, don't cry."

The pain that bloomed in Washington's eyes, the depth of his mother's grief, the very poignancy of the moment: all of these elements wrapped around Taylor with a sudden, terrifying pressure. And suddenly, she felt absolutely certain that Washington hadn't killed Joe Sessio.

Two cops led Washington out of the courtroom and Taylor slipped her arm around his mother's shoulders. "Let's talk outside, Mrs. Washington," she said gently, and the woman leaned against her, sobbing softly.

When they were on the sidewalk, Bertha dabbed at her eyes with a wadded up hanky. "You got to . . . to free my boy," she stammered, looking up at Taylor. "He done bad things, I can't deny that, but he's no killer, Ms. Brooke. My boy's no killer."

"You'll have a chance to testify to that, Mrs. Washington. Do you need a ride somewhere?"

She blew her nose and shook her head. "No, ma'am. Friend's pickin' me up."

Taylor squeezed her hand. "We'll talk soon."

Bertha waddled off to a car waiting at the curb and Taylor gazed after her, feeling lousy.

"You're not supposed to feel guilty about it, Taylor."

She glanced up at Stark, who stopped next to her. "You're right," she snapped. "You're the one who should be feeling guilty."

She walked away from him before he could reply and caught up with Kyle, who was waiting on the steps. "Mark my words, Stark thinks Washington is going to crack," Kyle murmured.

"He may crack, but he won't be talking about who hired him, because no one did."

They started walking toward his car. "We're going to have a hard time proving it, Taylor. Two of the witnesses the prosecution is calling claim to have heard Washington talking about his plans to kill Joe Sessio. They're both from Providence. Neither one has been in Boston very long."

"They're *both* from Providence? Are they buddies?"

"No. They came forward independently."

"So we'll just have to dig a little harder to find witnesses who can contradict them. Ask Burt Hallas to find out what he can on these two guys."

"I'll tell him."

Neither of them spoke for the next few moments. They reached her car, got in. Once she'd pulled out into traffic, she said, "It'd be great if Burt could zero in on whoever stole Tommy's gun."

"*If* someone stole it." Kyle gestured at the car directly in front of her. "Hey, watch out. He's about to turn."

"I see him, Kyle. Relax."

Spare me the backseat driving, she thought. But Kyle never took his eyes from the road. He sat upright and rigid in his seat, his body perpetually prepared for impact.

"Look, Kyle, let's get something straight. I think Washington is innocent and that someone out there would like us and the rest of the world to think otherwise. They want us to put up a paltry defense or no defense at all and I'm not going to do it. You're certainly entitled to your opinion about his guilt or innocence, but regardless of what you believe, he deserves the best defense we can give him."

"For Christ's sakes," Kyle snapped. "I wouldn't be a defense attorney if I couldn't separate my personal feelings from the case. So don't lecture me on moral points, Taylor."

Testy, she thought. "I'm not lecturing you."

Kyle ran his hand over his face, glanced out the window. They were at a stoplight, cars lined up in front of them. "Look, I'm sorry. I didn't mean to get short with you. I've been having some personal problems."

She waited for him to go on, to explain, however briefly, about his personal problems, but he didn't and she didn't press it. "The more I think about it, the more convinced I am that something very weird is going on in this case. These witnesses they've come up with, the vanishing phone call to DeCiccio's, the gun with Tommy's prints on it. It all seems too tidy, Kyle. Too neat."

"It's also possible that what you see is what you get."

She didn't think so. Every time she dwelled on the missing call, she thought of the tape. These two pieces of evidence were linked irrevocably in her mind. Someone had gone to a great deal of trouble to frame Washington and had carefully planned the entire scenario.

The ski mask he'd supposedly worn still had a partial tag on it that had been traced to a Salvation Army about six blocks from the kid's home. The gun could be bought on street corners in his neighborhood. And on and on it went, one perfectly orchestrated fact after another.

"We've still got one thing going for us," Taylor said. "They don't have a motive."

"Hey, Manson didn't have a motive. Bundy didn't have a motive. They were sick pups, end of story. Besides, one of these Providence boys claims that Washington was supposed to get twenty-five grand for offing Sessio. That's a solid motive for a kid from Roxbury."

"If that's the game Tommy was playing, he landed on the wrong square."

"What do you mean?"

"Monopoly. You know, collect twenty-five grand or go to jail. Tommy went to jail. As for these guys from Providence, I want to know who they are, where they come from, everything about them."

"Hallas will find out." His arm shot up, finger pointing through the windshield. "Watch out, that car on your left is trying to cut in front of you."

"I see him, Kyle."

"The speed limit's thirty here, you know."

Uh-huh.

"And the cops are always well hidden."

Yes, indeed.

Taylor deliberately stepped on the accelerator, swerved out of the right lane, darted in front of the car in the left lane, and flew through the next light. Kyle clutched the sides of the passenger seat and she turned her head away from him, stifling a smile.

Late that afternoon, Ogden Simpson buzzed Taylor's office. "Can you drop by for a cup of tea, Taylor?"

"Right now?"

"If you're free."

"Sure. I'll be down in a couple of minutes."

"Wonderful."

Whenever Simpson invited her to his office for tea, it usually meant he had something important to discuss with her. And she, naturally, drove herself nuts, trying to figure out what he wanted to discuss. She figured he'd found out about the tape—that she'd had it and, through her own negligence, had lost it, thus clearing the way to Washington's indictment and arraignment. Hardly exemplary, she thought, and worried that Simpson intended to put her on probation.

She left her office and on the way past Eileen's desk, her secretary said, "Oh, Taylor. Cathy Spelling just called. She wants to know if you can come over for dinner this evening.''

She thought a moment, then nodded. ''Tell her I'll be there and should be home by seven.''

''I'll call her back.''

''Thanks.''

The door to Simpson's office stood ajar and his secretary hovered over the coffee table in the sitting area. Simpson was on the phone, but gestured for her to come in.

''Hi, Taylor,'' Clara said. ''Do you take sugar or cream in your tea?''

''Just straight Earl Grey, thanks.''

She smiled. ''Coming right up.''

Simpson and his invitations to tea had always struck her as a distinctly New England custom, a throwback, perhaps, to colonial times. It made her feel as though she should be wearing a long cotton dress and have her hair swept up in a braided bun or something.

''Taylor, thanks for coming,'' Simpson said, hurrying over. ''Make yourself comfortable, please.'' He settled in a sitting area on the other side of his office. ''I understand Tommy Washington was arraigned this morning.''

She nodded and gave him a brief update on the case, but didn't mention that she felt certain Washington had been framed. Simpson's primary interest in the firm's cases focused on the legal specifics, not the attorney's personal feelings.

''There's something I've been meaning to speak to you about for some time. It's a rather sensitive topic, so I'm approaching it as delicately as I can.''

She'd messed up big time, she thought. That must be it. ''Delicate in what way?''

''It's about Franklin Morgan.''

''What about him?''

''That day we had the little celebration for you, he insisted that he make an appearance. I'd had a meeting with him over a business matter and mentioned I had to leave. He said he'd like to join us and I thought it'd be a nice surprise.''

Nice? She could think of better adjectives.

Simpson went on. ''The firm has enjoyed a cordial relationship with the political leadership of this state—not just with the governor's office, but on the federal level as well. Many of our clients come indirectly through the congressional offices.''

Taylor nodded, puzzled by his obvious hemming.

''I, uh, well, your heritage is something I took as a high recommendation for your employment here.''

''My heritage? I don't understand.''

''The Morgan name is respected in Boston. Frank Morgan has had an exemplary career in Congress. Important legislation has come out of his office, under his auspices. It seems to me that you've inherited his talent, his sure instincts for the law.''

She tried to swallow around the lump in her throat. ''How did you know?''

''I've known the Morgans for a long time. Frank told me about you years ago. He'd been concerned for some time about your welfare and spent years trying to find you. He confided in me because he thought I might be able to help him locate you. I sent out Burt Hallas, he's one of the best in the business, you know, and within a week he'd located you at Amherst, in your second year of law school. Despite the circumstances in which you'd grown up, you did well for yourself.''

Taylor's initial intimidation now collapsed into anger. She had cherished the hours she'd spent in the law library. It was one of the few places she'd felt secure, where she'd been able to lose herself so completely in something that the past faded away. The idea that she'd been spied upon, followed, and that her progress had been charted like a stock, incensed her.

''Why didn't you tell me you knew?'' she asked.

''Because I wanted to hire you and I knew you wouldn't take the job if you thought Frank Morgan had something to do with the offer that was made.''

''You're right. Damn right.''

Simpson paused briefly to sip at his tea. She tried to imagine this dignified man discussing her parentage with Morgan and it made her sick to her stomach. ''Frank was never malicious as a boy, Taylor. He was just headstrong. A very passionate young man. And one who wasn't always cognizant of the consequences of his actions. Let me assure you that the Frank Morgan of today would be the last one to condone his behavior during those years. Believe me, I've heard him castigate himself on this subject.''

Words, she thought. What the hell did words mean? When it counted, Morgan hadn't been there. ''Then why did he wait so long to approach me? If what you say is true, he's known how to reach me for several years now.''

''He'd made his father a promise and I think he needed to wait until Monroe passed away before he contacted you, Taylor.''

''That's a hell of a promise, Ogden. Ignore the little girl who needs you.''

His eyes softened and he leaned forward, speaking earnestly. ''People change. And Frank Morgan has definitely changed. There's nothing he wants more now than for you to be happy.''

Sure. He wanted it so much, he'd asked Simpson to have a ''little chat'' with her. She could just imagine these two men sitting over dinner in some expensive Boston restaurant, discussing her and how she should be approached. Their conversation undoubtedly had been steeped in proper New England syntax and grammar, the message as clear as glass.

''She's a lovely young woman, Frank. She has your talent for the law.''

''Would you talk to her, Ogden? She trusts you.''

''I'd be glad to.''

''I don't know how you'll explain about Dad and my promise to him, but—''

''Don't worry about it, Frank. I'll make it clear that you care.''

''May I be blunt, Ogden?''

''By all means.'' Simpson sat forward, his gaze intense, focused just on her. ''That's why we're here.''

''It's difficult for me to get past the fact that he destroyed my mother's life.''

She didn't mention the notes that Morgan had been sending her since the night she'd been knocked out. Nor did she mention the bouquets of flowers or the huge, potted plants that he'd sent. Morgan seemed to be trying, yes, she would give him that much, but his efforts had come about nineteen years too late.

And yet, that small, abandoned child inside of her felt thrilled by his attentions. Taylor didn't tell Simpson that, either.

The bottom line remained simple and succinct: Frank Morgan hadn't done the right thing nineteen years ago. He'd taken the easy way out and it had cost her mother's life. A part of her could never forgive him for that.

"I don't think you can blame him any more deeply for that than he blames himself, Taylor."

The words hung there in the air between them, weighted with what sounded like the truth. But Simpson, after all, had been a crack criminal attorney in his heyday, a man who manipulated language in such a powerful way that he often moved a jury to tears. Age hadn't diminished his gift for saying the right thing at the right moment. Her throat closed up.

"I'm glad we were able to have this chat, Taylor," Simpson went on. "I'm here if you need anything, anything at all, even a cup of good tea." He smiled at that and tipped his cup to his mouth, polishing off the rest of his tea.

It signaled the end of their tea party and she stood seconds after he did. She clasped his hand in both of her own and thanked him for his candor. It occurred to her that she'd said these same words to Michael Sessio weeks ago and that then, as now, she'd meant what she said.

11

Long, narrow shadows shot across the streets of Cambridge as Taylor pulled up to her townhouse. Everything looked peaceful, settled, predictable, just as it had this morning when she'd left. She liked that predictability, liked the counterpoint it made to her professional life, where nothing these days seemed predictable.

She wanted to take Lady for a run, grab a bite to eat, then chill out for the evening. But when she'd called Cathy back to beg off for tonight, she'd insisted that Taylor at least drop by to meet the new love of her life, a guy she'd met at her gym.

If this new guy followed Cathy's usual pattern with men, he would be married and this would be their second or third date. He would be good-looking, self-involved, financially stable, a taker rather than a giver. If the affair followed the usual course, Taylor thought, it would be over a month from now.

On the other hand, maybe this guy broke the usual mold. For Cathy's sake, she hoped so.

Lady greeted her at the door, dancing around on her hind

legs, her delight pure and uncontained. If people dealt with each other in the same direct way, she thought, life would certainly be simpler. Or, at any rate, *her* life would be simpler.

She took Lady for a run and it purged her frustration about the meeting with Simpson. She decided she would drop by Cathy's for a drink, meet her new friend, then excuse herself. In addition to Washington's defense, she had three other cases, one of which involved the embezzlement of funds from a bank.

As one of three attorneys on the case, her role barely counted, which suited her just fine, since she believed the defendant was guilty. At least with the Washington case, she felt the defendant was innocent, that he'd been framed. One way or another, she would prove it.

She showered when she got back to the townhouse, fed Lady, put on a pair of khaki shorts and a cotton shirt, and went over to Cathy's. Seconds after she rang the bell, Cathy opened the door. She looked stunning, a slight flush in her cheeks, her makeup just so, her dark frizzy hair as shiny as a wet street. She wore white designer jeans that hugged her hips and a black silk blouse with pearl-colored flowers on it.

"I can't stay long," Taylor said quickly. "I've got a ton of work to do tonight."

"You can stay long enough for a drink," Cathy said, and hurried her into the apartment.

And there, in the living room, stood Michael Sessio. "Taylor, nice to see you again." He smiled and came toward her, hand outstretched.

Taylor shook his hand and noted that it lingered longer than necessary. "This is a, uh, surprise, Mr. Sessio. I didn't realize you knew Cathy."

"We met a week or so ago at the gym."

Taylor glanced at Cathy. "I really don't think it's a good idea for me to be here, Cath. Because of the Tommy Washington case. It might be a conflict of interest."

"How is it a conflict of interest?" Sessio asked. "I don't understand."

She turned her eyes on him. "I don't know if it's a conflict of interest. I don't know what it is. But I'm just not comfortable with it.''

"Taylor, it's just a coincidence," Cathy said. "Michael didn't know you and I are friends. I didn't even make the connection between your case and Michael until the second time we saw each other.''

"Look, I know what you're thinking," Sessio said.

"No, you don't," Taylor snapped, irritated at his presumption.

But Sessio went on as though she hadn't spoken. "Ms. Brooke, if I wanted to speak to you, I could pick up my phone and call your office to make an appointment, just like I did before.''

She conceded the point. But in social situations, people tended to relax their guards. Things were said that might not be revealed in a business setting. The point, though, was that Michael Sessio remained a suspect. He knew it as well as she did.

"I'd prefer to keep it on a professional level, Mr. Sessio."

Before she turned around, he said, "May I ask you one question?''

"What's that?"

"Do you still have the tape?"

"What tape?" Cathy asked.

"It was stolen the night of the break-in to my apartment," Taylor replied, ignoring Cathy's question.

Sessio nodded, as though this confirmed what he'd expected. "I hope you realize that was the purpose of the break-in.''

"You sound awfully certain of that, Mr. Sessio."

"It should be obvious."

"What tape?" Cathy asked again, glancing from Sessio to Taylor.

"I'm not at liberty to discuss it, Cathy. It concerns the Washington case." She looked at Sessio again. "You sound like you know who was responsible for the break-in."

"The same people who are after me and who set up your client.''

The intensity of his gaze, that smoldering sexuality, made

her so acutely uncomfortable she simply said she had to get going and left the apartment. She spent the rest of the evening stewing over what had happened. Sessio, player, mover, master manipulator, would mold Cathy like putty. Taylor believed he'd known she and Cathy were friends, had known it since she'd been appointed to defend Washington, and that he'd joined Cathy's gym with the intention of meeting her. Clearly a setup.

And there wasn't a damn thing she could do about it.

Michael Sessio spent the next two days consumed with thoughts of Taylor. She haunted his dreams, prowled the corridors of his conscious thoughts, and surfaced at odd moments as though her very face were magic.

About seven A.M. on the third day after he'd seen her at Cathy's, Nikko called. "You alone, Mike?"

"Alone, with the door shut. What's up?"

"You're not going to believe this. Taylor Brooke's name used to be Talia Carlino. Her mother Eva was killed when she was nine . . ."

"Killed how?"

"Hit and run. They never found who did it. She spent the rest of her youth at St. Mary's Children's Home. It's primarily a Catholic school these days, but back then they also took in a certain number of orphans. She went to BU on a scholarship, got her law degree at Amherst. In between she married a guy named Eric Serle. Far as I can tell, they're still married."

Christ, Sessio thought. "Where's this Serle fellow now?"

"Last known address was in Fall River. In early June, he cleared out of his apartment and disappeared."

Sessio rubbed his forehead and swiveled around in his chair to gaze out the window at the harbor. "No trace of him?"

"Not that I've been able to run down yet."

"Stay on it and keep me posted. I'd like to see the file on Eva Carlino. Any chance you can get a copy?"

"I'll try."

"What about her father?"

"No listing on the birth certificate. It might be in the Children's Home records. It's a long shot, but I'll see if I can get a look."

"Great. Thanks again, Nikko."

"Mike?"

"Yeah?"

"Watch your ass. I got a bad feeling about this."

"Me, too."

A very bad feeling, he thought, and hung up.

Three days passed in which Taylor didn't see or hear from Cathy. She'd left a couple of messages on her machine at home, but she hadn't returned the calls. She'd stopped by Cathy's apartment last night and had rung the bell. Although her car had been parked out front, she hadn't answered the door.

In other words, she thought, it looked as if Michael Sessio had cost her friendship with Cathy.

Earlier today she'd gone to Simpson and told him what had happened. He felt as Taylor did, that Sessio had used Cathy to get to her. But he'd surprised her by suggesting that she find out what Sessio intended. However, as Simpson pointed out, it seemed entirely possible that once Sessio realized Taylor would keep her distance, he had moved on. Considering Cathy's track record, Taylor agreed.

She called Cathy's work number and she picked up on the second ring. "Hey, Cath. It's Taylor."

"Oh. Hi."

Chilly voice, Taylor thought.

"It's kind of short notice, but how about lunch on the wharf? We need to talk."

"Sorry, but I've got plans for lunch."

Several beats passed. "Look," Taylor said. "I apologize about the other night. But I just didn't feel it was appropriate for me to stay. You really caught me by surprise."

"I'm the one who should be apologizing, Taylor. I felt sort of weird about things as soon as I knew his last name. I should have been up front with you."

Taylor had been prepared to argue, to defend her actions. Instead, she now felt like an idiot for making such a big deal out of it. "I'm just sorry my job got wedged between us, Cathy."

"It hasn't. But you know, Mike's on your side. He doesn't think Washington is guilty, either."

She didn't find this particularly comforting. If anything, it made the prosecution's contention that Sessio hired Washington all the more plausible. "So how're you two getting along?"

"Just great. It's better than I thought possible. Listen, I've got to run. He just got here. We'll talk later."

And she hung up.

Taylor had stopped short of suggesting the three of them get together, stopped even though Simpson had urged her to do it. She couldn't bring herself to use Cathy the way she thought Sessio had been using her. Besides, she had the distinct feeling she wouldn't have to go looking for Sessio because he would come looking for her.

Hi, Ms. Brooke." Bobby Tee, the security guard, smiled as he greeted her and motioned her over to his desk in the lobby.

From the expression on his face, she didn't think he'd called her over for a wardrobe comment. "What's up, Bobby?"

"I just wanted to tell you that there was a man here earlier who was asking about you."

"Asking what?"

"When you usually came by here on your way to lunch. I told him I didn't know."

"Thanks, Bobby. I appreciate it. Any idea who he was?"

"No, sorry."

"What'd he look like?"

Bobby rubbed his jaw and frowned, thinking about it. Ever since the attack, her concern about Eric had never been far from her mind. Even though she'd heard nothing from him since he'd sent that rose with the card, the continued silence terrified her. Sometimes at night, when sleep refused to come, she could almost feel him out there somewhere, plotting and planning his next move against her. Worse, the cops had never found him in Fall River.

"Sort of tall," Bobby said. "Sort of . . . Hey, there he is now." He pointed and Taylor's head snapped around.

John Stark smiled; a wave of relief washed over her. "It's okay, Bobby. I know him."

"You have a nice day now, Ms. Brooke."

"You, too."

Stark stood there in a suit, his lean body loose and relaxed. As she strolled over to him, he eyed her so openly that it would be apparent to anyone that he had more than business in mind. Eat your heart out, pal, she thought. "What's up, John?"

"How about lunch?"

"You know my office number. You don't have to sneak around in the lobby, waiting for me."

Stark laughed. "I was in the building for a meeting and just asked the guard if you'd left yet for lunch. Why all the paranoia, Taylor?"

"Hey, you, too, may join the paranoid ranks after you've been knocked over the head in your own kitchen."

His mirth vanished. "Jesus, I'm sorry. I didn't mean—"

"Yeah, I know. Forget it. Look, I'd prefer a business meeting."

"You can have lunch with the opposition, you know. It's allowed." Then he touched her arm and walked her out of the building and into the warm July afternoon.

"Just so we understand this is business."

"I know where things stand, Taylor. I don't have to like it, but I'm aware of it, okay?"

When his arm dropped to his side, relief and regret struggled inside of her, each demanding equal say. The heat of his palm lingered against her arm.

They headed up the sidewalk, as they'd done in the past, in the early days of their relationship, when they were only friends. Unfortunately, that period hadn't lasted long. Their mutual attraction had seized them suddenly, intensely, and from the very first time they'd set eyes on each other, she'd known they would be lovers. It only had been a question of when.

The attraction persisted, but she reminded herself that nothing would come of it. He played on the opposing team and was still married. She knew her limits, understood the parameters within which she must live her life, and intended to abide by the unspoken rules.

The woman she'd been two years ago bore little resemblance to the woman beside him now. She no longer believed that if she'd loved Stark long enough, he eventually would leave his wife. Love didn't always solve the problem; sometimes it became the problem.

But then Stark dropped his bomb. "Did I tell you that I'm in the middle of a divorce?"

"You know you didn't."

He seemed briefly flustered—a quick, nervous smile, a quick, nervous glance at her. "Guilty."

"I hope it's better for you in the long run, John." Then she changed the subject. "So what's with your boss? She doesn't seem to like me very much."

"Debra got where she is by looking for the crack in her opponent's armor. When she finds it, she goes after it and tears the person to shreds. That's a friendly warning."

"I thought you were the lead attorney."

"I am. But she can jump in any time."

And would, Taylor thought.

They walked into an upscale diner where the cuisine was varied, delicious, and ridiculously expensive. Stark had made a reservation; the hostess showed them to a table. Since it was set for two, she assumed he'd made the reservation for two, and given the intimate little spot, he'd figured she would accept the lunch invitation. Arrogance or optimism? Either way, it annoyed her.

"So what's on your mind?" she asked, after they'd ordered.

"I know about the tape, Taylor. I know it was taken."

"So the grapevine is alive and well."

"I think the tape was faked. Ravigno says he doesn't play pool."

"Ravigno's a con man."

"Informers," he said with a wry, patronizing smile, "are rarely upstanding citizens. Otherwise they wouldn't be out on the street buying crack from the likes of Tommy Washington."

Her patience frayed; she felt like telling him to mind his own business, to go pound sand. Then it occurred to her that Gova had put him up to this. *"Browbeat her, John. Make her sweat."* And Stark, efficient foot soldier, carried out his orders well. "I think it'd be a good idea if we didn't talk about the case."

"Watch out for Michael Sessio."

It was as if she hadn't said a damn thing. Stark obviously had his agenda and intended to say his piece even if she didn't want to hear it. "Hang it up, John. I'm not in the mood right now for Gova games."

He leaned toward her, his eyes bright with emotion. "I'm not playing any goddamn game, okay?" Although he spoke softly, each word sounded sharp, crisp. "I'm concerned that you're getting sucked in by all the bullshit. And just so you know, one of my contacts found that Sessio hired a PI and . . ."

"I know about it," she interrupted.

The waitress returned with their lunches and as soon as she'd left, Stark continued as though there had been no interruption. "But you don't know what I know about him. The PI wasn't hired to tape Ravigno. Hell, he's not even a PI. He's worked for the Sessio family for years. I'm betting he was hired to find out everything he could about you, including who your friends and neighbors are."

Even if she considered the source, this didn't differ from what she'd suspected about Sessio. Setup, pure and simple. "Thanks for the tip. But I don't need your advice."

They ate in silence and, over coffee, he tried to strike up a conversation about other things, books, movies, cases in other parts of the country. She nodded, she murmured an opinion now and then, but mostly she kept quiet. And as soon as the waitress brought their bill, Taylor asked what she owed.

Stark, who could afford a fifty-five dollar lunch bill, said it was his treat and she thought, *Damn right.*

On the way back to the office, their hands brushed and moments later he caught her fingers and held them. "I miss you, Taylor."

"Get lost, John."

And she hurried on ahead and eventually lost him in pedestrian traffic.

That evening, she and Lady ran down to the river and she pounded out an extra mile. At one point, Lady wandered off, got spooked by something, and raced back to Taylor's side. Since the break-in, the dog had been frightened of men she didn't know, particularly large men, Taylor had noticed. She wondered what would happen if Lady saw the intruder again. Would she recognize the man? Whimper? Attack him? What?

She snapped Lady's leash back on. On the run back to the townhouse, though, she extended the leash to its full length. As they neared the townhouse, Taylor saw a black Mercedes parked behind Cathy's Honda Accord. Sessio's car. They seemed to be spending a lot of time together and she wondered at the sudden stab of envy she felt.

Sessio, a handsome, powerful, and wealthy man, seemed genuinely interested in Cathy. But Taylor couldn't move past the apparent coincidence that he'd fallen for a woman who happened to be her neighbor. On the other hand, if Stark was right that Sessio had hired someone to look into her life, how coincidental could Sessio's relationship with Cathy be? What had Sessio expected to find? Skeletons in her closets? Well, she had plenty of those. But what did he really want from her? That still puzzled her.

She headed over to a grassy area where many of the dog owners walked their dogs. A quiet stillness suffused the evening air. Too quiet, too still, she thought, and glanced around uneasily. Protected by nothing more than a dog that now feared strangers, she wouldn't scare off a potential attacker.

Eileen had urged her to get a gun, but Taylor felt that if you owned a gun, you attracted the circumstances in which you might have to use it. Superstitious, she supposed, but there you had it. Nix on the gun. Kyle had suggested that she buy Mace, one of those pocket-sized spray cans that she could keep in her purse or by her bed. She could live with Mace, she decided, and made a mental note to find out where she could buy the stuff.

Lady's head suddenly snapped up and she gazed toward the parking lot and began to growl softly. Taylor looked around and saw a shadowed figure leaning against a car and smoking a cigarette. In the dusk, the orange glow of the cigarette was just a point of light, floating toward the man's mouth.

"Big deal," she said to Lady. "Some guy sneaking a smoke. So what."

Lady moved forward, nose to the ground, pursuing a scent, and Taylor followed her, still holding on to the leash. She heard footsteps behind her, the back of her neck started to burn, Lady stopped and growled. Taylor looked back and there, less than a yard from her, stood Michael Sessio.

"Hi, Taylor."

Lady edged back, still growling and straining at the leash. "You spooked my dog," she said.

"Sorry." His dark eyes appraised her frankly, openly, taking in all of her. "How far do you run?"

"Usually a couple of miles."

"Good for you." He flicked his cigarette away from him and it arched through the dusk, etching a faint orange trail against the dusk. "I probably wouldn't make it a quarter of a mile. Cathy doesn't like me to smoke inside, so I duck out periodically." He looked at Lady and held out his hand. "Aren't you beautiful."

The lab whimpered and backed away.

"Not much of a watchdog," he remarked.

"She's been edgy since the break-in."

"Oh, that's right. Cathy said she got poisoned. So how're things moving along on the big case?" He asked as though one thought led naturally to the other.

"Moving along, just like you said."

Sessio smiled. "I really don't bite, Taylor."

"And I haven't changed my stance about discussing the

case with you.'' She heard the sharpness in her voice and knew he heard it, too.

''I understand. But if there's anything I can do for you, Taylor, let me know.''

''There is one thing,'' she blurted. ''Tell me why you faked that tape.''

''What? What're you talking about?'' He looked and sounded shocked, but there was something about his expression just then that tipped her off. She was right, she knew she was.

''Ravigno doesn't play pool,'' she said. ''So it couldn't have been him on the tape.''

Sessio glanced down at the ground and shook his head. When he raised his eyes again, the shock had vanished. ''I trust the investigator I hired and I doubt that he would fake evidence. But if he did, he'll answer for it.'' With that, Sessio walked away.

Taylor stared after him, wondering if she'd made a mistake. Maybe she should have kept that bit of information to herself. As one of her law professors used to say, the path to a conviction sometimes depended on what you didn't say.

But an astute businessman like Sessio would have kept a copy of the tape. And yet, he'd told her he'd sent her the only copy. Now she knew why. Then another thought occurred to her. Perhaps Sessio had realized she eventually would find out the tape was faked and had sent someone to retrieve it.

Later, as she got ready for bed, she remembered that Eileen had handed her a letter earlier today from Frank Morgan. This was the fourth she'd received from him since her stay in the hospital in early June; it was now mid-July. So, once a week, Morgan put his thoughts down on paper, mailed them to her, then she reciprocated.

Odd, but it had become the ideal way for her and Morgan to establish a relationship and attempt to mend the past. Taylor dug it out of her purse and sat down on the bed to read it.

This letter concerned his daughter, Melissa, who had been

stricken with leukemia. She'd been too ill to attend her grandfather's funeral and now spent most of her time in Palm Springs with her mother, under the care of a specialist. Her illness, coupled with the loss of his father, had forced Morgan to reexamine his life. Fine, Taylor had no problem with that. It just seemed that the bridge-building had come a little too late.

In the letter, Morgan referred to Taylor as his oldest daughter and remarked that very soon she might be his only living child. WHAT SEEMS OBVIOUS TO MOST PEOPLE HAS TAKEN ME YEARS TO LEARN, TAYLOR. FAMILY IS ALL THAT MATTERS.

She slipped the letter in the drawer of the nightstand, then brought out a pad of paper and a pen. She would reply, as she always did, but would keep it short, courteous. "Dear Senator Morgan," she began, then scratched through it, tore the sheet off the pad, crumpled it up.

Too formal.

"Dear Frank" was more appropriate.

She thanked him for his concern and offered her condolences on the death of his father and his daughter's illness. She said she'd been busy at work, then searched for a graceful way to close the note. She suggested, somewhat reluctantly, that perhaps they could have coffee sometime.

That night she dreamed she and Morgan sat in front of a crackling fire, in a cozy, book-lined den, the sort of room she'd always imagined to exist somewhere in the Morgan mansion. Everything moved in slow motion, even the flames in the fireplace. Her limbs felt heavy, weighted.

She heard a noise somewhere behind her and turned to look around. The firelight cast dense, dark shadows against the walls and windows. But Eric's face glowed like a pale moon in the windowpane and he grinned as he raised his gun. Her scream echoed in the room and suddenly the dream slammed into fast forward.

Morgan leaped in front of her as the gun went off. His eyes widened and he fell back with blood pouring from his chest. He crashed to the floor and Eric hurled himself through the window, glass exploding everywhere, and aimed the gun at her.

Taylor bolted out of the dream with a scream clawing its way up her throat.

12

The noise and the smoke and the press of the crowd ceased to exist for Kyle. He saw only the crap table, the dice he held in his hands, and his pile of chips in the center of the table. He blew into his hands, the fever seized him.

C'mon, baby, don't fail me now, he thought. Then he tossed the dice out onto the table.

His stomach turned inside out.

"Snake eyes," the dealer said, and swept all of Kyle's chips toward the dealer's end of the table.

Gone, seven hundred bucks gone in a flash. For seconds he couldn't move, couldn't wrench his eyes from the now empty table. Then his rigid muscles relaxed and he jerked back a step, spun, and lost himself in the crowd.

He dug through his pockets even though he knew he was busted, and pulled out a handful of loose change. Quarters for the ride home, for the tolls. Just one, he thought. If he played just one in a slot machine, maybe . . .

Maybe nothing. There would be no jackpot. There had never been a goddamn jackpot.

He'd driven more than two hours to Foxwoods in Ledyard, Connecticut, just to lose seven hundred bucks, the last money he had. Now what?

There had been a time when his room and board had been provided whenever he'd come here. He remembered the light, airy room way up on the thirtieth floor, remembered the soft peach carpeting, the Jacuzzi tub, the wet bar. He remembered how those sheets had felt against his body at night. He remembered the food, shrimp scampi flamed in sherry, steamed clams in cream sauce, the aged beefs, the Maine lobster tails in butter, the flambé desserts.

But all that was before his credit had gone bad. There were three creditors, loan sharks who looked like they were out of central casting. The bastards kept moving in on him, tightening the noose, calling him at all hours, demanding their money.

A few weeks ago, he'd relieved the pressure somewhat by paying each of the sharks five grand. The money had come from his work for Gova, work that had turned him into a Judas, the worst kind of betrayer, the lowest slime, a lawyer who turned on his own case.

But the ugly reality couldn't be ignored: he owed more than sixty grand and bankruptcy had never been an option, not with these creditors. They buried the people who owed them money.

Fortunately, Gova had come along with her fifty grand offer. He'd tried not to act too eager, tried to give himself time to think it over. But less than twenty-four hours after Gova had made her offer, he'd told her he would accept it.

At the time, it had seemed simple enough, just assure the conviction of Tommy Washington. But Christ, look where it had gotten him, busted again and on his way out of the casino with nowhere to go but home.

He continued to feed Gova information and tried to mislead Taylor whenever he could, wrestling with what remained of his conscience. His major success so far had been keeping her away from the restaurant's phone records. Once he'd convinced Taylor that no call had come in for Tommy, Gova had taken care of the rest.

Gova, he thought. Gova could get him more money and fast.

"Hey, Carrot Top, leaving so soon?" called a guy with a goatee. "You break the bank again?" He laughed and Kyle kept on walking.

Goatee, a buddy of one of the sharks, would spread the word that Kyle had dropped a few more bills. And tonight when he walked into his place, his phone would be ringing. Or the bastards would call him tomorrow at the office, which they'd already done a couple of times. Another one of the sharks had dropped by his condo a few days ago and asked a neighbor when he would be getting home.

They operated that way, putting a little pressure here, a little more pressure there. And some night, he thought, he would be walking down a dark street and they would jerk him into an alley and beat the piss out of him.

His beeper went off before he reached the front doors. A Boston number scrolled across the screen, not a number he recognized. The sharks had his beeper number, he thought.

No way they could get the number, since it wasn't even under his name. He stopped at the bank of phones and called the number.

"Hallas."

It took a moment for the name to register. "Burt, you called?"

"I found him."

"Found who?"

"Serle. Eric Serle."

Suddenly, the world looked a whole lot brighter. "Great, fantastic. Where is he?"

"In jail in Fall River. He beat up a hooker."

"How long's he been in?"

"Two days or so."

"Do the cops know he's wanted in Boston for questioning?"

"I don't think so. These small town cops don't give a shit about the big city. But the longer he's there, the more likely it is they'll find out. His bond is set at fifty grand, he can't pay it.''

"I'll be in touch.''

Debra Gova stretched out in bed, her back resting against pillows propped up against the headboard, a book open in her lap, the phone glued to her ear. "Don't worry, everything's in place,'' she said.

"Taylor isn't going to give up easily.''

Gova loved the sound of the man's voice, its smooth richness, its assurance. And tonight it would follow her into her dreams. "Kyle Nelson will keep her under control.''

"I get the impression that Nelson has trouble controlling himself, much less anyone else.''

"I'm keeping close tabs on him, don't worry.''

"When would you like to get together?''

"Next weekend?''

Now his voice licked at her ear. "Sure, that sounds good. We'll fly over to the hideaway.''

Perfect, she thought. The hideaway. "Great.'' Another call came in. "I've got to run. Talk to you soon. And don't worry, huh?'' She disconnected from this call and picked up the incoming call. "Debra Gova.''

"It's me.''

Shit, she thought. Kyle the Troublemaker. "What's up?''

"Eric Serle, that's what,'' Kyle replied, and told her what had happened.

Her mind raced, following an idea to its conclusion somewhere in the future. She decided it would work. "Bail him out. Direct him to Taylor's town house, take him by the hand, do whatever's necessary.''

"I need money to get him out, Debra.''

"You'll get it. Go over to Fall River now, to the office of a bondsman named Gerald Towers. He'll take care of everything and he'll also have a cash incentive, just in case Serle isn't cooperative.''

"What's he supposed to do when he finds Taylor?"

"Christ, Kyle," she snapped. "Let Serle figure it out. We want him to distract her, that's the whole point."

"Yeah, but this guy is dangerous and I'll be connected to him if I pay his bond."

"Your name won't appear anywhere in Towers's records. You go to him first, not to the cops, and everything will be just fine."

"I don't want Taylor hurt."

Gova rolled her eyes. Kyle Nelson, she thought, was beginning to sound like a broken record. He wanted the money she paid him, but he didn't want Taylor hurt. He wanted this, but wasn't willing to pay that. Yeah, she'd known plenty of Kyles in her life.

"Just do what I tell you, Kyle, and no one will get hurt."

"There's one other thing."

"Gee, let me guess. Dough." She wondered how much he'd blown during his latest casino visit.

"Right."

"Towers will have another fifteen for you. Now get moving."

"Debra?"

"Yeah?"

"I mean it about Taylor. She can't be hurt in any way. Not like the night of the break-in."

Gova's patience snapped. "Let's get something straight, Kyle. You bought into this when you accepted my offer. If you don't want Taylor hurt, then I suggest you make that real clear to Eric Serle. But if Serle doesn't do his part, if he doesn't make an impact, then I'll pursue other means, whatever's necessary." With that, she slammed down the phone.

13

Kyle arrived in Fall River at nearly one in the morning. His eyes burned from lack of sleep, his neck ached from tension, his stomach felt queasy. He'd gobbled so many Tums on the way up here his teeth felt strange, as if he'd been gnawing on aluminum foil.

He drove up and down streets near the city jail until he found the bondsman's office. The building needed a coat of paint, the windows hadn't been washed since the Cold War had ended, the neon sign hissed and sizzled like bacon on a hot griddle. Kyle drove around the block and parked on one of the side streets. He got out, locked his car, and walked quickly back to the building.

He didn't see any cars out front, but a dim light shone behind the venetian blinds. He rapped softly. The intercom to his right crackled with static, then a man said, "Yeah?"

"Gova sent me," Kyle said.

"Uh-huh."

The door buzzed, Kyle opened it, and stepped inside. The room was lit by a single floor lamp on the far side. It illuminated a robust man huddled over a desk littered with files, stacks of newspapers and magazines, notebooks, and boxes of computer disks. A dense cloud of smoke drifted through the light, so much smoke that Kyle waved his hand in front of his face and coughed.

The man glanced up and smiled, his lips pulling away from his teeth so that his smile seemed predatory. His plump cheeks puffed out, his bushy brows lifted, his small, dark eyes sank into their sockets. "Gerald Tower, Mr. Nelson." He waved a fat, dimpled hand at the only chair in front of his desk. "Have a seat."

Kyle didn't particularly want his body to touch anything in this office. No telling what sort of bacteria lived in here. He remained standing. Tower didn't remark on it one way or another.

"Let's see here. I've got two envelopes. . . ." He lifted papers and files and finally pulled out two bulging manila envelopes. He slipped on a pair of glasses with grimy lenses and glanced at the envelopes. "Uh-huh, here we go. This here's for you, Mr. Nelson." He held out one of the envelopes. "Fifteen thousand."

Kyle took it, slipped it inside his windbreaker.

"And this here is cash that Ms. Gova said you'll be needing." Tower flashed a big smile as he held out the second envelope. "I'll have Mr. Serle bailed out by eight tomorrow morning."

"Tomorrow? Ms. Gova led me to believe it would be tonight."

Tower sat forward, his plumps fingers laced together on the dirty desk. "Fall River is not Boston, Mr. Nelson. The earliest I can post bond is eight tomorrow morning. Rather than driving back to Boston tonight, you're welcome to sack out on my couch."

And contract a disease, Kyle thought. No thanks. He managed to smile. "Thanks for the offer, Mr. Tower. But a motel room will be fine."

"There's one just down the street. Nothing fancy, mind you, but it's clean." He glanced quickly around his office and laughed. "Lot cleaner than here."

"I'd appreciate it if you'd bring Mr. Serle to the motel when you bail him out."

"No problem."

"I'm curious about something, Mr. Tower."

Those small, insectile eyes impaled him. "What's that?"

"What do you get out of this?"

Tower looked at him for a long moment, his ugly eyes totally blank. Then he slammed his fat hand against his even fatter thigh and exploded with laughter. "Money, Nelson. I get money, same as you." Then he heaved himself to his feet. "You follow me to the motel and by eight A.M., things'll be rolling."

Rolling, Kyle thought, but in which direction?

The motel on the outskirts of town didn't look as bad as he expected. Thanks to his heavy gambling days, he carried an overnight bag in the trunk of his car, so he at least had a change of clothes, a toothbrush, and a few other essentials.

But once he got into bed, he couldn't sleep. Faces floated through his head: Gova, Taylor, Tommy Washington, Stark, the whole stinking parade.

He finally turned on the bedside lamp and opened the two envelopes Tower had given him. His envelope contained fifteen grand, just as Gova had promised. But the envelope for Serle—the incentive money, as Gova had put it—held another fifteen.

Gova, you snake, he thought.

He dumped all the bills on the bed and counted the money slowly, rolling the bills between his fingers. He mentally calculated the minimum he could pay off to the loan sharks to keep them off his back until he hit it big at the tables.

He dug out a pad of paper and a pen, scribbled numbers on a sheet, tore it off, scribbled more numbers, paced, thought, scribbled some more. *If* Serle would accept five grand to go after Taylor, then he would have twenty-five grand to work with, ten more than he'd figured.

Elated, he gathered up the bills, tucked twenty-five grand into one envelope, five into the other, and put both in his overnight bag. He shoved the bag under the bed, turned off the lamp, and lay there in the dark, smiling and plotting until he finally fell asleep.

The ringing phone snapped Taylor out of a sound sleep. She sat up and glanced at the clock. It was just past seven. A breather call?

She decided to let the machine answer.

"Hi, Taylor, it's Frank Morgan. Sorry I missed you, but . . ."

Taylor picked up the receiver. "Hi, Frank."

"I hope I didn't wake you."

"I was getting ready for work."

"I got your note. Instead of coffee, how about dinner tomorrow night?"

"I'm not sure what time I'm going to get off work."

"I'm flexible. I was thinking we could have dinner here at the house. My driver can pick you up at the firm or at your place, whatever is most convenient for you, Taylor."

She hesitated, but not for long. It was time to get this over with. "Here at seven."

"Great. My driver will pick you up. See you tomorrow night."

As she hung up, the thirteen-year-old girl who had been rejected all those years ago leaped around with glee inside of her.

Lady whined and jumped up on the bed, licking Taylor's face. "Just a minute, girl, then I'll take you out." She quickly called Cathy's number. She answered on the second ring, her voice chipper, energetic.

"Hey, it's me," Taylor said. "You have some free time today?"

"Around lunch, sure. Why? What's up?"

"Frank invited me to dinner at his place tomorrow night. I need something to wear."

Cathy let out a soft whistle. "Wow. This is like Cinderella time."

"Yeah, sort of."

"I'll meet you at Saks at noon, by the cosmetic counter."

"Great. Thanks."

"Taylor?"

"Yeah?"

"You realize we haven't gone shopping together in ages?"

"It'll be fun. See you then."

Eric picked at what passed for food in jail. The hash browns tasted like cardboard, the eggs looked half raw, the toast sagged in the middle, the bacon floated in a pool of grease. Even worse, the coffee tasted as weak as tea. He wondered if lunch could possibly be worse than this shit.

A guard dragged his nightstick against the bars of his cell. "You're outta here, Serle."

Eric sprang off his bunk. "I am?"

"Yup. Bondsman's out front. You must have a guardian angel out there somewhere, man. Your bail's been posted." He unlocked the cell door, tossed Eric his street clothes. "Take off the blues, leave 'em on the bunk."

Five minutes later, Eric followed the guard out front. Another guard handed him a wire basket that contained his wallet, car keys, and the other items he'd been carrying when he'd been brought in. "Sign here," the guard said, and thrust a form at him.

Eric scribbled his name at the bottom of the form, pocketed his belongings, and the double doors clicked open. He followed the guard into the lobby, where a fat man with a greasy smile waited for him. The fat man thrust out his fat hand. "Gerald Tower, bondsman."

"Who posted my bond?"

"We'll talk outside, Mr. Serle."

Tower shuffled toward the door and Eric fell into step beside him. Outside, a summer warmth hugged the air. A July warmth. Late July.

"My car's over here, Mr. Serle."

"Where're we going?"

"To see the gentleman who posted your bond."

"And who would that be?"

Tower flashed another greasy grin that dimpled his fat cheeks. "That's what you're about to find out, Mr. Serle." He opened the door of a filthy, ancient Volvo and Eric climbed into the front seat.

Empty paper bags and empty cups littered the floor. Empty containers from fast food restaurants gathered mold on the backseat. The inside of the car stank of old food, spilled sodas, smoke, coffee. Hygiene, personal or otherwise, seemed to be a foreign concept to Gerald Tower.

They didn't speak as Tower pulled away from the curb and headed up the street. "Where're we going?" Eric finally asked.

"Motel right near here."

Tower glanced over at him. He wore shades now and the lenses tossed back twin reflections of Eric's face. He needed a shave, he needed a shower, he needed dough, he needed to find out if the old woman had evicted him from his room. "So I meet this guy and then what?"

Tower shrugged. "Beats me."

A few minutes later, they pulled up in front of the motel. "Room ten, Mr. Serle. I'll wait until you're inside. Just knock on the door. And if I were you, I'd listen very closely to whatever your benefactor proposes. Opportunities like this don't come along every day and it seems to me you need a break."

"You got that right." Eric climbed out.

He knocked on the door of room ten. A guy with red hair opened it, waved at Tower, then said, "C'mon in, Mr. Serle."

"You bailed me out?" Eric asked as he walked into the room.

"That's right. And I have a business proposition for you."

"Uh-huh." Eric's eyes darted around the room, looking for anything that would tell him about this guy. But the room had about as much personality as a beach. "And what's it involve?"

"Your wife."

Eric's eyes snapped back to the guy's face. "My wife? What the hell do you know about my wife?"

"What's important, Mr. Serle, is what I'm going to tell you about your wife."

Eric straddled the desk chair and rested his arms along the back of it, watching Carrot Top as he paced. His heart hammered, his palms began to sweat. "She's in Boston, I already know that much. Saw her on the tube."

"Would you like to see her, Mr. Serle? Talk to her?"

Actually, he would like to smash the bitch's face. "Damn straight."

Carrot Top heard the vehemence in his voice, stopped, stared at him. "Then we're going to have some ground rules first, Mr. Serle."

"Yeah? Like what?"

"Number one." Carrot Top's index finger shot up. "No violence. She is *not* to be hurt. We clear on that, Mr. Serle?"

"Depends."

"On what?"

"On what's in it for me."

"You do what I tell you to do and you'll have five grand in your pocket, five grand that will take you way the hell out of Fall River."

"Jump bond, in other words."

"You got it."

"And what do I have to do for this five grand?"

"Scare the piss outta her, so that she goes into hiding. But don't harm her. If you harm her in any way, you'll find yourself back in jail so fast it'll make your cock spin. We clear on that?"

"Yeah. So where is she?"

"I'm not finished, Mr. Serle. You'll be paid two grand up front and the rest when she's gone into hiding."

"How do we stay in touch?"

"I'll give you a number to call. You ask for Watson. Don't call unless you've upheld your end of the deal."

"I'll need a place to stay in Boston. That can eat up the two grand real quick."

"I'll give you the name of a cheap hotel on the outskirts of town and an additional thousand to cover the motel and meals."

"And all I need to do is scare her outta town?"

"That's right."

"But without harming her."

"Yes."

"Okay. So what's her address?"

Carrot Top hesitated, then slipped an envelope out of his back pocket. "Everything you need is in there. I'll call you in a couple of days to make sure you're settled in at the motel."

Eric nodded, but his head raced toward the future, toward Talia, toward the showdown he'd been hoping for since the night she'd fled.

One of Michael Sessio's greatest joys involved the simple act of walking—specifically, walking around Boston. Except for the T, which he rarely used, your feet were the best way to get around the city.

This morning he'd walked from his office on the harbor to the Back Bay area, location of many of the specialty shops and art emporiums. He had come here for the art, but didn't know yet exactly what kind of art he wanted. He felt sure, however, that he would know it when he saw it.

He strolled along the storefronts, pausing here, there, admiring sculptures and oils, tapestries and African masks. He owned a number of exquisite paintings and sculptures in clay, iron, and stone, pieces that might mean nothing to another person but which spoke directly to him. Exactly what art should be, he thought. After all, if a piece of art didn't speak to *you*, what the hell good was it?

The trick would be finding the piece that spoke intimately to *her*.

Sessio entered one shop after another, poked around, wandered the aisles, paused over several pieces and decided none of them would do. After an hour and a half, he still hadn't found the right piece. Forget it, he thought. Try again later this week.

He crossed the street to head back toward the harbor and

then he saw it, a small shop on the corner which, at one time in his life, had carried the kind of art he liked. Worth a try, he decided, and went inside.

The piece stood just inside the door, a four-foot-high stone sculpture. It depicted a woman who seemed to be rising out of the stone, her arms lifted toward the heavens. One hand curled into a tight fist, as if from the exertion of reaching for something to grasp, to pull herself out of the stone. The other hand seemed to be flying open, as if expressing joy that the emergence from stone would be easier than she'd thought possible. He'd never heard of the sculptor, but the piece shone.

He paid fifteen hundred cash for it, which covered the delivery charges to Cambridge. He had absolutely no idea how Taylor would react. But it didn't matter, as long as she looked at it long enough to understand that in this piece, he'd recognized the source of who she was.

Saks had never been just a department store to Taylor. Since her childhood, when she'd stood outside the building and gawked at the window displays, it had represented a certain level of the American dream, an untouchable entity in her scarce, destitute world. And now, as she walked into the store, that same childhood wonder returned.

The delicious scents, the array of colors and clothes, even the shoppers themselves fascinated her. Cathy hadn't arrived yet, so Taylor circled the cosmetics counter, eyeing the vast selection of mascaras and eye shadows, creams and powders.

"With a face like yours, you don't need makeup," Cathy said, coming up behind her.

Taylor laughed and turned around. "Look who's talking."

"Ha." She pointed to the soft blue circles under her eyes. "Sleepless nights." She touched a corner of her mouth. "Wrinkles." She touched her forehead. "Worry lines."

"That's what late nights of great sex does to you."

Cathy ignored the remark and said, "C'mon, Yves St. Laurent has some great new evening dresses."

They spent twenty minutes picking through the clothes,

holding up this one or that one, chatting away about colors, cuts, designs. Cathy selected four evening dresses and Taylor chose another four, then they found a vacant dressing room.

As Taylor tried on various outfits, she realized Cathy hadn't mentioned Sessio. "So how're things going with Mike?"

"Great. We go out to dinner, we've been sailing, we flew up to Saratoga for the races, went to the Pops. . . . I've never been treated so well in my life."

"I hear a 'but'. . . ."

Cathy shrugged. "The guy's such a gentleman he's never laid a hand on me."

"What?"

Their eyes met in the mirror. "Yeah, surprising, huh."

To say the least, Taylor thought. "I figured you two had been lovers for weeks."

"He's never made a move."

"Is he involved with anyone else?"

Cathy shook her head. "He says no." She slipped on one of the dresses and smoothed the fabric over her narrow hips. "Maybe he's just an old world gentleman, you know? One year of courtship before anything happens."

Taylor doubted it. Whenever she saw Sessio's photo in the tabloids, he always had some gorgeous woman on his arm. "Have you asked him about it?"

"No. It'd be sort of awkward." She peeled off the dress and slipped on another one. "He actually talks a lot about you."

She noticed that Cathy avoided her eyes. "Since I'm defending the guy who allegedly killed his father, that isn't too surprising."

"No, it's not like that." Cathy regarded her in the mirror now. "It's . . . more personal."

"Like what?"

Cathy looked away. "It's like he has . . . a thing for you or, at the very least, that he's interested in you."

Taylor shook her head. "Men like Sessio are only interested in themselves, Cath." Then she quickly added, "No offense."

"He asked me if I knew you'd been married."

Taylor's eyes snapped to Cathy's face. "How the hell did he find that out?"

"Hey, it didn't come from me. He also knows your name used to be Talia Carlino."

Taylor went utterly cold inside. "Was he asking you for confirmation?"

"I don't know. But I acted surprised."

Her hands trembled as she put the dresses back on their hangers. "Did he say anything else?"

"He commended you for getting as far as you have."

"How generous," she said dryly.

"It's not like that." Heat rose in Cathy's voice.

"Oh, c'mon," Taylor snapped. "This information didn't just fall into his lap, for Christ's sakes. He had to dig for it." Dig deeply. "And why the hell would he bother, Cathy, unless he intends to use it against me somehow?"

"Keep your voice down." Cathy patted the air with her hands.

Taylor turned, grabbed another dress off the rack, put it on. Anger washed through her in waves. The nerve, the unmitigated gall. The bastard had no right poking around in her affairs. But at least she felt certain now that Sessio's primary interest in Cathy had to do with information.

She forced herself to focus on her reflection, on the fit of the black dress. Clean lines, a simple elegance. Yes, this would do. "What do you think?"

Cathy seemed taken back by the complete switch in Taylor's attitude. "I like it. Yeah, it's perfect."

"Fine. I'll get it."

As they left the dressing room, Cathy said: "Maybe I shouldn't have mentioned all this stuff."

"No, I'm glad you did. I'm just sorry this case has spilled over into your life. Did Mike tell you how he'd come by all this information?"

"No. And I didn't ask. There's one other thing, Taylor. Just so you know. He asked if I knew anything about your parents."

Another wave of anger and indignation crashed over her. "What'd you tell him?"

"That I, uh, didn't know anything."

Cathy's voice echoed with something that disturbed Taylor, but she let it go. "Do me a favor, Cathy. The next time he asks anything about me, tell him to give me a call."

Cathy nodded, but without conviction, and they got into the line at the register.

14

─────────

At seven the following evening, a black limo drew up in front of Taylor's townhouse. She saw it from her front window, its hood glinting in the glow of the streetlight, its windows so darkly tinted the glass caught the reflection of the trees.

A man in a black uniform got out, tugged at the bottom of his jacket, and hurried up the walk. He looked like the sort of man who would work for Frank Morgan—as solidly built as a boxer, not too tall, with a receding hairline. The kind of man, she thought, who followed orders quickly and efficiently. Taylor turned away from the window and glanced at herself in the mirror over the mantel. She brushed her hands self-consciously over her black dress, dabbed on fresh lipstick, started to run a brush through her hair, then shoved the brush back into her purse. Ridiculous. She felt like a teenager on her way to her first prom.

The doorbell rang and Lady bounded down the hall, barking. "It's okay, girl." Taylor patted her on the head, trying to calm her. Lady alternately snarled and whimpered, then backed away from the door with her tail between her legs. "You've got to get over this, Lady," she said sternly, then opened the door widely enough for her to slip outside.

"Good evening, Ms. Brooke. I'm Max, Mr. Morgan's driver."

He didn't offer his hand, but bowed his head slightly and gestured toward the car. He fell into step behind her, then opened the back door and she slipped into the scent of leather and money. It all smacked of old world manners, a scrupulous courtesy that seemed to be inherited.

The limo whispered through the streets and headed into Boston. Morgan still lived where he had when the thirteen-year-old Talia had come knocking at his door. Back then, it had looked like a castle; now it merely looked like the mansion it was, a splendid building rising toward the sky as if to embrace it.

The wrought-iron gate opened and Max pulled into the driveway and stopped. He opened the door for her and as she swung her legs out, the front door of the mansion opened and Morgan trotted down the steps to greet her. His obvious delight at seeing her contrasted so sharply with that terrible day fifteen years ago that a kind of unreality clamped down over her. Why couldn't this have happened when she'd needed him as a child?

"Taylor, it's wonderful to see you." He bussed her lightly on the cheek, then linked her arm through his own and walked her into the house.

The rarefied air inside the house seemed exquisitely attuned to the personalities of the people who lived here; she could barely breathe. The spacious, elegant rooms whispered tales of bygone days, when women wore long silk dresses with furs draped at their shoulders and the men wore tall hats and tuxedos and retired to the drawing room after dinner to smoke their cigars.

Antique furniture filled these rooms: pieces in dark, intricately carved wood with mauve and ivory cushions; ostentatious chairs with straight, beautifully carved backs that looked so uncomfortable they couldn't have been made to sit in; and numerous Biedermeier pieces with dark, wooden arms. Portraits of the family, rendered in oil and framed in glitzy gold, hung over the fireplace in the living room.

Every step she took across the polished wooden floors took her more deeply into the life she had been denied as a child. Resentment bubbled up inside of her, a fundamental resentment with which she'd thought she'd come to terms. She resented Melissa for living here like a princess for all the years that she'd been in the children's home. So now God seemed to be evening up the score, painfully at that, extreme role reversal. Missy's life was ending and Taylor's was just beginning.

She still resented Morgan's duplicity, his cold indifference to that thirteen-year-old girl who'd knocked at his door, and she resented the machinations that had brought them to this house, at this particular moment in time.

Seduced by the splendid accoutrements of Morgan's life, she felt that her own life seemed dull and silly in comparison. Men like Morgan, after all, built worlds; people like her merely kept the machinery in those worlds well-oiled.

Oddly, the taste in furnishings oppressed her. The dark wood, the heavily gilded frames, the formal, uncomfortable-looking chairs, left her with a terrible tightness in her chest; she felt smothered. Despite this, though, she enjoyed Morgan's vignettes about certain items in the house. The gold snuffbox on the fireplace mantel, for instance, had come from Saudi Arabia three generations ago. Presidents had dipped into its treasures.

Never mind that the bedroom set in Melissa's room reeked of gaudiness; it had been purchased at a Sotheby auction of the estate of a Maharishi. The Andrew Wyeth painting in Monroe Morgan's den, the place where Frank now worked, compensated for the ugly leopard rug on the floor and Morgan's hunting trophies on the walls.

Other than the painting, she could relate only to the computer that stood on the mahogany desk. But even it looked like an artifact from another, more advanced world.

''Are you on-line with any of the services?'' she asked.

As soon as the words left her mouth, she realized how inane it sounded and wished the floor would open up and swallow her. She somehow couldn't imagine men like Frank surfing the net. But Frank laughed, a soft, rolling chuckle that put her at ease, and shook his head.

"I'm not very good with computers. I can't even tell you what that computer does. It's here because Max uses it."

Max apparently did more than just drive Morgan around. Interesting, she decided, and wondered what, if anything, it meant.

The last room they toured was the kitchen, a chef's dream, everything arranged for ultimate convenience and efficiency. A pair of lobsters floated in a transparent tub of salt water on the counter, a pot of water boiled on the stove, a vegetable soufflé baked in the oven, wine chilled in the fridge. Time seemed to have slowed when he'd left this room and resumed its usual rhythm now that he'd returned.

"I hope you like lobster," he said, and plucked out the two lobsters from the transparent tub and dropped them into the boiling water.

They screeched, a sound of utter agony, and she winced and knew she wouldn't be eating much of the lobster. Then she heard only the noise of the boiling water.

When you showed up at my door fifteen years ago, Taylor, I was just entering my first race for a city council seat," Morgan said. "And my father was trying to get over my brother's death. The one thing that seemed to bring him back around was to focus on my career. He refused to accept a relationship between Eva and me."

"So he ran your life."

Her bluntness brought resignation to Morgan's eyes. "More or less. I'm not trying to excuse what I did, Taylor. But at the time I walked out on your mother, I didn't know she was pregnant."

By 1980, Morgan went on, he'd been married to Alicia for five years, Melissa had just turned two, and the elder Morgan had immersed himself in cementing the political alliances necessary for his son to make a successful run in politics.

"I thought my life had finally settled down. Then that day

you came to the door, I was watching from an upstairs window. Something about the way you carried yourself—the tilt of your head, the color of your hair—I just froze. When you started screaming at Maria, I knew I had to see for myself if you were who I thought you were.''

''And what did you decide?''

''I knew it as soon as I saw your eyes. You were my child in more ways than one. Your persistence, the stance you took . . . my God, you were so full of courage it terrified me. I never forgot the expression on your face. It has haunted me for years.''

The remark struck her as shamelessly emotional, a blatant attempt to win her over. And yet, she softened inside, softened just as he'd intended, she thought.

''After a week or so, I convinced my father at least to look for you, to make sure you were all right. From his point of view, you were the sum total of every mistake I'd made in my life. It's painful to even say this, Taylor, but he was afraid you'd cause a scandal. God forbid that Roe Morgan or the Morgan family should suffer any more scandal, they'd had their share. The family looked at me as though I'd committed some heinous crime. They were afraid the public would once again smear the family name.''

Ironic, Taylor thought. ''It never even occurred to me to go public. I was used to rejection, Frank. I never would have told anyone my father didn't want me. It made me ashamed.''

Morgan now looked ashamed. ''My lack of courage back then remains one of my deepest regrets. I can't forgive myself for it. The truth is that I just couldn't handle it. My father was a strong, persistent man. No, not just that. He was a *domineering* man. When my brother died, well, I had to do what I could to please him. I hope you can somehow understand all this and forgive me.''

Taylor's capacity to understand Morgan's actions far surpassed her ability to forgive him for what he'd done. But she didn't say it. Morgan, at the very least, attempted to make amends and, frankly, she enjoyed being here with him.

The evening passed quickly. Although she remained aware of the presence of other people in the house, the servants appeared only to bring in coffee and dessert. The phone rang frequently, but Morgan apparently had left instructions not to be disturbed. She appreciated his efforts.

After dessert, they went into the library for a nightcap, cognac served in small glasses made of crystal as delicate as an angel's wings. Mozart played from unseen speakers, the music drifting softly through the air. Morgan showed her his campaign album, a collection of photos and newspaper clippings that captured the frenetic activity preceding his election.

"By the way, how's your case proceeding with Tommy Washington?" he asked.

Taylor shrugged. "Okay."

Morgan smiled gently. "Just okay?"

"Things could be better. But I really don't feel comfortable talking about it with anyone outside of the defense team, Frank."

"Of course. I understand. You're quite right."

The phone in the library rang. He murmured, "Excuse me," and got up to answer it. "Frank Morgan . . . right . . . okay, give me five minutes." He hung up. "I'm afraid I'm going to have to cut our evening short, Taylor. I've got to call Alicia back. Melissa saw a new doctor today and I need to speak to him."

"Of course." She stood quickly, set her crystal glass on an end table. "I've certainly enjoyed it."

"So have I." He gave her a quick hug. "Perhaps you'd consider coming over to the Vineyard some weekend to visit. It's a pleasant place to get away to."

Martha's Vineyard. She hadn't known he had a place at the Vineyard. "I'll think about it."

"Good. Max will drive you home."

He pressed a buzzer on the phone, then walked her out into the front room, where Max waited. They agreed to have dinner again soon, he squeezed her hand, and hurried away.

Outside, the distant sound of traffic punctuated the quiet. Max seemed to be in a more talkative mood than he'd been earlier and asked if she enjoyed the evening. "Very much," she replied.

"Good. It was real important to him."

"How long have you worked for him?"

"Years. Monroe Morgan hired me when I was twenty-one. And that was twenty-five years ago."

"You were driving for Monroe?"

"Yes, ma'am. Driving, doing whatever was needed."

He opened the back door for her and she slipped into the scent of leather and money again. Once they pulled out onto the road, Taylor leaned forward and said, "Max, did you ever meet my mother?"

He eyed her in the rearview mirror and for a brief, terrible moment she felt fear—of Max, of Morgan, of the entire situation that had evolved since she'd been assigned to Tommy Washington's defense. Then Max smiled and when she spoke, his voice seemed changed, softer somehow. "Yes, ma'am, I met her a couple of times. She was a fine woman."

Taylor suddenly wanted to prod him for more details—where had he met her? When? What circumstances surrounded that meeting? But she didn't ask, couldn't. It would be a breach of the unspoken etiquette that had been established.

"Yes, she *was* a fine woman." Regret for her mother and all that could have been filled the inside of her mouth with a foul, bitter taste.

Eric's car, silent and dark, stood at the curb at the end of Taylor's street. He'd been parked here for nearly two hours now, watching Taylor's townhouse, noting the people who entered and left the building and the cars they drove. A car turned down the street and he sank low in his seat, baseball cap tugged low over his forehead, his eyes glued to the rearview mirror.

A black stretch came into view, a car fit for royalty. He figured it would cruise on past the row of townhouses and continue for several blocks to a neighborhood where the homes got larger. To his utter shock, the limo drew up in front of Taylor's townhouse and she stepped out of the back.

Jesus God, he thought. Look at her, just look at her.

Adjectives raced through his head: stunning, exquisite, beautiful. But none of them adequately described the woman who strode up the sidewalk to the townhouse. He sat up slowly, unable to wrench his eyes away from her.

Now, sneak up behind the bitch now, whispered the devil inside of him.

But he refused to listen to the devil; he could feel the weight of all that money lining his wallet. So he sat there, drinking her in, his senses scrambling. He could taste her skin, smell her voice, hear her smile. Images flashed through him, memories from the months of their marriage, good memories, then the bad. But by then she'd vanished into the townhouse, the corner apartment.

A light winked on inside, her shadow passed across the curtains. His fingers curled into fists against his thighs, blood rushed into his ears, pounding, hammering until it became a thunderous roar.

Eric didn't know how many minutes had passed before she appeared again, wearing jogging shorts and a tank top, a black lab on a leash trotting along beside her. She went over to an aging Saab parked at the curb, unlocked it, leaned inside for something. Then she shut the door and jogged along the sidewalk, fiddling with a pair of headphones and a transistor radio hooked to her waistband.

Taylor, cruising home in a limo.

Taylor, jogger.

Taylor, hotshot attorney.

Taylor, his wife.

Taylor, the bitch who'd walked out on him.

How could she have changed so drastically in just under five years? How? His life had remained pretty much the same, but hers . . . Christ, her life had charged ahead into countries he'd never imagined.

A wave of regret mingled with disappointment washed through him, then collapsed into a grief that approached despair. The woman he'd known had ceased to exist and in her place loomed this . . . this stranger.

She passed under the street light and for seconds, Eric saw her clearly. Her blond hair, caught up in a ponytail, bounced as she jogged, her breasts strained against her tank top, her long legs ate up the concrete.

Then he sank down so low in his seat he could no longer see her and began to count by the thousands. On twenty-five, he slipped upward again. Taylor had vanished. And his rage surfaced again.

His fingers closed over the door handle, he jerked it toward him, the door opened a crack. He would break into her place while she jogged for health and longevity. He would hide until she returned. And then he would teach her what the whores in Fall River knew, he would . . .

A car turned onto the street; Eric wrenched the door shut and sank down in his seat again.

A black Mercedes.

First a limo, now a Mercedes.

These people definitely moved in better circles than he did.

The Mercedes stopped at the curb, the light inside came on as someone opened a door. He saw a man behind the wheel, a woman in the passenger seat. They seemed to be arguing. The woman started to exit the car, the man apparently drew her back, they embraced, then the door shut and the light inside went out. Only their silhouettes remained visible.

Minutes ticked by. He began to get antsy, nervous, he wanted to get the hell out of here and think things over.

Now the door opened again, the woman got out. Even from where Eric sat, he could see that God had sculpted her.

The man climbed out, too, and fell into step beside her, his arm at her waist. At one point, they paused on the sidewalk, beneath the glow of a streetlight, and the man threw his head back, laughing. In that moment, Eric saw his face clearly and recognized him.

Michael Sessio, son of murdered Joe, whose killer Taylor was defending.

He barely had time to think about this before the two of them disappeared into the apartment next door to Taylor's.

Eric waited as long as he could, then he cranked up his Charger and got the hell out of there.

15

Taylor spent the morning with Kyle, reviewing various aspects of their defense. The overall picture looked grim. They simply hadn't answered the most basic questions yet and until they did, Tommy Washington faced a certain conviction.

She listed the major points they needed to get to immediately and the question of Richard Adler loomed as a priority. Even though the lead on the dead corporate attorney had come from Mike Sessio, whom she didn't trust, she needed to investigate it. Taylor had called the Adler home several times, only to be told Mrs. Adler wasn't in. Not surprisingly, she hadn't returned any of Taylor's calls. It would be more difficult to ignore a personal visit, she thought.

"I'll go with you," Kyle said. "She can't shut the door in our faces."

"If she does, she'll be subpoenaed. No sense in both of us going. I'd like you to check in with Tommy, find out if he's remembered anything else about the day of Sessio's murder."

Kyle made a face; he disliked going to the jail as much as

she did. "Hell, he hasn't remembered anything because there's nothing to remember."

Taylor winked. "Next time it's my turn."

"I'll hold you to it." He glanced at his watch. "Guess I'd better get going. See you back here this afternoon."

"Right."

Shortly after Kyle left, Taylor booted up the office computer and went on-line. She accessed the Boston Public Library reference desk and searched for information on Richard Adler. Best to be prepared in the event Mrs. Adler agreed to see her, she thought.

Considering Adler's high-powered profile, she expected to find more information than she needed. But other than biographical data and quite a bit of information about the carjacking that killed him, her search turned up very little.

Taylor thought back to her meeting with Michael Sessio that Friday weeks ago on the wharf. Important papers, he'd said. Legal documents. Since Adler had practiced corporate law, it seemed logical that the papers would relate to corporate law. Michael Sessio hadn't said that Adler had been his father's attorney, only that they'd been friends. Perhaps Adler had advised Sessio about certain corporate proceedings.

She entered a new search phrase: Sessio Shipping.

This yielded more than seventy-five articles. She thought a moment, then specified "early history." This narrowed the original seventy-five to twenty. She downloaded these and began to read them on the screen.

Halfway through, she found a reference to Richard Adler, buried in the business section of the *Boston Globe,* a short piece dated twenty years ago, part of a courthouse roundup of news. On May 10, 1977, incorporation papers had been filed in district court by Richard Adler for the creation of Sessio Shipping. It provided a brief description of the company, with a list of its officers. Mike Sessio headed the list as CEO.

She read on, hoping to find another reference to Adler and Sessio. Instead, in the courthouse roundup for May 13, she found Adler's name linked with Monroe Morgan's. Adler had filed incorporation papers for the creation of Dovecote, the fine china company which Morgan Senior had passed on to Frank.

Ironic, she thought. The two men who had been buried on the same day had each seen one of their many family business holdings incorporated in the same week two decades ago. Their lives had been linked by forces larger than both of them, a kind of karmic brotherhood that undoubtedly would have amused them both.

But even more intriguing, Adler had represented them both. And she, the illegitimate granddaughter of one man, would defend the killer of the other man. A cosmic chuckle, she thought. The universe and its jokes.

She shut down the computer, picked up her briefcase, and left her office. Eileen stopped her on her way out. ''Kyle just called from the jail. He said to tell you he's going to be there awhile. Apparently the inmates and their cells are being deloused.'' She wrinkled her nose. ''Can you imagine? Lice. Christ.''

''I should be back after lunch. You can always get me on the cell phone.''

''Right.''

Taylor wondered what Eileen would think if she knew that a little girl named Talia had put up with worse things than lice. There had been days when her mother had been so drunk, so totally out of it, that dirty dishes had been left in the sink, on the counters, on the table, dishes with food crusted on them. The ants and the roaches and the other disgusting bugs that had lived in those apartment walls had gotten a whiff of all that old food and converged.

They couldn't afford bug spray, so she had used her mother's hair spray to kill the suckers. She'd sprayed until the bugs had turned white and weighted with the stuff and they'd weaved across the filthy floor, stopped, and collapsed.

When her mother had sobered up, she'd noticed the empty hair spray can. She didn't give a damn about the bugs, she hadn't been there. She'd shouted at Taylor, called her terrible names, and had locked her in her room as punishment.

Taylor hadn't killed a bug since.

———————

Newton lay just twenty minutes up the road from Boston. Affluent and green, home to some of the best schools and oldest homes in New England, it felt like a town to Taylor, even though it was a city.

A lot of the faculty from the various colleges and universities lived here. Perhaps that explained why it possessed a certain arrogance. Even though the arrogance had a typically New England taste and subtlety, she resented it a little. Resented the old brick houses with the huge, graceful trees, the trikes and kids' wagons in the yards and driveways, the tidy rows of shops.

Adler's home, an old colonial, occupied a lovely estate. A cast-iron fence enclosed it. Behind the gate stood a pair of chocolate colored cars, a BMW and a Mercedes. A Rottweiler prowled the fence. Nothing like living in a fortress, she thought, and pulled up to the gate.

She got out and rang the intercom bell. A female voice said, "Adler residence. Your name, please?"

"Taylor Brooke, with the law firm of Simpson and Willis. I'd like to see Mrs. Adler."

"One moment, please."

The "moment" stretched out into five minutes. Just as Taylor started to punch the intercom button again, the woman spoke. "Mrs. Adler can't see you now, Ms. Brooke. If you'd like to call later in the week, she—"

"I've called repeatedly and she hasn't returned my calls. Please tell her that if she doesn't see me today, I'm going to have her subpoenaed to testify at the trial of Tommy Washington."

"I'll, uh, relay the message, Ms. Brooke."

"Good. I'll wait."

She resigned herself to another five minute wait. But thirty seconds later, the woman said, "Mrs. Adler will see you. Please drive up to the front steps and don't get out of your car until I restrain the dogs."

"Fine."

She hurried back to her car and drove through as the gate

opened. The Rottweiler she'd seen earlier galloped alongside the Saab, barking fiercely. A pair of Dobermans joined him, lean, muscular dogs that added to the fracas. As soon as she stopped, the dogs surrounded the car, leaping and snarling, clawing at the windows and the side of the Saab. She honked the horn twice to frighten them away, but it didn't daunt them.

A slight woman in a white uniform appeared on the steps with leashes draped over her arm. She stuck two fingers into her mouth and emitted a piercing whistle that brought the dogs running. She snapped on their leashes, led them over to a shaded area under a beautiful oak tree, and secured the leashes to a line that ran from the trees to the side of the house. Only then did Taylor open her door and step out.

The woman hurried over, her white shoes squeaking. Taylor realized she was a nurse, not a maid, and wondered if Mike Sessio knew about Mrs. Adler's failing health. "Thanks for your patience," the woman said pleasantly, and extended her hand. "I'm Jennifer Griffin, Mrs. Adler's nurse."

"Taylor Brooke. Has Mrs. Adler been ill very long?"

"When you're confined to a wheelchair, even a week is a long time, Ms. Brooke. I suspect that's why she hasn't returned your calls. She hasn't gone out at all since Mr. Adler's death."

"What's wrong with her?"

"Multiple sclerosis. She was diagnosed shortly after Mr. Adler's death. She tires easily, so I would appreciate it if you kept your visit short."

"I only have a few questions."

They headed up the steps. "She'll do her best. Part of the problem with MS is that memory is affected. So keep that in mind when you talk to her."

"I certainly will."

The inside of the house struck her much differently than Morgan's had. Despite the formal furnishings and the numerous accoutrements of vast wealth, she could breathe in these rooms. Sunlight streamed through the tall front windows and pooled on the polished wooden floors. The doorways had been widened to accommodate a wheelchair, ramps and handlebars had been added.

Jennifer motioned toward the tidy sitting area near the fireplace. "Make yourself comfortable. I'll go get Mrs. Adler."

"No need," said a voice from the doorway, and Mrs. Adler propelled her wheelchair into the room.

She seemed impossibly slight and frail, probably no more than five feet tall when she stood. Her salt and pepper hair looked freshly brushed, her slacks and silk blouse looked expensive, designer chic. She wore a minimum of makeup. Taylor guessed her age as early seventies.

"Stephanie Adler," she said, but didn't offer her hand. "Please, have a seat, Mrs. Brooke. Would you like coffee? Cold juice?"

"Coffee would be fine."

"Coffee for Mrs. Brooke, Jennifer, and a glass of cold water for me."

"Coming right up," Jennifer replied, and left the room.

"I apologize for not returning your calls. But I've been under the weather."

"I understand. I'm defending Tommy Washington, Mrs. Adler, the man who's accused of—"

"Yes, I know who he is." A small smile tugged at her mouth. "I'm not so addled that I've lost touch with the world. So what may I do for you, Mrs. Brooke?"

The "Mrs." business bugged her, but she didn't bother correcting it. "I understand that your husband sometimes represented Joe Sessio in business matters."

"My husband represented a great many business people, but I can't begin to tell you who they were or the specifics involved. Richard didn't discuss his legal practice with me."

"Never?"

The woman's smile smacked of decades of resignation and a certain regret. "We were married nearly fifty years, so perhaps I should rectify the 'never' with 'rarely.' "

"Specifically, I'm concerned about some legal documents that Joe Sessio may have entrusted to your husband. Documents that may have something to do with the car-jacking that killed him."

Even though the cops hadn't come up with any evidence that Adler's death had been related to his work, Taylor sensed a connection, just as Sessio did. But as soon as she said the words, Stephanie Adler's expression changed, as if a door had slammed open somewhere inside of her and distasteful memories now poured out.

"The police found nothing at all to indicate the car-jacking was anything but a random act of violence. They . . . they . . ." Her eyes brimmed suddenly with tears. "He was in the wrong place at the wrong time, that's why he died."

"Did you run across any legal documents when your husband died, Mrs. Adler?"

She sniffled, dabbed at her nose with a piece of Kleenex that she pulled out of a pocket in her slacks. "His safe was crammed with papers. I turned them over to our estate attorney."

"Without looking at them?"

Jennifer walked back into the room before she replied and set a tray on the coffee table between them. She handed Mrs. Adler her glass of water, a linen napkin folded carefully around the bottom of it.

"Cream or sugar, Ms. Brooke?" asked Jennifer.

"Nothing, thanks." Actually, she took both. But she didn't want to prolong the nurse's presence in the room; she sensed an agitation in Mrs. Adler now that might play to her advantage. "I'm fine."

"You doing all right, Mrs. Adler?" Jennifer asked.

"Okay, yes, I'm okay."

She didn't sound okay and tears kept brimming in her eyes, facts that didn't escape Jennifer. She tapped her watch. "Five more minutes, Ms. Brooke."

"Sure."

She left again, her shoes squeaking against the floor. Mrs. Adler, gripping the bottom of her glass, seemed to be listening intently to her nurse's receding footsteps. As soon as they faded completely, she leaned forward and hissed, "Joe Sessio was a despicable man, a hoodlum, and frankly, I applaud whoever killed him."

Mrs. Adler uttered this with uncontained vehemence, as though she'd been waiting most of her life to spit it out. It took Taylor by surprise; several moments passed before she spoke. "Then you knew him personally."

Visibly agitated now, she snapped, "I didn't say that. I'm giving you my opinion of the man."

"Based on what? Hearsay? The news? Your opinion sounded very personal."

"Personal?" She laughed, a hard, bitter sound. "You don't know the meaning of the word, young lady. Now if you'll excuse me, I'm quite tired."

She set her glass in a round hole in the wheelchair's arm, pressed the lever that operated it, and whipped the chair around. Taylor shot to her feet, grabbed onto the handles, and stopped the chair. Then she moved around in front of it, blocking the woman's access to the doorway.

"You're terrified, aren't you," Taylor said softly, leaning toward her. "You're so terrified you hide out in this house."

"Get out of my way," she said, tears filling her eyes again.

"I'll have you subpoenaed and then you're going to have to face your terrors in public. Think about that, Mrs. Adler."

Emotions flicked through the woman's eye, fury, fear, despair. Then she slammed the lever into reverse and called, "Jennifer, Mrs. Brooke is ready to leave now."

"It's *Ms.* Brooke," Taylor snapped. "In the event you change your mind, here's my card." She strode over to the wheelchair, dropped her card into Mrs. Adler's lap. "Otherwise I'll see you in court." She strode past the nurse. "I'll see myself out."

Eric killed ten minutes cruising up and down the neighboring streets, waiting for Taylor to leave the estate. He thought he might attract unwanted attention if he kept driving past the place. No telling what kind of sophisticated crime watch they had in a community like this.

He finally pulled into the lot of a small playground on the main road and parked where he would still be able to see her car when she left. He got out his maps and spread them open against the steering wheel, just in case a cop happened by. He kept his shades and baseball cap on; he didn't want Taylor to recognize him.

While he waited, he checked the estate's address and the name he'd seen on the mailbox, which he'd scribbled on a piece of paper. A trip to the library would tell him what he needed to know about the Adler family. But that aside, he now knew one thing for sure. With this kind of wealth involved, good ole Carrot Top would have to cough up additional cash for Eric to carry out their agreement.

When Taylor drove up to her townhouse at six that evening, a delivery van stood at the curb, engine idling. One man unloaded a carton from the rear of the van to a dolly, while the other hurried over to her with a clipboard in his hand.

"Excuse me, ma'am, I'm looking for Taylor Brooke's apartment."

"I'm Taylor Brooke."

"Package here for you, ma'am."

"I'm not expecting a package."

The man looked exasperated. "Just sign here, ma'am, and tell us where you'd like it."

"Who's it from?"

He showed her the order on the clipboard; the name of an art store in Back Bay graced the top, nothing more. "Isn't there a card with it?"

"Probably inside, ma'am."

"Where we putting this?" the other guy called out, pushing the dolly up the sidewalk.

The guy with the clipboard looked at her. "You accepting the package or not, ma'am?"

"Yeah, sure, okay." She would look for the card when they got the package inside. "Apartment four, there on the end."

Taylor led the way to the apartment, unlocked the door, and put Lady in the bedroom before she admitted the guy with the dolly. She directed him to put the box in the living room, where he and his companion cut it along the sides. The cardboard panels and stuffing fell away, revealing the most exquisite stone sculpture she'd ever seen.

Morgan, she thought. Had to be.

One of the men emitted a soft whistle. "Incredible."

"I don't see a card," Taylor said, and the three of them dropped to their knees and pawed through the stuffing and bubble wraps until she found the card. "Here it is." She rocked back on her heels and eagerly opened the card. It read:

> *This reminded me of you. Enjoy.*
> *Best wishes,*
> *Mike Sessio*

Blood rushed into her face and hammered in her ears. For moments, she literally saw red and couldn't speak. Then she turned to the men and said, "Take it back. I don't want it."

They exchanged a glance, then the taller of the two men spoke. "You don't *want* it?"

"Absolutely not," she snapped. "Take it back."

The short man stammered, "But the box is—"

"Forget it," the taller man said. "We'll just put it on the dolly and take it back out to the truck." He handed Taylor the clipboard. "Please note that you refused the package, ma'am."

"You bet." She scrawled a note to that effect on the clipboard, then scooped up the stuffing and cardboard and carried it out into the kitchen. She jammed it into the trash can, marched down the hall and opened the door for the two men as they carted the sculpture back outside.

As soon as they'd left, she released Lady from the bedroom, snapped on her leash, grabbed the card, and punched out the number for the art shop. She explained that she'd received a delivery from a Mike Sessio and needed his home address to send a thank you note. The clerk checked the records, then returned to the phone with Sessio's address.

He lived downtown, in a lovely brownstone that looked as if it had stood here since Paul Revere had ridden through. She parked, left Lady in the car, with the window down, and propelled by her fury, headed into the building.

She rode the elevator to the penthouse, where the entire floor belonged to Sessio. A maid in a crisp black and white uniform answered the door. "Is Mr. Sessio in?" Taylor asked.

"Yes, ma'am. Your name?"

"Taylor Brooke."

"One moment, please. I'll find out if he's available."

She shut the door most of the way and Taylor stood there in the hall, fuming. Screw it, she thought, and pushed the door open and walked into a wide hall with a marble floor. The grandeur of the penthouse shocked her. She suddenly remembered reading about it somewhere. If memory served her correctly, the penthouse boasted ten thousand square feet of space, four marble fireplaces, seven bathrooms, six bedrooms, a two thousand bottle wine collection, servants' quarters, and a secretarial suite. Now she believed every word of it.

Priceless art lined the walls, classical music drifted from invisible speakers, the very air smelled of unimaginable wealth.

She continued into the living room, her eyes drawn instantly to the portrait of Joseph Sessio that dominated the room. A younger Joe Sessio, proud and arrogant. It unnerved her, disturbed her at a level too deep for words, and yet she couldn't explain why. She felt an almost overwhelming urge to flee. Everywhere she looked, the evidence of Sessio's wealth seemed to mock her: the Persian throw rugs; the Steinway baby grand piano next to a picture window that overlooked Boston Harbor; the sculptures, the paintings, the utter perfection of the waning light. She felt as if she'd walked into a movie.

"Ms. Brooke?"

Taylor spun around, flustered. "Is he available?"

"Uh, yes, ma'am. Come with me."

Taylor followed her across the living room to the doorway of a library. The maid rapped softly, then opened the door and Taylor stepped into the most incredible library she'd ever seen. Books covered three of the four walls from floor to ceiling. A chandelier hung from the ceiling. And against the picture window stood a long mahogany desk, where Sessio sat, a phone fixed to his ear.

He hung up, stood, his smoldering eyes locked on hers. He didn't come toward her, didn't do anything except stare at her. He seemed to be suspended in the evening light that streamed through the window behind him. Taylor strode quickly over to his desk, slapped down the card that had come with the sculpture. "I don't know what the hell game you're playing, Mr. Sessio. But count me out. And do *not* send any more surprise packages to my house and stop asking my neighbor about me. If you have any questions, ask *me*, Mr. Sessio, not Cathy. Understand?"

Those smoldering eyes never left her face; he still hadn't moved. She felt the heat of his gaze down to her toes. It tore through her like a current and surged upward through her soul, forcing her finally to avert her eyes simply to break the connection.

"I thought you'd like the sculpture," he said finally. "But I'll certainly abide by your wishes. As for the questions . . ." He shrugged. "It wasn't my intention to snoop around in your life."

"Then what *is* your intention?" She glanced back at him and wished that she hadn't.

"Just to get to know you."

"Frankly, Mr. Sessio, I think you set out to gather information on me, which included finding out who my friends are. Once you knew about Cathy, you engineered a meeting. And now here we are. I don't like your maneuvers. I don't like any of it."

With that, she headed for the door. But as she passed Sessio, he caught her hand. "Wait a second."

She turned, fire spat from her eyes, and he released her hand. "Make it quick. My dog's downstairs in the car." The magnetic pull of his eyes worked on her like a drug. She felt herself falling into the smoldering dark pools, mesmerized by the ineffable pull of his sensuality.

"You've misjudged me."

The sound of his voice broke the moment. "I doubt it," she replied, and swept past him.

16

Taylor jogged through the warm August evening at a fraction of her usual pace. Her body felt heavy and weighted, as if she carried twenty extra pounds. She felt like heading back to her townhouse and spending the rest of this Friday evening vegging out with a good book and a bowl of popcorn. But she hadn't run all week.

It had been that kind of week, days that began early and ended late. She'd seen Tommy Washington, spoken to his mother and sister again, managed to squeeze in a lunch with Cathy, had spoken several times to Frank Morgan, had tea with Simpson, and had waited for Stephanie Adler to change her mind.

It had been more than a week since Taylor had spoken to her. Since Taylor hadn't heard from her, she would have to get the ball rolling on the subpoena. She simply couldn't cut the woman any more slack. *Tempus fugit* had never seemed more immediate and personal.

At the end of her block, she jogged across the road, headed toward the river. Cars drove past her in both directions, the usual traffic for a Friday evening, commuters on their way home. But she couldn't shake the feeling that had plagued her for more than a week, that someone watched her every move.

She wrote off part of it to the break-in and assault way back in June. It had left her as uneasy as it had Lady. She now jogged with a can of Mace in her hand, had changed the locks on the apartment, and put in an alarm system. She hated barricading herself in like that, but frankly, she slept better at night knowing that bells and whistles would sound if someone broke in.

Thoughts of Eric had plagued her, too, this week, with one incident in particular unrolling in her head like an old home movie. It had happened shortly after she'd started taking law classes. She'd been studying in the front room when Eric had suddenly shouted her name above the din of music from the living room. Taylor had jumped up quickly and hurried out into the hall.

He'd stood there with a half-full beer bottle clutched in one hand and his belt wrapped around the other. *"Where's my dinner?"* he'd snapped, tapping the belt against his thigh.

"I've got a test tomorrow, I—"

"I don't give a goddamn about your test. I'm hungry, bitch. . . ."

Taylor had backed away from him, terror balled in the center of her chest, but it was too late. Moments later, he struck her, the leather sharp and burning against her skin. . . .

A door slammed shut in her head.

No, she thought. All that lay in the past.

She and Lady ran down the slope to the sidewalk that paralleled the river and she heard footfalls behind her. Lady barked and Taylor's body tensed up. She ran faster and reached into her pocket for the can of Mace. The footfalls drew closer, louder, and she broke into a flat out run, shoes slapping the sidewalk, arms pumping at her sides.

But suddenly, the man reached her and she whirled, the can of Mace aimed, and Stark threw up his hands as if to defend himself. Lady backed up, snarling softly. "Hey, dog, it's okay." He glanced quickly at Taylor. "Call off your hound, Taylor."

"Christ, John. You should've called out or something."

"If you'd known it was me, you would've run like hell."

She laughed and pressed her hand to the stitch in her side. "That's not true." She held up the can of Mace. "You almost got a faceful of this."

"Wicked stuff."

She eyed his clothes; he looked terrific in a tank top and jogging clothes. "I don't suppose it's any coincidence that you're in my neighborhood dressed like that."

"Guilty. I didn't feel like jogging alone."

"Since when are you a jogger?"

"Since Gova assigned me the Tommy Washington case."

Interesting, she thought, but didn't comment. They walked briskly along the river, through a light breeze that blew in over the water. Lady bounded along beside them, apparently accustomed to Stark now.

"See, I don't bite, pooch," Stark said, glancing down at the lab.

Lady barked and wagged her tail. "I guess she believes you."

"Hey, dogs usually like me," Stark remarked. "Dogs, cats, kids. It's just women I have problems with."

You've got that right, Taylor thought.

"She's been spooked ever since the break-in," Taylor said.

"Can't blame her for that. What about you? Have you been spooked, too?"

"I have my moments."

She felt certain about one thing now: Stark hadn't assaulted her and poisoned her dog. He hadn't been a serious contender, but it comforted her to be able to scratch him off the list of suspects.

They walked in silence for a few minutes. Taylor expected him to ask her about the defense's case, so she beat him to it. "How's the case going against Washington?"

Stark shrugged. "It's going."

She waited for him to continue or to ask about the defense's case, but he didn't, which surprised her. "You seem, I don't know, sort of circumspect tonight."

"Circumspect. Yeah, I guess I am. I was going to stop by

the hospital after I heard about the break-in and assault, but I figured you'd toss me out.''

''Hardly.''

Stark caught her hand as they walked and held it lightly in his own. She didn't object, didn't withdraw her hand. The gesture acknowledged their past and felt right, almost like a truce. ''How's the divorce coming along?''

''Pretty good. She's being more reasonable than I expected. I may get out with a quarter of our assets.''

''Is it worth it?''

''Christ, yes. I realized I'd been dying in the marriage for a long time.''

She wondered about that. She knew Stark had political aspirations and that his wife, who came from an old-time Boston family, might be helpful in the achievement of those aspirations. She wanted to ask about it, but didn't.

''Taylor, is it possible for us to talk about the Tommy Washington thing off the record?''

Six or eight weeks ago, this particular question would have triggered her internal alarms. But she heard a sincerity in his voice now that had been absent back then.

''I guess we can, if we don't discuss particulars. What's bothering you?''

''Gova. Something's not right with her. I can't put my finger on it, but every instinct I have says she's not playing this on the up and up.''

''In what way?''

''That's just it. I don't know. Sometimes she's too quick to reach conclusions. Other times, she refuses to look at what's obvious.'' He paused, glanced at Taylor. ''You're a threat to her, Taylor. I'm sure of that much.''

''Me? A threat?'' She laughed. ''Hell, I'm the one sweating bullets over this defense.''

''That's the whole point,'' Stark said. ''Based on the evidence as it exists now, she should be fairly confident of a conviction. But she's uptight about it. It's like she's hiding something.''

''What could she possibly be hiding?''

He shrugged. ''I don't know. But I can tell you right now

that if there's something underhanded involved, I'll go to the judge and request to be removed from the case.''

Her old mistrust suddenly surfaced. It seemed entirely possible that Stark had been setting her up all along, that he and Gova intended to seed a suspicion that, ultimately, might prompt *her* to request removal from the case. But just how much of a threat could she possibly be? She hardly measured up to a Clarence Darrow.

She let go of Stark's hand. "Are you setting me up for something, John?"

He stopped. The glow of the lights along the street struck his face in such a way so that she could see the remark had wounded him. She immediately felt guilty and wanted to take her words back.

"Christ, Taylor, is that what you think?"

"It crossed my mind."

He kicked at a fallen leaf and shook his head. "I'm sorry you feel that way. I was hoping that by being honest and open about this, you wouldn't suspect me of having a private agenda. But I guess that's too much to ask."

The testiness in his voice irritated her. If anyone had a reason to be annoyed, she did. "Correct me if I'm wrong, but your private agenda was always an issue with us."

"A private issue," he snapped. "It never related to work. You're essentially calling me a liar, Taylor, and I resent it."

"What the hell am I supposed to think? Right from the start, you and Gova have tried to intimidate me and frankly, I'm sick of it. So if you honestly believe she's up to something, then you'd better find out what's going on and go to the judge, if that's what you need to do. But don't try to compromise me."

With that, she turned, whistled for Lady, and headed away from the river, Lady trotting alongside her. Anger slammed around inside of her.

"It's like she's hiding something."

Maybe. But it seemed just as likely that Stark and Gova had united against her and that Gova's master scheme involved undermining her, as the defense attorney, by chipping away at her armor. If nothing else, she supposed she ought to be flattered that Gova felt so threatened.

But her instincts told her that the truth of it had little to do with her. Taylor sensed that in Gova's mind, she remained peripheral to the larger picture, a bit player, an annoying bug that should be squashed at some point during her own ride to victory.

Eric seethed. He'd seen her with the guy in jogging clothes. Seen them holding hands. Seen them arguing. And now, as he watched Taylor run back to her townhouse with her goddamn dog, he felt like leaping out of the car and sinking his fist into her pretty face.

Instead, he hunkered down in his seat, fingers clenched around the steering wheel, and counted slowly to fifty. Then he eased upward slightly, just enough to peer over the edge of his window.

Gone.

But in the rearview mirror, he now saw the man she'd been with, jogging up the sidewalk. As he approached her townhouse, he slowed, and Eric recognized him.

John Stark, one of the prosecutors in the Tommy Washington case.

Stark, Sessio, Richard Adler's widow, some very mighty players, he thought. Carrot Top would pay up because he would have no choice. And then Eric would seek his just revenge on the woman who had walked out on him.

"Scare her," Carrot Top had said.

For sure, Eric thought, and smiled.

At 8:55, the doorbell rang. Taylor doubted that Stark would approach her so soon after the scene in the park, but looked through the peephole just to be sure.

Cathy stood outside the door, one hand raised in greeting, her grin slicing her face in half. "Hey, it's me."

"Hold on, let me get the chain." The chain and the two

deadbolts and the puny lock in the knob. She opened the door and Cathy held up a bottle of wine and a bag of microwave popcorn. "Girl's night out? We'll finish watching *Gone with the Wind.*"

"Sounds great, c'mon in."

"You and Lady come over to my place," said Cathy. "We're always messing up your apartment."

Taylor grabbed her keys, whistled for Lady, and they went next door. "Where's Mike tonight?" Taylor asked, flopping back into the recliner.

"Working." She tore open the bag of popcorn and dumped it into a bowl on the coffee table. "He's married to his job."

"Well, it's better than him being married to another woman."

"True, true." She popped the cork on the wine, filled a pair of wineglasses, passed Taylor one. "Let's drink to Scarlett and Rhett."

Taylor laughed and they made their toast. She wondered if Sessio had told Cathy about the little scene in his office last week, when she'd told him off. Probably not. Sessio didn't impress her as the kind of man who talked about battles he hadn't won.

"You won't believe who I ran into in the park while I was out running."

"Frank Morgan?"

"John Stark."

Cathy's eyes widened. "Kind of a long ways from home, isn't he?"

Without elaborating on detail, Taylor related what had happened, that she felt Stark and Gova had been setting her up for a fall. But she didn't discuss the particulars of the case with Cathy, couldn't as long as she and Sessio dated. It seemed to be the easiest way to keep the friendship intact. "Your life is awfully complicated, Taylor."

"Yeah, sometimes it seems that way."

"The other night, Mike and I were calculating the odds of our meeting and we got into this conversation about the number of coincidences around our relationship."

"Like what?" Taylor tried not to sound too interested and

glanced toward the TV, where Rhett was about to kiss Scarlett.

"Well, first of all, I live next door to you and you *just happen* to be defending the kid who allegedly killed Mike's father. Then you *just happen* to be the granddaughter of Monroe Morgan, whose life—"

Taylor snapped upright, her fury burning like some bright, new sun. "You *told* Mike Sessio that Frank's my father?"

Cathy looked stunned, as though the enormity of what she'd said just hit her. "I . . . he . . . ," she stammered, color rushing into her cheeks. "Jesus, Taylor, it just came out, okay? We'd had a couple of drinks, we were talking, and—"

"And he said the right thing and you blurted it out."

Cathy stared at her, guilt burning in her eyes. "Yeah, more or less," she said softly.

The ticking of the clock on the wall filled the subsequent silence. Cathy broke it. "Jesus, Taylor, so what? What's the big fucking deal? Mike doesn't give a damn who your old man is. He—"

Taylor shot to her feet and Lady immediately scrambled up, whining softly, watching Taylor, glancing at Cathy, whining some more. "*I* care. You were the only person who knew that, Cathy. I trusted you. You . . . you had no right to tell that to anyone."

Cathy lost her temper then. "Everything with you is so complicated. I have to censor myself every time I have a conversation with Michael." She wrinkled up her face. 'Oops, can't say that, Taylor might get offended. Uh-oh, better not get into that, I might say something about Taylor.' Frankly, I'm sick of it. It's always a secret to keep. Your whole life is a secret. I'm sick of protecting poor Taylor, everyone feeling sorry for her, even Michael."

Taylor felt as if glass had exploded inside her chest. "I never meant to burden you," she said quietly, then whistled for Lady and hurried toward the door. Cathy didn't stop her, didn't hurry after her.

Taylor opened the door and Lady raced past her, out into the dark. She chased after her, got halfway across the parking lot when a car turned in, its headlights impaling Lady like a deer. "Lady, come here!" Taylor shouted, but the lab had frozen.

The driver slammed on the brakes, the door flew open, and Michael Sessio leaped out. "Want me to get her?" Sessio called out.

"Thanks, but I'll do it." Taylor ran over to Lady, whose snout trailed over the ground, pursuing a scent. "Bad girl. You can't just run away like that." Taylor took hold of the lab's collar. "C'mon."

Sessio walked over. "I thought I was going to hit her."

Lady glanced up at him, growled softly, and sat back, waiting for Taylor to release her collar or get moving. "She darted out of the apartment."

Sessio nodded, slipped his hands in the pockets of his slacks. As usual, he radiated a bristling sexuality that both attracted and repelled her. "How've you been?"

"Okay." She released Lady's collar and told her to stay.

Their confrontation last week seemed to move between them, a wall too thick and weighted to break through. Then Sessio said, "By the way, did you ever get in touch with Mrs. Adler?"

"Why?"

"Just curious."

"As a matter of fact, I went over to the house and told her if she didn't speak to me, I'd subpoena her. Did you know she has MS?"

"I knew she was ill. But I didn't know about the MS."

"She also hated your father."

"I think she hated everyone who had any claim on Richard's time."

"My sense is that she *does* know something, but that she's scared to death. I've given her more than a week to get back to me and she hasn't, so I'm going to subpoena her."

"Good luck. It probably won't do any good."

"She'll have to appear in court."

"Or her attorneys will use her health problems as a way around it."

Taylor nodded. "Maybe. I didn't realize that Richard Adler was responsible for incorporating Sessio Shipping."

"Yeah, twenty-five years ago. It gives you some idea how far back he and my father went. But he hadn't done any work for us since I took over Sessio Shipping."

Translation: My hands are clean, she thought. "Did you know that during that same week, Adler also filed incorporation papers for Morgan's company, Dovecote?"

"I didn't know about that, but it doesn't surprise me. I suspect that Adler's list of clients probably read like a Who's Who of the corporate world. Why don't you ask Frank Morgan about him?"

She heard no snideness in his voice, but it rankled her nonetheless. "We've already covered this ground, Mr. Sessio. Cathy had no business telling you about my relationship to Frank. And I'd appreciate it if you kept it to yourself."

He raised his hands, patting the air. "Hey, I'm not the enemy, Taylor. I don't give a damn if your father is a Martian. But if you're trying to establish a relationship with him after all these years, then take advantage of it. He may be a good source of information."

She didn't reply. She took hold of Lady's collar and walked away, aware of Sessio's eyes burning a hole in her spine.

17

Kyle negotiated the Monday morning traffic as though he owned the road. He drove too fast, cut in front of other cars, and nearly clipped a fender when the guy in front of him suddenly put on his brakes.

"Asshole," Kyle muttered, and darted into the right lane. He sped ahead, ducked into the left lane again, and hit sixty on an open stretch of road.

Morons, he thought. Morons filled the road, Boston, the entire goddamn state. And the king of morons sat right here, driving this car. He never should've listened to Gova about using Eric Serle. The guy had been in town for nearly three weeks and he hadn't done squat about Taylor yet.

Kyle pulled into the motel that Eric seemed to consider home now. He parked between a pair of vans that would hide his car from anyone passing on the road and got out. He wore sunglasses and a baseball cap and kept his head bowed.

He doubted that any of his law colleagues hung out in this part of town, but some of the loan sharks did and he definitely didn't want to be recognized by any of them. Although they'd backed off since he'd paid them a portion of what he owed, he knew it would be just a matter of time before they came knocking at his door again.

Eric opened the door before Kyle knocked, grinned, and motioned him into the room. "We have to stop meeting like this," Eric quipped.

"Very funny. What's so urgent, Mr. Serle?"

"It's actually more urgent for you, Mr. Nelson."

A chill licked its way up Kyle's spine. Until now, Eric had known him only as 'Watson.' "The name's Watson."

Eric shrugged and paced back and forth across the room, arms swinging at his sides. "Hey, you wanna call yourself Spiderman, that's okay with me."

"So far, you haven't upheld your end of the deal."

"Well, first I wanted to see what was going on, you know what I mean? The lay of the land and all that. And from what I've seen, Watson, I'm not getting paid enough."

Shit shit shit. I don't need this, Kyle thought. "Suit yourself. I'll find someone else to do it."

Eric stopped in the middle of the room, his biceps flexing, anger shadowing his eyes. "Hear me out, Watson. It'll be worth your while. Taylor's dealing with major heavies—the widow of Richard Adler, Michael Sessio, John Stark—"

He'd found Frankenstein, no doubt about it. "You're not being paid to spy on the woman," he spat. "You're being paid to scare the shit out of her so she leaves town for awhile. And so far, you haven't done that."

"I've decided it's worth more than five grand."

"Like I said, Mr. Serle. If you don't want to do it, I'll find someone else."

Eric pressed his fingertips together, which made the tendons in his wrists and forearms stand out. It struck Kyle as vaguely threatening. "Let me put it this way. Taylor has met with John Stark. Now I realize I'm not up on all the specifics of the law, Watson, but it seems to me that when a prosecutor and a defense attorney are working the same case, that shouldn't happen."

Kyle's thoughts raced through a dozen options, none of them suitable. "They run into each other all the time. So what?

That doesn't mean they're discussing the case. Taylor wouldn't compromise herself that way."

"Jogging together along the Charles isn't quite the same as meeting in a courthouse, Watson. We both know that."

Jogging? Sweet Christ. If Taylor and Stark had been meeting on the sly. . . . Not good, not good at all. He started to reply, but Eric hadn't finished.

"I'm sure it would shock Taylor if she knew her assistant had paid her husband five grand to scare the shit out of her, Watson."

"Don't threaten me," Kyle snapped. "One call and you'll be back in jail."

"Exactly. We each have something over the other, Watson. So it makes sense for us to work, well, cooperatively. But I also think I deserve more money."

Kyle knew, to the penny, how much more he could afford to pay Eric. "I'll pay you another five grand, but you don't get it until she's out of the picture. And this time I want a time frame. A very narrow time frame, Mr. Serle."

Eric frowned. "In other words, seventy-five hundred on the other end."

Kyle nodded.

"Okay. She'll be gone in a month."

"A *month?* In another month, we'll be going to trial. That's not soon enough."

"Within two weeks."

By early September: yes, that would do. He would take over the defense and, of course, would lose. "Okay, Mr. Serle. Two weeks. And don't call me again until she's out of the picture."

Eric laughed, pointed his finger like a gun, and aimed it at Kyle. "You got it."

Shortly before noon, Eileen buzzed Taylor. "Burt Hallas is on the line for Kyle. You want to take the call, Taylor? Kyle isn't back yet."

"Where is he?"

"He just said he'd be in the field for a while today."

"Sure, I'll take it." The phone clicked, then: "Hi, Mr. Hallas. This is Taylor Brooke. Kyle's not in right now. Is there something I can help you with?"

"Yes, there is. I've got some information on those two prosecution witnesses from Providence. I was able to find where they lived. Would you like to take a ride out there?"

"Now?"

"If it's convenient."

"I'll meet you in the lobby in ten minutes, Mr. Hallas. What do you look like?"

He chuckled. "Big and balding."

Ten minutes later, she strolled into the lobby just as a large man with a receding hairline came through the front door of the building. His jeans had seen better days, his wrinkled shirt looked as if it had come from the Salvation Army, his new Reeboks squeaked as he moved. He reminded her of an ex-boxer whose body had gone to seed, not like a crack private eye.

Taylor went over to him. "Hi, Mr. Hallas. I'm Taylor Brooke."

He flipped up his shades, stuck out his beefy hand, pumped her arm as though he hoped to draw water. "Burt, please call me Burt." His grin created a pair of identical Gerber baby dimples at either side of his mouth. "I'm parked right out front."

Hallas's car seemed an extension of Hallas himself, a stout, friendly minivan. The backseats had been removed and equipment filled the rear of the van. Miniblinds hung over the windows, shielding the equipment from view.

"What's all that stuff in back?" she asked.

He flashed a quick smile. "Tools of the trade. Directional mikes, recording equipment, cameras, videocameras, you name it, it's back there. What isn't there, is here." He patted the dashboard, a dizzying array of switches, buttons, and electronic gizmos. Mounted just above their heads was a small TV-VCR unit.

"You watch TV when you drive?" she asked.

Hallas laughed. "Naw, the van used to be the family car. Whenever we took off for vacation, we piled the kids into the back, popped in movies, and hit the road. Works like a charm.''

"So what've you found out about these two prosecution witnesses?''

Hallas seemed delighted to talk business. "Real interesting pair. Wilbur Cane and Gerald Maltais. They're both from Providence, live in the same neighborhood, but claim they don't know each other.'' He pulled a tape from a side pocket in the driver's door, slid it into the VCR, turned on the TV. "If you slide your seat back as far as it goes, you'll be able to see better.''

Taylor took his advice. On the tape, a tall, very pale young man dribbled a basketball across a court somewhere. He wore baggy pants, an even baggier shirt, and shoes that looked to be about two sizes too large for his feet. He had a shaved head, with a heart tattoo clearly visible above his left ear.

"Wilbur Cane,'' said Hallas. "He likes to be called Wilt, after Chamberlain, right?''

"And this other kid?'' She motioned toward the screen, where a dark, sullen kid had appeared on the other side of the court.

"Gerald Maltais. He's originally from Quebec.''

They appeared to be about the same age, in their late twenties or early thirties. But Maltais stood half a foot shorter than Cane and had dark, shoulder-length hair that looked as if it hadn't been washed in about six months. He dribbled his basketball to the center of the court, he and Cane glanced at each other, and without uttering a word, they switched basketballs. Then they spun simultaneously, neither of them missing a beat in their dribbles, and shot at the basket.

Cane's ball dropped through the net a breath before Maltais's. They caught their balls, grinned at each other, then dribbled toward opposite ends of the court. Street choreography, she thought, the kind that happens between punks who hang together.

"And they supposedly don't know each other? Ha,'' she scoffed.

"Yeah, ain't it grand?'' Hallas laughed. "They both belonged to a union up in Providence, worked the same dock.''

Which pointed, again, to Mike Sessio.

If memory served her, Maltais claimed he'd shot a couple of games of pool with Washington several days before Joe Sessio's murder. Tommy supposedly had been badmouthing Sessio's organization and threatened retaliation because he'd been turned down for a job by one of the local chapters of the longshoreman's union.

Cane also claimed to have heard Tommy threaten to shoot Sessio one day when they cruised the streets. And yet, Cane and Maltais had given separate statements swearing that they didn't know each other. The fact that they evidently knew each other well led her to wonder who the hell had paid them to lie.

Stark, as the chief prosecutor in the case, seemed the obvious choice. But suppose he'd been telling her the truth about Gova? Despite Taylor's mistrust of Stark, she found it easier to believe that Gova would buy off witnesses than believing Stark could be capable of such a thing.

If nothing else, this tape would discredit two of the prosecution's witnesses. "Without these two bozos, the prosecution has a weaker case," she remarked, thinking out loud.

"True. You still have Ravigno to deal with, but from what Kyle's told me, he doesn't sound too much more reliable than Cane and Maltais." He ejected the tape, handed it to her. "I heard about what happened with that other tape," Hallas said. "Kyle told me. So just keep this to yourself, okay? I've got the original stashed away and you and I are the only ones who know about it."

"I shouldn't even tell Kyle?"

"Hey, it's up to you, Taylor. I'm just suggesting we keep it between you and me. That way if anything happens to either of us, we'll know the only way that could've happened was because my van's bugged." He glanced at her and grinned. "And I can tell you now, it's clean. I sweep it every morning and night like clockwork."

"Deal." She shoved the tape deep into her purse.

Moments later, Hallas turned into a neighborhood on the fringes of Charlestown. He gestured at a basketball court on his right. "That's the court on the videotape. This is Cane's neighborhood, but Maltais lives about a mile or two east.''

"When did you shoot the tape, Burt?"

"Two weeks ago. You'll see some other stuff on there of Cane and Maltais separately, going about their normal lives. Or at least, what passes for normal with these punks. But the court was the first time I'd seen them together." He slowed as he approached an ugly tenement building. "That's where Cane lives. Right now, he's a stock boy at a grocery store near here. Makes minimum wage. But he drives a brand new Harley that he bought about six weeks ago."

"And Maltais?"

"He works at a garage and drives a two-year-old Camaro, souped up to the gills. There's no lien against it, he doesn't have a credit history, so he must've paid cash for it."

"How much cash?"

"Around eight grand." He pointed out where Maltais lived, a spavined three-story building that shrieked for fresh paint and basic repairs. "Doesn't look like the kind of place where people save that kind of money, does it."

She shook her head. "Any theories, Burt?"

He laughed good-naturedly. "Hell, that's your job. But based just on experience, I'd say they were paid off. All you got to do is prove it."

"No, I don't have to prove it. I just have to cast aspersions on them as witnesses."

"Tape should do that." He swung into a U-turn in the middle of the road and headed back in the direction from which they'd just come. "Say, whatever happened with that fellow I tracked down in Fall River?"

"Which fellow?"

"Serle, Eric Serle."

Blood pounded in her ears, her throat closed up. Moments passed before she could speak. "I have no idea. It must be an angle Kyle's working on." She tried to keep her tone normal, not too inquisitive. "Where'd you find him?"

"In jail. He'd beaten up a hooker. I was just curious about what Kyle did."

"I don't know. I'll ask him. He and I have been running in opposite directions lately."

Eric. Fall River. Jail. A hooker. What the hell had been going on, anyway? Maybe after the break-in, when she'd told Kyle about Eric, he'd taken it upon himself to track him down. But why hadn't he told her anything about it?

"I thought you, uh, knew about it, Taylor, since Serle was wanted for questioning here in Boston for the break-in to your place."

"Kyle probably thought it would upset me or something. Do you remember how long ago you located Serle?"

"Not offhand. But I got it in here somewhere." He slipped a notepad out of his shirt pocket and flipped through it as he drove. "Yeah, here it is. About three weeks ago. I beeped him late that night, he said fine, that was it. It wasn't Serle's first arrest. He seems to have a history of beating up hookers. In just the last four years, there were five arrests for the same thing. You want the dates?"

"You have them?"

"Right here." He wagged the notepad, then handed it to her. "Just copy 'em down."

As she copied the dates onto another sheet of paper, the date of June 7 leaped out at her. *Suspected in beating of hooker on 6/7. Believed to have gone into hiding until arrest for this beating three wks. ago.*

It seemed a stretch, even for Eric, to have beaten up a hooker on the same night her place had been broken into. And besides, her original impression of the man had been that of someone larger than Eric. But if he hadn't done it, then who had assaulted her and stolen the tape? She tore the sheet out of the notepad, folded it, slipped it into her wallet, and handed the notepad back to Burt.

"Do you have any idea if Serle's still in jail?" she asked.

"He got bailed out the day after I spoke to Kyle and has since disappeared. I went by the rooming house where he was living and the landlady said he moved his stuff out four or five days after his arrest. He didn't leave any forwarding address."

She felt a terrible, abrupt cramping in the pit of her stomach. "Who was the bondsman?"

Hallas flipped through the notepad again. "Gerald Tower,

Tower Bonds. Old timer, that's all I know about him."

She filed the information away in her head, not entirely certain what, if anything, she would do about it. But one thing had become clear to her: she needed to keep closer tabs on Kyle.

Debra Gova leaned back in her chair and massaged the throbbing ache in the middle of her forehead. She'd just gotten off the phone with Kyle, who had provided an unwelcome bit of news about Stark and Taylor Brooke.

Christ, she didn't need this shit. She pushed away from her desk, rummaged in her bag for several Tylenol, and took them with water from the cooler outside her office. Then she headed up the hall to Stark's office. Through his partially closed door, she heard him talking on the phone. Instead of knocking, she pushed the door open and strolled in.

Stark glanced at her and mouthed: *Be with you in a second.* The courteous thing to do, of course, would be to step out of the office until he finished his call. But she wasn't feeling particularly courteous right now.

She went over to one of the chairs in front of his desk and stood behind it. Her eyes roamed the room—furniture designed with comfort in mind; tasteful pen and ink drawings done by local artists; a pair of poster-size photographs of Boston Harbor; a framed Doonesbury comic strip. The photos of his wife that had once stood on his desk had vanished. Otherwise, though, the room looked pretty much as it had ever since Stark had come to work here.

"Right, I understand . . . look, let me call you back. Yes, that'd be fine. Bye." Stark hung up and shook his head. "My wife's attorney."

"Divorce attorneys are always bloodsuckers, John."

"This guy sure as hell is. So what's on your mind?"

Gova ran her hand over the back edge of the chair, stepped out from behind it, and leaned into Stark's desk. "Just one thing, actually. Taylor Brooke."

"What about her?"

"I understand you've been seeing her. I hope I don't have to remind you that it's the kind of behavior that could—"

Fury seized his face. "Back off. Just back the hell off, Debra. You're way out of line."

"Out of line?" She laughed and leaned into his face. "No, I don't think so. Jogging with the lead defense attorney in the Washington case makes *you* out of line. I want a conviction in this case and I won't tolerate impropriety from anyone on this team. Do I make myself clear?"

Stark's fury had spread to his eyes. "Before you lecture me on ethics, Debra, you'd better be damn sure your own behavior is above board."

He knows, she thought. No, impossible.

"What the hell's that supposed to mean?" she snapped.

"I'm just making *myself* clear."

"Look, if you've got a problem prosecuting this case, fine. I'll do it."

"Seems to me you're the one with the problems. Now, if you'll excuse me, I've got some calls to make." With that, Stark spun his chair around, his back to her, and picked up the receiver.

"You'd better be damn sure your own behavior is above board." The words echoed in her head as she hurried back down the hall to her office. She shut the door, pulled her secure phone out of the bottom drawer, and punched out a number. She left a message and two minutes later the phone rang.

"I hope this isn't another problem," he said without preface.

"A potential problem. John Stark." She explained quickly, her voice soft, hushed.

"Is he actually dating her again?"

"I don't know. But that's how Kyle made it sound."

"And who did Kyle hear this from?"

"Eric Serle."

"Interesting. Let's keep an eye on Stark. If he's feeding her information, remove him from the case."

"Will do."

"Maybe there's a way we can use this Eric fellow. Something Kyle doesn't need to know about."

"I've considered that as an option."

"Let's give it some more thought. We'll talk soon."

"Great."

"Hey, wait." His voice softened.

"Yeah?"

"I enjoyed this weekend."

"Me, too."

"When can we do it again?"

His hands and mouth still burned against her skin, phantom touches, rising like fire in her blood. "My weekends are looking pretty good until the trial starts."

"Then we'll have to do it soon."

"I'd love it."

Once they'd hung up, Gova's hand lingered on the receiver, as if to sustain the connection between them.

18

Taylor peered out the living room window and glanced up and down the road in front of her building. She didn't see anything unusual for a Wednesday morning in August: neighbors leaving for work, a young man walking his dog, a pair of joggers headed down to the river.

And yet, that same sensation persisted, of being watched, observed. It surpassed mere paranoia. Ever since Monday, when Burt Hallas had told her about Eric, she'd been *feeling* Eric's proximity. He'd bailed himself out of jail and then had come here to Boston, looking for her.

Maybe he'd seen her on TV, maybe he'd been searching for her since the day she'd fled, she didn't know, didn't care. It seemed she'd spent a good chunk of her life being terrified of him and suddenly thought of the night she'd left him. She clearly remembered standing alone in the dark, in a shabby part of town, waiting for the train that would whisk her to freedom.

Now look at her, she thought. The same fear.

She moved away from the window and went to the kitchen

window at the rear of the apartment. Lady waited on the steps to be let in. Taylor unlocked the door and the lab bounded in, leaped up. Taylor hugged her, inhaling the scent of her fur, sweet with the smells of the August morning.

"I'll try to get home around noon to take you for a walk or I'll ask Cathy to come in."

Lady barked and ran to her bowl, which brimmed with food. Taylor picked up her purse and briefcase, checked the windows to make sure they were locked, double-checked the alarm system, then stepped outside.

The skin on the back of her neck tightened; she glanced uneasily up and down the street. A few empty cars stood at the curb, a woman on a bicycle whizzed past.

She hurried down the steps to the parking lot at the side of the building, pressed the button on her key chain that unlocked the Saab's doors. Moments later, she slid inside, locked the doors, dropped her briefcase on the passenger seat, and her purse on top of it. Then she sat there, her breath balled in her chest, her fists resting against the steering wheel.

Get moving, get out of here, get on with your day, she thought.

Right. Her day.

As she backed out of the parking space, her purse toppled off her briefcase and everything spilled out. A note from Frank Morgan lay on top of the mess. It had been in her mailbox when she'd gotten home last night and she still hadn't read it.

Taylor opened it as she drove. Morgan's smooth, controlled script covered the expensive, monogrammed card:

HOPE YOU CAN MAKE IT OVER TO THE VINEYARD FOR A WEEKEND. LADY IS MORE THAN WELCOME. MAX CAN PICK YOU UP, JUST LET ME KNOW WHEN IT'S CONVENIENT FOR YOU. BEST. FRANK

The rarefied air of Martha's Vineyard: yes, she could stand that for a weekend. She needed a break, needed to get out of here for awhile. But with the trial starting in less than a month . . .

No, she wouldn't think like that.

All the way into Boston, she kept checking her rearview mirror, certain she would see Eric's face leering from the windshield of some super-charged car. But no one followed her.

She stopped first at the jail, to talk to Tommy Washington. Even though she hadn't called ahead, a guard ushered her quickly into the room where attorneys met with their clients. Tommy ambled in about five minutes later, his left eye swollen shut, his shoulders slumped as if with an unbearable weight.

"My God, what happened to your eye?"

"I got in the way of some dude's fist."

"I thought you were still in isolation."

"They done moved me two days ago."

"Do you want me to request that you be moved out of the population again, Tommy?"

"No, ma'am." He sank into the chair on the other side of the table. "I'm okay. I didn't get blamed for the fight. Just got the swelled eye." He attempted a smile, then laced his fingers together on the tabletop and fell silent.

"Tommy, I need some answers."

"Yes, ma'am. Me, too."

She turned on the tape recorder, noted the date, time, and her location. "Do you play pool, Tommy?"

"No, ma'am. Never learned."

"Do you know a guy named Gerald Maltais?"

He frowned, shook his head. "Name don't sound familiar. Why?"

"I'll get to that in a second. Did you ever apply for a job at the docks?"

His frown deepened. "Yeah, back when I wasn't workin' and the state was tellin' me that if I was gonna collect unemployment I had to apply for a bunch of jobs a week. But I knew I'd never get on with that particular union, you hear what I'm sayin'? I'm black, they're white."

"Do you know a guy named Wilbur Cane? They call him Wilt, because he's tall like Chamberlain."

"I know a couple dudes named Cane, black dudes. But no Wilburs who call theirselves Wilt."

"You're sure?"

"Yeah, I'm sure."

"Well, this Gerald Maltais claims that several days before Joe Sessio's murder, you two were playing pool and you were badmouthing Sessio's organization. He says you threatened to get even with Sessio because you'd been turned down for a job by one of the local chapters of the longshoremen's union. And this Cane kid said that one day when you were cruising the streets, you threatened to shoot Sessio and—"

"That's bullshit," he hissed. "They're lyin', whole bunch of 'em is lyin'. I never met no Ravigno, no Cane, no Maltais. I swear it. I don't play pool and I ain't cruised the streets for a year, that's the God's honest truth."

And right then, Taylor knew she would put Tommy Washington on the stand. She turned off the recorder. "I believe you, Tommy. I think you've been set up big time. Until the trial, you just stay out of trouble and speak only to me. I'm going to give you a number where you can always get a message to me if you have to." She jotted her cellular number on a scrap of paper, told Tommy to memorize it, asked him to repeat it to her, then put it into her purse. "I'd like you to call me if any of the prosecutors show up here to talk to you."

"Stark, you mean."

"Stark or a woman named Debra Gova."

"What about Mr. Kyle?"

"You'll be speaking to me directly from now on, Tommy. Kyle is going to be pursuing other angles on the defense. If he shows up, though, call that number."

"Yes, ma'am."

"You just sit tight. We're going to get you acquitted."

He nodded, his eyes filling with tears. "I hope so, ma'am, I sure hope so."

Taylor stopped next at the bank, where she put the tape Burt Hallas had given her into her safe-deposit box. She'd made two copies, stashed one in her apartment, and the other in her office.

Before she showed it to Kyle, she wanted an explanation

about why he hadn't told her about his search for Eric. If his explanation didn't satisfy her, she intended to go to Simpson and request a new assistant. Drastic, perhaps, at least for her, but she couldn't work with an assistant whom she couldn't trust.

Shortly after leaving the bank, she pulled into a parking spot across the street from DeCiccio's Restaurant. Before she got out, she opened her briefcase and glanced through the crime-scene report to make sure she hadn't overlooked any detail. She compared it to the schematic she'd drawn of the inside of the restaurant and the escape route Tommy supposedly had taken when he'd fled.

Sessio had been here later in the day than it was now, but the time concerned her less than the specifics about what had happened inside the restaurant. She crossed the street, eyeing the six blocks to her right, where Tommy allegedly had fled. Six blocks that led to the wharf.

Inside DeCiccio's, business looked good, every table occupied, busboys hustling, waiters and waitresses hurrying back and forth. Apparently Sessio's murder hadn't kept the customers away.

The maître d' asked if she had a reservation. "Actually, I'd like to speak to Mr. DeCiccio, if he's in."

"Your name?"

"Taylor Brooke, with the law firm of Simpson and Willis."

The woman's eyes widened. "Oh. You're defending Tommy. He's a nice kid. None of us believes for a minute that he killed Mr. Sessio." She smiled quickly, self-conscious about her impromptu little speech. "He's in his office off the kitchen, Ms. Taylor. Go on back and I'll buzz him that you're coming."

"Thanks very much."

As Taylor walked to the rear of the restaurant, she passed Joe Sessio's booth, occupied by a well-heeled couple sipping coffee. She noted that it took her about fifty-five seconds to move from Sessio's booth to the kitchen doorway. As she entered, she spotted the public phone on the wall to her left.

DeCiccio's office stood at the far end of the noisy kitchen, a cubicle of glass that provided him with a clear view of most of the kitchen, including the phone. He moved toward the door, where he stood, waiting for her, his arms folded across his chest, as if to block her entrance.

"Ms. Taylor." His thickly accented voice conjured images of Mediterranean sunlight, of water so blue it made your heart ache with the beauty of it. "Nice to see you again."

"You, too, Mr. DeCiccio. Do you have a minute?"

"Certainly." He gestured toward his office and stepped aside so she could walk through the doorway first. They settled in the only two chairs in the room, DeCiccio behind his cluttered desk. "What may I do for you?" he asked.

"According to the police report, you were here in the kitchen at the time of Joe Sessio's murder. Is that correct?"

"In the freezer." He pointed through the glass at the walk-in freezer on the other side of the kitchen. "The door it was shut. I heard nothing. When I come out, I see chaos." His hands flew dramatically through the air, conveying chaos. "Everywhere there is chaos. People screaming, my chefs running around. . . ." He shook his head. "Terrible," he added softly.

"About how long were you in the freezer?"

His bushy brows jutted together. "How should I know? It was a busy day. I go in and out of the freezer many times on a busy day."

"I thought the lunch crowd had tapered off by then, that Mr. Sessio was out there alone, finishing his lunch."

"But in here it was busy."

"So you were in the freezer—what? Five minutes? Ten? Give me some idea."

DeCiccio sat forward, smiling at her as though she were a young and not very bright child. "I have no idea, that is what I just said."

"Do you recall seeing Tommy Washington in here, using the phone, shortly before you went into the freezer?"

He waved his hand impatiently. "I have many busboys working here. I don't know them all. I told that to Ms. Gova. I told that to Mr. Stark. I told it to, what's his name." He waved his hand impatiently. "The man with the red hair."

"Kyle Nelson."

"Yes, him, too. My employees use that phone all the time. I think I remember seeing someone on the phone, but I don't know who it was."

"Do you recall if the person was male or female, Mr. DeCiccio?"

"A man. I only saw him from the back."

"Was he black or white?"

"Black. Yes, I think he was black."

Taylor could barely contain her excitement. She'd never come this close to verifying Tommy's story that he received a call. "Did you tell that to Ms. Gova or Mr. Stark?"

If he had, then she would know for sure that Gova or Stark or both of them had buried information.

He frowned, he rubbed his temple, he shrugged. "I talked to so many people. I can't remember what I told to who."

"Did you tell Mr. Nelson? The man with the red hair?"

"I can't remember. That was in June. Now it is August, young lady." He tapped his temple. "The mind slips."

"Okay, so then you went into the freezer and when you came out, things were chaos."

"Yes, that I remember clearly."

DeCiccio's phone rang. "I should get this," he said.

"Just one more thing, Mr. DeCiccio. May I have Tommy's time cards for the month of May?"

"One minute, okay?" He took his call, got off quickly, then riffled through his desk drawer until he found a stack of time cards. He shuffled through them, handed one to Taylor.

"Did any of the other attorneys ask for this?"

"No one."

Someone in the kitchen called for DeCiccio, he shouted back in Italian. Taylor got to her feet. "Thanks so much for your time, Mr. DeCiccio."

On her way back through the kitchen, she glanced at the number on the phone and jotted it down. She noted the instructions posted on the wall next to it:

- long distance calls can't be made from this phone
- 3 minute limit on calls
- using this phone is a privilege, not a right

Taylor did a quick head count: eleven people in the kitchen. And yet, according to the police report, none of the employees remembered taking a call for Tommy. The prosecution would use that in court, but she felt confident that DeCiccio's testimony would outweigh it.

As she came out of the kitchen, she saw Cathy and Mike Sessio in Joe Sessio's old booth. They looked—what? Divided? At odds? As though they were mired in the aftermath of a disagreement?

Don't look this way, she thought. But Cathy spotted her and waved and she couldn't very well just wave back and leave without at least saying hello. Taylor strolled over to the booth.

"Taylor, good to see you," Cathy exclaimed, as though they hadn't seen each other in weeks. As though the breach of confidence about her father hadn't happened. "What're you doing here?"

She stabbed a thumb over her shoulder. "Washing dishes back there."

Mike Sessio laughed. "Join us for lunch."

"Thanks, but I can't." She felt the magnetic scrutiny of Sessio's eyes—on her face, her breasts, her hips—and knew that Cathy noticed it. "I've got a million things to tie up today."

"At least join us for coffee or something," Cathy said.

"I really can't."

"Oh, I nearly forgot," Cathy said. "My car's got to go into the garage over the weekend and I've got a consultation on Saturday. If the garage can't give me a loaner, would you mind if I borrowed your car for a couple of hours?"

"Of course not. Remind me tomorrow, okay?"

"Sure thing."

Taylor glanced at Sessio, his eyes fixed on her. "Good seeing you, Mike."

"You, too."

She felt relieved to get outside, away from Sessio's scrutiny and the tension between him and Cathy. She sensed the problem between them echoed Cathy's previous patterns with men. Sessio's roving eye spoke tomes. Besides, she wondered, what kind of man could have lunch at the very same restaurant, at the very same table, where his father was killed? It didn't say much for Sessio's character, and, if anything, put even more questions in Taylor's mind.

She walked quickly toward the wharf, following Tommy's path the day of the shooting. It took her about five minutes to reach the wharf and another minute and half to get to the dock for the airport taxi. Tommy said he'd raced to the wharf, so call it three or four minutes, she thought. Then he'd waited for the caller to show up. Instead, a cruiser had pulled in, with Billy Boy from the kitchen in the back seat, pointing at him, identifying him for the cops.

And with that, Tommy Washington had become a temporary ward of the state.

Taylor bought a plate of fresh scrod and Boston brown bread from one of the fast food stands and sat down at a table on the wharf. The sun felt good against the back of her head. A breeze blew off the harbor, thick with the scent of August. Sailboats glided across the water.

Taylor opened her briefcase, removed a notebook, and wrote up what she'd found out. Suddenly, someone bumped into the back of her chair, a tray fell, food spilled all over the ground to the right, and she scrambled to get out of the way.

Then she glanced at the offender. Stark murmured, "Jesus, I'm sorry," and crouched to clean up the mess.

"If I didn't know better, I'd say that was intentional," Taylor remarked, stooping to help him.

"It was. I think Gova's having me followed. She knew we were jogging together last Friday. I'm not taking any chances. Can you meet me in the parking garage? We need to talk."

Shocked by his admission, a dozen questions leaped to mind. "Definitely. Where and when?"

"Third level, give me at least a ten-minute lead when I leave the wharf. Make sure you aren't followed."

"Got it."

Then his eyes met hers, eyes torn with conflict. Whatever Stark had or hadn't been in the past, she knew that right now he told the truth. He got up and walked off toward the trash can. Taylor sat down again and tried to immerse herself in her notes.

But she couldn't concentrate. She flipped through a mental Rolodex of people she might have told about running into Stark in the park. Kyle, Frank Morgan, Cathy: no, no, and yes. Cathy.

Cathy didn't know Debra Gova. They'd met the day she and Cathy had lunch at the Cornucopia. But even if they *did* know each other, Cathy wouldn't feed Gova information, would she?

She told Mike who your father is, whispered an ugly little voice inside of her.

But this involved professional ethics, not personal issues.

So what? snickered the little voice. *Maybe Gova offered her something she couldn't refuse.*

Like what? Money? Endless decorating jobs? What the hell would entice Cathy to do such a thing?

Nothing, she thought. Nothing.

And yet.

Taylor glanced around uneasily, eyeing the faces of the people around her.

"I think Gova is having me followed," Stark had said.

Gova, the gaping unknown.

19

━━━━━━━━━━

An erotic thrill whipped through Eric. He hadn't been this close to Taylor in nearly five years and now he stared, drinking in the sight of her—shiny blond hair where he remembered black; skin that looked so soft he could almost feel it between his fingers; and that mouth, that lovely, kissable mouth.

Then his vision telescoped and he seemed to be looking at her as if from a great distance, a slender blond woman busy writing at one of the tables. Her clothes looked expensive, her shoes looked expensive, everything about her looked expensive.

Fraud, he thought. Phony. A made up person. You aren't real, Taylor Brooke, he thought at her.

She glanced around as though she'd heard his thoughts. Eric quickly turned his back and gazed out at the harbor again. He, too, had donned a disguise, dressed as pretty little Talia had never seen him, slacks and a shirt and tie, all of it courtesy of "Watson" Nelson's dirty money, thank you very much. He looked like a lawyer. He'd let his beard and a mustache grow and wore a pair of expensive shades.

He counted slowly to fifty, then glanced back.

Gone.

He shot to his feet and hurried through the crowd, looking about frantically. Where?

Stark, of course. He'd seen Stark and the food fiasco. Stark had left about ten minutes ago. Eric felt certain that Taylor had slipped off to meet him at some preordained spot.

He sprang free of the crowd and broke into a run, his new, shiny shoes squeaking, his tie slapping softly against his shirt. He stopped at the curb, looked wildly in either direction. Nothing, no sign of her.

Eric darted through the traffic, his frustration and rage propelling him. Bitch. She'd left to meet with the fancy lawyer. He reached his car, hurled himself inside, and swung away from the curb, into the traffic. The driver behind him honked; Eric shot him the finger and swerved into the left lane.

She'd walked to the wharf from her office; he guessed he would find her Saab parked within a block of Simpson & Willis or in the garage. He drove past the office and circled the block. And then he saw it, her pathetic little Saab with the rusting rear fender, dried mud shooting out across the sides like crooked zippers. It stood at the curb, just as it usually did, the windows sealed.

His fury surged—then seized him. He pulled up parallel to the Saab, got out, raised his hood. He slipped between the two cars, crouched, pulled out a switchblade, clicked it open, and jabbed the blade into the front left tire. It felt so goddamn good he jabbed again and again and again. Air hissed out, he plunged the blade a final time, twisted it, and jerked the blade upward, slicing through rubber.

He quickly folded the knife, hastened back to his car, and drove away, hands clenched to the steering wheel.

Stark's Volvo sped through sunlight and shadows, deeper into the heart of Roxbury, Tommy Washington's world.

Taylor felt strange being in this car with him again. Memories of the past crowded around her like eager spectators at a baseball game. The faded rabbit's foot that hung from the rearview mirror had once been a joke between them. The yellow smiling face sticker on the glove compartment door echoed an afternoon they'd visited museums. The cool leather seat had cradled her head on innumerable occasions.

To her relief, Stark didn't make any references to their past. Almost immediately, he launched into his confrontation with Gova and his deepening suspicion about her. The quiet power of his voice swept away whatever doubts she'd had about his sincerity.

"I wanted to give you a call as soon as it happened, to warn you, but after the other night, I thought you would suspect me of double-dealing."

"I apologize for that, John. Right now, I feel like we're both pawns in Gova's game, whatever it is. Where're we going, anyway?"

"Someplace that's going to even the score. It'll give you a little more ammunition in your defense."

She glanced at him, his face rendered in profile against the light, strands of his blond hair burned almost white by the sun. "In other words, you're doing exactly what she accused you of doing."

"You got it. I intend to stay on the prosecution team as long as I can and figure out what the hell Gova's doing. Until then, I've got to be able to live with myself."

She felt a rush of warmth for Stark that had nothing to do with their previous relationship. This struck her as a new emotion, a deep affection for a man she once had loved and no longer did. The sudden realization both liberated and saddened her.

Moments later, Stark turned into a youth center, a one-story concrete building painted in shades of blue. Along the entire east wall, aspiring artists had painted street scenes that literally exploded with color and personality.

"The guy who runs this place is a friend of mine," Stark said as they got out of the car. "Malcolm Eubanks."

"I didn't realize you ever left your social circles."

Stark laughed. ''Christ, that was blunt.''

She shrugged. ''Sorry, it's just an observation.''

''Actually, I volunteer here a couple of times a month. These kids are trying to steer clear of the local gang culture and most of them have been busted for drugs at one time or another.''

The idea that Stark volunteered for anything, much less at a youth center, shocked her. She'd never seen this side of him.

''Tommy Washington ended up here when he was twelve.''

She nodded. ''I saw his juvenile record, but didn't realize this was the place.''

A bell tinkled as Stark opened the door for her. Taylor walked in and immediately smiled; the atmosphere triggered a rush of pleasant feelings. Everywhere she looked, she saw color—the walls, the paintings that adorned them, the furniture, even the concrete floor.

On one side of the room, a tall, lanky black man with graying hair stood over two kids working on a pair of computers that looked like early Radio Shack models, Neanderthals. ''That's Malcolm.'' Stark touched her elbow. ''C'mon, I'll introduce you.''

Eubanks glanced around before they reached him and his face lit up like the Fourth of July. ''Johnny, boy, good to see you, m'man.'' He grabbed Stark's hand, pumping it vigorously, and slapped him on the shoulder. ''Just saw you two nights ago, what gives?''

''Malcolm, this is the defense lawyer I told you about, Taylor Brooke.''

He grasped her hand between both of his own. ''The lady who's going to save Tommy. Mighty nice to meet you, ma'am. You give that boy a fair shake.''

''Talk to John about that. He's the prosecutor.''

''Shee-it, he's got nothing but lies to work with. I set him straight on that one.'' He touched her arm and they moved away from the two kids working on the computers. ''Listen, I known that boy since he was twelve, you hear what I'm saying? He got busted for possession when he was this high.'' His hand chopped through the air in front of Taylor's waist. ''Got caught holding a dime bag, which he was deliverin' to an older dude who was selling the shit on the streets.

"So Tommy's ma brings him down here to me. She wants her boy to get out of Roxbury, away from the dudes, the drugs. Wants him to get an education. So up until he finished high school, he checked in here with me every afternoon. He's a good boy, Tommy is. Gotten himself into some scrapes, but he never killed no one."

"What about the arrest related to that kid who was set on fire?" she asked.

"He saw what them kids were up to, tried to stop it, and got cut with a knife. The kid who died? His brother saw the whole thing and told the cops what happened. That's why the charges was dropped."

"Do you know if Tommy ever applied for a job at the docks?" Taylor asked.

"Lady, he applied for jobs everywhere. State said he had to. But what's a black kid from Roxbury gonna be doing in a place fulla micks and Italians, huh? They're not gonna be rolling out no welcome mat, that's for sure. So he applies at the shoe factory, the MBTA, he applies at the docks. That's the way you play the game. But bottom line? He don't know Joe Sessio from Madonna, 'cept to clean off his table when he's finished eating. This kid's been set up."

"I agree," she said, and Malcolm Eubanks beamed.

"She's okay," Eubanks said to Stark, as though she weren't present.

Stark laughed. "I wouldn't lie about a thing like that."

Eubanks rocked onto the balls of his feet and poked a long bony finger into Stark's chest. "I think you'd best get on the right side of things, John."

Stark held up his hands in surrender. "Hey, I'm trying. I'm trying."

"Would you be willing to testify about Tommy in court, Mr. Eubanks?"

"Lady, I'd testify to the good Lord Hisself about Tommy Washington."

You may have put yourself at risk by doing this," Taylor said later, when they were back in the Volvo.

Stark shrugged. "For once in my life, I'm trying to do the right thing."

"But how's this going to affect things in court? You and I are still going to be up against each other."

"I'm hoping we'll nail the right guy before it gets to court, Taylor."

"And who's the right guy? Mike Sessio?"

"It makes sense, I just don't have any proof."

"How do you figure it makes sense? Why would he have his own father killed? What was his motive?"

He looked over at her, aware of what she'd heard in her own voice, a defense of Mike Sessio. "You really think that guy is innocent, Taylor?"

"Give me a reason to think otherwise."

"You're taken in by his charm and you're seduced by the mystery that surrounds him. Hey, understandable. The man has had more women than Macy's has had shoe sales. But the fact is that Mike Sessio is the only one with a strong enough motive. He wanted his old man's empire."

Somewhere along the way, Stark had concluded that Tommy Washington had been set up. But instead of digging more deeply for the truth, he'd transferred blame to Sessio. It disappointed her; she'd hoped for more than this from Stark. Yet, some of what he said about her attraction to Sessio had struck home, despite her reluctance to admit it.

The bottom line, she thought, was that right now her emotions concerning Mike Sessio and Stark vacillated wildly between trust and distrust.

They fell silent after that, Taylor gazing out the window, Stark staring straight ahead. Their differing opinion about Sessio had created a new breach between them. It underscored the very basic problem that always had existed between them. Their timing stank.

His marriage, their opposing sides of the law, the age difference: if not that, it would be something else. It simply confirmed her sense earlier today that all the passion she'd felt for this man had died somewhere along the way and only this quiet affection remained. A part of her mourned its passing.

Awhile later, Stark pulled into the parking garage where he'd picked her up. Before she got out of the car, she reached for his hand, gave it a quick squeeze. "I appreciate what you've done."

He pushed his sunglasses back onto the top of his head and turned those incredible eyes on her. "I hear a *but* in your voice."

"We'll always disagree on basics."

He drew her hand to his face, rubbed the back of it over his cheeks, and squeezed his eyes shut, as though he were memorizing the contours of bone and tendons, the texture of her skin. Taylor slipped her arms around him. "Christ, Taylor," he whispered, and encircled her in his arms.

The past assaulted her, seized her, turned her inside out. This was one of those vacillating, confusing moments, she thought, but didn't pull away. The scent of his skin, of his hair, the utter clarity of the embrace, all of it burned with memory. His mouth soft and as familiar to her as her own bones.

Perhaps the absence of intimacy in her life had left her vulnerable, perhaps Stark's body merely felt wonderfully familiar to her, but she melted into the embrace, and briefly lost herself in it.

Then, suddenly, something snapped inside of her and she pulled back gently. She didn't want this, didn't want more empty nights in which she waited for the phone to ring, waited for Stark to fill the hollow pockets in her life. "I don't think this is a good idea."

"But . . ."

Taylor touched her index finger to his mouth, silencing him. "Let's just leave it at that." Before he could object, she got out of the car, rapped her knuckles once against the windshield, and hurried toward the garage's exit, the taste of his mouth lingering against hers.

On her way to her office, Taylor stopped by Eileen's desk to pick up her messages. Eileen whispered, ''Kyle's buzzed me four times. You're supposed to call him.''

''Why're you whispering?''

''Trouble, Taylor. Debra Gova has been in Simpson's office for about twenty minutes.''

''Just what I don't need.''

''That's not the worst of it. I'm supposed to buzz him as soon as you get in. I told him you were doing some fieldwork and weren't expected in today.''

''I'm not about to get put on the spot by Gova. Wait until she leaves, then buzz Simpson and tell him I'm here.''

''You bet. By the way, Armand Assante called again. He asked for your voice mail.'' Her voice dropped to a conspiratorial whisper. ''Did you ask him if he had any single friends?''

Taylor laughed. ''Not yet, but I will.''

She went into her office, shut the door, and unlocked her filing cabinet. She checked to make sure the tape remained where she'd stashed it, then picked up her voice mail messages.

Two hang-ups, then Sessio's voice: ''Hi, Taylor. It's Mike. Can you give me a call? It's important. Thanks.''

How important could it be when she'd run into him only a few hours ago at DeCiccio's? She resented Sessio putting her in a compromising position with Cathy. On the other hand, she needed to pursue every lead at this point.

She punched out his number, his secretary informed her he was in a meeting. Relieved, she left her name, hung up, and buzzed Kyle. ''Kyle Nelson.''

''You have a few minutes?''

''Where the hell have you been?''

''Doing footwork. I've got something to show you.''

''Did Eileen tell you Gova's in with Simpson?''

''Yeah.''

''You don't sound too concerned.''

"Hey, Kyle, I take it an hour at a time with this case."

"I'll be right over."

Kyle breezed in thirty seconds later, his red hair tousled, as though he'd just come in from the street, his eyes bright with youth and enthusiasm. With that Tom Sawyer face, how could she possibly suspect him of duplicity?

"So what's going on?" he asked, flopping down into the chair in front of her desk.

"I saw Burt Hallas on Monday and—"

"I thought you'd never met."

Perhaps her imagination and paranoia had veered into hyperdrive, but it seemed that the color drained from Kyle's face. "Monday was the first time I've spoken to him. He actually called looking for you. He was wondering what happened with the Eric Serle matter."

For a full fifteen seconds, Kyle said nothing, he simply stared straight ahead, unblinking. It looked as if he'd suffered a petit mal. Then he blinked and stammered, "I, uh, didn't want to bother you with all that, Taylor. I . . . I thought Hallas could track him down and then I'd tell the cops where they could find him and they . . . I mean, he's still under suspicion for the assault on you and . . ."

"I appreciate your good intentions, Kyle. But the fact is that you should have told me. This concerns my personal life."

"I don't know, I just couldn't stand it that day in the hospital, seeing you there . . . I . . . I apologize, Taylor. You're absolutely right. I shouldn't have interfered."

He sounded sincere; his good intentions had simply gone to extremes. And yet, now that doubt had been seeded, she couldn't trust him as easily. She wished, suddenly, that she had some way of testing him. If she showed him the tape that Hallas had given her, of Cane and Maltais, and the information got back to her somehow, then she would know that Kyle had leaked it. But it might jeopardize her defense and she couldn't do that to Tommy Washington.

"From now on, just be up front with me, Kyle." Even though she couldn't afford to be entirely up front with him.

"You bet. I understand. I never intended to create any mistrust between us."

"I know you didn't. But according to Burt, Eric was bailed out of jail and has disappeared. That makes me real uncomfortable."

"I doubt very much that he has any idea where to look for you, Taylor. He's probably two thousand miles away from Fall River by now."

She hoped he'd pegged it, but doubted it.

Her phone buzzed and she answered it. "Taylor Brooke."

"Taylor, it's Ogden. Could you come down to my office for a few minutes?"

He'd bypassed Eileen, she thought. That meant Gova hadn't left yet. "Kyle and I are right in the middle of something, Ogden."

"Bring him, too," he replied, and hung up.

She dropped the receiver in the cradle and looked at Kyle. "The shit hits the fan," she said. "Gova's still in there with him."

"Christ." Kyle rubbed his hand over his face.

Taylor, Kyle, make yourselves comfortable," said Simpson in his usual gracious manner. "I believe you both know Ms. Gova."

Kyle's rage seethed from someplace so deep inside of him he thought for sure it would leap away from him. He knew what Gova's little visit here concerned and felt that she'd double-crossed him. He managed to mutter a greeting, then joined the others in the sitting room. Gova, he noticed, didn't look at him, avoided his gaze completely.

"Ms. Gova stopped by to discuss her concerns about the upcoming Washington trial," Simpson said.

You Judas, Kyle thought, but couldn't think of anything to say. Taylor, however, got right to the point.

"Other than the fact that we're on opposite teams," she said bluntly, "what concerns do you have, Ms. Gova?"

And Gova, the witch, looked at Taylor with an utterly mask-like face and replied: "Your relationship with John Stark, the prosecutor on this case."

Shit, Kyle thought, and wished the floor would open up and swallow him.

Simpson, the unofficial mediator, looked at Taylor. "Is there anything you'd like to say?"

Taylor shrugged. "Frankly, I don't know what you're referring to, Ms. Gova. My relationship with Mr. Stark is strictly professional, just as it is with other attorneys I know."

Gova, ever the prosecuting ball breaker, sat forward slightly and pinned Taylor with her small, hot eyes. "Do you deny that your present relationship is intimate?"

Taylor looked at her as though she'd lost her mind and burst out laughing. "I'd have to be certifiable to have an intimate relationship with the man who intends to convict my client, Ms. Gova." And she smiled sweetly and opened her hands, palms up, a woman with nothing to hide. "And I don't think the practice of law has driven me over the edge yet."

Kyle laughed, laughed perhaps a tad too loudly, and Gova glared at him. But Simpson smiled, tried to hide it, then stood. "I don't think we have a problem here, Ms. Gova. But if you feel we do, then perhaps you should take your concerns to Judge Cornwell."

Even Gova, relentless cutthroat, Kyle thought, realized she'd lost this round and that she probably shouldn't have come to Simpson in the first place. Kyle nearly cheered.

Gova stood, tugged at the hem of her cotton blazer, and said, "As you know, Ogden, my main concern is that we go to trial on time. A change in attorneys at this point might delay things."

Horseshit, witch, Kyle thought.

Simpson nodded, glanced at Taylor. "I don't anticipate any delays. Do you, Taylor?"

"No, sir. I actually anticipate an acquittal." Then she looked pointedly at Gova and flashed a brilliant smile.

Gova didn't find it the least bit amusing. Her mouth twitched, then she turned and left.

Several beats passed. Kyle heard footsteps in the hall, a

phone ringing somewhere. "We just won round one," he remarked dryly.

"Excuse us for a moment, will you, Kyle?" Simpson asked.

"Uh, sure. Buzz me when you're done, Taylor."

She nodded and he hurried out of the office, shutting the door behind him. He hesitated briefly, then loped down the hall after Gova. He caught up with her just as the elevator doors were shutting, slammed his hand against the door, and darted inside before the doors shut again.

Gova snapped, "Just what the hell do you—"

Kyle smashed his fist against the STOP button, the elevator ground to a halt. He poked her in the chest with his index finger, poked so hard she winced and wrenched back. "Don't *ever* pull shit like that again," he hissed, spittle flying in her face. "What the hell were you going to do? Tell Simpson you saw them jogging? Or that some snitch you're paying saw them jogging? Or maybe you were going to tell him her husband is stalking her. Just what the fuck were you thinking of, Gova?"

Her eyes had widened with incredulity, she looked to be on the verge of a stroke. Then she slammed her knee into Kyle's groin. Stars exploded inside his eyes and he doubled over, groaning, his body on fire from the waist down. She grabbed him by the hair and threw his head back, forcing him to look at her.

"Don't fuck with me, Kyle. I won't just break you. I'll obliterate you."

Then she released her grip on his hair, pushed him away from her, and Kyle fell back against the wall of the elevator. His testicles throbbed, sweat flooded from his pores. The elevator lurched downward. He somehow got to his feet and leaned into the wall, and stood upright when the doors opened.

20

Ogden Simpson didn't look happy with the situation and when he began to speak, his voice held a hint of sternness that she'd never heard before.

"Your personal life is certainly your own, Taylor. But in the event that Ms. Gova convinces Judge Cornwell to have you removed as Washington's defense attorney, it's going to cast the firm in a negative light."

Taylor felt like a three-year-old who had been given a time out for something she hadn't done. Even though her innocence remained questionable, the extenuating circumstances outweighed Gova's accusations. And yet, she hesitated saying too much to Simpson. What certainty did she have that she could trust him? At this point, she didn't know who to trust about anything.

On the other hand, if Gova went to the judge and succeeded in removing her from the case, she could write off her career at this firm. She doubted that Simpson would fire her, but his confidence in her would be shot.

"Taylor?" Simpson frowned. "Is there anything you want to say?"

"Actually, yes. There are some things about the prosecution's case that don't add up." She told him what Burt Hallas had discovered about the two witnesses from Providence, then explained about Malcolm Eubanks at the youth center, but without mentioning Stark. "In other words, sir, I believe that Tommy was set up."

"Do you have the tape Mr. Hallas took?"

"Yes."

"Keep it in a secure place. We'll show it in court if we have to. Will this Eubanks fellow testify in Washington's defense?"

"Yes. There's something else, Mr. Simpson," she said, and told him about Richard Adler.

"Have you gotten the subpoena?"

"It's in the works."

"I knew Richard quite well and until his death, had a rather pleasant relationship with his wife. Then she became a recluse. I didn't know about her medical problem. But perhaps it's time to pay her a neighborly visit. I'll see what I can do."

"Thanks. That'd be a great help. Maybe she'll listen to you."

"It's worth a try. But if she doesn't, we'll just subpoena her." Simpson paced some more, then paused at the long window, then resumed his pacing. "Off the record, Taylor." He stopped, looked at her. "Are you and Mr. Stark involved?"

"Absolutely not, sir."

"Were you jogging together?"

"He showed up where I was jogging, yes." She didn't want to implicate Stark, so she chose her words carefully. "He's in the midst of a divorce and wanted some legal advice."

Simpson smiled. "Ironic. When lawyers get divorced, they always turn to other lawyers."

"What bothers me is that Ms. Gova knew about our jog. The only way she could possibly know that is if she's having me or Mr. Stark followed. Now why would she be doing that?"

"Good point. Look, just keep me apprised of the situation, Taylor. I'm here if you need me."

"Thanks. I appreciate your support."

Off the hook, she thought, and with Simpson's confidence in her restored. But for how long? She hurried back to her office and gathered up her things. Go home, she thought. On her way out, she passed the closed door of Kyle's office. He'd left already.

Outside, violet bled across the eastern sky. A brisk breeze swept through the street, stirring up dust and cellophane wrappers. Evening traffic crawled out of the city, horns blared, pedestrians hurried past her.

Taylor focused so intensely on Gova and her machinations, she failed to notice the flat tire on her car until she came around to the driver's side. "Shit," she muttered, and crouched to take a closer look.

She ran her fingers over the slashed rubber, the punctures, and a chill whipped up her spine. Whoever had done this had gone after the tire as though it were a living thing. She jerked her hand back, rubbed it against her skirt, and glanced around uneasily at the lengthening shadows.

Eric, out there somewhere. She knew it.

A surge of near panic shot her to her feet. She quickly unlocked the car, got inside, shut and locked the door. As she dug her Triple A card out of her wallet, her cell phone rang, a soft, muffled ring from deep inside her briefcase. She opened her briefcase, grabbed the phone.

"Yes? Hello?"

"Taylor?"

"Oh. Frank."

"I wasn't sure it was you. You sounded different."

Different. She nearly laughed. "I've got a slashed tire, that's why, and I'm about to call Triple A."

"Slashed?" Alarm riddled his voice. "Give me your address. Max and I are in town, we'll swing by and pick you up and get the tire taken care of."

"Thanks, Frank. But I don't want to impose."

"It's no imposition. Really."

Okay, so maybe it wouldn't be an imposition. But if she

accepted his favor, then he would expect something in return—
dinner, conversation, whatever. She just wanted to be alone
this evening.

"No strings attached," he added with a laugh, as though
he'd read her mind. "Where are you?"

She told him.

"We're about three minutes away. Sit tight."

They hung up and she waited in the car, waited with the
windows rolled up and the doors locked, waited like a prisoner
for an eleventh hour reprieve. Sure enough, three minutes
later, a shiny Mercedes pulled alongside her Saab.

Dad arrives to take care of things, she thought. Ironic. As
a child, she'd dreamed of moments like this, being rescued
by the father she'd never known. Now he'd arrived in the
flesh, the solicitous senator and his loyal chauffeur, clucking
about the ruined tire.

"The slashes are neat and narrow," Max remarked, exam-
ining them. "My guess is a switchblade. Any other damage
to your car, Ms. Brooke?"

"I don't think so."

"The tire's bad enough," Morgan said. "Do you have a
spare?"

"In the trunk. But I don't have a jack."

"No problem," Max said. "We've got one."

"Why don't we let Max tend to your tire," Morgan said.
"And I'll drive you home. You look beat."

Taylor glanced at Max. "I hate putting you out like this,
Max."

He smiled and she liked the way it softened his face,
rounded out his square jaw, and brought a certain humanity
to his otherwise dark and somehow menacing eyes. "My pleasure, ma'am. One of my first cars was an old Saab. It'll be a
pleasure to drive one again. I need your key, though."

"Oh. Right."

She handed it to him, retrieved her briefcase and purse, and
Max tossed the Mercedes keys to Morgan. "Just drop the car
by her place when you're done," Morgan said.

"Yes, sir. Let me get that jack."

As Taylor slipped into the Mercedes, she drank in the details of Morgan's world. The soft leather seats. The spotless dashboard. The pristine floor carpet. The campaign magnet stuck to the door of the glove compartment. She noted the maps tucked neatly into a pouch on the driver's door, the absolute clarity of the glass, not a speck of dirt or mud to mar the view.

Compared to this, the inside of her Saab looked like the aftermath of a violent storm. But then, she didn't have a chauffeur or a battalion of hired help.

Morgan got in, glanced at her, and smiled. "Now *this* is a treat." With that, the Mercedes whispered to life and he pulled away from the curb. "Have you eaten?"

She shook her head. "I just left work."

"Good. I'll fix you dinner."

"I really need to get home, Frank. My dog hasn't been walked since. . . ."

"I meant I'd fix you dinner at your place. If that's okay." A quick smile. "I'm a pretty decent cook."

His infectious enthusiasm made her laugh. "How can I possibly refuse an offer like that?"

They made one stop, at a fish market, then headed toward Cambridge. She felt self-consciousness when they entered her apartment and suddenly wished she'd straightened up before she'd left this morning.

But Morgan didn't seem to notice the details that suddenly struck her as shabby. He made friends with her dog, commented on the handmade quilt tossed over the back of an antique chair, admired a painting by a local artist that hung on her dining room wall.

"So lead me to your kitchen and then you go relax," he said.

She laughed. "You may have to conjure up magic with what I've got in the pantry."

He winked. "I'm a resourceful man."

Taylor familiarized him with the kitchen, then he donned a chef's apron that Stark had given her and shooed her out of the kitchen. It felt strange to have her father in her kitchen and stranger still to hear him humming to himself as he bustled around, clanging pots and pans, preparing their dinner.

She didn't want to turn on the TV, didn't want to plop down

on the couch, couldn't just stand in the doorway and watch. So she kicked off her shoes and padded down the hall to her bathroom. A shower, clean clothes, and then dinner with her father. She smiled at the thought and so did the little girl inside of her.

Jesus God Jesus God Jesus God. . . . The words ran through Kyle's head like a recording caught in an endless loop. He paced and worried and tried to think, to plan. But he felt like a character in *Waiting for Godot*, hopeless and helpless, rammed up against something so much larger than himself he couldn't even imagine how to get out of it. And yet, there had to be a way out. The practice of law had taught him that much.

Kyle went into his bedroom closet, dropped to his knees, moved the shoe rack to one side. He raised a loose floorboard, exposing a small opening between the foundation of the house and the wooden planks that formed the floor. Inside was a shoebox. He lifted it out and sat back on the floor, holding the box like a kid with a favorite toy. He peeled back the masking tape and the lid popped free.

On top lay a .38, polished and bright and never used. Kyle's father had bought it for him, along with a box of ammunition, when he'd left home. He set the gun aside and dipped his fingers into the hundred dollar bills. He pressed his face into the sweet scent of money. It abraded his panic, took off the terrible, thick edge of it, and within moments, a strange calmness embraced him.

Eight grand and change in here. Enough to get him somewhere, he thought. If it came to that.

But it wouldn't come to that. It couldn't. He'd worked too hard to get through law school and signed up with a firm like Simpson & Willis. There had to be a way out; he simply hadn't thought of it yet.

Fresh scrod in an herb sauce, French bread with garlic butter, a salad with a homemade dressing, and red wine: the cuisine made her stomach growl. "You're hired," she blurted, and Morgan laughed.

"Since Melissa got sick, I've been spending more time in the kitchen. We experimented with different diets, natural foods, no preservatives or artificial color, the whole gamut. Anyway, this has been the year when my culinary talents have blossomed."

"How often do you fly to D.C.?"

"For awhile, I was practically commuting, flying back and forth on the red-eye so I could spend time with Melissa. But since she and my wife left for the clinic, I've been flying down two or three times a week, as needed." He filled her wineglass, then his own, and lifted his glass. "Toast."

"To Melissa's improved health," Taylor said. Morgan's smile shrank. "That's generous, Taylor. Considering my behavior in the past, that's incredibly generous."

"I'd like to put the past behind us, where it belongs."

Morgan looked—what? Surprised? Relieved? Happy? All of the above? Then he said, "To a new chapter in both our lives, Taylor."

They clinked glasses, sipped, and for the first time in her life, the notion of father ceased to be just a fantasy to her. Her father now sat across from her, Frank Morgan in living Technicolor.

From that point on, the evening opened up, a doorway to some enchanted place. They talked about books and movies, the law and politics, music and the symphony, his relationship with her mother and her marriage to Eric. The exchanged confidences liberated her in a way that few other things had; her life had finally come full circle.

Max drove up in her Saab around 9:45. It didn't look like the same car. It had four new tires, had been washed and waxed, and the inside had been vacuumed. "It can't be my car," she exclaimed, standing out on the sidewalk with Morgan.

"Like I said, ma'am, I have a special fondness for these cars. Yours needed an oil change in the worst way. I hope you don't mind that I took the liberty."

"Of course not. How much do I owe you?"

"Nothing, ma'am."

"C'mon, Max. Four new tires, an oil change . . . Let me pay you something."

"Don't be ridiculous," Morgan replied. "It's our pleasure."

Disarmed by their generosity, Taylor leaned forward and bussed Max on the cheek, then put her arms around Morgan and hugged him. "Thanks so much for dinner and all your help," she said softly. "It's been a wonderful evening."

"Then you'll come to the symphony with me Friday?"

"You bet. I'd love to."

She still stood on the sidewalk as the Mercedes drove away. Despite the upheavals in her life since June, she drew an almost savage comfort from her renewed relationship with her father. Somehow, it compensated for her vastly altered friendship with Cathy, the change in her feelings toward Stark, her unsettled reaction to Sessio, even the uncertainty of Eric.

21

She struggles *against the wall of blowing snow, her feet slipping and sliding, her hand clutching her mother's. But Talia can no longer see her mother, the snow falls too fast and furiously. "Mama," she calls. "Go slower, I can't see you."*

Her mother slows down, then stops. They stand at the curb, waiting for the light to change. Her mother fusses over her, buttoning her jacket, raising the collar. Talia wants desperately to bury her face in her mother's skirt, to wrap herself up inside the fabric. But her mother mutters something about the light being broken, and steps off the curb, gripping Talia's hand tightly.

Suddenly, a car races toward them and Talia's mother gasps and shoves her out of the way. She falls back, arms pinwheeling, snow flying into her face, and smacks the ground. The air abruptly clears and she sees the car clearly, a Saab flying toward her mother.

At the wheel, his face close to the windshield, is Michael Sessio.

A heartbeat later, the Saab slams into her mother, hurling her body into the air, and she screams. . . .

Taylor's eyes snapped open to moonlight and the memory of Mike Sessio's face burned into her retina. The sheets had wrapped around her legs, trapping her like a caterpillar in a cocoon. Her heart hammered, perspiration dampened her nightshirt.

She kicked off the covers, sat up, and glanced at the clock. 2:40 A.M. Her head felt fuzzy from the wine she'd had at dinner with Frank. Lady whined and leaped onto her bed, nudging her hand, begging for attention. Taylor wrapped an arm around the lab and pressed her face into the dog's fur.

Sessio, she thought. Ridiculous.

She didn't have to be Freud to figure this one out. Sessio represented the unknown, the mysterious, the dangerous. The Saab symbolized her own car. On a deeper level, it also symbolized the *vehicle* of her guilt about her mother's death, i.e., that she, the bastard child, had been the burden that ultimately killed her mother.

She sensed more than that, but couldn't decipher it at the moment. Perhaps it would come to her later.

The phone rang and she reached across Lady to answer it. "Hello?"

"Taylor, it's Mike Sessio."

Out of my dream and into the real world, she thought. It spooked her. "It's a bit late for a social call. What gives?"

"I tried you earlier, but got no answer. I didn't want to leave a message on your machine."

"I called you back yesterday, but you were in a meeting."

"I didn't get home until nearly midnight. Look, I'm at the all-night diner a couple blocks away. You know the place I mean?"

"Yes."

"Would you mind if I stopped by?"

"Let's just talk now."

"I'd rather not talk over the phone."

"Mike, it's nearly three o'clock in the morning."

"Cathy isn't home, if that's what you're worried about, Taylor."

The smoldering sexuality of his voice disturbed her at a level too deep for words. "Look, I need to go back to sleep. We'll meet tomorrow."

But it was as if she hadn't said anything. "How about if you meet me here?" he asked.

Christ, she thought. "Give me ten minutes, then come on over here."

"Got it."

He hung up and she slammed down the receiver. It irritated her that Sessio seemed to think he could invade her private space. And yet, at the same time, she felt—what? Intrigued? Secretly thrilled? Deeply attracted to him?

All of the above, none of them.

Ha.

She put on a pair of Anne Klein slacks, a pale silk blouse, soft Gucci flats, and brushed her hair back from her face, so that it fell in waves to her shoulders. She primped in front of the mirror, then abruptly stopped. No way would she primp for the likes of Sessio, she thought. She exchanged the slacks and blouse for jeans and a cotton blouse. Plain denim, plain cotton, no makeup.

When the doorbell rang, Lady barked and ran down the hall. Instead of growling or whimpering when she saw Sessio this time, the lab sniffed at his shoes, then wagged her tail and greeted him.

"The lab's stamp of approval," Sessio said with a laugh, scratching Lady behind the ears. "I guess that's a good sign."

Better than he realized, Taylor thought. "C'mon in. Coffee's on."

He looked good; but then, the way he looked had never been the problem. Tonight he wasn't wearing an Armani suit, just jeans and a blue work shirt. She wouldn't have recognized him on the street. But perhaps that was the point: Sessio traveling incognito. He toted a briefcase, though, which puzzled her, considering the time.

She felt as self-conscious as she had when Frank Morgan

had entered the apartment for the first time. But Sessio, like Morgan, merely remarked on certain items and followed her into the kitchen.

Taylor filled two mugs with coffee, which he took black, then they settled at the butcher block table next to the window. "So what's all the urgency, Mr. Sessio?"

"I really wish you'd drop the mister," he said with a smile.

She met his eyes and instantly felt a tightness in her chest, a kind of breathlessness. "Okay, Mike. What's going on?"

"A couple of things. The first part's about the prosecution's two witnesses from Providence."

"I suppose you know about them through the same source that told you about my real name."

Her bluntness seemed to surprise him. "Yes, that's right. If my source is correct, they claim they don't know each other."

He paused, waiting for her to confirm or deny this point, but she didn't, so he continued. "They're from the same union up in Providence. Worked at the same dock."

Thanks to Burt Hallas, Taylor already knew this, but acted surprised. "What else?"

"This." He picked up his briefcase, set it on the table, snapped it open, lifted the lid. He removed a folder, handed it to her. She hesitated, her hand resting on it for a moment. She felt, just then, like Pandora with her box. Once she opened this, she couldn't go back. She looked down at the folder, then glanced up at Sessio. She couldn't decipher the expression on his face.

"Go ahead," he said. "You need to know this."

She dropped her gaze again, then opened the folder. A police file, a Boston police file. Then she saw the name on it and her heart seemed to stop, her blood pressure plunged, her ears began to ring, her every movement felt trapped in a weird slow motion. She couldn't wrench her eyes from the words across the top of the page: *2/15/77, Eva Carlino: SWF, Hit & Run.*

"Dear God," she whispered, and began to read.

Time screeched to a halt, everything around her shrank, then vanished. Only the words existed, the stark, dry language that some cop had typed out nineteen years ago on a portable type-writer.

Sessio watched her as she read slowly through the thirty-six-page report. Line by line, she worked her way back through nineteen years of questions and doubts. Emotions flickered like shadows across her face, her mouth twitched, her fingers turned the pages.

He got up only once, to fill their mugs from the pot on the counter. He lingered at the window over the kitchen sink, gazing out into the August moonlight.

Some would argue, he knew, that he had no business meddling in her psyche like this. But those same people failed to understand what had taken him a lifetime to grasp. Your parents weren't simply the people who had given you life. Somewhere in the process of growing up, they became the measurement of the life you built for yourself.

He knew this as well as anyone. His father had belonged, in a very real sense, to other people—the housewives who had come up to him in cafes, begging for justice; to the bereaved, the ailing, the forlorn, all of whom had placed their hope in him, as though Joe Sessio belonged in a pantheon of gods, the mythological magician.

But on the other end of the scale, his father had been the devil's apprentice, a man who often had wielded his power with a complete absence of mercy. If you harmed his family, lied to him, betrayed his trust, or did something that he misconstrued, you bore the mark. In the grand scheme of things, ol' Joe had been seriously flawed.

As flawed as Taylor's father.

And yet, good or bad, Joe Sessio had been his father and that connection, of blood and bone, of genes and chromosomes, spoke louder than all the rest of it.

Sessio turned away from the window, walked back to the table, and set down the fresh mugs of coffee. The lab, sprawled on the floor next to the table, lifted her head, whimpered, and shut her eyes again. Somewhere in the apartment, a clock ticked.

Two witnesses reported that a dark Saab struck Eva Carlino. . . . Those words rolled across the inner screen of her eyes. At least she didn't humiliate herself by crying. She'd done enough of that over the years.

She set the police report aside and picked up several other sheets of paper—a letter to Mike from someone named Nikko and copies of various documents. Taylor frowned and read slowly and carefully through everything. Her incredulity mounted with each word, each sentence. When she finally set the papers aside, she looked up and met Sessio's eyes.

"Your father and my mother," she whispered, shaking her head. "So your father was the guy I remembered as Bob—"

"Who took you to St. Mary's," Sessio finished, his voice soft, but hoarse with emotion. "He funded your stay at St. Mary's."

Taylor ran her hands over her face, her emotions so confused, so tangled, she couldn't speak for several moments. "But it wasn't in the police report about Mom's death."

Sessio shook his head. "Even if the police had known, they wouldn't have included it in a police record."

"How long have you known?"

"Since Nikko handed me this stuff around midnight."

"You never suspected?"

"Never."

"My God," she whispered.

For long moments, neither of them spoke. Taylor finally broke the silence. "I need to know something. Did you fake that Ravigno tape?"

"No. I swear it."

The conviction in his voice, the nakedness in his eyes: she believed him. "May I keep this?"

He nodded and she ran her palm over the front of the file, a gesture like a caress, and told Sessio about the dream she'd been having when he'd called. No, she didn't just tell him;

she blurted it, blurted it detail by detail, the snow, the mal-
functioning streetlight, her mother's gasp, the Saab tearing toward her with Sessio himself behind the wheel.

He looked . . . she didn't know, she couldn't read him.

"I'm no shrink," he replied, sitting across from her. "But
even your subconscious seems to be telling you there's a connection between us, Taylor, and somehow it's all . . . I don't
know. . . ." His hands moved, as if seeking to pluck the right
phrase out of the air. "It seems to be all wound up with the
strange relationship between my father and your mother."

She winced inwardly at that, winced even though she knew
he'd hit it. "I need to give this a lot of thought, Mike."

Evasive, yes, but she didn't care. She wanted to read
through everything again, needed to dissect it free of her emotions, if she could. And she hoped that somewhere in the process the remembering plundered the deepest levels of her
being. Only then would she be healed of her past.

Sessio leaned forward, arms against the edge of the table,
parallel to it, his eyes so naked it pained her to look at him.
When he spoke, his quiet voice seemed to ring out in the
silence.

"Look, I know you don't believe it, but I'm on your side.
You're into some very heavy shit here, Taylor, with players
who can run circles around you. It's not that they're smarter
than you; they're only more experienced. This is how they
play the game. It's the only game they know. And they are
very, very good at it." He pushed to his feet then, his shoulders slumped as if to sustain an incomprehensible burden, and
managed to smile. "Thanks for the coffee."

Her hand slipped over the top of the file once more and she
nodded and remained seated. She listened to his footfalls in
the hallway, heard the tap of Lady's claws against the floor as
she followed him to the door. And suddenly she shot to her
feet and hurried after him.

"Mike, wait."

She didn't intend to put her arms around him; she only
wanted to thank him. But her body acted as if of its own
volition, arms encircling him, senses drinking in the reality of

his body pressed against hers, voice whispering, "I appreciate what you've done, Mike."

And suddenly, his mouth found hers, his hands moved across her back, the scent of him flooded her awareness. Her mouth opened against his and, locked together, they stumbled back, hands fumbling at each other's clothes, urgent yet not rushed, insistent yet not demanding. They weaved down the hall, neither of them uttering a sound, and fell back on her unmade bed.

Their clothes melted away, they rolled, the mattress creaked. His hands explored her skin as though her body were an unknown continent; she read the contours of his bones like a blind woman discovering braille for the very first time. Her obligations, her job, her career, the essentials of her daily routine, all of it ceased to exist.

She lost herself in the touch of his skin, the heat of his hands, the exquisite taste of his mouth. The pressure of his fingers inside of her brought her to the electric edge. Then he entered her, just slid inside of her as though he belonged, and nudged her over the edge.

As she slipped away, her nails dug into his back, dug deeply into the flesh that she had denied too long.

After that, she remembered nothing.

She woke sometime later to Lady whimpering in her face and Sessio curled up against her, the two of them pressed together like old spoons in a drawer. His arm lay motionless across her waist, her right leg had gone numb between his legs, she wanted him again. With Stark, she thought, she'd felt fulfilled and sated after lovemaking; but with Sessio, her emotions went well beyond that.

Taylor lay very still, eyes squeezed shut against her desire, and barely resisted the urge to stroke his arm. After a while, she extricated herself and padded, naked, across the floor to her closet. She pulled a terrycloth robe from a hanger, looked at Lady and patted her thigh. The lab rose instantly to her feet and followed Taylor out of the room, into the kitchen, and slipped out the back door when she opened it.

She glanced at the wall clock. Past nine. So what. She paused briefly at the kitchen table, ran her hand over the file, and returned to the bedroom and the forbidden pool of her desires.

Debra Gova despised this neighborhood, the poor fringe of town. Here, ice machines didn't work right, if at all, the bedsheets probably hadn't been changed since Clinton entered office. The golden arches of McDonald's loomed in front of her, symbol of America's wasteland. Christ, what the hell had brought her to this?

But she didn't stop, didn't swerve into a U-turn. She pulled into the parking lot of the cheap motel, parked on the far side, plucked a briefcase off the passenger seat. Onward and upward, she thought.

She knew Eric Serle was here; she'd called his room from her cell phone a few minutes ago just to be sure.

Debra paused outside room fourteen, glanced up and down the corridor, then rapped on the door. "Housekeeping," she said.

A moment later, the door opened. She didn't know what she'd expected Serle to look like, but it wasn't this—brawn, hair the color of straw, dangerous eyes. "You don't look like a maid," he said with a sly grin.

"That's right, Mr. Serle, I'm not. Do you have a few minutes to discuss a business proposition?"

He looked her over once, apparently decided she couldn't possibly be a threat, and opened the door wider. "Sure, c'mon in. Excuse the mess. You look familiar. Have we met before?"

"No."

The TV droned, clothes and sections of a newspaper covered one of the beds. Serle gestured to one of the faded, stained chairs next to the window. "Have a seat."

They settled on either side of the round table. Gova opened her briefcase, removed a bulging envelope. "You got a name?" Serle asked.

"Debra Gova."

Serle frowned, then snapped his fingers. "Sure, I've seen you on the local news. You're the DA."

"Very good, Mr. Serle. Have you spoken to Kyle Nelson recently?"

Something changed in his expression as pieces of the larger picture fell into place. "Nope, not in awhile. Why?"

"Well, you won't be working with him anymore. In fact, you'll be leaving this dump." She opened the envelope and brought out a leather pouch. "In here, you'll find credit cards under your new name. Once we get a good photo of you, this pouch will include a driver's license, passport, and other ID that will back up that identity. You'll be staying at a four star hotel on the harbor. Your new vehicle is there now, registered under your new name."

Serle's eyes had widened throughout her discourse. Now they narrowed and he leaned forward, his voice low, almost mocking. "Just what do I have to do to get all this?"

"Kill Taylor Brooke."

He looked incredulous, then exploded with laughter. "Well, that'll be a fucking pleasure. But Kyle said all I had to do was scare the piss outta her so she'd leave town."

"Forget what Kyle said, Mr. Serle. This has to be done within the next twenty-four hours."

"And what do I get paid for this?"

"A hundred thousand—and, of course, your new identity."

"Cash?"

"Yes."

"How much up front?"

"Twenty-five. When it's done, you'll receive the rest of the I.D. and the rest of the money. But her death has to be carried out in a particular way."

"How?"

Gova proceeded to explain, step by step, what had to happen. Serle nodded, asked a couple of questions, nodded some more. When she left half an hour later, she felt disgusted, relieved, exultant, all these emotions rolled into one tight, throbbing ball in the center of her chest.

22

At five Friday afternoon, a package arrived at Taylor's apartment with a Valentino gown inside and a note from Frank:

I COULDN'T RESIST. IT WAS MADE FOR YOU. LOVE, FRANK.

Thrilled, elated, beside herself with delight, Taylor lovingly ran her hands over the black fabric. She'd never owned anything as lovely as this and the fact that her father had picked it out made it that much more special.

When she tried it on, it fit as though it had been made with her in mind. She hurried into her bedroom to pick out the right pair of shoes, the right touch of jewelry. By eight o'clock, when Frank Morgan's black limo stopped in front of Taylor's building, she was ready.

Taylor took one last glance at herself in the mirror. She had added a string of pearls and a beautiful lace shawl that added a feminine touch to the outfit. The dress, though, had nothing to do with the salubrious glow in her face; she credited Sessio for that.

He'd wanted to see her tonight, but when she told him about her date with Frank, he said he understood and asked her to call him as soon as she got in. Just thinking about him, about the day they'd spent here in these rooms, brought a flush to her cheeks.

On her way up the hall, she picked up the envelope for Cathy, with her car key and a note inside. Cathy had left a message on her machine several hours ago, reminding her that she needed to use Taylor's car tomorrow because her car would be in the garage. She expected to leave Northampton, where she was involved in a decorating job, later this evening.

Despite the minor inconvenience for Taylor, she felt so guilty about what had happened with Mike, she would have lent the car to Cathy under almost any condition. She still had no idea how she should handle her altered relationship with Mike in terms of Cathy.

She slid the envelope under Cathy's front door, then went down the steps to greet Max, who strolled up the walk. "Hi, Max."

"Evening, Ms. Brooke. How's the Saab running?"

"The best it's run since the day I bought it."

He laughed. "Great."

"Where's Frank?"

"We've got to swing back by the house to pick him up. He was in the middle of a call with Melissa's doctor."

"How's she doing?"

"Hard to say, ma'am. She has good days and bad."

Taylor slipped into the backseat and moments later, the limo pulled away from the curb.

As they approached the Morgan mansion, Taylor saw him standing outside, beneath a streetlight, a solitary figure, almost forlorn. She guessed the news about Melissa hadn't been good.

Max pulled up to the curb and Morgan opened the back door, slid in beside her, and the limo began moving again. Morgan hugged her hello, then held her at an arm's length and remarked, "There's something different about you tonight."

Lovemaking, she thought. "Really? Different bad or good?"

He smiled. "Good, for sure. You look terrific. I'm glad the dress fits."

"It's just beautiful. Thank you. How's Melissa doing?"

He shook his head. "Not very good. The new treatment doesn't seem to be working." Then he slipped her arm through his own and patted her hand. "But let's not talk about that. Tonight's our night."

She nodded, vaguely disturbed by something she couldn't explain. She shook it off once they got to the symphony, but now and then she felt it rolling around inside of her like a loose marble.

Eric congratulated himself on his impeccable timing. On this pleasant Friday evening at the tail end of August, most of the people in Taylor's building had gone out. The sparse traffic along the road barely counted as an obstacle.

Dressed in dark coveralls and a dark baseball cap, so that he blended with the darkness, Eric moved quickly up the sidewalk, a canvas bag hanging from his shoulder. He went about his task and, fifteen minutes later, strolled up the sidewalk, whistling softly to himself.

His single regret had more to do with his ego than anything else; he wished he could confront the bitch before she died. But what the hell. For a hundred grand, he could live with it.

Kyle panicked. "What do you mean he checked out?"

"This morning, sir," replied the motel clerk, and turned the register so that Kyle could see it. "Right there." She pointed at the square for room fourteen. "Settled his account in cash, didn't leave a forwarding address."

Sweet Christ, Kyle thought. "Did he make or receive any calls before he left?"

The clerk, an aging matron with a bulbous nose riddled with broken blood vessels, smiled and shook her head. "I'm not at liberty to give out that kind of information, sir."

Kyle slipped his wallet out of his back pocket, removed a fifty, set it on the counter in front of the woman. "What were you saying?"

Her grubby little hand covered the bill, drew it toward her. She hit a couple of keys on the computer. "I remember seeing a woman at his door." Her description fit Gova.

His blood turned to ice. "Thanks for your help," he murmured, and hastened out of the lobby.

Gova and Eric: it didn't take a nuclear physicist to figure this one out. His brain urged him to drive over to her place and confront her. But his instinct for self-preservation told him to wait, to bide his time, to let Gova make the first move.

The music enveloped Taylor, intoxicated her, and ultimately whisked her away, right out of herself and into some other place. At the break, the memory of the music buoyed her, sustaining the mood as she and Morgan walked out into the lobby.

The opulence, the grandeur, seemed surreal to Taylor. She felt a part of this world, the world of the Morgans, the Sessios, and all the others like them. She glanced around the room, at the gilded, handpainted walls, at the celebrities, the politicians, the society matrons. She experienced a pang of conceit, then utter amazement, as she realized that people kept looking at her, that she was, indeed, the belle of the ball, Cinderella in the flesh. And Frank, she thought, beamed like the proud father he was.

Her mood lasted until she spotted Stark and his wife in the crowd, the two of them looking quite chummy for a couple locked in the throes of divorce. Liar, she thought, and suddenly wondered about everything he'd told her concerning Gova and "doing the right thing."

"That's John Stark, isn't it?" Morgan asked, noting her interest.

"Yes. With his wife."

"You say that oddly," Morgan remarked.

Taylor glanced at him. "I'm worried about being up against him in court."

"That's all that's worrying you." He chuckled, a soft, paternal chuckle. "You'll do fine against him, Taylor." His cell phone rang. "Excuse me, this might be Melissa's doctor."

He turned his back on her and spoke quietly into the phone. Taylor glanced at Stark once more, a quick, almost surreptitious glance, and he saw her. Zeroed in on her. He started to make his way through the crowd, toward her, when his wife joined him. Taylor turned away and walked over to Morgan just as he slipped his cell phone into his jacket pocket.

"Taylor, I hate like hell to cut our evening short, but something's come up."

"I hope it's not Melissa."

"No, just business. I'll have Max drive you home and I'll take a cab."

"I'll hail a taxi, you get going." She hugged him, then watched him vanish into the crowd.

Taylor stood there for a moment, debating about whether to go back inside for the rest of the symphony.

"Taylor?" Stark fell into step beside her. "It's not how it looks."

"And how *does* it look, John?"

"Like I'm not getting divorced."

"Frankly, I don't care one way or the other." She stopped, impaled him with her eyes. "I've realized that you can't be true to any woman. Hell, you can't even be true to yourself. And frankly, I think everything else you told me is also bullshit. Have a nice evening, John."

Outside, she hailed a cab and gave the driver Sessio's address.

Sessio wandered through the rooms, as restless as a ghost in chains. Tonight he hated this penthouse, hated its memories, its grandeur, its silence.

His employees had left for the weekend and the silence stretched through ten thousand square feet of space. In the library, dominated by the imposing portrait of his father, Sessio opened the new file that Nikko, his trusted friend, had sent by messenger only an hour ago.

It contained a listing of Monroe Morgan's corporate holdings. The one that interested him the most was Dovecote, a manufacturer of fine china that had cornered an impressive share of the market. Nikko, like Taylor, had noted that Dovecote had been incorporated officially in the same week as Sessio Shipping, and that Richard Adler had filed the papers.

A recent article in *Business Week* had estimated Dovecote's earnings last year to be around $800 million. He owned several pieces himself, including an original prototype for the famous Peace Dove, the company's logo. Monroe Morgan had given it to Joe Sessio years ago, after the election which had ushered his son into the U.S. Senate. That triumph wouldn't have happened without Joe's help in winning the union vote for Frank.

One more connection between the two men, Sessio thought, though he sensed the link went deeper.

He read through the rest of Nikko's report, searching for something he couldn't explain, but which he sensed. He became so engrossed in his search that when the doorbell rang, it seemed intrusive.

Sessio hurried through the cavernous rooms, flicking on lights, and opened the door. Taylor stood there in a stunning black gown with a black lace shawl around her shoulders, her blond hair falling to her shoulders like a river of light.

"Hi," she said. "I hope you don't mind my stopping by without calling. Frank had to—"

Sessio touched his finger to her lovely mouth. "Don't explain," he said, and drew her inside the door and kissed her.

Never in his life had he felt like this about a woman. Since he'd first touched her, she'd unlocked an insatiable hunger in him for her body, the sight of her face, the sound of her voice, the entire complex package. "Would you like a drink?" he asked. "Something to eat?"

"Water with tons of ice," she said. "And a tour."

And so he gave her the tour, leading her from room to room. He told her the stories connected with various pieces of art, including the priceless Picasso that hung in the living room, one of his father's first art purchases. He showed her the private wine collection and asked her to choose a bottle.

"I read about your Beacon Hill penthouse somewhere," she admitted, then laughed softly. "But I never thought I'd be sampling a bottle of wine from the Sessio collection."

They savored a glass during the tour, which included a swing through the library. While she stood staring at the portrait of his father, Sessio quickly shut the file he'd been reading and locked it in the bottom drawer of his desk.

They ended up in his bedroom and made love by the light of the moon. The taste of her skin, the texture of her hair, the shape of her mouth against his, the very heat of her: all of it sated his hunger, but not for long.

Afterward, they talked quietly, propped up against the pillows. They exchanged memories of their vastly different childhoods, spoke in hushed voices of their dreams, and he kept stroking her body and hair, luring her into his arms again.

At some point in the long, luxurious journey toward dawn, Taylor said, "One of us needs to tell Cathy what's going on."

"We're supposed to go out to dinner tomorrow night. I plan on telling her then. She and I have never been lovers, Taylor."

"She told me." Taylor turned on her side, touching his face as if to define it. "Look, when the trial starts in two weeks, we can't see each other."

Sessio nodded; he'd been expecting something like this. "I understand. How's your defense shaping up?"

"Better than I hoped, but I still need a miracle to get him acquitted."

"You'll find it," he said, then drew her against him and began to make love to her again.

Taylor left his penthouse about seven-thirty Saturday morning, wearing one of his blue work shirts and a pair of jeans that had belonged to a woman somewhere in his past. She carried a plastic bag that held her dress, shawl, and purse.

She felt like a teenager sneaking home after a night of forbidden pleasures and hoped that Cathy had already gone off to her appointment. She didn't want to lie about why she'd come home in a cab, wearing someone else's clothes. She needed time to mull everything over.

As the cab turned down her street, she saw her Saab at the curb at the other end. Cathy stood outside it, unlocking the door, sliding behind the wheel. "What's the address again, ma'am?" the driver asked.

"The last building on the right at the end of the block."

"Got it."

He slowed, then stopped about six yards away from the Saab. Taylor fumbled in her bag for money, trying to delay getting out of the cab until Cathy had driven away. "My money's in here somewhere," she muttered, and glanced around the cabbie's head at the Saab.

She glimpsed Cathy's face in the windshield, heard the Saab's engine turned over. Then, suddenly, the car exploded, and the explosion hurled pieces of metal and glass in every direction. Flames leaped through the clouds of gray, putrid smoke.

The driver threw the cab into reverse to escape the ball of fire, people poured out of the buildings on either side of the street. Taylor froze to the seat, unable to move or scream, unable to do anything except stare at the flaming ruin in front of her.

PART THREE

The Trial

SEPTEMBER

23

In the weeks since the explosion, Taylor Brooke had grown to detest the news—radio, TV, newspapers, it didn't matter. One seemed as bad as the other. She winced as the firm's driver turned up the volume on his radio, flooding the car with the WBZ announcer's voice.

"The trial of Tommy Washington, accused of killing union strongman, Joe Sessio, got underway Monday, despite enormous controversy. Prosecutor John Stark and defense attorney Taylor Brooke gave impassioned opening arguments, and today the prosecution will present its first witness.

"Judge Cornwell ruled against live TV coverage of the trial, citing her concern that the trial would turn into a media circus. This hasn't stopped the flocks of paparazzi from descending daily on the courthouse steps. Security is very tight around the courthouse, due in large part to the explosion of Ms. Brooke's car at the end of August. A neighbor was in the car at the time and died in that explosion.

"A large crowd of dock workers is expected outside the

courthouse again today. For the last three days, they have held a silent vigil for Joseph Sessio. The . . .''

Taylor leaned forward. "Could you turn that off, Bobby?"

"Sure thing, ma'am."

Bobby Tee had been promoted from security guard to the firm's driver and his first assignment had been to drive Taylor to and from the courthouse as long as the trial lasted. She appreciated Simpson's concern for her safety. But, quite frankly, she felt most vulnerable at night, alone with Lady in her townhouse.

She'd rented a car to use until she had the time to look around for a new one. Just to be safe, she kept it behind her building, hidden from the street. But since the explosion, she hadn't used the car much.

Frank Morgan had insisted on putting Max at her disposal and kept pestering her about moving into his mansion as a security measure until the trial ended. She'd resisted because it would mean cutting off all contact with Mike Sessio. But she'd accepted his invitation to come to the Vineyard for the weekend.

With the explosion that had ended Cathy's life and the media blitz that followed, her affair with Mike Sessio had come to a screeching halt. Even though they still talked daily by phone, neither of them could risk exposure.

Sessio's standing with the dock workers would suffer irreparable damage if it got out that he was romantically involved with the woman defending his father's alleged killer. The consequences for her would be even worse.

She touched the emerald and diamond heart pendant Sessio had sent her. Inscribed inside were the words: YOU ARE ALWAYS IN MY THOUGHTS.

A goddamn mess, she thought, all of it. This case had cost the life of her friend, possible exposure of her past, and could end up costing her a job she loved. Meanwhile, Eric still roamed the streets of Boston and the clock ticked relentlessly, marking the time that stood between Tommy Washington and the jury's verdict.

Bobby Tee drove past the courthouse, where the media vultures gathered like gawkers at an ancient Roman game.

"Looks worse than yesterday," Bobby remarked. "I'll try the rear entrance."

She doubted it would be much better. She slipped on her sunglasses, snapped her briefcase shut, and braced herself for the dash into the courthouse. The vultures, of course, had spotted the car and some of them managed to reach the rear entrance before she did, joining forces with the predators who had guessed where she would enter.

"When you're ready, buzz me on your cell phone and I'll pick you up at the side entrance," Bobby said.

"Thanks, I appreciate it."

The vultures closed in on her as soon as she got out, all of them shouting questions and shoving mikes in her face.

"Ms. Brooke, do you have anything to say about—"

"What do you think of—"

"Ms. Brooke, what about—"

"How will you—"

The cacophony of their shouts rose around her, a wave that threatened to crush her. Then she ducked into the courthouse and the din fell away from her.

She spotted Stark at the other end of the lobby, speaking to Gova and one of the other prosecutors. Just beyond them stood Mike Sessio.

He saw Taylor and made a beeline toward her. For a terrible moment, they simply looked at each other, circumstances looming between them, an invisible wall. Then he smiled. "Jesus, I miss you. I hate not being able to touch you, Taylor."

"Gova would have you drawn and quartered if she heard you say that."

"Any way we can see each other?"

"How?" She felt as helpless and frustrated as she sounded. "It's too dangerous. Tomorrow or Saturday I'm going up to the Vineyard to stay the weekend with Frank."

"It'll do you good to get away. But I wish it were with me."

"Me, too." She nearly reached for his hand, but caught herself before she could. "Someone's going to see us talking."

"Here, take this." His hand came out of his jacket pocket and pressed an envelope into her hand. "It'll blow their witness out of the water."

Without another word, he turned away and Taylor dropped the envelope into her purse, then went into the ladies' room. She locked herself in a stall, tore open the envelope, and read Sessio's note. It nearly shot her into orbit. How had he gotten this bit of information? Through whom? His sources on the streets?

Yes, maybe.

Her head spun, her hands trembled as she tore the note into tiny pieces and flushed it down the toilet. She hurried out of the stall, the smell of triumph thick in her nostrils.

Sal Ravigno didn't look like a thug, at least not today. He obviously had been coached about how to dress and act in court—his neatly trimmed hair combed back, his jacket and slacks spotless, his nails clean. He took the stand with the assured confidence of a man who knew exactly what questions he would be asked and how he would respond.

Stark strolled up to the stand with the same sort of confidence. "Mr. Ravigno, I'd like you to tell the court about your relationship with the accused, Tommy Washington."

Ravigno didn't look toward Washington; he kept his eyes on Stark. "I know him because I've bought crack from him a few times on this corner over in Roxbury. On the evening of May twentieth, I was on my way home from work and I saw him hanging on the corner, so I stopped to buy a couple hits from him."

Tommy leaned toward Taylor and whispered. "He's lyin'. I never seen him before."

"Let him finish. Then it'll be our turn," she whispered back.

"And what happened during the course of this sale, Mr. Ravigno?" asked Stark.

Ravigno, unflustered, crossed his legs at the knees. "He was real high at the time and started talking about how he was going to off Joseph Sessio. I asked him why he'd want to do that and he says, 'Ain't my idea, dude. You wouldn't believe who I'm doin' it for. . . . ' Those were his exact words.''

Murmurs rippled through the courtroom. Judge Cornwell tapped her gavel and the murmurs faded away. Kyle leaned toward Taylor. "You should've objected to that. The witness drew a conclusion about Tommy being high."

Taylor merely nodded. Kyle, exasperated, sat back. Taylor glanced at Gova, who hung on Stark's every word, her eyes narrowed, intense.

"And what happened after Tommy Washington said this to you, Mr. Ravigno?''

"I asked him how he was going to off a dude like Joe Sessio. And he said he was going to do it when Sessio was having lunch at the restaurant where he bussed tables. He said he was getting paid five grand to do it."

More murmurs, another, more insistent tap of the gavel. Stark waited until the murmurs died down, then looked pointedly at Taylor. "Your witness."

Taylor stood and strolled up to the witness stand. She felt the jury watching her, appraising her, felt the chill of Gova's gaze, the warmth of Sessio's eyes. Her body had become a surface that emotions struck like missiles.

"You said it was the evening of May twentieth when you bought crack from Tommy Washington, is that correct, Mr. Ravigno?''

Those surly eyes fixed on her. "Yes, ma'am. That's right.''

"About what time in the evening would you say that was?''

"Around six-thirty, seven," he replied without hesitation.

Sloppy, Stark, very sloppy, she thought. "Really. I'm a little unclear on how that could be, Mr. Ravigno. Mr. Washington works from eleven A.M. to seven P.M. At the quickest, it would take him at least fifteen minutes to get to Roxbury. Perhaps you'd like to rethink the time?''

Stark shot to his feet. "Objection, Your Honor. The defense is assuming the accused worked those hours on May twentieth.''

"Ms. Brooke?'' asked Judge Cornwell.

Taylor returned to the defense table and removed an envelope from her briefcase. "I'm submitting Tommy Washington's time cards for the month of May as defense exhibit eighteen, Your Honor. On May twentieth, he punched in an ten fifty-eight A.M. and punched out at seven oh two."

She handed the envelope to the judge, then turned her attention back to Ravigno. He didn't look quite as self-confident now. "So tell me again, Mr. Ravigno, about what time you bought crack from Tommy Washington."

His eyes darted to Gova, then he said, "Six thirty or seven, maybe a little later."

"How much later might it have been, Mr. Ravigno?"

"I don't know exactly. But it was still light out."

"On the evening of May twentieth, between the hours of six and eight P.M., you were with a prostitute in Roxbury, isn't that right?"

The courtroom erupted with noise and Stark shot to his feet again. "Objection, Your Honor. The defense is badgering the witness."

"Approach the bench, counselors."

Stark and Taylor came forward. She felt certain now that Stark had been in Gova's court since the beginning, that he'd set her up all along. The judge removed her glasses, revealing eyes like chips of dry ice. "Do you have proof of that, Ms. Brooke? Or are you shooting in the dark?"

"I have a witness who will testify if need be."

"A witness who wasn't on the list, Your Honor," Stark said stiffly.

"Because she just came forward," Taylor replied without looking at him.

"Then proceed with your questioning, Ms. Brooke."

They moved away from the bench and the judge said, "Repeat your question, Ms. Brooke."

"Were you with a prostitute between six and eight on the evening of May twentieth, Mr. Ravigno?"

"I . . . I . . ." Blood had drained from his face.

"A simple yes or no, Mr. Ravigno," said the judge.

"Y-yes," he said softly.

"I have no further questions, Your Honor."

This turn of events sent Gova into a tailspin. As noise raced through the courtroom, Gova and Stark consulted frantically; she looked to be on the verge of a stroke. The judge slammed her gavel, an uneasy hush descended over the room, and Stark got to his feet. "Your Honor, we'd like a recess."

She brought the gavel down hard. "This court is adjourned until Tuesday morning. I'd like the defense and the prosecution teams to meet in my chambers immediately."

Correct me if I'm wrong, Ms. Gova. But Sal Ravigno's original statement led to the accused's arrest, isn't that right?" the judge snapped.

Gova, visibly rattled, said: "Yes, Your Honor. But we have two other witnesses who corroborate his story."

"Then let's hope they aren't as confused as Mr. Ravigno. Frankly, counselor, it looks as if you haven't done your homework and that the trial date may have been premature for the prosecution."

"Not at all," Gova said quickly.

Judge Cornwell regarded Kyle, Stark, and Taylor. "From now on, any exhibits or witnesses that aren't already included in the list will have to be discussed with me before they're presented. Are we clear on that, counselors?"

They nodded in unison.

"Great," Cornwell said. "See you tomorrow morning at nine sharp."

Once they left the courtroom, Gova fell into step alongside Taylor. "Nicely done. That's quite a trick to pull out of your hat. Too bad it won't make a difference in the long run."

Taylor noted her outfit, the touch of makeup, the gold bracelet she wore. Even Gova attempted to look feminine for court. "What worked for you in June, Ms. Gova, doesn't work now. See you in court tomorrow."

Kyle caught up with her before she walked outside. "What'd Gova say?" he asked.

"Not much. She's just trying her ole 'psych out the opposition' routine."

"That was some wrench you threw into things, Taylor. But how come I didn't know about it?"

"Because I just found out this morning."

Kyle nodded, but didn't look convinced. "So how about if we go back to the office and prepare for tomorrow?"

"We're on track, Kyle, don't worry about it."

"Who's this mysterious witness?"

"I'd rather not say."

Kyle looked at her strangely. "Christ, Taylor, I'm the assistant defense attorney on this."

"Yes, you are. And God forbid that any of the things that have happened to me in the last few weeks should happen to you or the people you care about. I'm just trying to protect you."

"But Simpson . . ."

"Simpson appointed *me*. And right now, I'm calling the shots."

He looked so stricken, she reached out impulsively and squeezed his hand. "Hey, trust me, okay?"

As she hurried to the side door, she brought out her cell phone and called Bobby Tee. A few minutes later, she escaped into the autumn sunlight. She didn't see the firm's car, but spotted a maroon Cherokee Jeep coming around the corner, Bobby Tee waving at her. She ran over to the passenger side, hopped in, and laughed.

"Great idea. Whose car is it?"

"My daughter's." He grinned at her. "I figured it'd make it harder for them to spot you." As they passed the front of the courthouse, he gestured at the crush of media people surrounding Mike Sessio. "He needs something like this, Mr. Sessio does. Work? Home? What's your pleasure, ma'am?"

Her gaze settled briefly on Sessio. "Home." Home where she would barricade herself inside and consider the possible ramifications if she filed an affidavit citing wrongdoing by the prosecution. And while she considered it, she seized a perverse pleasure at the thought of the shit hitting the fan for Stark and Gova.

Gova paced back and forth across her living room, her head pounding, her stomach knotted. How the hell had things gotten so messed up?

Eric Serle had killed the wrong woman, Ravigno had been discredited as a witness, Taylor seemed to have cut Kyle off completely, and no telling what sort of stunt Stark might pull next. She needed help badly—and she needed it now.

She punched out his number, but hung up before anyone answered. He wouldn't help at this point; the decision about where to go next rested solely with her. Then she changed her mind and called his number again.

"It's bad," she said without preface.

"It's never that bad."

"Ha," she replied, and proceeded to explain.

The subsequent silence stretched like an elastic band, then popped when he spoke. "Ravigno has to be eliminated, that's fairly obvious. Get Eric Serle on it. He owes us."

"He's a wild card."

"At this point, I think Kyle is the true wild card."

"I'm not going to pay *him* to do it."

"I'm not suggesting that you should."

"Then what the hell *are* you suggesting?"

He told her, outlined his plan simply, brilliantly. But as soon as they'd hung up, her doubts crept back. Was it worth it? she wondered. Was any of this worth it?

She didn't know. She realized she'd lost sight of the goal and, for that matter, couldn't even remember what the hell it had been.

Taylor spent most of the afternoon down by the river with Lady. While the dog frolicked, she went through her notes on the case and reviewed her tactics for tomorrow Up until today in court, she'd figured Stark would call the boys from Providence next. But given the holes she'd blown in Ravigno as a witness, perhaps he would focus on some of the other witnesses.

She glanced at the witness sheet and tried to put herself in Stark's head. At the peak of their relationship, that had been relatively easy for her to do; now she couldn't second guess him.

Put yourself in his shoes, she thought. *What would I do?*

Easy. She would focus on building the evidence against Tommy Washington. She would have some sort of visual time line for the jury to see that would fix the events in their minds: when Joe Sessio had sat down for lunch, when the hit occurred, when Washington had been arrested.

Stark's best move for tomorrow, she decided, would be to put Detective Schultz on the stand, as well as the busboy who'd identified him for the arresting officers. But then what? She didn't know. She would have to wing it.

If the defense could present their case first, she mused, she would call DeCiccio simply because he had seen a black man using the public phone in the kitchen shortly before Joe Sessio had been shot.

Taylor lay back on the grass, an arm over her eyes, and moved the many pieces around in her mind, trying to make them fit. Even if she won an acquittal for Washington, the real question remained: who ordered the hit on Joe Sessio?

Stark would say that Mike Sessio had ordered it. But neither he nor Gova had been able to gather enough evidence to indict Sessio. And yet, Wilbur Cane and Gerald Maltais hailed from a union in Providence; Mike would have the clout to get them to Boston and definitely had the money to pay them to make incriminating statements against Washington.

Her heart said no, but her head insisted it was logical. What better way to win what you wanted than to seduce the defense attorney?

But then why had he given her the tip on the hooker? Why had he given her the tape of Ravigno admitting that he knew Washington didn't shoot anyone. *"I know for a fact that the whole thing was set up to make it look like he did it."*

She rubbed her hands over her face, trying to bury the memory of Sessio's hands, his mouth, the heat of his body.

He couldn't make love to her the way that he had if he were guilty, she thought.

Stark would call her naive for a thought like that. Hell, maybe he was right.

Only three people had known about the tape—the man who'd recorded it, Sessio, and Kyle.

This brought her back to her the conclusion she'd made before she and Sessio had become lovers: that he'd used the tape to plant doubt in her mind, then had stolen it back, which explained why he'd never made a copy.

Kyle, on the other hand, seemed damned unlikely, except that he'd withheld vital information from her about tracking down Eric. But why would Kyle work against her? What possible motive could he have? She pulled her cell phone out of her briefcase and called Burt Hallas's number.

"Hallas here."

"Burt, hi, it's Taylor Brooke."

"I was just thinking of you. Saw the fracas outside the courthouse today."

"Yeah, it's been ridiculous. Listen, I was wondering if you can do something for me."

"Shoot."

"You remember that bondsman you mentioned up in Fall River? Gerald Tower?"

"Sure thing. What about him?"

"I'd like to know who bailed Eric Serle out of jail. I think it may be related to the Washington case. Do you think you can find out something like that?"

"Depends."

"On what?"

"Whether you're talking about a finding it out on the up-and-up or in some other way."

"Your call, Burt. I just don't want anyone to get hurt. All I need is the information."

"No problem. I'll do my best. This being a weekend and all, I should be able to get you something by Sunday at the latest. Where can I contact you?"

"My cell phone or this number on the Vineyard," she replied, and ticked off Morgan's number.

It probably wouldn't win an acquittal for Washington, she thought. At the very least, though, it would settle her doubts about Kyle one way or the other.

24

Eric had been waiting for his chance ever since he'd seen Taylor and her dog head off toward the river. So now he climbed through an open window of her townhouse. The alarm system either didn't extend to screens or it didn't work because she'd left the window open.

He simply raised the kitchen screen, with his handkerchief between his fingers and the edge of the metal, and crawled in over the kitchen sink. The scent of her struck him immediately, a faint hint of perfume, something far more expensive than when he'd known her. He also caught a fragrance of shampoo, soap, and dog.

He removed his sneakers, tied them to his belt, then pulled out a pair of latex gloves, which he worked onto his hands. He padded across her kitchen floor in his stocking feet and kept inhaling the air that she breathed, as though the act would somehow bring her closer.

Eric paused in the kitchen doorway, glanced out into the living room. He barely noticed the furnishings, the decorations; none of that interested him. He headed down the hall to her bedroom. It would be the heart of her, filled with the mystery of Taylor, of who she had been and who she had become.

He stepped into her bedroom and drank in everything in sight—the four poster mahogany bed, the rocker near the window, the chest of drawers with four small, framed photos lined up across the middle of it. Her scent seemed most powerful here, overwhelmingly thick, as if she'd sprayed her perfume into the air before she'd left or rubbed aromatic oils into the pillows.

Eric crossed the room, looked at the photos on her dresser. Taylor had labeled each one: MOM & ME, THE YR. SHE DIED; LAW SCHOOL GRADUATION; CATHY & ME, WHARF; MOM & DAD, AROUND 1965.

Dad? What dad? She'd always told him her father had abandoned her mother when she'd gotten pregnant, that she didn't even know his name. Eric picked up the black and white photo and carried it over to the window, where the late afternoon light fell through the glass.

The grainy images, the yellowing at the edges of the photo: this sucker looked old, all right. The woman bore a definite resemblance to Taylor, but interested him less than the man.

Eric looked more closely at the man, rubbed his thumb over his face to clear away a fine skin of dust. He recognized this guy.

Senator Frank Morgan, minus about thirty years, fifteen pounds slimmer, and no gray hair.

Taylor, the illegitimate daughter of a senator.

It explained the limo he'd seen. It explained the odd silences that had often greeted his questions about the father she'd claimed she'd never known. It also might explain a great many other things.

Eric set the photo back on the chest of drawers, went over to her dresser, opened a drawer. Just a quick look, he thought. He couldn't be sure when she would be back and didn't want to be here when she returned. On the other hand, he intended to leave behind a momento.

He thrust his hands into a hill of softness. Slips, panties, bras, nightgowns, and T-shirts slipped like water through his fingers, over the sides of his hands. He buried his face in the fabrics, inhaling the sweet, feminine scent of Taylor.

Memories flashed through him, each one brilliant and vivid. They seized his heart, squeezing it dry, then suffused him with such rage that he hurled the lingerie across the room and plunged his hands into the next drawer and the next.

Bitch, bitch, bitch: the word charged through him, fueling his rage, feeding it until only the rage existed, a demon that rode him, that sucked away everything else inside of him. His rage, now distilled to its purest form, filled him like some explosive fuel and then ignited.

At some point, he stumbled back, breathing hard, sweat pouring down his face, his Eddie Bauer hunting knife clutched in his hand. He couldn't remember pulling out the knife, but it felt like an extension of his hand, hard and powerful. He spun, eyes flicking around the room, seeking something else to destroy.

The closet.

Bitch bitch bitch . . .

Eric flew over to the closet, jerked the door open, and went after her clothes with the same unmitigated rage that had driven him moments ago. He ransacked the shoeboxes, throwing shoes over his shoulders, stabbing at a pair of leather pumps.

He wrenched open a drawer of the nightstand, dumped the contents on the floor, and pawed through them. Letters. Love letters? He cut through the string that bound them, tore open one of them. His eyes dropped to the signature at the bottom of the first letter: *Best, Frank Morgan.*

"Daddy dearest," he spat, and stuffed the letters in the pockets of his windbreaker.

He stabbed her pillows until feathers bled out of them. He tore the quilt off her bed, plunged the blade into the mattress, slit it open down the middle. He grabbed the wooden rocking chair near the window and threw it across the room. It struck a floor lamp, knocking it over, and slammed into the wall. Splinters of wood flew away from it.

Then he grabbed the corner of the quilt, pressed his face into it, drinking in the smells of her again, and unzipped his jeans.

Mike Sessio understood the risk, but he needed to see her, to talk to her in person, to touch her, hold her. His hunger for her had grown like a tumor inside of him these past weeks. He just couldn't imagine waiting until the trial ended.

As he hurried up the sidewalk, he glanced uneasily toward Cathy's apartment, empty now, a FOR RENT sign already in the front window. He felt guilt and a deep, unrelenting regret about Cathy. He'd used her to get closer to Taylor, then discovered that if it hadn't been for Taylor, he might have grown to love her.

In the dusky light, the glass offered an imperfect reflection of the street and the trees that lined it. The absence of Taylor's car at the curb struck him as an uncanny parallel to the vacant apartment where Cathy had lived. Even though he knew Taylor now parked her car elsewhere, it disturbed him nonetheless.

In the moment before he looked away from Cathy's apartment, he imagined that he saw her face, pressed up against the glass, smiling at him. Maudlin, he thought, and rang Taylor's doorbell.

He heard its peal inside, but didn't hear Lady barking. He turned, glanced up and down the street. Maybe they'd gone running. He debated driving along the river until he spotted her, then decided to check behind the building first to see if she'd left her car there.

Sessio went around the side of the building. As she reached the back, he saw a man scrambling out of Taylor's kitchen window. "Hey, you!" he shouted.

The man's head snapped around, his homicidal eyes locked briefly with Sessio's, and in a moment of blinding clarity, Sessio recognized him. Serle, Eric Serle.

Serle spun around and took off at a crisp clip across the grass. Sessio ran after him, arms pumping at his sides, legs eating up the distance between them. Adrenaline rushed through him and suddenly everything in him opened wide and he hurled himself at Serle.

Sessio slammed into him, tackling him at the knees, and

they crashed to the ground. Serle's strength astonished him, arms like lead pipes, legs as solid as cement pillars, his fists as hard and compact as bowling balls. Sessio clung to him, trying to gain an advantageous position, but Serle sank those fists into his ribs, pummeled his kidneys, and finally got his hands around Sessio's throat and pressed so hard against his Adam's apple that he cut off Sessio's air.

Stars exploded inside Sessio's eyes, his peripheral vision blurred, his brain shrieked for oxygen. Then, somehow, he managed to jackknife one of his legs and drove his knee into Serle's groin. Serle gasped, his grip loosened on Sessio's throat, air rushed back into his lungs, and the world snapped into clarity.

Sessio grabbed Serle's hair, jerked his head back, and Serle grunted, snorted, raged like a stuck bull, and tried to seize his throat again. They rolled across the grass and through a flower bed, struggling now on their sides, Sessio's bent legs between them.

Sessio caught the glint of a blade in the waning light and realized Serle had pulled a hunting knife. Every instinct inside of him slammed into gear and reservoirs of strength he didn't know he had suddenly rushed through him. His legs snapped open, his shoes struck Serle's hard, flat stomach, and Sessio threw him off.

He scrambled to his feet and Serle shot after him, screeching like a banshee, the knife raised, his face burning with rage. Sessio scooped up a handful of dirt from the flower bed and hurled it. The stuff struck Serle in the face and he howled and stumbled back, clawing at his eyes.

Sessio charged him, charged when he should have run in the other direction as fast as he could. His body slammed into Serle's, knocking him sideways, but not before the edge of the knife slashed across Sessio's forearm. It felt like a hot poker burning a path across his skin. Blood streamed out of the gash and kept streaming as he swept up a large rock and threw it.

The rock grazed Serle's temple, he stumbled, and then he ran like a man fleeing his own perdition, his powerful legs carrying him away at the speed of light. Sessio stood there for a moment, everything inside of him screaming to give chase, to follow the fucker. Then his knees buckled and he sank to the ground clutching his wounded arm, the stink of his own blood suffusing the twilight, nauseating him. A burning pain lit up his right side and he realized he had at least one cracked rib.

He finally looked down at his arm, at the blood seeping through his fingers. He fumbled for a handkerchief and wrapped it around the gash to stem the flow of blood. Cell phone, he thought. Get to the cell phone in the car.

As he stood, he gasped at the stab in his side. His head spun. He steadied himself, clutched his wounded arm to his side, then weaved through the twilight, stumbled across the sidewalk, and nearly collapsed against his car.

Keys, he needed his keys. Right pocket, he thought. Good. Insert key in lock. Open door. Cell phone. 9-1-1. When someone on the other end picked up, he muttered Taylor's address, then disconnected and crawled into the front seat of his car. And there he passed out.

Dark pockets of shadows suffused her street as Taylor returned from her day by the river. Then she saw the paramedic truck, she flashed on the explosion that had killed Cathy.

She swerved to the curb, slammed on the brakes, and leaped out of the Saab, Lady bounding along behind her.

She ran toward the paramedic truck, barely noticing the people who had gathered at windows and doorways. She stopped at the rear of the truck and her heart nearly seized up with horror.

Sessio sat at the edge of a stretcher, his face pale and wan. A paramedic was wrapping his midriff; the upper part of his right arm was also bandaged. "Mike, my God, what—"

At the sound of her voice, his head rolled and he looked at her, his face as pale as a rising new moon. "Bastard tried to grab my wallet. . . ." he murmured.

"Hold still, sir," said the paramedic. "I'm nearly done. I wish you'd reconsider and have your ribs X-rayed. . . ."

"I'm fine," Sessio murmured.

"My partner took the liberty of calling the police to report the assault. They'll be along shortly."

More publicity, she thought. And just the kind neither of them needed right now. She knew by Sessio's expression that the same thing ran through his mind and that he didn't feel any happier about it than she did.

Sessio watched as the paramedic finished wrapping him up and filled out a form. Then he got out of the vehicle and the two of them walked over to Sessio's car, out of hearing range.

"What the hell really happened?" she asked softly. "What were you doing over in this neighborhood?"

"I just wanted to see you," he replied, then told her everything. "It was Eric. I caught him climbing out your kitchen window. We—"

His name froze at the back of her throat. She couldn't spit it out. "I . . . how . . . how do you know what he looks like?"

Sessio shrugged. "The same way I got the file on your mother."

"I have a security alarm inside the apartment."

"Which probably doesn't work on an open window."

She rubbed a hand over her face, then glanced toward the apartment, a ball of dread rising in her chest. "I . . . what're you going to tell the cops?"

"The same thing I told the paramedics. I'd parked here to walk along the river and this guy came up behind me, grabbed my wallet, and I ran after him. He cut me, end of story."

"The end unless they realize I live here."

"And what the hell are they going to do about it? Question you? I doubt it. Grab Lady and go on inside."

The ball of dread had moved into her throat. She glanced toward the apartment again, looked at Sessio. "You're sure he ran away?"

"Positive. I'll be up as soon as the police leave." He squeezed her hand, then she whistled for Lady and headed for the townhouse.

Fear seized her as she slipped the key into the lock. She swallowed it back, pushed the door open with her foot, and Lady trotted in snout to the floor. Taylor hesitated in the doorway, waiting to see if the lab growled. When she didn't, Taylor finally entered the apartment.

Forty minutes later, Sessio rang Taylor's doorbell, then turned the knob and stepped inside. "Taylor?"

"Back here," she called.

He found her in the bedroom, stuffing clothes into a suitcase, surrounded by an unimaginable ruin. Her movements stirred the feathers that seemed to cover everything. Drawers lolled like tongues from the dresser and the nightstand, clothes and personal belongings spilling out of them. He stepped over a shoe that had been sliced to ribbons. He kicked aside a pillow bleeding feathers and stuffing. He picked up the pieces of a shattered ceramic figurine and paused at the foot of the bed.

A wet stain soiled the middle of the sheet. It and the expression on Taylor's face told him everything he needed to know about what Eric had done here.

"Jesus, Taylor," he whispered, and touched her shoulders.

She wrenched away and spun around, tears spilling down her cheeks, trailing smudges of mascara. "Leave me alone, don't touch me."

"Hey, sorry." He held up his hands, stepped back, and suddenly translated the look in her eyes. "You think *I* did this? You think I crawled through the kitchen window and did *this?* Christ almighty, Taylor."

"I don't know what to think anymore, okay? I don't know who the hell to trust. You have some detective gather information on me, find out who my friends are, then you show up in Cathy's life. You feed me information, bring me the police file on my mother, become my . . . lover, then . . . you claim you saw Eric, fought with him, that he cut you, that . . . Aw, screw it."

She swept past him to her closet, jerked a dress off a hanger, scooped T-shirts and jeans off the floor, and shoved everything into the bag. Sessio, shocked into silence, stood there and watched her, his heart breaking piece by pitiful piece.

Finally, he said, "It started because I knew I had information that could make a difference in Tommy Washington's trial. But once I met you, I was . . . fascinated by you. I wanted to know everything about you. I—''

''And you've always used your wealth and your power to get what you want,'' she finished.

''You make it sound dirty, Taylor. I never promised Cathy anything, I never slept with her, I never took advantage of her. I liked her and we enjoyed each other's company.''

''But you befriended her because she lived next door to *me*.''

''Yes, I did.''

She seemed surprised that he admitted it. ''And now she's dead.''

''I'm not responsible for that.'' His voice rose sharply and he immediately regretted it.

''I know.'' Tears rushed into her eyes again. ''I'm responsible.'' She slung her bag over her shoulder. ''I need to get out of here.'' She hurried past him, into the hall, and whistled for Lady.

Sessio caught up with her in the kitchen, where she loaded dog food into a paper bag and snapped Lady's leash to her collar. She reached across the sink, shut and locked the window. She glanced at him, said nothing, continued into the living room. She picked up her briefcase, took a final, slow look around, and turned on the alarm system. She opened the door and motioned it.

''After you,'' she said.

He walked past her and didn't look back.

For an hour, she drove aimlessly, music issuing from the radio, Lady ensconced in the passenger seat, her head stuck out the window. She felt torn up inside, as if some monster tractor had run amok across the fields of her heart.

Questions roared through her skull, each one more difficult to answer than its predecessor. How well did she really know Sessio, anyway? Could she say with any certainty that he hadn't set her up for something, just as Stark had? But could he be capable of the savagery she'd seen in her apartment? Of the rage?

The rage, she thought, smacked of Eric. But the manipulation, the intricate machinations, the emotional games: what the hell did all that add up to? Was this the sum total of Michael Sessio?

Who could she trust? The question rolled around in her head, begging for an answer.

A few minutes later, she realized where she'd driven. She pulled up to the gate, left her engine running, and got out to ring the intercom. "May I help you?" asked a female voice.

"Is Senator Morgan in?"

"Who may I say is calling?"

"His daughter," Taylor replied.

25

Taylor Brooke and her father settled in the dining room, just the two of them at a long table that probably seated two dozen. A virtual feast had been laid out—spicy duck soup, a rack of lamb, piping hot French bread, some sort of vegetable soufflé.

Max served everything with the stiff courtesy of an Englishman, stiff except for the full apron he wore that had a red, grinning devil on it. His mood seemed distinctly British as well, pleasant but circumspect. He did, however, set a bowl filled with sliced lamb on the floor in front of Lady and she gobbled it up, then sprawled on the floor next to the table, and promptly fell asleep.

Taylor picked at her food, tried to make small talk and failed. Frank Morgan apparently noticed it, because he finally said, ''What is it, Taylor? The trial?''

''In part, I guess.''

''According to the news, you scored some points today.''

''Only because the prosecution was sloppy. I'm going to file an affidavit of wrongdoing over the weekend.''

"You *are*? For what?"

"A number of things."

"Is that wise?"

"I think it's my only recourse at this point." She didn't want to talk about it and changed the subject. "Actually, I'm looking forward to coming up to the Vineyard this weekend."

"Max can pick you up whenever it's convenient for you. He'll take you to the airport and my pilot will fly you over."

His driver, his plane, his wealth and power. This heady stuff seduced that part of her which had grown up dirt poor and needy. But another part of her wanted something simpler: could she sleep here tonight?

"My townhouse was broken into," she blurted. "I . . . I think it was Eric who did it. My drawers were ripped out, my clothes thrown around, my mattress and pillows were sliced to shreds, my . . ."

To her utter horror, she started to cry, then to sob, and pressed her hands to her face, trying to stifle it. But she couldn't stop. Her emotions seemed to twist in on themselves, excessive, dark, dangerous, leading her into areas of her past that had nothing to do with this particular moment.

Morgan suddenly moved to her side and smoothed his hand over her hair, patted her shoulder, drew her head against him. "It's okay," he repeated softly, again and again. "You'll stay here tonight, Taylor. And tomorrow Max will drive you to the courthouse, pick you up, and get you and Lady to the Vineyard. We'll have a wonderful weekend. There's so much to show you. . . ."

She surrendered herself to the sound of his voice and the touch of his hand against her hair. She allowed herself to be comforted and reassured and after a few minutes, she felt better. Not great, but definitely better.

"I'm sorry, I didn't mean to dump on you like this."

"Don't be ridiculous. You're not dumping on me. C'mon, let's go have coffee in the library."

He whistled for Lady and the lab heaved herself to her feet and followed them through the cavernous house to the library. Her claws clicked against the floors. A clock somewhere in the house chimed nine. Taylor realized she felt cold. The first hint of autumn embraced the darkness outside and seeped into the mansion.

In the library, a fire roared in the fireplace, twigs crackling, hissing, sending up plumes of smoke. Taylor and Morgan pulled chairs over in front of the fireplace, Lady collapsed between them, and Max brought in mugs of strong coffee and a bottle of Grand Marnier. Morgan splashed some into their coffee, then Max left.

The flames leaped and crackled and the fire's warmth finally penetrated the chill lodged in the center of her. She wanted to curl up in the chair and sleep. She wanted to forget about court, about her suspicions concerning Kyle and Stark, Gova and Sessio, about what had happened to her apartment.

But Morgan began to talk about his relationship with her mother, how difficult and yet intoxicating it had been and how he'd carried his guilt for all these years over the way he'd treated her—and Taylor. She closed her eyes as he spoke and tried to conjure her mother's face, the face of the woman he described so eloquently. She saw the Saab racing toward her mother that snowy day nineteen years ago. She heard the sickening thud as the car had struck her mother.

Perhaps she dozed, perhaps she only thought that she did. But suddenly, she snapped into full awareness and realized Morgan had fallen into a strange silence. Taylor looked over at him, at his profile against the bright, lambent firelight. On impulse, she recited several lines of the Byron poem her mother used to read her. " 'And all that's best of dark and light, meet in her aspect and her eyes.' "

Morgan looked at her. "That's beautiful," he said softly.

"Byron. 'She Walks in Beauty.' My mother used to read me that sometimes at night."

An air of silence fell between them. Then she changed the subject. "I'm curious, Frank. What was the nature of your father's friendship with Joe Sessio?"

He turned his head slowly, like a man in a dream, and said, "What?"

Taylor repeated her question. Morgan sipped from his mug of coffee and turned his eyes back to the fire. Several moments passed before he replied. "Joe Sessio was like Dad's wild side, what he would have been if he'd cut loose. And Dad was Joe's disciplined side. They complemented each other, I guess that's the best way to describe it. Why?''

''There're some curious parallels between their lives.''

''Like what?''

''Richard Adler, for one. I found it curious that twenty-years ago, Adler filed incorporation papers for Sessio Shipping and Dovecote within three days of each other.''

''Sessio Shipping has always been Mike's company, not Joe's.''

''But it's the same family. Then their funerals botched up traffic on the same day. It's like they were karmicly linked or something.''

''Karmicly?''

Taylor raised her hand from the armrest. ''You know, past-life stuff.''

''You believe in that?'' He seemed genuinely interested.

She opened her arms, a gesture that encompassed not just the room, but the entire physical universe. ''You think this is all there is?''

He glanced back at the fire. ''I really don't think about it one way or another.'' Then, more softly, he said, ''Given Melissa's condition, I'd rather not think about death at all.''

Taylor nodded, but she didn't really understand what he meant. If anything, his response should have been that Melissa's illness had precipitated exactly these kinds of questions. Even if you didn't buy into past lives, any man in Morgan's position should be questioning the ultimate meaning of existence. Did he have religious convictions? Did he attend a church? She didn't know, but felt good that she would finally have a chance to find out.

''How do you find time to oversee Dovecote, plus be a senator, a husband, and a father?''

He thought a moment, then laughed. ''These days, I don't seem to be anything very well. I'm just getting by.''

Taylor reached across the small distance that separated them and squeezed his hand. ''I think you're doing great,'' she said softly.

''You don't realize how much having you here means to

me.'' For a moment, he clung to her hand like a drowning man, then got up to refill their mugs.

To Eric, Gova's task smacked of simplicity. Kill Ravigno, make it look good. In other words, this had to be the kind of death that didn't raise any questions.

Given Ravigno's role in the prosecution's case, though, there would be plenty of questions. But he didn't care. Why should he? He would collect a shitload of money for silencing the man and, frankly, he would enjoy making it look like the kind of hit Mike Sessio might pull.

The other side of it, however, bothered him. Since Washington had supposedly killed Sessio's father, why would Sessio want to silence the guy whose testimony would send Tommy Washington to Death Row?

But it didn't bother him enough to turn down the job. He needed the money. He had plans. He had his entire goddamn life in front of him and money would surely make that future easier.

So he drove to Ravigno's neighborhood and wired a bomb to his car. He just hoped that Ravigno didn't lend his wheels to anyone, as Taylor had done. The bitch, he thought, had nine lives and the way he figured it, she'd used up about eight of them.

When he got back to his place, he reread the notes that Frank Morgan had sent his illegitimate daughter and he laughed.

Mike Sessio couldn't sleep. He wandered through his penthouse possessed of something he couldn't explain, that he didn't fully understand, knowing only that his thoughts were always consumed by the very thought of one magnificent woman. Taylor, it all came back to Taylor, he decided, and sat down in front of his computer and constructed a time line of events that had happened since his father's death.

The sky began to fade to gray and light the color of milk

spilled through his den. Taylor and Adler, Adler and Taylor. He sensed the connection, but couldn't see it, couldn't find it, couldn't draw it out into the light so that he could scrutinize it. He realized he should never have gotten this personally involved. She was only supposed to help fill in the blanks—not succeed at winning his heart. He'd never let a memory, a scent, or for that matter a name linger in his thoughts more than even a day. Now he was defeated. Taylor had touched places in his heart, his very being, that no one had ever gotten near. He let his guard down and now he wondered if he'd be made to pay the consequences.

He finally collapsed on the couch in his den, drew a worn afghan up over himself, and lay awake, his head pounding. His arm ached and throbbed, memories of his father flashed through his head. The answer, he thought. It seemed close, yet not close enough for him to seize.

When Kyle Nelson's phone rang at six Friday morning, he had been awake for hours, lying in bed with his plots, his plans, his miserable future. He didn't feel like answering the phone; he felt sure it would be one of the sharks on the line, threatening him. But if he didn't answer it, they might come over here.

"Hello?"

"Have you heard the news?" Gova asked without preface.

"There's been so much news lately, it's hard to keep up," he said, dryly.

"Ravigno's car blew up about an hour ago."

"So what? You were finished with his testimony."

"I figured Ms. Brooke would want to know, in the event that she planned on cross-examining him again."

"I don't know what her plans are. She's stopped talking to me about the defense."

"You'd better find out what the hell her plans are, Kyle. I've been paying you to botch up the defense and so far, nothing's been botched. We lost points in court yesterday, in case you didn't notice."

Kyle squeezed the bridge of his nose and quietly replaced the receiver.

The phone rang again moments later. He reached down to the cord and jerked it out of the wall.

Taylor thought John Stark looked supremely confident that morning. He strolled back and forth in front of the witness stand in a three-piece suit, his voice crisp and clear. Even to an unpracticed eye, she thought, he cut an impressive figure.

Detective Schultz, the chief detective at the 13th Precinct, testified first. If the jury judged witnesses by how they looked, then Schultz would end up at the bottom of the list. His square jaw, his beefy arms, the hint of a sneer on his face: none of it made you like the man, she thought.

Schultz recounted the events that had unfolded at DeCiccio's Restaurant on the Thursday before Memorial Day weekend. He drew no conclusions that went beyond his jurisdiction, said nothing that she could object to. Stark had coached him well. She glanced through her notes, then leaned toward Tommy and whispered, "What time did you leave the restaurant, Tommy? Do you remember?"

"Yes ma'am, jus' like I told you before. I lit outta there at nine minutes to two. I remember because I looked at the clock. I wanted to be able to tell Mr. DeCiccio how much time to dock me."

"Your witness," Stark said, and walked back over to the defense table and sat down.

Taylor got up and approached the witness stand. This is it, she thought. "Detective Schultz, I'd like you to clarify a couple of points."

Schultz smiled. "Sure thing."

"How long after the shooting did you arrive at the restaurant?"

"A squad car answered the nine-one-one almost immediately. I got there right afterward, took a look around, and called District Attorney Gova."

"And when did Ms. Gova arrive?"

"Not too long after I called her."

"About how long, Detective Schultz? Fifteen minutes? Twenty?"

"Twenty, twenty-five."

"Had you located Tommy Washington by then?"

"No, ma'am."

"But you had squad cars out looking for him."

"That's right."

"And in one of those squad cars was a busboy from the restaurant."

"Right. Billy Schultz."

"Any relationship to you?" she asked, just to lighten the mood.

The question got a few soft chuckles and Schultz smiled. "No, ma'am. No relationship."

"And why was he with the police, Detective Schultz?"

"We needed someone to identify Tommy Washington."

"So, let me get this straight. Joseph Sessio was shot between one fifty-five and two o'clock that afternoon. Ms. Gova arrived about two twenty-five. Would you say that's correct?"

"More or less, yes."

"According to the arrest report, Detective Schultz, Tommy was taken into custody at two twenty, before Ms. Gova had arrived. But you just finished telling me the police were still looking for Tommy."

"Objection, Your Honor," snapped Stark. "Except for the time of Washington's arrest, these are approximate times. The witness can't be expected to recall exact times of arrivals."

Judge Cornwell hesitated, then looked at Taylor. "Is this line of questioning pertinent to a point you're trying to make, Counselor?"

"Yes, Your Honor."

"And what point is that?"

"I'm trying to show that the police knew Tommy Washington was at the wharf, Your Honor."

Noise erupted in the courtroom and Judge Cornwell slammed her gavel several times before the din faded. "This court is recessing for fifteen minutes. I want all four attorneys to meet me in my chambers. You're excused for now, Detective Schultz.''

With that, she left the courtroom, her robes rustling, the four attorneys trailing behind her.

"What the fuck are you doing?" Stark whispered to her.

"What I should have done yesterday," she replied.

Inside the judge's chambers, Cornwell gestured to the chairs in front of her desk, then lit into Taylor. "Are you making an accusation against the prosecution, Ms. Brooke? Or am I misunderstanding you?"

"I'm going to file an affidavit citing wrongdoing by the prosecution, Your Honor."

"What?" Gova exclaimed. "What wrongdoing? Your Honor, this is clearly an attempt to stall for time, to—"

"When I want your opinion, Ms. Gova, I'll ask for it," the judge barked, and Gova shut up. Cornwell turned her icy eyes on Taylor. "And when are you filing this affidavit, Ms. Brooke?"

"I'll fax it to you over the weekend."

"This is an outrage," Gova burst out.

"I agree," Stark piped up. "Your Honor, we've followed the—"

"Excuse me, Mr. Stark. I haven't finished speaking yet. Court will be adjourned for today. Once I've read Ms. Brooke's affidavit, I'll decide how to proceed. I want the four of you to know, however, that I'm disgusted with some of the antics I've seen in the courtroom this week." She looked at Kyle. "You haven't said a word, Mr. Nelson."

"I have nothing to say, Your Honor."

"I take it you weren't told about Ms. Brooke's plans to file an affidavit?"

"No, I wasn't."

"Do you agree with it?"

"She's the attorney on the case, Your Honor. I'm merely assisting."

"I see. Very well. You're free to go. Ms. Brooke, I'd like to speak to you privately."

The other three got up and shuffled out of the chambers. Taylor remained seated, her palms damp with perspiration, the inside of her mouth as dry as the Sahara. She expected Judge Cornwell to read her the riot act. Instead, Cornwell came out from behind her desk, leaned against the edge of it, and said, "May I be frank, Ms. Brooke?"

"I wish someone would be."

Cornwell smiled at that. "What wrongdoing do you intend to cite in your affidavit?"

"Off the record?"

"Certainly."

"I think some of the prosecution witnesses have been paid to testify, that evidence has been tampered with and, in some cases, obliterated altogether. I also don't think it's a coincidence that the prosecution's witness, Sal Ravigno, was killed in a car explosion earlier this morning."

"These are serious accusations, Ms. Brooke. Can you give me any specific examples?"

Taylor hesitated. Could she trust this woman? Did she have a choice? One way or another, Judge Cornwell would be the one who decided whether the affidavit warranted further investigation. "Yes, I'll give you an example. My client insists he received a threatening phone call about his sister, that she was in danger. When I checked, I couldn't find any record of an incoming call at that time. Yet, Mr. DeCiccio clearly remembers a black man receiving a call shortly before Sessio was shot. In other words, a call came in—but the record of it vanished. And that's just one example."

Cornwell nodded thoughtfully. "All right. So I can expect it over the weekend?"

"Yes."

"Frankly, I hope you're wrong about this, Taylor. Because if you aren't. . . ."

She shook her head and didn't finish the sentence; she didn't have to. Taylor understood the implications as well as Cornwell did. Wrongdoing on the part of the prosecution could result in a mistrial and an investigation into the DA's office, exactly what she hoped would happen.

———

*K*yle *hurried* into the parking garage to get his car. He kept thinking about what had happened in the judge's chambers, kept seeing Cornwell's face, those icy blue eyes, the suspicion. Immersed in his fear, he didn't hear her until she fell into step beside him.

"Why didn't you tell me this was going to happen, Kyle?" snapped Gova.

"Because I didn't know. I told you this morning on the phone that she'd cut me out of the defense proceedings."

"This could mean a mistrial."

Or worse, he thought.

"It could bring certain, uh, information to light, Kyle."

He didn't say anything.

"Our arrangement, for instance."

He stayed silent, kept walking, reached his car and unlocked it. Gova suddenly grabbed his arm. "Say something, will you?"

Kyle wrenched his arm free. "The biggest goddamn mistake I ever made was buying into your fucked up scheme, Gova. The defense was supposed to be botched; people weren't supposed to be killed. Taylor's maniac husband wasn't supposed to blow up her goddamn car.

"And just in case you've got the same thing planned for me, my records of everything that has transpired between us are in safekeeping. In the event that I die under mysterious circumstances, those records will be released to the press and to the state attorney general."

He started to get into his car, but she grabbed his arm again and this time, her nails dug into the skin. "If I go down, you're going with me, Kyle. Count on it."

He just looked at her, his contempt so obvious she pulled back a little. "You've got farther to fall."

With that, he got into his car, slammed the door, locked it, and backed out of the parking space.

26

_____

Max picked up Taylor and her dog at two on the nose and drove them to the general aviation area at Logan Airport. "You'll be making the flight in that single engine Bonanza over there," Max explained.

Taylor glanced off in the direction that he pointed, but she didn't know a single engine Bonanza from a Cessna. "How long does the flight take?"

"An hour tops, depending on the weather. You'll miss the ferry this way, lucky you. On Fridays, that ferry's always jammed to the hilt."

"Are you driving the car over?"

"No, ma'am. Mr. Morgan keeps a car at the Vineyard. He's going to keep you so busy, you won't have time to work."

Nice thought, but she wouldn't have a choice, not if she wanted to fax the affidavit to Judge Cornwell by Sunday, at the latest. "That'll be nice for a change."

Max pulled up to the general aviation building, hopped out, opened the back door for her and Lady, then got Taylor's shoulder bag and laptop out of the trunk. "Plane's fueling up at the pumps," Max said. "I'll walk you over."

Lady strained at her leash, tugging Taylor toward a nearby patch of grass. "I'll meet you over there. Let me walk Lady first."

Max nodded, handed her the bag and laptop, and strolled off toward the plane. As she walked Lady over to the patch of grass, her cell phone rang and she fished it out of her purse.

"Taylor Brooke."

"It's Burt Hallas. Can you talk?"

"For the moment. What's up?"

"Something weird's going on."

You've got no idea, Burt, she thought. "How weird?"

"Gerald Tower has a file called 'special cases,' in which he keeps a running bookkeeper's record on sums he's paid under the table. Considering how much of a slob he is personally, it's astonishing that his financial records in this area are quite tidy.

"The day before Eric Serle was bailed out, Tower made an entry of fifty grand. Next to it, in the loss column, fifteen went to ES and another fifteen went to KN."

KN: Kyle Nelson. Taylor squeezed her eyes shut. How the hell could he do it? And why? "What about the remaining twenty?"

"It shows up in Tower's profit column."

"Any indication who the fifty grand came from?"

"There're only the two sets of initials and both of them were paid *from* the fifty grand. By later tonight, I should have a copy of his phone bill for the month of July. That might provide a clue about where the money came from. Want me to fax it to you?"

"Can you scan it and send it through my E-mail? I'm on my way to Martha's Vineyard, so this'll be the easiest way for me to get it."

"Sure thing. Give it to me."

She ticked off her E-mail address, then said: "Burt, I'd appreciate it if you kept this between us."

"No problem. I understand completely. I'll buzz you at this number when I've sent it."

"Great. And thanks again."

She disconnected, started to punch out Kyle's number, then saw Max headed toward her and changed her mind. She would call him later, when she knew what to say to him.

"The weather looks good for the flight over," Max said. "A storm is supposed to move in with a cold front later tonight. It'll come in over Boston first, then out to the islands. But tomorrow and Sunday are supposed to be just beautiful. Real fall weather. I hope you brought warm clothes."

Taylor patted her bulging bag. "I brought too many clothes."

They stopped at the plane, he introduced her to the pilot, put her things into the baggage compartment, then shook her hand. "Have a nice flight, Ms. Brooke."

"Thanks, Max."

From the air, Martha's Vineyard, Nantucket, and a pocket of smaller islands stretched out against the sea like a string of soft green pearls. The view left her breathless.

Two years ago, she and Cathy had come out here for a weekend, her first and only trip to the Vineyard. The absence of high rises and luxury hotels had struck her nearly as deeply as the untouched beaches, protected woodlands, and early American architecture. Then, as now, the geography of the Vineyard echoed that of another continent: steep cliffs, lush plains, thick forests, and rocky farmland.

As the largest island in New England, twenty-four miles long and ten miles wide, it boasted a cultural diversity that equaled that of its geography. She envied Melissa Morgan for the idyllic weekends she'd undoubtedly spent here as a child and resented the fact that her own mother, who had deserved part of this life, had been denied it. But she needed to put the past where it belonged—behind her.

The airport, located at the south edge of the island, had once been a naval training station. Decaying Quonset huts rose like mutant anthills from the area around the runways. The terminal looked dilapidated. But the control tower, a modern concrete structure, testified to the renovation in progress.

She spotted Frank Morgan as soon as the plane taxied to a
tie-down spot. He looked as though island life suited him. He
wore casual chinos, a blue shirt, a lightweight jacket, and deck
shoes.

"It's so great to have you here," he said, hugging her
quickly as she and Lady got off the plane. Lady barked and
he laughed and patted her. "You, too, girl." He picked up her
bags, spoke briefly to the pilot, then they walked off toward
the parking lot.

"How was your flight?" he asked.

"Great. The island is beautiful from the air."

"It's even lovelier down here. You feel like driving around
a bit?"

"Sure. I'd love to."

They piled into a blue Chevrolet Suburban and drove east
along a picturesque road that climbed steadily upward. "I
thought I'd take you out to Gay Head Cliffs first. It's the
highest spot on the island."

"Gay Head Indians," she said suddenly. "Herman Mel-
ville. He wrote eloquently about the Gay Heads and the Vineyard."

Morgan looked delighted. "Right. At one time, the tribe
populated the entire island. They eventually sold most of their
land and settled on Chappaquiddick and Gay Head."

"I guess you're planning on working this weekend," Morgan remarked, gesturing toward her laptop.

"I've decided to file that affidavit we talked about last night.
I need to write it up."

"So you're going through with it?"

"It's the right thing to do."

He seemed vaguely amused by this. "Right and wrong are
rarely so black and white, Taylor. Politics and law taught me
that."

His remark bothered her. "Something is either right or it's
wrong," she said. "It can't be both ways."

"It's all perspective. Look at your own situation. You're
defending a man who's allegedly guilty of murder. Your job
is to convince the jury that he's innocent. To do that, you have
to *change their perspective* about what happened. If you're

successful, he's acquitted. But that doesn't mean he isn't guilty of the crime.''

"It's not the same thing," she argued. "You're mixing up constitutional rights with personal values. But using your example, it's *wrong* for the prosecution to tamper with and obliterate evidence. It's wrong for them to pay off witnesses, to—''

"You need proof, Taylor.''

"No. I need sufficient evidence to cast serious doubt on the way the prosecution has handled this case. And I have that.''

"It's going to mean more delays for your client.''

"A delay is preferable to a prison term or the death penalty.''

He smiled then, a quick, almost resigned smile. "Your mother was a lot like you in that respect, Taylor. For Eva, something was either right or wrong, true or not true, black or white.''

"So you're saying it's genetic," she said with a laugh, trying to lighten the mood.

But Morgan didn't laugh. He merely smiled and kept on driving.

As soon as they passed Chilmark, the road weaved precipitously, up and down hills, higher and higher. At one point, she could see the Vineyard Sound to the north and the Atlantic Ocean to the south, with a lighthouse looming eerily against the sky, a vestige of another century.

Morgan turned onto Lighthouse Road and a few minutes later, the lighthouse rose in front of them, close enough to touch. Morgan swung into a parking lot with half a dozen other cars and they got out. Lady tugged furiously on her leash, dragging Taylor forward. Morgan grabbed the leash and snapped, "No, Lady. Heel.''

The harshness in his voice astonished Taylor and made Lady whimper. She quickly took the leash from Morgan. "I'll walk her, Frank.''

"She needs to go to obedience school.''

His unsolicited opinion annoyed her; he might as well have criticized her child. She felt like telling him he had no right to intrude into her affairs. "She's just rambunctious," Taylor remarked.

Dark clouds gathered in the distance, the breeze had picked up. The cold front, she thought, would be here by dark. She peered down a hundred and fifty feet, over the red clay cliffs, to the sea below. The clay colored the frothing water, a testimony to the erosion that had taken place over the centuries.

"In the winter," Morgan said, stopping beside her, "you can sometimes spot whales from here."

Taylor nodded and kept a tight hold on Lady's leash as she stuck her snout through the railing and sniffed at the wind. Suddenly, rocks and dirt underfoot gave way, tumbling over the edge. Lady began to slide, pulling Taylor with her.

She jerked back on the chain leash, stumbled and struck the ground hard on her buttocks. Air rushed from her lungs and for a moment, she simply sat there, stunned. Lady ran around her, barking and licking her face, the leash wrapping around Taylor. Morgan rushed over, shouting at the lab, who instantly cowered, and helped Taylor to her feet. "Are you all right?" he asked, anxiety thickening his voice.

"Yes." She untangled herself from the leash, brushed off her clothes, then looked at him. "I would appreciate it if you wouldn't shout at my dog, Frank."

"My God, the dog nearly took you over the cliff."

Lady sat back on her haunches, growling softly, her lips pulling away from her teeth. "It's okay, girl," Taylor said softly, stroking the lab's head, her eyes still glued to Morgan. "If you didn't want me to bring her, you should have said so."

He seemed momentarily flustered. "Forgive me, Taylor. I'm new at this. I . . . I want this to be a wonderful weekend for both of us. I'm sorry for scolding Lady. I . . . I thought you were hurt. Call it fatherly concern, I guess. I apologize." He looked at Lady. "Sorry, girl."

Lady growled and backed away, not ready to make friends yet. He started to say something, but his cell phone rang. "Excuse me, let me get this."

"Sure." Taylor walked Lady over to a grassy area to give Morgan privacy. "He wants to be friends, Lady," Taylor said. "You've got to at least be polite."

The lab barked and nudged Taylor's leg, making her laugh. "Yeah, yeah, I know. You're sorry."

She watched Morgan from a distance. He seemed agitated, pacing back and forth along the railing, his body tight, almost rigid. More bad news about Melissa, she thought. Or about business. Or about politics. When he disconnected, he hurried over to her and said, "Sorry. How about if we drive to the house and have an early dinner?"

"That sounds great. I hope that wasn't bad news about Melissa."

"Unfortunately, that's exactly what it was. Her doctors say she's taken a turn for the worse. I'm going to have to fly back tonight."

"I'll go with you," Taylor said.

He shook his head. "No, you stay here, enjoy yourself. This has happened before—a turn for the worse, then she improves."

But Taylor noticed how he bit at his lower lip and knew that he didn't believe she would improve this time. Although she didn't know Melissa, she felt terrible for Frank. On impulse, she reached over and squeezed his arm. "Promise that you'll call me if you need to talk."

He caught her hand and returned the pressure. "You have my word."

They drove on toward the house, beneath a rapidly clouding sky.

A light rain fell as Michael Sessio drove through the Newton neighborhood where Richard Adler's wife lived. The dark, sagging clouds had swallowed most of the twilight, so that a kind of pall had settled over the city.

His windshield wipers whipped back and forth across the glass, a steady, monotonous sound that nearly mesmerized him. He found the house easily enough, the lights in its windows glowing like moons in the wet twilight.

He knew Stephanie Adler was in because he'd called the house a few minutes ago and she'd answered the phone. She'd locked the gate, however, and if he rang the intercom, she probably would refuse to see him. He saw only one car parked in the driveway and wondered if it belonged to Mrs. Adler or the nurse Taylor had mentioned.

Maybe the nurse had weekends off, he thought.

He hoped so.

He parked at the curb, turned off the headlights, slipped on his raincoat, slung a canvas bag over his shoulder. Outside, a breeze slapped the corners of the raincoat against his jeans. His Reeboks squashed through the standing pools of water on the sidewalk. He followed the fence around to the back of the house, checking for the dogs Taylor had told him about. The rain apparently had driven them indoors.

The house backed up to an alley, with tall hedges separating it from the houses beyond it. He wouldn't be seen. Sessio grabbed onto one of the vertical iron bars and scrambled over the fence, his injured arm protesting the pressure and abuse. He dropped silently into the yard and ran, hunkered over, toward the rear of the house.

He expected the dogs to start barking as soon as he stepped onto the porch. They didn't. He guessed they hadn't caught his scent. He removed his soggy shoes, tucked one in either pocket of his raincoat, and turned the knob. Locked, of course. He reached inside his raincoat for a leather pouch and brought out a long, slender tool that could pick virtually any lock.

He'd bought it years ago from a pawnshop—not because he planned on breaking into houses, but simply because the craftsmanship had struck him. He inserted it into the lock and moments later, the door yawned open. He stepped into the dark kitchen, shut the door, listened. The drone of the TV, someone speaking on the phone in another room, no sign or sound of the dogs. Move it, he thought, and crept forward.

Lightning flashed, followed by a distant roll of thunder. As he started past the cellar door, a frenzied barking broke out. He realized the dogs were in the cellar. He quickly passed the cellar and ducked into a twilit hallway.

He could hear Stephanie Adler clearly now. "I'd better scoot. The dogs are starting up again. You know how much they hate storms. . . . That's sweet of you, Jennifer, but I'm fine, really. You just take care of your mother and I'll see you Sunday afternoon. Thanks so much for preparing those casseroles. . . . Right, we'll talk tomorrow.''

She hung up. He heard her wheelchair rolling across the floor, headed this way. Seconds before she reached the hall, he stepped out. "Good evening, Mrs. Adler.''

She made a startled, choking sound, slammed the heel of her hand against the lever that operated the wheelchair, and rolled back at an astonishing speed, making a beeline for the phone. Sessio lunged past her, grabbed the handholds of the chair, and held it in place, the electrical engine whirring, the chair going nowhere.

"I'm not going to hurt you, Mrs. Adler,'' he said, and leaned forward and hit the switch that turned off the engine. "I just want to talk to you and you've made that difficult by never returning my calls.''

"You broke in here,'' she snapped. "You're trespassing. That's at least two laws you've broken, Mr. Sessio. Keep this up and I'll throw the book at you.''

"All I want is the file my father gave to your husband.''

"I don't have any files.''

"Taylor Brooke may have bought that story, Mrs. Adler, but I don't. I know for a fact my father turned over a file to your husband about six weeks before he was killed. I also know you've been subpoenaed to testify for the defense and—''

"I won't have to testify,'' she said quickly. "My health isn't good and—''

"It won't cut it this time,'' Sessio said. "You'll have to testify or face contempt charges and go to jail.''

"Testify to what? I don't know a damn thing. That's what I told Ms. Brooke and that's what I'm telling you. My husband's business was exactly that—*his* business.''

"Then you have nothing to lose by giving me the file.''

"You're as despicable as your father,'' she said softly.

"Your husband didn't think my father was despicable.''

She laughed, a harsh, ugly sound. "That's true. Richard didn't think he was despicable; he rarely thought in those terms when it came to other people. But he was terrified of Joe.''

"Oh, for Christ's sakes," Sessio exclaimed. "They were friends. They'd been friends for nearly thirty years, Mrs. Adler. People don't remain friends that long if one feels such terror of the other.''

Lightning flashed in the windows again, illuminating Stephanie Adler's face, the wrinkles of age, of worry, of disease. "You don't understand," she said softly, miserably.

"Help me to understand." Sessio leaned toward her, his tone pleading. "Please. Tell me what you know."

She turned her face away from him, knuckles pressed to her mouth, her eyes so filled with pain that it hurt him to look at her. "I can't," she whispered.

"Why? Has someone threatened you?"

She shook her head.

"Then what?"

She looked at him again, the conflict in her eyes like some raw, oozing wound. "I can't help you, Mr. Sessio. Please leave."

"I can't leave." He got up, walked behind her wheelchair, pushed it out into the middle of the living room. God forgive me, he thought, turning her wheelchair as he turned. "Where's the safe, Mrs. Adler? Behind that painting? Or that one? Let's take a look behind the pastoral scene." He pushed her chair over to the wall, reached up and pushed the painting to one side. "No safe there. How about over here?"

She began to weep, soft, pathetic sobs that tore him apart inside. But he didn't stop. He pushed the chair over to the next painting, then the next and the next. "There's more at stake here, Mrs. Adler, than just you and your fear. While you're hiding in your house, behind your disease, other people's lives are suspended. People who don't have the luxury or the means to hide.''

He pushed her out into the hall, past the cellar door. Her hand shot out, trying to turn the knob, to let the dogs out, but Sessio spun the chair away from the door. Then he turned the skeleton key in the lock and pocketed it. "No, Mrs. Adler.

I'm your nightmare. I'm here to stay until you give me what I want.''

Lightning burned across the windows, lighting up the inside of the house. Thunder roared through the rapidly encroaching darkness. He pushed the wheelchair into the spacious den. ''In here. I bet the safe is in here.'' He shut the door and locked it so she couldn't get out and pushed the wheelchair into the middle of the room, where he could keep an eye on her. ''One last time, Mrs. Adler. Where's the file?''

''It doesn't concern you!'' she shouted. ''It's not your life at risk, it's mine, don't you understand? *I'm* at risk. That's what I inherited from my husband. *Risk,* Mr. Sessio.''

Sessio jerked open desk drawers, riffled through papers, tore folders out of the filing cabinet. And when he glimpsed movement in his peripheral vision, he lunged for the wheelchair that sped across the room, and stopped it dead. And suddenly Stephanie Adler shot to her feet and stumbled toward the door, a cripple no more.

He reached her seconds before she got to the door, grabbed her around the waist, and lifted her off the floor. She weighed practically nothing, just a wisp of a thing, all bone and terror, flesh and desolation.

He set her in the chair; she wept softly, face hidden behind her hands. ''Did you really believe you'd protect yourself by concocting an illness, Mrs. Adler?''

''I . . . I don't know what I believe anymore.'' Her hands dropped away from her face. She looked utterly defeated, worn out. ''Just leave me alone. Please.''

''I can't.'' Sessio crouched in front of her. ''Please help me. I'm begging you, Mrs. Adler.''

She regarded him for long, terrible moments. ''You know why my husband died, Mr. Sessio?'' Her voice softened so much it was barely audible. ''Because he knew too much. But since I can't prove it, I say nothing.'' Her mouth trembled, tears brimmed in her eyes. ''I've learned to live with my compromises. Now you sweep in here with your noble pleas and expect me to sacrifice myself for you and your needs, Mr. Sessio.''

He wondered what the hell he had to do to get through to

his woman. "I believe there's a connection between my father's murder and your husband's death, Mrs. Adler. But I can't prove it without knowing what my father entrusted to your husband. So please, let me see the file so that their deaths can be vindicated."

She sniffled and blew her nose, punctuating the silence. Her struggle showed in her eyes, emotions cresting like waves, crashing, rising again. Finally, she said, "Two conditions. You never saw me walk and you never reveal where this information came from."

"Agreed."

"That may be more difficult than you think."

"Where it came from is going to be less important overall than the information itself, Mrs. Adler."

She hesitated, measuring him against some criteria in her own mind, then pointed her long bony finger upward. "It's taped to the fan. Richard scanned the file onto the computer, copied it onto a disk, then wiped out the file on the computer and destroyed the file. The disk is all that remains."

Sessio pushed a chair under the fan, climbed onto it, and untaped the disk from one of the blades. He removed it from its plastic covering, gestured toward the computer. "May I?"

She blew her nose. "Why bother asking at this point?"

Sessio booted up the computer, inserted the disk, and began to read.

His father's words leaped off the computer screen, familiar in tone, in cadence. Sessio could almost hear his voice, tracing his long history with the Morgan family.

It had begun during Prohibition, when Monroe Morgan had made his initial fortune through bootlegging. Joe Sessio had known about it because he ran the docks, knowledge that had prompted Morgan to cut Sessio in for a share of the profits. This was the first of many such deals that had tied the two men together.

Once a bootlegger, always a bootlegger, Sessio thought, and Monroe Morgan proved the adage. Over the decades, the product he ran had changed, but the business deal between Joe and Monroe had remained the same.

In the early seventies, Richard Adler set up Dovecote as a

funnel for profits from Monroe Morgan's various illegal enterprises. Today, those profits came primarily from the illegal exportation of high tech products to foreign countries, with Max, Monroe's trusted servant as the middle man, collecting more than a fair share of profits for himself.

Joe had known about it, of course, because he and Adler were close friends. This money laundering operation had funded Frank Morgan's political rise to power. But Joe had noted that Frank wouldn't have won without his support, which had garnered the union vote in the state. Monroe Morgan had already approached Joe about doing the same for his son's reelection campaign. Joe expressed reservation, however, about supporting the son again. Perhaps it was because he was getting old, and starting to wonder about his own mortality and where he stood in God's eyes. Or perhaps he merely wanted finally to settle an old grudge, but either way, the effect was the same when he told Frank, "Forever go to hell."

Sessio sensed his father had loved Eva Carlino deeply, but that he realized he couldn't compete with memories of her affair with Frank. After her death, he asked Adler to set up the trust fund that had paid for Taylor's stay at St. Mary's.

If Joe had suspected that Eva Carlino's death was anything more than a hit and run, he didn't say, didn't even speculate, which struck Sessio as odd. After all, he'd spelled out everything else, facts and speculations alike, so why exclude this?

Because he knew the answer, Sessio thought. Because he was a part of the complicity of silence that surrounded her death.

"Dear God," he whispered, and ejected the disk. He pocketed it and turned to look at Stephanie Adler. "Did you see my father after your husband was killed?" he asked.

"Only once. He asked me about the file. I told him I didn't have any idea what he was talking about."

"And he believed you?"

"No. He told me Richard died because he knew too much and that if I knew what was in that file, I'd best keep it to myself or I might be next. He . . . he threatened me."

"No, Mrs. Adler," Sessio said softly, gently. "He was warning you."

Sessio sped through the blinding rain to his penthouse. While he made multiple copies of the disk on his laptop, he called Taylor's townhouse, reached her machine, hung up, and tried her cell phone number. It apparently wasn't working due to the weather.

The Vineyard, he thought. She'd gone to the Vineyard.

He hurried into his den and put one of the disks in his safe. He dropped another in an envelope with a note to his attorney, mailed a third to Taylor's address, and pocketed the fourth. At his next stop, the bedroom, he stuffed clothes in a bag, hesitated about taking a gun he'd never used, then tossed it in the bag and hoped he wouldn't have to use it. Then he called the company pilot.

IFR weather, said the pilot. Not a good night to fly to the Vineyard. But he didn't recommend driving, either. Fog would be rolling in over the highways on the Cape, the weekend tourists would be out in throngs, and there would be a long wait for the ferry to the Vineyard.

"So we'll fly," Sessio said. "I'll be at the airport in forty minutes to an hour."

"You're the boss."

Yeah, I am, Sessio thought, and hung up.

He tried Taylor's cell phone again; no connection. He called John Stark's home next. The woman who answered, presumably a housekeeper, informed him that Mr. and Mrs. Stark had gone out for the evening.

"Look, this is an emergency. I need to know where I can get in touch with him."

She hemmed, she hawed. "Leave your number, sir, and I'll have Mr. Stark return your call."

"By then it will be too late. Thank you for your—"

"Okay, hold on. Here's the number. It's Mrs. Stark's birthday. They're celebrating." She gave Sessio the number, he thanked her, hung up, dialed it.

"The Rowes Wharf Bar." The man who answered shouted over the background din.

"John Stark, please."

"Who?"

"John Stark."

"Stark. Yeah, the birthday party. Just a second."

"Wait, you can help me. I was supposed to be there an hour ago. Can you give me directions?"

"Sure thing."

The man reeled off the directions, Sessio hung up, and flew out the door.

Despite the inclement weather, Sessio found the place easily enough, an Irish bar within the Boston Harbor Hotel that was known for its excellent food and wide selection of brews. He remembered reading somewhere that Mrs. Stark's family hailed originally from Ireland. But that failed to explain why Stark had attended; according to Taylor, he and the Missus were in the midst of a divorce.

Sessio made his way through the rowdy crowd, to a back room where the Stark birthday celebration had throttled into full gear. Clouds of smoke drifted through the red and blue lights. Old sixties tunes pumped from a Wurlitzer. And there, in the middle of the very small dance floor, Stark and his wife were twisting the night away to Chubby Checker.

He waited at the edge of the crowd until the tune ended, then threaded his way through the throngs of people, to where Stark stood. "Excuse me, Mr. Stark."

He held a martini, his eyes looked glazed. A beat or two passed in which he seemed to be struggling to place Sessio's face. Then fire leaped into those eyes, an electric current seemed to tear up through his spine. "You," he said, and swung at Sessio.

Fortunately, Stark's swing lagged well behind Sessio's reflexes. He ducked, caught Stark's arm on the downward arc, and jerked him forward. "Take it easy, man. You don't want to do anything stupid," Sessio hissed.

Stark wrenched his arm free of Sessio's grasp, took a long, deep gulp at his martini, pinned Sessio with his gaze. "You set up Washington, you seduced Taylor, and you ought to be on trial for your old man's murder.''

His words slurred, but he seemed to be sober enough to understand the basics, Sessio thought. "It concerns Taylor, Gova, this whole stinking mess. You going to listen or not?''

"John?" His wife appeared at his side, glanced uneasily at Sessio, then back at her husband. "Everything okay?''

"Sure, everything's fine," Stark replied without looking at her, and nodded toward the nearest doorway.

Sessio followed his cue and they went into the pool room. Less smoke, less noise, fewer people. Sessio could finally breathe again. Stark glanced around, tipped the martini to his mouth, polished it off, and set the empty glass on the table. "So?" Stark said.

Sessio began to talk, choosing his words carefully, couching them in a language Stark could understand. It occurred to him that Taylor had once loved this man, that she might love him still. That alone nearly drove him over the edge, made him want to smash the bastard's polished white teeth down his goddamn throat.

He finished what he had to say, then pressed the disk into Stark's clammy hands. "Read it, mull it over, do whatever it is you lawyers do. Then go make a difference, John.''

Stark looked at the disk as though he hadn't quite made the connection between what Sessio had said and what the disk contained. Then he looked at Sessio, glanced toward his wife, standing in the doorway, saying his name, then his eyes returned to Sessio again.

In that brief glance, Sessio understood that John Stark, hotshot prosecutor, understood exactly how everything connected, that he had already calculated the odds, that he had glimpsed his choices.

"So where the hell did you get this information?" Stark asked.

"As long as it's accurate, who cares?''

The machinations of ambition whirled in Stark's eyes. "She loved me, you know.''

Sessio nodded.

"I couldn't deal with it.''

Another nod, one man to another. "I know."

"She told you?"

"Enough."

He looked contrite then, but his guilt smacked of a post-script. "I did what I had to do."

"I understand," Sessio replied, even though he didn't understand at all. "Go find yourself a laptop and read the disk, John."

Stark reached for Sessio's hand and gripped it tightly in both of his own. "Get your ass to the Vineyard before Gova does something to harm her, Mike."

Mike and John, two peas in a pod, their lives linked by the daughter of the woman who had connected the lives of his father and Monroe Morgan. Full circle, Sessio thought.

He hastened from the bar and sped through the pouring rain to the airport.

27

The rambling farmhouse, more than a century *
old, occupied twenty acres of land in West Tisbury. Taylor
Brooke's upstairs room overlooked rolling hills and a barn,
both of which had been swallowed by the darkness, the storm,
and a rapidly thickening fog.

Morgan had left shortly before dinner to be at Missy's side.
Now she sat at her computer, waiting to connect with the local
access number for America Online. Lady lay on the floor next
to her, apparently content to be alone in the house, undisturbed
by the rain that continued to fall outside. The old house
creaked in the wind. Branches slapped and scratched at the
windows.

The computer finally connected to AOL and announced that
she had mail. She went into the mailbox and found a note
from Burt Hallas. *The phone bill follows. Let me know if you
need anything else. Best. Burt.* Taylor scrolled through the
long list of phone numbers, looking for Kyle's home number.
It didn't appear. So I'm wrong, she thought. Just the same,

she printed out the list, logged off, then sat back, studying the numbers.

On the day of and the day before Eric's release, Gerald Tower had made thirteen long-distance calls, eight of them to Boston. She decided to begin with the number closest to the time of his release and work her way backward through the list until she either ran out of numbers or found what she needed.

She dug her cell phone from her purse, turned it on, but the connection buzzed and crackled. The storm, she thought, and wondered suddenly if Sessio had called her. She picked up the receiver of the phone she'd been using on-line, started to dial his number, then hung up. Not now, she decided, and pushed him out of her mind and went to work.

The first number she called turned out to be a bank in Boston. At the second number, a woman answered. Taylor didn't recognize her voice, but played along for a few moments. "MCI calling," she said. "Are you the head of the household?"

"Sure am," the woman replied.

"Are you interested in changing your long distance service, ma'am?"

"Nope," she replied, and hung up.

So much for her detective work; she moved on to the next number. On the fourth, she reached an answering machine.

"This is five-five-five, seventeen hundred. Please leave a message at the tone and I'll get back to you."

Taylor quickly disconnected. "Can't be," she whispered, and punched out the number again. She listened closely to the message, everything inside of her turning cold.

Debra Gova, no doubt about it.

She disconnected again, her head roaring. She immediately called Kyle's home number. It rang and rang before the machine finally clicked on. At the sound of the tone, she said, "Kyle, it's Taylor. Are you there?"

He picked up immediately. "I'm here." His voice slurred; he'd been drinking. "I was just on my way out. What's up?"

"How the hell could you do it, Kyle?" Her voice nearly broke, but she didn't stop. "You . . . you sold out to Gova, sold out the defense, sold out Tommy Washington, sold out your career—and for what? My God, I trusted you, I—"

"What're you talking about, Taylor?"

"Gerald Tower, fifty thousand bucks, bailing out Eric for Gova. And you were the one who tipped off Gova about the Ravigno tape. Were you the one who attacked me? Who fed Lady bad meat? Gova . . . she hired you to screw up the defense, she—"

She heard muffled sobs, then the soft explosion of his words. "I didn't have any choice. . . . I . . . I needed the money, she had me by the balls, she . . . she said she'd ruin me, she—"

"You're finished, Kyle," she spat, and hung up.

Dead air. Kyle slammed down the receiver and backed away from the phone. The bottle of scotch he gripped slipped out of his grasp and crashed to the floor. Waves of despair and self-loathing crashed over him. Images of his future flashed through his head—his arrest, his trial, the public humiliation, the jail time, his disbarment, the disgrace to his family, particularly to his father.

Kyle began to sob uncontrollably. He stumbled down the hall to his bedroom, threw open his closet door, dropped to his knees and pulled up the loose plank in the floor. He brought out the shoebox, knocked off the lid, dumped the contents on the floor. Bills fluttered out, his secret stash, his getaway money.

He ignored the bills and picked up the .38. He turned it over in his hands, ran his thumb over the hard, cool metal of the barrel. Kyle pressed the end of the barrel to his head, squeezed his eyes shut, and pulled back on the trigger.

The gunshot exploded through the room and echoed through the emptiness.

Taylor started to call Judge Cornwell, then realized she needed to speak to the judge in person. A phone call just wouldn't cut it, not for this. She needed to get off the island now, not tomorrow, not Sunday, but now. She needed a car, she needed . . .

"Stop it," she whispered, running her hands over her face. "Think it through."

Lady looked up at Taylor, whined softly.

"It's okay, girl. We've got to get out of here. Now." She rushed into the bathroom to gather up her makeup, shampoo, and hair dryer. She would call a cab. Get to the airport. Take a flight back to Boston.

Would planes be flying in weather like this? If not, she would rent a car at the airport and drive back to Boston. One way or another, she would get there tonight, speak to the judge tonight.

In her rush to gather up her toiletries, she accidently knocked a soap disk off the counter. As she stooped to pick it up, a gold earring glinted against the floor. Taylor picked it up, turned it over in her palm. A clover leaf with an emerald in the middle: she knew she'd seen it somewhere before, but couldn't place it. She put it on the counter and ran back into the bedroom.

Computer, clothes, printer, everything zipped up and ready. She buckled her fanny pack around her waist, with money and odds and ends inside, then glanced out the front window, hoping that Morgan had gotten back. No car in the driveway. She peered out toward the road, but a thick fog had rolled in, swallowing it and everything around it.

Cab, she thought. She would call a cab.

Her cell phone suddenly rang, startling her. She answered it. "Yes? Burt?"

Instead, she heard Mike Sessio's voice, chopped by static. "Taylor . . . get . . . the island . . ." The connection erupted with more static. ". . . Max, he's. . . ."

The line went dead. She waited a few seconds for him to call back, but the cell phone didn't ring. She dialed his penthouse number, reached his machine, hung up without leaving a message. *"Get the island . . . Max . . ."*

It didn't make sense.

Lady suddenly growled softly, scrambled to her feet, and

trotted over to the closed door. She pawed at it. Alarmed, Taylor grabbed her bags and Lady's leash and hurried over to the dog. "What is it?" she whispered, snapping on Lady's leash.

Lady kept scratching at the door, snarling softly. Taylor opened the door, poked her head into the dark hall, and listened, straining to hear something, anything but the relentless drumming of the rain, the moan of the wind. "It's just the storm," she whispered. "C'mon, let's go downstairs. I'll call the cab from there."

She moved quickly through the hall, spooked by something she couldn't explain, and turned on the stairwell light. The stairs seemed to descend forever into shadows. "Frank?" she called. "Max?"

Her voice echoed in the silence. Lady emitted soft, menacing growls and tugged on her leash, trying to hurry Taylor along. She walked slowly down the stairs, the skin tightening at the back of her neck, a wall of perspiration sweeping across her spine. At the bottom of the staircase, she stopped, listening again. The lab's growls punctuated the silence.

"One call, Lady, then we're gone," she whispered, and headed for the phone in the front room.

Lady tugged in the opposite direction, toward the foyer and front door. Taylor jerked on the leash, forcing the lab to follow her. But before she reached the front room, she felt a draft licking at her ankles. An open window? An open door?

She stopped. Turned. Frowned. Lady suddenly broke free and charged toward the foyer, barking fiercely. Taylor shouted at her to come back, but the dog vanished around the corner. Taylor ran after her, ran to the sound of a shutter or a door banging in the wind. The front door stood open, the screen door whipped open and shut, and Lady had vanished.

Taylor propped the door open with a tall copper can that held half a dozen umbrellas. "Hi, Talia," said a voice behind her, and she spun around to face Eric.

Her shock paralyzed her, rendered her completely mute. She simply stared at him, her thoughts racing, jammed into an endless loop of questions.

"Cat got your tongue, Talia?" He grinned. "Oh, I forgot.

It's Taylor. Taylor Brooke, not Talia Carlino Serle." He laughed, stepped closer to her, and she saw the hunting knife gripped in his right hand. "You shouldn't have run, bitch. No one runs out on me."

He took another step toward her and her body finally snapped free of its paralysis and she stepped back. Forward and back, again and again, the two of them locked into a grotesque prelude to a dance until her spine touched the door and she couldn't move any farther.

"And you've been unfaithful to me, Talia," he said. "First Stark, then Sessio . . ." He clicked his tongue against his teeth, shook his head, and unbuckled his belt with his free hand. "It makes me sick to think of those guys fucking my wife." He whipped off the belt, wound it around his hand. "Remember this? Remember how you used to beg me to stop?" And suddenly he lunged toward her and she grabbed one of the umbrellas and jabbed the end into his groin.

Eric fell back, shrieking, and Taylor tore out the door, stumbled down the porch steps, and ran into the rain, the wind, the impossible fog. She ran wildly, blindly, arms pumping hard at her sides. The shoulder bag and computer slowed her down, weighted her, and she dropped them and charged along the side of the house, into a hedge.

Headlights suddenly illumined the fog. Through the branches, she saw Max leap out of a car. Eric raced into her view, Max shouted at him, Eric stopped, turned, and Max fired.

Eric seemed to fall back in slow motion, a figure in a nightmare, his hands clutched to his chest. He crashed to the ground and didn't get up. Didn't move. A sob exploded from Taylor's mouth, she pushed back through the hedge until her back pressed up against the side of the house.

"Taylor?" called Max. "You're safe. He's dead. Taylor?"

Something didn't fit, something prevented her from leaving the safety of the hedge. How had Eric found her?

"Get off the island . . . Max . . ."

Sessio had been trying to warn her about Max.

Max had led Eric to her, Max was Morgan's Judas. And the earring, she suddenly remembered where she'd seen it—hanging from Gova's ears. Max and Gova, out here screwing around when no one else was around. Max, sweet Christ, Max.

She flattened out against the ground, fog swirling around her like some sort of ectoplasmic substance. The fog would hide her.

"Taylor?" Max called again.

Don't move, she thought. Don't breathe.

The headlights went off.

Her nails dug into the wet dirt.

She waited, her heart pounding in her throat.

Then she heard his footfalls on the porch.

Taylor, chilled and shivering, crawled out from under the hedge and tore through the fog, away from the house, away from Max and Eric's fallen body, toward the barn.

It had taken Mike Sessio's pilot nearly two hours to negotiate the bad weather. Throughout much of the flight, Sessio had been on the phone—first, trying to reach Taylor, then talking with several people who owed him favors. He needed to find the location of Frank Morgan's home on the Vineyard.

"Did Dad know any cops on the Vineyard?" he asked the pilot.

"Hell, yeah. The chief of police in Edgartown. I figured you'd already called him."

Sessio grinned and punched out information. As soon as he'd gotten the number, the pilot said, "Christ. We can't land. Fog's closed off the airport."

"Tell them it's a Mayday."

"You got it." The pilot fiddled with the radio controls. "This is Cessna four-seven-seven-niner. We've got a Mayday. A Mayday. Request permission to land. I repeat . . ."

Sessio peered below at the dense fog that now covered much of the Vineyard. Don't let me be too late, he thought, and called the number for Edgartown's chief of police.

The barn appeared suddenly in the fog, a large, restored building with a padlock on the door. Desperate, Taylor ran around to the back, praying she would find a window, another door, some way of getting inside.

She did find a door, but it, too, had been padlocked.

At the bottom of it, however, someone had put in a swinging door for a dog. She dropped to her knees, pushed at it. It looked large enough for a German shepherd, she thought, and quickly rocked back on her buttocks, pressed her feet to the swinging door and began working her body through it.

Taylor got stuck at the hips, had to back out, and go in on her side, with her right hip pressing painfully against the bottom edge of the opening. By pulling her arms in close to her body, she compressed her shoulders enough to squeeze through.

Inside, she literally couldn't see an inch in front of her. She crawled to her left, along the wall, then patted her way up to the wall to a standing position. A light, she desperately needed a light. She felt for the zipper on the fanny pack, opened it, and dug around through the change, certain she'd put a penlight inside.

Her fingers found it, she brought it out, zipped the fanny pack shut. She aimed the penlight at the floor of the barn, turned it on. Exhilaration rushed through her. If she could find a place to hide or find something she could use as a weapon, then maybe she would be able to stay alive until Frank returned.

Except that he wouldn't be back tonight.

She moved farther into the barn, made out the shape of a car covered with a cloth canopy, and reached a mountain of hay. To the left of it stood an empty stall, with a length of rope still tied to one of the beams, and a rusted pitchfork lying on the ground.

Taylor ducked into the stall, scooped up the pitchfork, and scrambled into the hay to wait for Max.

The chief of police met Sessio as soon as the plane landed. Sessio briefly explained what he needed, what he knew. The chief looked at him, not entirely convinced, then said, "Your old man paid for my son's dialysis. The least I can do is look into it."

"It's got to be now."

"I understand. My car's parked over there. Let's go."

Max called her and moments later, the barn doors flew open and the wind rushed in.

Taylor couldn't see him; she'd sunk down too deeply into the hay. But she saw the beam of his flashlight, poking here and there into the shadowed recesses of the barn. The beam climbed up the mountain of hay, struck the ceiling, and fell again.

She couldn't hear him, the wind swallowed whatever noises he made. But she felt him out there in the barn, not far from her now. "In here?" he shouted. "Hiding in the car, sweetheart?"

And just then, Lady raced into the barn, charging silently toward Max, and struck him in the back, knocking him to the floor. His gun went off, Lady's fierce and savage growls filled the air, and Taylor sprang out of the hay and tumbled forward, still clutching the pitch-fork.

Max struggled with the lab and tried to get to his feet. Taylor swung the pitchfork and slammed it hard against the backs of his legs. He shrieked and went down, falling like a giant, the floor shuddering as he struck it. His head hit a post, knocking him out.

Lady backed away, growling. "Good girl," Taylor said softly.

She swept up Max's gun and flashlight and hurried over to where he lay. Out cold. Lady whimpered and Taylor threw her arms around the lab, crying with relief. "Good girl," she said over and over again. "Good girl. Stay here, Lady. Bark if he wakes up. Okay?"

Lady whimpered, pawed at the ground, and sat back.

Taylor ran over to the car and started lifting the corners of the fitted canopy, working it off the vehicle, hoping it would start. Once she got the corners loose, she found the driver's side unlocked. She scrambled in, praying she would find a key. She looked in the glove compartment, on the visor, in the ashtray, under the seat. Nothing, of course not. That only happened in the movies.

She leaped out of the car, shouted at Lady to follow her, and they ran toward the barn doors. But they exploded open before she reached them. Headlights impaled her and Morgan seemed to glide through the light like an angel or an apparition. He tipped a flask to his mouth, pocketed it, and stopped in front of her.

"Taylor," he said.

Lady broke loose and charged past Morgan; Taylor flung her arms around her father and caught the scent of the booze he'd been drinking. Then words tumbled out of her mouth— Eric, Max, Gova, everything all mixed up and crazy.

He disentangled himself from Taylor and gazed past her, at Max, still dead to the world. "Is he dead? Is Max dead?" His words slurred.

"No. I . . . he . . ." Confused, she turned to look at Max and, suddenly, the car was all that she saw, the car she'd uncovered when she'd removed the canopy, the car now illumined in the wash of the headlights.

Everything inside of her suddenly began to rumble and shake as the memory of this car broke loose, rushed toward her, and slammed into her. She recognized it, the Saab from her dreams, the Saab that had run down her mother nineteen years ago.

Numb with horror, her eyes sought Morgan's face. "You," she whispered. "You killed her. You killed my mother. You were driving the Saab that killed her."

"No, no," Frank said softly, thickly, tilting the flask to his mouth again. "Max was driving. Your mother wouldn't accept the money my father offered her. She would've made trouble ater on. Then she and Joe Sessio got involved. . . .''

Taylor's heart shattered in her chest, her feet took root in he barn floor, her body seemed so heavy she couldn't even ift her arms. Tears spilled down her cheeks, his face blurred, he couldn't speak around the terrible lump in her throat. But er head raced—Joe Sessio, Richard Adler, Monroe and Frank Morgan, and her mother. The ugly pieces slid together, forming an even uglier and more terrifying whole. And even hough she knew the answer, she needed to hear him say it.

"Who . . . who killed Joe Sessio?" she stammered.

"Joe knew too much. He . . . he was a threat to me. He vasn't going to support me in the reelection. He wanted to uin me.''

"He knew you killed Adler," she said.

Morgan flashed a quick, drunken smile. "You were always oo smart for your own good, Taylor. You'd make any father proud." He staggered toward her, clutching a gun in one hand, he flask in another.

The only salient thought she had was to keep him talking. 'And who called DeCiccio's kitchen?''

"Max paid some punk to do it. It wasn't supposed to end ike this, Taylor. You were supposed to lose the Washington case, then you and I—'' He took another swig from the flask. 'But you were too smart, too curious. It could've been so good for us, so good.''

"Why court me? Why come after me all these years and get me into the firm? All that stuff about wanting to claim me as your daughter . . . it was all lies.''

Frank looked bemused. "I saw you that day, coming up the walk, those eyes—my eyes, my God, it was like looking into a mirror. I knew you were my child. I never got you out of my mind. It was a damn long time before Simpson finally located you. Studying to be a lawyer . . . how ironic. I wanted you back. We could've been happy. You, darling, could've had everything. All of this.'' His arms swept through the air.

He leaned in close to her. The warm stink of his breath swirled into her nostrils; she wanted to vomit. "You've never called me Daddy," he said softly.

Tears coursed down her cheeks. She pressed the back of her

hand to her mouth to stifle her sobs. "And you and Gova—"

"Debra has been my eyes and ears. But you've been my joy, Taylor. It could've been so different for us, so very different. I admit you've given me some real turns, my dear, but as far as my mental state goes, I'm not around the bend yet."

Taylor remained numb. "That first attack on me," she said softly, through her sobs, "that rose . . ."

Once more, a smile crossed his lips. "A nice touch, don't you think? You see, darling, I've fought so hard to get where I am. I couldn't let you ruin it. I couldn't let you take it all away from me. I'm a senator." He smiled. "I'm the best they've got. There's no room for scandal. . . . A bastard child whose mother was a drunk. Sympathy, now that's my angle. Missy's death. The public loves a sob story. The public loves me." His stare turned icy. "But you are so beautiful."

She stared back and noticed his eyes were filled with tears.

"I've lost both my daughters," he whispered.

Taylor, sobbing loudly, pressed her hands over her mouth. "Please," she begged. "Please don't kill me."

Then he put an arm around her and pulled her against him. Her body felt like wood, heavy, rigid, paralyzed. But her right hand moved, as if of its own volition, into the pocket of her sweater. Her fingers tightened around the gun. Max's gun.

"A kiss for daddy," he whispered, his gun sinking into her side.

The explosion of gunfire echoed through the rain and the fog, then faded away until only the damp, chilled stillness remained.

Mike Sessio descended on the Morgan estate with a battalion of squad cars, their sirens shrieking, their lights flashing. He sat in the lead car, with Edgartown's chief of police, who drove his squad car like a maniac on the autobahn.

As the chief tore into the driveway, Sessio saw lights about four hundred yards from the house. "Over there!" he shouted, and the chief swerved the car onto the grass and raced across it.

Inches short of a collision with a car parked in front of the open barn doors, the chief slammed on his brakes and Sessio leaped out. He ran into the barn, expecting the worst—and seeing it. Two bodies lay slumped together several yards away, the woman's soft blond hair shielding their faces like a shimmering veil.

"Christ, no," he whispered, then he saw the lab huddled up against Taylor and ran over to them.

Taylor raised her head, blood smeared across her cheeks and forehead, her eyes glazed with a pain so intense, so private, he lost his ability to speak. He dropped to his knees in front of her, rolled Morgan's body away from her, took the gun out of her hand and hurled it across the barn.

Then he put his arms around her and held her, their bodies rocking slowly back and forth, back and forth, until he couldn't tell whether he comforted her or she comforted him. And sometime later, he helped her to her feet and they walked out of the barn and away from her past.

Epilogue

_____

The trick-or-treaters came out in full force that evening, goblins, witches on broomsticks, princes from make-believe lands. They rang Taylor's doorbell every few minutes, the autumnal air echoing with their chants. In between, Taylor caught segments of the evening news.

The top story locally focused on Stark's campaign to win the DA slot. He'd been appointed to the position after Gova was indicted, but it looked as if he would win it fair and square in next week's election. He appeared on the steps of the courthouse, his attractive wife slightly behind him, the perfect political couple, she thought.

On the courthouse steps, Stark pontificated to reporters on the ramifications of Tommy Washington's acquittal, which he'd turned to his own advantage.

"Good luck, John," she said softly, with a shake of her head.

The doorbell rang again and she grabbed a basket of candy for the next round of hungry goblins. But when she opened the door, Mike Sessio stood there. "I've come for trick or treat," he said in a thick accent that echoed Boris Karloff or Lon Chaney. Then he whipped out a bouquet of flowers from behind his back. "And to bring you these."

Taylor smiled, then ushered him inside. He looked as handsome as ever, draped in head-to-toe Armani, Michael's signature. Some time had passed between the night at the Vineyard and now, enough for her to sort out her emotions, to realize what she really needed from her life—security, warmth, the need to be wanted, all things she'd searched and longed for. She had realized all these things must come from within and that they'd been there all along, though she'd had to find out the hard way.

She had entered the Washington case alone, gained a family, a sense of belonging—a father. In the blink of an eye, it had all disappeared. She'd walked away with none of it, had gone out the way she'd come in, independent, self-reliant, calm if not happy.

She moved toward Sessio, arms outstretched, closer and closer until she was locked in his embrace. "I'm embarrassed at my mistrusting you," she said.

Michael tilted his head back and looked into her eyes. "Dad's affair with your mother began an ongoing feud with the Morgans. A silent feud. Only the key players knew. Dad, Frank, and Roe."

"You figured it out," she interrupted.

"With your help," he added.

"I love you," she said. For the first time in her life she meant it.

"Oh?" He smiled. "Is that what they call this . . . love?"

His eyes locked with hers, embracing her, pulling her even deeper into his trance. She watched the images of her past fade into nothingness, blocking out all that had happened to her, the love, deaths, joy and pain. For in the end, none of it was able to destroy her. She was a survivor. Her world once again was serene. She'd made her peace, wrestled with her demons, and took a chance on destiny—Michael Sessio.

> The smiles that win, the tints that glow,
> But tell of days in goodness spent,
> A mind at peace with all below,
> A heart whose love is innocent!

> —*Lord Byron*

Available by mail from

BURNING DOWN THE HOUSE • Merry McInerny

Burning Down the House is a novel of dazzling storytelling power that peers into the psyche of today's woman with razor-sharp insight and sparkling wit.

CHOSEN FOR DEATH • Kate Flora

"I enjoyed *Chosen for Death* immensely. Kate Flora is a fine new talent."
—Barbara D'Amato, author of *Hard Tack*

PLAY IT AGAIN • Stephen Humphrey Bogart

In the classic style of a Bogart and Bacall movie, Stephen Humphrey Bogart delivers a gripping, fast-paced mystery.

IRISH GOLD • Andrew M. Greeley

"May be Andrew M. Greeley's best effort yet....A first-rate adventure story with the love interest intertwined in the mystery."—*Baltimore Sun*

COLUMBO: THE HELTER SKELTER MURDERS •
William Harrington

The most popular detective on television returns to face the legacy of one of history's most infamous killers.

STAGE FRIGHT • McNally

For five years, Hayley's been tormented by guilt over the murder of her fiancé. Now a vengeful ghost has come to claim her, and Hayley must defend her life and the man she has come to love.

"Gotti's fevered plot is in overdrive from the very first page, and it's a wild and crazy ride."

—*The New York Times*

"Plenty of intrigue in this page-turning whodunit."

—*American Woman*

"[Gotti supplies] the prime ingredient for a good murder mystery—a surprise ending. . . . Written in engaging, entertaining style."

—*Times Record News* (Wichita Falls, Texas)

"Hypnotic charm."

—*Amarillo News-Globe*

"[Gotti] has crafted an interesting and compelling first novel."

—*Crime & Justice*

"Gotti offers a very complicated story line that is amazingly straightforward."

—*Las Vegas Sun*

"Articulate. . . . [Gotti] has the potential to go as far as such lady authors as Jackie Collins, Judith Krantz, and Daniel Steel."

—*The New York Post*

"All of [the] elements are carefully woven into an intriguingly complex plot, which Gotti unfolds at just the right place."

—*The South Bend Tribune*